The PARIS COOKING SCHOOL

The PARIS COOKING SCHOOL

SOPHIE BEAUMONT

ultimo press

Published in 2023 by Ultimo Press,
an imprint of Hardie Grant Publishing

Ultimo Press
Gadigal Country
7, 45 Jones Street
Ultimo, NSW 2007
ultimopress.com.au

Ultimo Press (London)
5th & 6th Floors
52–54 Southwark Street
London SE1 1UN

ultimopress

A catalogue record for this book is available from the National Library of Australia

The Paris Cooking School
ISBN 978 1 76115 141 5 (paperback)

Cover design Christabella Designs
Cover illustrations Strawberry tart by Cheryl Orsini; Paris by grop / Shutterstock
Author photograph Courtesy of Lorena Carrington
Text design Simon Paterson, Bookhouse
Typesetting Bookhouse, Sydney | 12/18.9 pt Minion Pro
Copyeditor Deonie Fiford
Proofreader Pamela Dunne

10 9 8 7 6 5 4 3 2 1

Printed in Australia by Opus Group Pty Ltd, an Accredited ISO AS/NZS 14001 Environmental Management System printer.

The paper this book is printed on is certified against the Forest Stewardship Council® Standards. Griffin Press – a member of the Opus Group – holds chain of custody certification SCS-COC-001185. FSC® promotes environmentally responsible, socially beneficial and economically viable management of the world's forests.

Ultimo Press acknowledges the Traditional Owners of the Country on which we work, the Gadigal People of the Eora Nation and the Wurundjeri People of the Kulin Nation, and recognises their continuing connection to the land, waters and culture. We pay our respects to their Elders past and present.

Respirer Paris, cela conserve l'âme.

Breathe in Paris, it preserves the soul.

VICTOR HUGO

One

A millisecond. That's all it took. One glance away, and the red leather case and everything it contained was gone. Gabi hadn't even caught a glimpse of the thief. Well, they'd be disappointed when they examined their booty. Sure, the case looked expensive—because it was, a gift from that heady period last year—but all it held was Gabi's battered work iPad, bereft of any thief-friendly information; a sketchbook with a couple of scribbled and crossed-out pages, but otherwise blank; and a new set of pencils her twin seven-year-old nieces had given her as a going-away present. The pencils were the only things she minded losing. Everything else was a reminder, a reproach, a refrain she could do without.

Draining the last of her strong coffee, Gabi hoisted her backpack onto her shoulders and stood up. The Gare du Nord heaved with people going in all directions and echoed with loud, confusing announcements. On the Eurostar from London earlier that morning, she'd been warned by her chatty seat neighbour that this busy station was Thief Central and to keep an eye out. She'd nodded politely, thinking she'd hardly present a tempting target. Her backpack was ancient, and her passport, cards and what cash she had were all stowed away in the money belt she carried under her jumper. The red leather case had clearly figured so little in her thoughts that she'd not even factored it in. And now, as she strode away from the station and out into the busy street, she felt as though it was a sign. Just as the case had vanished, so would her burden . . .

Come *on*. Get real, Gabi. The case might be gone but the Thing didn't disappear so easily. At that moment, she caught the startled eye of a passer-by and realised that she'd spoken aloud. *Oh great. Talking aloud to yourself in public now.* And imagining that a station thief was an instrument of fate. She could add those things to her growing shame parade. Like telling her agent that she was 'taking a stand on digital distraction' and would not only be turning off social media but that she would not be reachable. Like telling her family that her local mobile number was only to be used for emergencies and on no account given to anyone else. Like not telling anyone what this trip was really about or what was really going on. Hiding, ducking, dodging, deceiving, pretending. The old Gabi would never have done any of that stuff. *But I'm not that person anymore, and I don't know if I can ever be again*, Gabi thought, as the unspoken anxiety that had become all too familiar surged through her. What if it was all over and she—

Cut that out. Focus. You are in Paris now, she told herself, sternly, as she walked through the crowded streets. *And you really like this city, even though your father would scoff and say Paris is just that place you fly over on the way to his beloved Basque country.* The thought made her smile for the first time that day. Okay. For four weeks, she was going to forget everything else but being here, doing something that didn't make her feel anxious, something far away from expectations. It would be an escape. A real one.

She took a deep breath, and immediately sneezed. Then again. She stopped, pulling out a tissue, blowing her nose, before sneezing once more, the sneeze turning into a laugh. Hayfever now, for God's sake. And no wonder. Just look at those street trees, budding, no, absolutely *bursting* into bloom. The pollen count must be off the charts. And it was warmer than you'd think, for Paris in April. London had been chilly, and she'd dressed accordingly. Now she was starting to sweat with the heavy pack against her padded jacket. She pulled the jacket off and stuffed it into her bag. Pushing stray strands of blunt-cut black hair away from her face, she consulted the map on her phone. Bugger, still a fair way to go before she reached the hotel. She should have caught the Metro, not stalked out of the Gare du Nord like some drama queen. Ah well. *Serves you right, grumpy guts*, she thought, adjusting the straps of her pack and walking on.

Kate's bag bumped against the steps as she climbed up. She'd decided to get off at the station before her destination, just so she could get a proper first look at the neighbourhood as a whole. Plus the long flight and then the train and Metro ride from the airport had left her dazed and disorientated. She needed fresh air to reset her body clock. She needed to know she really was in Paris and not in interminable transit through draughty tunnels and platforms and airport halls that could have been pretty much anywhere in the world.

Emerging into the street from the dim underground, she felt the blissful shock of the colours, the smells, the sounds. It was the most beautiful afternoon, the sky was deep blue, and against it the lovely old pale stone buildings glowed, trees flung up armfuls of white and pink blossoms, the soft air was full of fragrance, there were people seated at the outside tables of cafés, chatting and laughing, and not one of them was wearing black. Imagine! Then she heard the melodious cooing of a wood pigeon from somewhere nearby, and she had a memory of her parents dancing to an old jazz song called 'April in Paris', which was about the charm of spring in this city. *I understand it now,* she thought, her pulse quickening, barely even noticing when an impatient commuter surged past her, muttering about *les touristes.* Kate didn't care. Joy filled her from top to toe.

The hotel wasn't far away but she took her time getting there. There was so much to see and she kept stopping all the time, taking it all in, and taking photo after photo. Yes, she'd been to Paris before, once. But that had been sixteen years ago, when she was twenty-five. And she'd only been here three days, rushing around, taking in a dizzying number of classic sights, the tourist magnets such as the Eiffel Tower and Notre Dame, the Opera and the Champs-Élysées . . . That hadn't been her choice, she'd wanted to take it more slowly, to see less and yet see more in a way, to take it in properly. But, of course, Josh had other ideas. He wanted to 'do' Paris, to say he'd been there, to tick off all the sights in the three days he had planned so tightly, before they moved on to the next 'iconic' European city. She hadn't had the heart to tell him that wasn't what she'd dreamed of when she'd mentioned wanting to go to Paris. *Oh well,* she'd thought, *we've had a little taster, and though I'm still hungry to see more, there'll be a next time, and it will be different, I'll make sure of it.* But years had passed, and there'd never been a next time . . .

Until now. And even though it was the beginning, already it felt different, like a real adventure starting in a place she was going to get to know well. Her heart skipped a beat at the thought. This would be her neighbourhood, her actual home, for the next month—would you just look at it! Here was a café whose awning was covered in stunning waterfalls of silk cherry blossom, while across the street rakish rows of multicoloured bikes looked as though they were about to take off by themselves. Over there a small greengrocery showed off its fruit and vegetables as though they were still-life paintings, while not far away oysters and scallops, still in their shells, ferried a heady smell of the sea. A little further on, a flower shop boasted bouquets of pale violet roses that looked unreal until you touched them, and another shop presented quirky gifts and attractively odd objects. In backstreets, there were quiet public gardens tucked away, and cobblestones, and more birds singing, and the massive, photogenic doors of old apartment buildings. On the big street she'd also seen imposing churches, a strange medieval tower, the magnificent Hôtel de Ville . . . The backstreets were quiet but even on the big street there wasn't much traffic so it was easy to cross and recross streets, even dragging a bag behind you.

She stopped by a patisserie with an enticing display: cakes like fragile jewels perched on gilded stands, or lined up in mouth-watering single file, their names written in that curly handwriting that made everything look so deliciously, so perfectly, French. But 'window-licking', as the French called it, wasn't enough and she couldn't resist going in to buy the most beautiful little strawberry tart that had surely ever existed. She ate it there and then out on the pavement, sheer bliss in the glorious mix of flavour, texture and aroma: meltingly sweet fruit, creamy vanilla-fragrant custard, buttery soft pastry. It was truly perfect and, when she finished, she couldn't help licking her fingers.

Through the window of the patisserie, she met the amused glance of a shop assistant. She just smiled back, green eyes alight with mischief. It didn't matter one bit that she'd been caught out acting like a kid. She hadn't done anything so spontaneous in years. She hadn't done much of anything except dance to someone else's tune. But now—well, she was where she was meant to be. No matter what happened, no one could take that feeling from her. Certainly not Josh, far away in Australia. In another world. Another life.

Not *her* life, now. And in this moment, blessedly, that thought held no pain at all.

Sylvie took another sip of her favourite Burgundy pinot noir and looked once more through the folder that her PA Yasmine had compiled. The fresh supplies had been ordered and would arrive first thing tomorrow morning, arrangements had been made with the guest presenters for the month, and the list of students was fully confirmed. *Ouf.* Phew. The last three weeks had been something of a nightmare, a couple of bookings falling through, and then someone emailed to say they'd been about to book but had seen the bad review on Tripadvisor, and what could Sylvie tell him about that?

Sylvie couldn't tell him anything because she hadn't actually known the review existed. When she did click on to it, she was both angry and puzzled, because it was clear that whoever wrote it had never attended the Paris Cooking School. They mentioned things that never happened, and ways of working she never used. On her neighbour Serge's advice—one of his other friends had gone through the same thing—she'd got in touch with Tripadvisor and complained. The bad review would be removed, they assured her. And so it was. The person who'd hesitated about booking had signed up, and shortly after that the last vacant spot had also been filled. So it had all worked out in the end. But it had left a lingering unease.

It was very quiet in Sylvie's office, just off the big high-ceilinged kitchen and dining room where all the main action of the Paris Cooking School took place. Right now, those spaces were quiet too. But tomorrow morning it would all start up again, with a new class of eight students. Eight new faces; eight new ways of doing things, seeing things. Eight people who would present challenges but who, by the end of the four weeks, would hopefully work as colleagues, yet still keep their differences.

In the fifteen years since Sylvie had founded the Paris Cooking School, there had been nearly a hundred such classes, each with their eager batch of students. There had been dramas and personality clashes over the years, but also many friendships had been forged, and several romances had even sparked off across the workbenches. Most of the students simply wanted to learn how to cook the French way for their own sake, but a few had gone on to have successful foodie careers. The most prominent was now a famous food writer with her own spin-off TV show in the US, who'd dedicated her first cookbook to Sylvie and sent her a signed copy. She still kept in touch, as did a number of others, who wrote and emailed to say that the month they'd spent at the school had been one of the great experiences of their lives. Sylvie's son, Julien, who had pretty much grown up in this environment—he was only seven when she'd started the school—had said it was not surprising they felt that way. 'For you, Maman, it's your everyday life. For them, it's a magical holiday *away* from their everyday lives.' And he was right, of course. But lately she'd found herself thinking that it might be time for things to run their course, as it were.

But right now wasn't the time for that, any more than it was the time to think properly about her troubled relationship with Claude and the ultimatum she really must give him, for her own self-respect. Finishing off her wine, she shuffled the student list and other papers back into the folder, stretched and got up. She caught her own glance in the mirror opposite. The woman in the mirror looked so sure of herself, and so effortlessly chic with her shining chestnut hair, slim dark pants and silky green shirt, but the woman looking into the reflection knew just how much the mirror could lie. Shrugging, amused at her own unexpected fancy, Sylvie turned away. Picking up her empty glass, she went into the kitchen, washed and dried the glass and put it away. She glanced around her. Everything was in its place. Everything ready. Everything waiting, in suspended animation, for the noise and bustle and questions and, yes, the *magic*, to start.

Two

Ten years ago, when Gabi had first visited Paris, she'd stayed in Montmartre, in a converted attic room. Back then, she'd imagined it was still the haunt of bohemian artists and had been disappointed to find it so touristy, especially around the Sacré-Coeur. But she had discovered other, less hyped spots in Montmartre, and in particular the amazing fabric shops that rambled down both sides of one winding street. She'd spent many happy hours there sketching quick impressions in her visual diary, then painting them up later in her room. Another of her favourite sketching spots had been at her attic window, looking out over the pigeon-haunted roofs and down into the crowded street. She'd really felt a part of the Paris story then, finding her own small but inspirational cameo within it.

Ten years later, here she was standing at her present-day Parisian hotel window in the Quartier Saint-Paul. In the southern part of the famous Marais district of Paris, the quartier had a maze of cobbled backstreets, remnants of medieval walls and ancient mansions, known as *hôtels particuliers.* It preserved some of the old character of the city, prior to its nineteenth-century transformation by Baron Haussmann. But though the pace was relaxed, less consciously 'buzzy' than other areas of the Marais, the quartier didn't live in the past. It was a lively and animated scene she looked down on, full of colour and movement. But this time there would be no inspirational cameo. No sketching herself into the story. She wasn't a part of it; she was *apart.*

Abruptly, she turned away. Enough. She'd overslept and had to get going right away, without breakfast. That was hardship enough, never mind getting into a funk over *if only*s. Gabi loved her food, and the thought of coffee and a croissant made her mouth water. This was Paris so there was sure to be a bakery on the way. And so there was—a lovely one with Art Nouveau rural scenes painted on glass panels at the entrance. A minute later, hurriedly brushing croissant crumbs from her mouth and her clothes, she was at the door of the school's apartment building. It was only then that she realised what she'd left behind. Her phone, where she'd noted the entry code for the school doors, still lay on the bedside table where she'd left it last night. Squinting at the entry pad, she tried to remember the code. Was it 445AS? Or 554SA? She tried both, to no avail. She couldn't even call anyone to let her in. Bugger. She'd have to go back for the phone.

'*Ça va*?' The voice behind her made her jump. Turning, she saw a man around her age, thirty or so, tall, with wavy light brown hair curling irrepressibly around his ears, and eyes so dark they were almost black. Dressed in a leather jacket over a T-shirt and jeans, he was carrying a large flattish wooden box. Before she could answer he added, in English, 'You are for the Paris Cooking School?'

'Yes. *Oui.* But the code . . .'

His dark eyes twinkled. 'Of course. Allow me.' As he came closer, she caught a whiff of something strong. He saw her nose wrinkling and laughed. 'Goat's cheese, Mademoiselle. For the school.'

Of course. To cover her embarrassment, she retorted, in French, 'Good. I love goat's cheese. Especially the strong, smelly ones.'

His eyebrows rose fractionally, and she saw with some satisfaction that her perfect French had surprised him. But he said nothing, only gave a darting smile and punched in the entry code. The door opened with a click and he held it open for her. He headed for the lift but she bypassed it. She wasn't keen on the narrow wooden lifts you found in old French apartment buildings. Instead, she took the stairs to the third floor two at a time, just for the heck of it, and got there hardly even panting. That had at least been a rare benefit of the last few months. She'd taken to running every morning as a respite from her oppressive thoughts and had become quite fit as a result.

At the entry door of the school, on the third floor, there was a buzzer. Its call was answered almost immediately by a brisk young brunette carrying an iPad. She introduced herself as *Yasmine Berada, personal assistant to Madame Sylvie Morel*, in excellent English, and looked only momentarily surprised when Gabi responded in fluent French, introducing herself in turn and apologising for being late. 'It is not a problem,' Yasmine replied smoothly in French, ushering her in, 'nothing has started yet. Now, if you would please leave your shoes here,' she continued, 'and put on a pair of these—' pointing to a rack of soft-soled black slip-on shoes—'that would be much appreciated.'

'Of course.' Gabi took off her boots and selected a pair of the slip-ons in her size. Glancing at the golden, creaking parquet floor, she could see why they wouldn't want people tramping around in street shoes. And though the slip-ons didn't look all that elegant paired with her dark red skirt, they would be much less tiring on the feet than her heeled boots, especially if she was standing around for hours in a kitchen.

As she slipped the shoes on, the man who'd let her in downstairs came down the hall, minus the box he'd been carrying. He nodded at Yasmine and gave Gabi another of those darting smiles. 'I hope the cheese is up to your high standards, Mademoiselle,' he said, in French. 'And if you'd like more, come visit me at the Bastille markets—I'm there every Thursday and Sunday!'

'Perhaps I might do that,' Gabi replied, 'if the cheese is satisfactory. Or even perhaps if I need to complain about it!'

I'm flirting, she thought, *and I haven't done that for ages*. She'd forgotten how fun it was. Especially in Paris, where everybody understood how it worked. No strings attached, just a nice moment.

He laughed. 'You do that, Mademoiselle.' And then, with a cheerful goodbye to them both, he was gone, clanging the door shut behind him.

As if anticipating a question from Gabi, Yasmine said, 'That's Max. He's a bit of an *original*.' A character, that meant, in French:

a word that could be used with approval or not. Yasmine's tone was neutral, so Gabi wasn't sure.

She took Gabi to a storage room lined with shelves on two sides and lockers on another side. On the shelves were all kinds of kitchen linen—aprons, tea towels, napkins, tablecloths—as well as large boxes of kitchen paper, aluminium foil and disposable gloves. 'You can leave any belongings you won't need in a locker,' Yasmine said, 'the key always stays with you. And take an apron and gloves.'

Obediently, Gabi divested herself of her chunky cardigan, and locked it and her money belt safely away. From the pile of aprons, she chose a cheerful flowery one, which was not only practical but looked good against her black top. The apron also had a front pocket where she stashed a pair of gloves. Then she followed Yasmine out of the storage room and down the hall.

Her first impression, as they entered the large kitchen, was of golden light. The sun poured in through the window, picking out the mellow tones inside: shades of wood and cork and tiles. She had half-expected impersonal pristine whites and gleaming steel, not this warm, intimate feel. It was almost as though you were stepping into someone's home kitchen, despite the size of the room, and the discreetly positioned twin glass-topped cookers and double sinks, the double fridges in a recess and the shelf holding professional-looking cooking implements. A large walk-in pantry with double doors was on one side of the room and above its entrance hung a painting of a market scene: it was naïve but full of colour and vigour. A feeling of both peace and cheerful busyness

pervaded the kitchen, and it made Gabi say, 'Oh,
beautiful room!'

'Yes.' Yasmine smiled. 'It is inspired by the kitchen o
grandparents, where she first learned to cook as a child. Up ...ed
equipment, of course, but otherwise with that same *ambiance*. And it's at the heart of everything we do here.'

'I can see that,' Gabi said, softly, a pang going through her as she thought of the kitchen back in her parents' house—of being enveloped in a warm bustle of practical beauty and homely pleasures. 'Does Sylvie use the kitchen when there's no class on?'

'Oh yes. Sylvie lives on the premises. As does her son, Julien, when he's here. But come,' Yasmine said, 'let us find the others.' She held open a door at one end of the kitchen, where a babble of voices was coming from. Taking a deep breath, Gabi followed her into another large, pleasant room, dominated by a long oak dining table and a dresser, above which hung a reproduction of a painting by Claude Monet, showing people seated around a dining table enjoying a meal. At the real table, people were also seated, not eating, but talking.

In the past, Gabi had a reputation for being extroverted, able to enter any room full of people with confidence. It had been a façade. Today, as she took the only vacant chair, with a 'hello' all round, people nodded pleasantly, then the chatter started up again, and she relaxed and scanned the group discreetly. Eight people all up: four men and four women, including herself. A door at the end of the room opened and two other people came in.

It was clear who the newcomers were, for their names and faces, like Yasmine's, had been featured on the Paris Cooking

School's website. In her simple white shirt, black pants and green and white stripy apron, chestnut-coloured hair tied back in a thick plait, Sylvie Morel managed to look both practical and stylish. Her assistant/sous-chef, Damien Arty, had a young face but prematurely thinning fair hair and was immaculately dressed in the traditional chef's attire of short-sleeved white tunic shirt worn over grey trousers, and a black apron tied at the waist.

'*Mesdames, messieurs, bienvenue*! Ladies and gentlemen, welcome!' Sylvie's voice was deep and clear, her English perfect, with a soft, attractive accent. The classes at the Paris Cooking School were always conducted in English, because students either came from English-speaking countries or from those where English was taught as a second language more often than French. 'You have come to Paris from six different countries: Australia, Japan, Germany, Canada, the USA and Britain,' she went on. 'We thank you for joining us from so far away. And we hope that, after this month, you will all think of our city as your second home. Well, at least as your second kitchen,' she added, earning smiles and a smattering of applause.

She spoke for a little while after that, about timetables and schedules, and after a moment Gabi's attention wandered. But she was jerked from her thoughts by Sylvie saying, 'Well, enough from me. Let's hear from you now.'

'From *me*?' Gabi blurted out.

Sylvie smiled. 'I meant *you* in the plural, Ms Picabea. But by all means, let us start with you.'

Three

Kate listened to the others' stories and thought she'd have nothing interesting to add. Everyone else's reasons for being at the school seemed to stretch back into fascinating pasts and enchanted, or sometimes haunting, memories. But her own suburban childhood had been ordinary, her family history unexotic and her adult life mostly contented, without real drama. Until Josh's bombshell. But even that wasn't something you could truthfully say was exceptional. It was probably the oldest story in the world, being dumped for a younger woman. And it wasn't something she wanted to talk about, anyway. So when it was her turn, she simply said, 'I'm from Melbourne, Australia, where talking about food has become something of a religion. But I love cooking itself. And I really wanted to cook in Paris. That's all.' She smiled. 'I still can't believe I'm actually here though.'

Lots of smiles and nods back. She had hit a chord without trying to. And as Yasmine came in with a tray of coffees and Sylvie invited them to take their cups with them into the kitchen, Kate fell into conversation with the friendly German couple in their sixties who told her they'd loved what she said. 'It is so honest. And why we are all here, really,' the woman, Anja, said. She and her husband Stefan spoke excellent English, with a slight German accent.

'We try to be interesting and different,' he added, 'but really we are all alike inside, yes?'

'I suppose so,' said Kate, politely.

'You know the other Australian person?' Anja asked.

Kate glanced across the room at the young woman who'd given her name as *Gabrielle, but everyone calls me Gabi.* Quite a complicated, exotic mix of family history there, plus something about an ancestral link to Paris and food, back in the 1900s? Lucky her. Plenty to draw on. No, Kate had never actually met her before. But she had a nagging feeling that she had seen the other woman's face somewhere. It was an unusual face, not traditionally pretty but certainly striking, with jet-black hair framing distinctive features, including an aquiline nose and long-lashed hazel eyes. Not a face you'd easily forget. *Unlike mine*, Kate thought, ruefully. Maybe they'd been on the same plane and she'd spotted her in transit. 'Australia's a big country,' she told the Germans. 'And Gabi lives in Sydney. I live in Melbourne. And you know what they say: never the twain shall meet.' She saw their expressions and added, 'I mean, the cities are far apart, not only in distance but also because there's a rivalry between them.'

'Oh, that is so interesting,' Stefan remarked, and looked like he was about to say more, only just then Sylvie called for their attention and the class began in earnest.

Sylvie told them the Paris Cooking School was not about teaching *cordon bleu* cooking, but about helping people discover and apply the French way of home cooking to their own lives. 'The French way of home cooking is not *fancy*, or difficult,' she said, 'or even necessarily time-consuming. In this school, you will find what may seem like an unusual way of learning, and which may not always seem serious. But it's designed to immerse you immediately, and help you understand what underlies the French approach to food. Understanding needs to come not only through the mind, but also the heart and the imagination. And the hands, of course!'

Kate wasn't the only one smiling at that, as Sylvie went on, 'I know you all already love to cook, and a couple of you—' nodding at Misaki, who was a retired chef from Japan, and Ethan, who ran a gastropub in England—'are actually professionals. You already have a good understanding of cooking. And you have your own ways of doing things. We don't ask you to forget any of those things. But we encourage you to go beyond. To start with an open mind and be willing to be surprised.' She gestured to Damien, who disappeared into the pantry. 'And that is why we're starting this first session with a bit of a game. Humble and simple this food item may be, but without it, French cooking could hardly exist. Can you guess what it is?'

Everyone stared at her, then a chorus of voices threw out ideas. 'Garlic!' 'Cream!' 'Herbs!' 'Wine!' 'Butter!' 'Bouillon!'

'Snails,' said Ethan, in his posh drawl.

'Frogs' legs,' put in Mike, the burly American who had introduced himself earlier with a twinkle in his eye as *Ethan's partner, or kept man—take your pick*.

Chuckling, Pete, the fiftyish Canadian who already reminded Kate irresistibly of Tigger from *Winnie the Pooh*, contributed, '*Je ne sais quoi*,' making everyone laugh.

'All right,' Sylvie said, breaking into the hilarity, 'then, as we say in French, will you give your tongue to the cat? It means to give up,' she explained, smiling.

'But in English we say, if the cat's got your tongue that means you have to keep quiet,' said Kate, cheekily.

Everyone laughed, including Sylvie. 'Very true,' she said, giving Kate an appreciative look. 'Okay, Damien, show them.' Her assistant came out from the pantry, arms full of egg cartons. The room erupted in exclamations and cheers.

'This is my contention: that the humble egg is a cornerstone of French cooking,' Sylvie said, when the noise had died down. 'Let's talk, then, about the egg and its many stories.'

Pulling up a banner printed with a map of France, Sylvie produced four little paper flags, each labelled with the name of an egg dish. She pinned a flag on a place on the map, then recounted a lively story about that particular dish in local culture and folklore. Then Sylvie and Damien together made a couple of those stories come to delicious life, creating the stuffed eggs known as *oeufs mimosa*, first made in a modest 1950s Parisian café, 'owned by a man from Provence homesick for the golden mimosa trees of his home village', and eggs *en cocotte*, baked eggs with tarragon and cream, 'made in a Norman farmhouse kitchen, overlooking a busy barnyard and small herb garden, the lowing of dairy cows in the fields beyond'. It was an unusual and imaginative way to demonstrate a recipe, and the class clustered enthusiastically around the stove, watching Sylvie and Damien work and occasionally asking questions. Some people made notes in small notepads or on their phones, others took pictures, but Kate simply looked and listened, trying to memorise it all. The heartfelt simplicity of it, yet also the imaginative, playful attention to detail—it was just brilliant!

Afterwards, they all got to try samples of the *mimosa* and *en cocotte* eggs: they tasted every bit as good as they looked and smelled. Then Damien handed out some cards with recipes of each of the egg dishes and Sylvie set the class the task of choosing one, thinking about a place it might have come from and making it. 'You can do this individually or as a pair,' she added, when someone—Kate thought it might have been Gabi—sighed. 'And you are welcome to try the same things we made, if you'd like. Don't overdo quantities; we're just looking for small portions. And don't worry about getting facts right in your stories, that's not what we're after. Damien and I will be here to help and advise. After we finish, your creations will be the centrepiece of our lunch.'

It was quite a daunting task at first glance and Kate couldn't make her mind up whether she wanted to go it alone to make her own mistakes or be with someone else for moral support. She saw Gabi gathering certain ingredients and realised she must be preparing to make a *piperade*. She remembered Gabi saying her father came from the French Basque country, so she probably already knew how to whip up the hearty, aromatic mix of eggs, air-dried ham, onions, tomatoes and long green peppers that was so characteristic of that region. She'd probably also have a good story to go with it, ready-made. So it might be easy to join in with her. On the other hand, she'd be riding on someone else's coat-tails and that was something she'd sworn never to do again. By then, everyone else had already started: Stefan and Anja, and Ethan and Mike, expectedly paired up, and Misaki, Pete and Gabi were each doing it on their lonesome. And it seemed she was too.

Scanning the recipe cards, she decided on a mushroom omelette, with the button mushrooms known as *champignons de Paris* cooked quickly in butter and garlic, and then tipped into the almost-cooked omelette, which would then be folded over. The result would be a luscious creamy egg top with the savoury, garlicky mushrooms inside. Just the thought made her mouth water.

But what about the story to go with it? Mushrooms were normally found in the woods, but these little numbers were likely not called 'Paris mushrooms' for nothing, so the story needed to be something set here. What about a young housemaid who dreams of being a cook and who, at night, sneaks into the kitchen of the grand Parisian house where she works to create this dish? And so delicious is the smell emanating from the kitchen that it wakes a guest in the house who happens to be a great chef. He comes down in search of the source of the smell and is so impressed that he offers the maid a place in his famous restaurant! Grinning to herself, Kate set to work. This was truly the most fun she'd had in years.

Four

Gabi wound her way through the backstreets to the hotel in the late afternoon. She'd politely declined an invitation from some of the other students to go for a drink after class. They all seemed nice enough but she didn't feel like sharing time outside of class with them right now. Besides, people might start asking questions about what she did, and she didn't want that. Talking about her family history and how it intersected with her love of cooking, now that was safe. And the weird fact that both her Basque ancestors on her father's side *and* her Channel Islands forebears on her mother's side had coincidentally had little food businesses in Paris at the time of the 1900 World Exposition always intrigued people. She hadn't had to explain what she did back home; she hadn't had to go into any tiresome explanations about her own recent history. Everyone thought they understood her reason for being here: cooking in the place her ancestors had worked *and* finding out a bit more about them. And she intended to keep it that way. It was a fine reason, and it wasn't altogether untrue, anyway. No need to elaborate on the context.

She didn't wonder about what any of the others might be hiding. She had no headspace to think about anyone else's problems right now. They seemed like an ordinary bunch, nice enough, generally speaking, though Pete could be irritating and Ethan rather snarky. Lunch had been a lively affair as everyone sampled each other's eggy creations, washed down with some pretty decent wine and accompanied by a big bowl of deliciously simple green salad mixing together different types of lettuce, from mignonette to chicory, seasoned with a tangy vinaigrette and chopped chives. And lots of fabulous bread, of course! Gabi had hoped the goat's cheeses might make an appearance but, according to Sylvie, those would be used in tomorrow's class, so she'd have to wait to sample them.

She'd enjoyed the clever way Sylvie and Damien had wound their teaching around stories, turning what could have been a 'Do this, then that' type of cookery class into something that felt more like the natural way you absorbed things as a child. 'Be willing to be surprised,' Sylvie had said, and that had certainly been the case for Gabi today. The *piperade* was her dad's signature dish and, until today, she'd never attempted to make it herself. His was always so good, what was the point? But somehow she'd found herself drawn to it, and found, too, that she didn't need to do more than glance at the recipe. She even knew exactly how much *piment d'Espelette* to put in—that beautiful, aromatic red pepper powder that was found in practically all Basque cooking and was a must in the *piperade*, a moist, succulent scrambled mix of egg, tomato, peppers, herbs, onion and garlic. She seemed to already know what to do, though before then she'd not consciously been aware she had learned it just by seeing him make it during her childhood. And it had turned out perfectly.

She turned the corner into another street and the window display of a bric-a-brac shop caught her eye. Arrayed on an old sewing machine against deep blue velvet drapery was an eclectic collection of objects: Art Nouveau ebony and rhinestone brooches shaped like cicadas; a stuffed white mouse wearing a jewelled cap; a 1950s hat whose tight green plumes made it look like an artichoke; an odd-shaped, brightly coloured cup and saucer; a pair of enormous 1970s purple suede platform boots; and a small, subtly coloured pencil drawing of a bowl of fruit, which had an arrestingly strange perspective. Gabi caught her breath. She peered at it, trying to see a signature, but either it was too faint to see from this distance, or there wasn't one. But if it was what she thought . . .

The shop was an Aladdin's cave inside, every centimetre of its small space stuffed full, objects scattered on tables, spilling out of drawers, perched on shelves. Behind the counter, reading a newspaper, sat an elderly man. With his large ears, spindly limbs, stringy hair and glum expression, he reminded Gabi of an illustration in one of her favourite childhood books, C.S. Lewis's *The Silver Chair*. All that was missing was the pointy hat. The illustration had been of the character called Puddleglum the Marsh-wiggle, known for his indefatigable gloominess.

'*Bonjour, Monsieur*,' she said, trying not to grin as he lifted his head reluctantly and muttered, ungraciously, '*Bonjour, Mademoiselle*.'

'I would like to have a look at the drawing in the window, please.'

'A look at the drawing in the window?' echoed Monsieur Marsh-wiggle, as if this was the strangest request. He sighed. 'Okay.' Putting the newspaper down, he came out from behind the counter, reached a long arm into the window display and plucked out the drawing. Ignoring Gabi's outstretched hand, he placed it on the countertop, indicating that Gabi could have a look. But he kept a close eye on her. She couldn't be sure if that was because he knew what she thought it was, or if he was just displaying reflex suspiciousness.

She picked up the drawing. Still no signature visible, but the colours, the subject, the whole feel of the painting, made her skin prickle. She turned it over to see if there might be any clue as to its provenance. There was a faded sticker on the back of the black frame, probably the name of the framer, but unreadable, smudged by age. Okay, so no proof yet—but she had to buy it, anyway.

'How much, Monsieur?' she asked.

He frowned. 'What do you think it's worth?'

Chancing her arm, she said, 'Er—twenty euros?'

'Thirty,' he said, at once. 'But I'll keep the frame.'

She stared. 'Excuse me?'

'The frame is ebony, which is rare these days, and there are other pictures it can be used for,' he said, sharply. It was then that she knew for sure he had no idea what the drawing was. Or at least what she *thought* it was.

'Okay,' she said. 'I'm travelling, so it will be easier to carry that way.'

'I knew you weren't from Paris,' he said, becoming more voluble now he thought he'd got one over her. 'You're from the South, right? I can hear the sunshine in your voice.'

'Yes, I am,' Gabi said, smiling politely, but not wanting to be drawn. She watched as he carefully unscrewed the frame, lifted off the glass and took out the drawing in its cream mount. Putting a sheet of tissue paper around it, he slid it into a carboard sleeve, then looked at her. 'All right?'

'Yes, thank you. That's fine.' She took out her credit card, but he shook his head.

'Cash, please.'

'Oh. I'm not sure if I . . .' Gabi took out her wallet, as he watched her imperturbably. Thank God—by adding the few cents of change she'd got from the bakery that morning, she could scrape together thirty euros exactly. She was damn sure Monsieur Marsh-wiggle would not have accepted one cent less. As it was, he counted every bit before he handed her the parcel and she took her leave.

Back in her room, she carefully took out the painting and looked at it again. No signature on the front, but at the back, on the edge of the paper, just under the mount . . . She squinted. Was that some writing in a tiny, crabbed hand, or just a scribble? She peered more closely but still couldn't make it out. She needed a magnifying glass. Then she had a brainwave. Picking up her phone, she took a photo of the writing and zoomed in. Yes! Finally she could just about make it out. It read *Pour OS*—or was that *GS*, it was hard to be sure—*affectueusement, MY, '38*. That last bit was much clearer. Gabi sat back, her pulse quickening.

Back in art school in Sydney, ten years ago, Gabi had first come across the work of Marguerite Yonan, an elusive artist born in France to an Assyrian father and Belgian mother. Yonan had lived in Montmartre, but left France in 1939, not long before war broke out, then wandered through Asia, and eventually ended up in Sydney. She'd taught for a short while at the art school and exhibited in a number of galleries in Sydney and Melbourne before she vanished without a trace, presumed drowned, off a beach on the NSW north coast in 1953. Her paintings and drawings, distinguished by a surreal, almost sinister sense of perspective that turned ordinary objects into bizarre fragments of another world, survived in a few public and private collections—including at the art school.

Although Yonan's work was not regarded by art critics as being of the highest rank, it was still considered interesting and quite collectable, and certainly worth a good deal more than thirty euros. But Gabi didn't care whether it was collectable or highly regarded by snobby critics. Marguerite Yonan's work had been one of her early influences, helping her find her own path, her own style, and knowing that she now owned an actual Yonan work filled her with elation. Even better, this was an early work that predated Marguerite's departure from France, let alone her professional artistic career. Among the works Gabi had seen in Australia, there was none as early as this. The artist's actual birthdate was hazy, but she couldn't have been more than twenty-three or twenty-four in 1938. Gabi had no idea who GS—or OS—was, but they had clearly been someone dear to Marguerite. Very little was known of Marguerite Yonan's private life, other than she'd been an only child, and orphaned at a young age when her parents died in a car crash. She had never married, never had children. There was speculation she'd left France as the result of a failed love affair, but no one knew for sure. She had been a very private person.

Propping the drawing up on the table near the window, Gabi looked at it for a long moment. Surely this was a sign that things were going to change. She had been right to come here. So right! It was time to go buy a new sketchbook.

Later, back at the table in her room with the small sketchbook and pencils she'd bought from a shop down the road, Gabi started drawing—a few rapid strokes conjuring up an image of Monsieur Marsh-wiggle sitting at his counter, a bowl of bizarre fruit perched on his head. Yes, it was happening, it really was. That strange encounter, that unexpected find: it was unlocking something. It was the beginning of something new, she was sure of it.

She bought a takeaway dinner of roast chicken and potatoes from the local *rotisserie*, and ate it straight from the bag on a quay down by the river, a short walk from the hotel. The early evening was cool, but it was still light. It was a postcard-perfect scene, the river gleaming softly, the famous skyline of the Île de la Cité rising opposite.

Once the food was finished, she wiped her fingers and started on another drawing, this time of a bowl of fruit floating on a flooded river, smudged buildings crowding in on it. But she had only just begun sketching in the fruit, half-visible in ripples of water, when she stopped, the pencil hovering, then coming down hard, jabbing into the paper, furious black dots all over the half-started lines. No. No. This was all wrong. This was way too—whimsical. Self-consciously quirky. Facile. She was trying to pastiche Yonan and not succeeding. It was lifeless. Dull. Second-hand. No, third-rate. Angrily, she ripped the page out and scrunched it up. Then she turned back to the first drawing and scrunched that up too. Jamming the sketchbook and pencil into her jacket pocket, she found a bin and chucked in the pages along with the takeaway bag, then walked rapidly away, head throbbing, heart beating fast.

She walked for a long time along the river, passing small groups of picnicking families and interlaced couples. She tried to calm herself, to stop the familiar cold trickle of fear. This wasn't the first time she'd seen a false dawn, gone down a dead end. She'd tried any number of ways to whip that bitch of a muse back into shape, this was just the latest. But somehow it felt different. As though the universe was mocking her, sending her a shining sliver of hope, only to snatch it away again. Who was she to know if that drawing really *was* a genuine Yonan? There could have been any number of amateur artists with those initials, and surrealism was quite the go back then, in the heyday of Magritte and Dalí.

Treacherous thoughts coursed through her. *I'm just as bad at spotting the genuinely inspired in others now as in myself. That's because I've lost it. The understanding, the instinct. I'm not a real artist. Not anymore. But if I'm not that, what the hell am I?* She fought against the thoughts—the corrosive fear, the futile questions—just as she'd done for months now. She had to deal with it in the only way she knew: push it into a fog at the back of her mind.

When she finally decided it was time to go back to the hotel, it was getting quite late, and she felt calmer. The mind-fog had worked.

She got the Metro, and as she got off at the Saint-Paul stop, she saw, ahead of her in the crowd of people flooding out from the train, Sylvie from the cooking school, with a good-looking silver-haired man in a navy-blue coat. He was no taller than Sylvie; in fact, if she had been wearing heels, he would definitely have been shorter. His arm was around her, and Gabi kept well back, not wanting to intrude. By the time she got up the steps and into the street, they had disappeared.

Five

'So we're agreed, then?' Sylvie turned at the street door and looked searchingly at Claude.

'Of course, my love,' he said, smiling at her in that way that used to make her pulse go faster. Now it mostly irritated her.

'It will be so much better once everything is clear,' she said, firmly. 'We will all know where we stand.'

'You are absolutely right, my darling. And I will do it, exactly as we agreed. But it isn't easy. Poor Marie-Laure, she still lives in the past. You understand.'

No. She didn't. She was fed up with 'understanding'. From what she could tell, Marie-Laure, from whom Claude had been separated for over a year, was an entitled, narcissistic cow who enjoyed seeing him twist on the cunning hook of her own manipulative neediness. Sylvie had never met her in the flesh, but Claude had shown her a photo once, revealing her to be one of those fine-boned, haughty, look-down-the-nose types. She certainly hadn't behaved with any kind of upper-class *sangfroid*, though. She hadn't accepted the separation well, and was blocking any attempt at divorce by jamming sticks in the wheels, as the French saying had it. Worse than that, she rang Claude in tears late at night, and constantly wanted him to come over to her flat to fix a litany of household issues (amazing in itself, considering Claude's total lack of DIY skills). And because she had been known to turn up unexpectedly at Claude's flat, he and Sylvie never met there, but at Sylvie's, or in some neutral spot, like a café or restaurant or hotel. So far, Marie-Laure had not found out he was seeing someone else, and Claude said it was imperative that she didn't, because she was morbidly jealous and would make life unbearable for them both.

Sylvie had had to agree with all the skulking-around nonsense because she didn't want to precipitate a melodramatic confrontation with an obviously unstable woman. But this situation had been dragging on for far too long now. It was one thing to have a clandestine affair with a married man—you went into that with your eyes open, knowing he might never leave his wife, and you might not even want him to. It was quite another to be having a relationship with a man whose *ex-wife* still controlled his life to the extent that he had to hide all signs that he had a new partner. She'd put up with it long enough, but now it had become intolerable. That was why she'd finally told Claude tonight that she was no longer prepared to wait. 'Either you tell her about us *and* you cut ties with her, or it's over between us.'

He'd protested, saying that he needed more time, but Sylvie had shook her head. 'I've given you long enough, Claude. It's absolutely absurd that we have to hide and skulk in corners as if we were teenagers trying to deceive strict parents, not adults who are perfectly free to conduct a relationship.'

'I know, I know,' he'd said, taking her hand in his over the restaurant table, his rueful green eyes gazing directly into her cross brown ones. 'It is a source of great distress to me that we have needed to do this.'

'Then end that distress. No more waiting.'

He'd sighed. 'You can be a hard woman, Sylvie, when you want to be.'

'And you can be a weak man, Claude,' she'd flashed back.

An angry glint had come into his eyes. 'You don't know what it's like, trying to deal with Marie-Laure.'

'No, I don't. It's not my concern. And it shouldn't be yours any longer,' Sylvie had said, tightly.

'You know how soft-hearted I am,' he'd said. And he'd squeezed her hand and smiled sadly at her. 'Please give me more time. Losing you would be like losing part of my soul.'

A cool part of her had cringed at the sentimentality, even though it gave her a little twinge. She'd said, briskly, to cover it, 'I don't want to lose you either, Claude. But this can't go on.'

'Of course,' he'd said. 'And it won't. I promise.'

Now, on the threshold of her building, he looked at her and said, 'How about we go up and toast our agreement?'

She shook her head. 'Not tonight. I'm very tired. And you know what it's like, the first week of a new class. I have to be absolutely focused.'

Irritation gleamed in his eyes. 'Of course. I'd forgotten it was one of *those* weeks. I'm glad you could spare some time for me tonight.' Definitely a bit of vinegar there.

'I'm sorry, Claude,' she said. 'But I do have to work.'

'Of course you do,' he said, giving her another of those smiles. 'You're a real businesswoman. Unlike . . .' He stopped, hurriedly, but Sylvie's hackles rose. *Unlike poor Marie-Laure.* Bloody Marie-Laure, a spoiled *fille à Papa*, a daddy's girl, a rich man's daughter who'd never had to work for a living. She'd always got everything she wanted, including Claude—and was furious that her luck was running out now. Why did Claude always make excuses for her? 'Good night, then,' Sylvie said, coolly.

'Good night,' he said, kissing her on the cheek. 'We'll speak soon.'

She watched for a moment as he went off up the street. He had definitely been put out by being sent off, when he'd clearly expected to stay the night, but the last thing she needed right now was to be ministering to his hurt feelings.

She'd first met Claude Bollon at the launch of a new perfume brand, nine months ago. He was the editor of an ultra-chic magazine but didn't seem like the pretentious type she associated with that world. He had a natural charm, and his good looks, those amazing green eyes against thick, prematurely silver hair, didn't exactly hinder him either. He'd come up to her with two flutes of Champagne, handed her one and said, with a smile, 'You look as if you might need this. As do I.'

And that was it. Embarrassingly for her self-respect, she had fallen for him that night. He had only been separated from

Marie-Laure for three months, and was very eligible. Yet somehow he had chosen her. And she was so out of practice with men! She hadn't had a serious relationship in years. She'd always been too busy running the business, and looking after Julien. His father had never been a part of their life, so she'd had to bring her son up as a single mother. Love affairs had been the last priority in her hectic life. Occasionally, there had been a short-lived fling, yet even that had tailed off in the last two or three years, because she just couldn't be bothered with it. When she met Claude, Julien had been about to finish university, and though he hadn't left home, he was pretty independent. And the business ran like clockwork. Mostly.

And so she and Claude had become lovers. He was just as good in bed as she'd imagined, and out of bed he was attentive, interesting and sophisticated. And though she soon learned what Marie-Laure was like, she'd thought it would pass and the woman would see sense. But months and months had passed and nothing had changed . . .

Tapping in the entry code, she pushed open the door and went in. She had just got off the lift on the third floor when a door along the passageway opened and Serge poked his head out. 'Ah, Sylvie, I hoped it might be you. We have a problem.'

'What's up?' she asked, immediately alert. Serge wasn't just a neighbour and friend; he also supplied the school, and several restaurants around Paris, with high-quality organic vegetables and fruit, which he sourced from a range of producers in the regions around the city.

'I've just had a call from that new guy who was meant to deliver the asparagus for your class tomorrow morning.' He pushed his glasses up his nose, the normally cheerful grey eyes behind them filled with annoyance. 'He's run out, apparently. I'm so sorry, Sylvie. I've rung around to source some others, but it's going to be hard to get the same quality at this short notice. I could go to Rungis first thing tomorrow, see if I can get some there.' Rungis was the huge wholesale produce market on the outskirts of Paris.

'Don't worry,' she said, thinking quickly. 'We'll simply switch from the asparagus dish to one that uses something you do have on hand. What about fresh peas?'

He looked relieved. 'Absolutely. No problem with that. We have excellent ones, the sweetest your students will ever have tasted, I'm sure.'

'Then it's settled.' She smiled. 'Please bring me a box tomorrow at eight.'

His eyes lit up with a smile. 'Done!' Then his expression changed. 'I'm so furious with that *mec*, that guy. I suppose a bigger order came along, and mine was too small. I won't use him again, I'll just go back to my original supplier. Honestly, you try to give someone new a chance and they fling it in your face. I'm sorry. I know you have things planned.'

'It's okay, Serge, really,' she said, gently. 'It might even freshen up our presentation a bit.' An idea for a vignette around the peas was already firming up in her mind. She'd have to send Damien a text about the change, but he was a flexible sort of guy.

'Then I'm glad.' Running his hand absent-mindedly through his wiry red hair, he added, 'If you're sure.'

'Absolutely.' She gave him a mock-stern look. 'Don't worry. The panic's over.'

He gave her a sideways glance. 'Sure it is. Till next time.'

'That's how it is in our business, *hein*?' she said, and they both laughed.

'Fancy a small cognac?' he asked. 'I feel like I need it.'

'What a good idea.' She smiled and followed him into the apartment.

And it was indeed a good idea. By the time they'd finished their cognacs, while cheerfully chatting about what the upcoming week might bring, the last of the tension had left Sylvie.

Six

Kate was woken early from a deep sleep by the strident call of her mobile. She usually put it on silent to sleep but last night she'd forgotten. Her jet lag had finally caught up with her after a lively night out with some of the other students. They'd gone from an after-class drink to a great meal in a local restaurant and then another drink in one of the cool little bars that dotted the Marais. It wasn't very late when she got back to her room but late enough. She'd fallen into bed and not opened her eyes till the phone rudely jerked her awake, anxiety gripping her throat as she saw who was voice-calling on WhatsApp.

'Dad, what's up? Is Mum okay?' Her mother had recently been diagnosed with high blood pressure, which, she assured the family, was being managed perfectly well with medication. But she was also perfectly capable of pretending all was well so as not to worry anyone. It drove Kate to distraction, though her older sister, Leah, was more philosophical. *No point in fretting with Mum*, she'd say. *You'll just raise your own blood pressure and make no impact on her.*

'She's fine, don't worry.' He paused. 'It's Josh.'

Kate stiffened. 'What about him?' Despite their many differences, her father had got on with Josh. Of course he'd been shocked at his son-in-law's betrayal and had supported his daughter, but Kate suspected that, deep down, he still had a soft spot for her ex.

'Look, Kate, don't take this the wrong way,' her father said, 'but it's about those Resmond shares you still hold.'

Kate said nothing. She'd seen the increasingly urgent emails from the company but had decided to ignore them.

'Have you even had a look at the offer?'

'Haven't had time,' she replied, tightly.

He sighed. 'You just need to decide, sweetheart. One way or the other. Your mother and I . . .' He broke off, but she wasn't going to let him get away with it.

'What, Dad? What do you and Mum think I should do? Reward my cheating husband by selling him my shares at a bargain basement price?'

'Hardly,' he said, 'they are paying above the odds, and—'

'Are you doing Josh's dirty work for him,' she hissed, 'is that it?'

'Oh, Katie, sweetheart. That's not fair, and you know it.'

She took a deep breath. 'I'm sorry, Dad. I didn't mean . . . I really don't want to be thinking about this right now. I'm having such a lovely time here and that's the headspace I want to be in, not . . . not stuff that I . . .' To her annoyance, her voice quivered, and she stopped.

'I know,' he said, quietly. 'And I wouldn't have called if Josh hadn't been on my back about it. It's worrying your mother, and you know how it's no good for her if she worries . . .'

'That bastard!' she said, furiously. 'How dare he put the hard word on you and Mum, I'll bloody well kill him—no, I'll sic my lawyer on to him!'

Her father gave a brief laugh. 'Sweetheart, calm down. No killing, no lawyers required. Just answer your emails and give them a decision. Then we can all take a breath. And forget about Josh.'

Kate's stomach churned as the pain of the last few months surged through her. 'I would love to do that,' she whispered. 'I wish I could wipe him from my memory so that the sound of his name doesn't ring a single bell. But I can't. He betrayed me in the worst possible way.' Her voice shook. 'You know that. So don't ask me to do anything that would make his life easier.'

'Oh, sweetheart, not his,' her father said, softly, 'yours.'

'How does it make it easier for me? I helped to build that company,' she retorted. 'Its success was at least partly due to me. I don't see why I should simply let that bastard take everything.'

'Of course not!' Her father's voice rose. 'Listen, Katie. Your mother and I sold our shares back to them at a good profit, because you know what? Since you left the board, no one has dared to rein in Josh's extravagances and wilder ideas. We reckon that Resmond's over-hyped and over-extended and that in not very long, maybe a year, maybe less, its stock will plummet.'

'Really?' Kate couldn't quite keep the scepticism from her voice, though she was touched by his affirmation of her management skills.

'Look, I know we're not professional investors, but we know what's going on and we keep up with trends. I'm telling you, now's the time to get out, while you can.'

'Okay, Dad.' His words made sense. Besides, she was tired of it all. And she'd be late for today's class if she didn't get her skates on. 'I'll tell them I want to sell. But at the price I want.'

'You're doing the right thing, sweetheart. You really are.' A pause, then he went on, 'And you're enjoying yourself over in gay Paree, then?'

'Oh, Dad.' He could be such a dag, with his outdated sayings. A wave of love for him and her mother filled her as she went on, 'It's wonderful. I wish you and Mum could be here too.'

'No, you don't,' he said, laughing. 'We'd only cramp your style. You want to say a word to the old girl? She's around somewhere.'

'Dad!' she reproved. 'That's so sexist! How would you like it if she referred to you as old boy?'

'I'd be delighted,' he said, chortling, 'it would make a change from being called old bastard! Hey, Pat, come and say a quick word to your daughter before she goes off for another day of frogs' legs and cancan!'

He was impossible, Kate thought, grinning, which was exactly what her mother said as she came on the line. 'Your dad's imposs-ible. I told him it was probably silly o'clock over in France but he just had to call.'

'It's okay, Mum. I had to be up anyway, we start classes early, you know. Anyway, how are you?'

'Never better,' said her mother, airily, 'but let's not talk about me. How are you coping over there? How's your French going?'

'Okay, so far.' She'd had basic French but had to do a refresher course before coming. 'But I haven't had to do much more than order in a restaurant and simple conversation. The classes are all in English, there are people from everywhere. Even another Australian, but she's from Sydney.'

'Oh well, then,' said her mother, dismissively, and Kate smiled to herself. Her mother was a convinced Melburnian born and bred. 'How's the course going?'

'It's early days, but great. Really different from any other cooking class I've ever been to. The woman who runs it, she's amazing. I had a bit of a chat to her yesterday over lunch and guess what? She backpacked in Australia for a year when she was in her twenties and got a job as a kitchen hand in that pasta place you used to like, Benny's or whatever it was called?'

'Well, well, small world, eh!' Kate's mother sighed. 'Wish we could head out to Benny's for dinner tonight. Life was simple, then.' A pause, then she went on, 'Your father's not been going on at you about those shares, has he?'

'He *might* have mentioned them,' Kate said, lightly, 'but don't worry, Mum, he's right. I'm going to sell. And draw a line under you know who.'

'Ugh,' said her mother, 'that line's sure to be crooked, if it has to do with you know who. But seriously, darling, it's a good move.'

'Yes,' Kate said, and not wanting to go over it again, she changed the subject. 'So how are my favourite kids? Still causing chaos, I hope?'

'They sure are,' said her mother, laughing fondly, 'especially Billy, jeez, he's a character that one! Marches to the beat of his own drum, that's for sure.'

'Best way to be,' said Kate, firmly. Her nephew, Billy, Leah's youngest child, held a special place in her heart, though she also adored Billy's sweetheart of a big sister, Mia. But Billy reminded her of herself when she was his age, always getting into mischief out of sheer curiosity about the world.

They talked about Paris and the cooking classes for a while before Kate had to end the call. She was glad now that her father had called. She felt refreshed and determined. Ready to start a new day. And to draw a line under Josh and that part of her life. So before she headed to the shower, she brought up the latest unanswered email from Resmond, hit reply and quickly keyed in *Try 300 per cent more than your current offer and it might be considered. Sincerely, Kate Evans*, and sent it.

Seven

'Superb simplicity, that's what spring is about,' Sylvie said, 'coloured in shades of green. Just look.' And she gestured towards the array of vegetables on the table: the bright green of podded peas, dramatic in a pure white bowl; a raffia basket of olive-green artichokes; bunches of deep green spinach; new fresh garlic, their long light green stems making them look like tiny leeks; the small, soft, dark green salad vegetable known as *mâche* or *doucette* in France, which you saw everywhere at this time of the year. There were several herbs, too, in different gradations of green: feathery dill and lacy parsley; small-leaved thyme and large-leaved mint; a bunch of chives and a picking of tarragon and chervil. Next to all the green, by way of contrast, was a latticed wooden box filled with small new potatoes whose skins would just rub off, revealing delicious waxy yellow flesh underneath; a tall bottle of organic olive oil from Provence next to a beautiful round pat of Norman farmhouse butter; the bright red of *piment d'Espelette* in a jar; and a long platter of blue-green glass on which reposed a series of small round fresh goat's cheeses, no doubt the ones brought yesterday by that guy Gabi had met at the door.

It was a beautiful sight, a classic still life fit to be captured in a riot of paint. *But that won't happen*, thought Gabi, determinedly keeping the self-pity at bay. After a restless night, she'd woken with a clear knowledge. She'd lost it. Not the urge to capture life in lines and colour—no, that kept coming, nagging away like an unresolvable itch. But the more you scratched at it, the worse it became. You were left aching, your skin sorer than before, and you still couldn't get rid of the itch. So she hadn't lost that urge, no, but she'd lost the capacity to discriminate, to know when inspiration would lead somewhere: that deep-set knowledge which made you an artist. She'd felt it instinctively before. Inspiration to process to finished work: it had been seamless. It hadn't always resulted in great work or even good work, but that had been okay, because that was all part of it. She'd worked away all those years, feeling her way into her art, deeply, so it became embedded in her bones and blood. She'd worked tirelessly, not afraid to make mistakes, or experiment, or start again, but always, always, trusting in her art. And eventually, all that work had culminated in *Shadow Life*. Her breakthrough. Her big success. Her curse . . .

'This spring symphony of green, with notes of other colours, is what we'll be working on today,' Sylvie was saying, 'partly as a preparation for choosing your own ingredients on our first visit to a local market on Thursday. Now, before we start, are there any questions or thoughts about yesterday's class?'

'Yes,' said Pete. 'A bunch of us went to a café last night for dinner, and they had those eggs *mimosa* on the menu, but they weren't anything as good as the ones we had here. Maybe you should go and give them a masterclass!'

There was a bit of a laugh at that, and Sylvie smiled. 'Thank you. That is much appreciated. But I wouldn't dream of it. And do beware of thinking we have the *only* right recipe, the *only* right way to do things. Although we do have a pretty good one,' she added, with a twinkle in her eye, 'and we're glad you approve of it!'

'But if you don't think you have the only right way,' Gabi began, 'what are you doing teaching it to others?' As soon as the words were out of her mouth, she wished she could call them back. She'd sounded rude and aggressive. And judging by the expressions on the other students' faces, they thought exactly that. But she hadn't intended to be insulting, it had just slipped out like that. And now it was too late to backtrack.

'It's a good question,' Sylvie said, sounding quite unruffled. 'And if I say that teaching the way that I am confident about, which I know best, is the only reason I *can* teach it, will that be a good enough answer?'

She looked at Gabi. *Everyone* looked at Gabi. She swallowed, flushed, and said, 'Of course. I understand. Totally.'

Now I sound gushing and insincere, she thought, crossly.

But Sylvie smiled. 'Then I'm glad. Not only about that, but that you asked the question in the first place. Because it made me think about what I'd said before and crystallise why I believe it. Thank you!'

'No worries,' mumbled Gabi, wishing they could just move on so she could stop being the centre of attention. And little by little, as the morning wore on and the cheerful kitchen clatter began, Gabi took her own advice and moved on into the real enjoyment of watching and listening and cooking up a storm.

Lunchtime was late again but just as cheerful as yesterday, as the class chattered animatedly about the morning's lesson, and tasted each other's creations. The goat's cheese, deservedly, was very popular as a 'note' in the 'green symphony'. It featured as the centrepiece of a warm cheese salad on chopped spinach braised in olive oil, with fresh garlic; stirred through a dish of new potatoes, with butter and dill; and as a side to a bowlful of sweet, buttered tiny peas dotted with mint, and a fragrant platter of simple steamed artichokes, served with vinaigrette. The vinaigrette itself had been a side-lesson within the morning's work, and even Gabi, used to her family's classic version, had to admit this one, with its addition of tarragon mustard, a grating of garlic and a hint of lemon juice to the base of olive oil and white wine vinegar, was pretty damn good. Her own contribution had been that glorious bowl of peas; it had almost felt like cheating, because there was so little that could go wrong. But she'd still been pretty chuffed when Sylvie and Damien, tasting a spoonful, had pronounced it to be 'absolute perfection'. The class hadn't been far behind in their appreciation. At least there was one thing she could still get right!

Even the kids wouldn't turn up their noses at these greens, Kate wrote to the family WhatsApp group, inserting photos of the various dishes that had been on the table but were now well and truly demolished. It was after lunch and she was about to head off. *And those peas, OMG! Like green caviar, bursting in your mouth with a pop of absolute sweetness and freshness, just amazing!*

She was about to send the message when the front door buzzer sounded. From where she stood, in the hall just outside the bathroom, she could hear it very clearly, but as nobody came to answer, it seemed nobody else had heard it. She realised most of the other students had already left, and the staff must be busy. The ring came again, insistently, and she hesitated. She could just go and get Sylvie, but she'd left the dining room soon after lunch. Damien and the assistant, Yasmine, must be about though, it'd be better if they spoke to whoever was at the door, rather than her with her imperfect French. Then the buzzer rang once more, and she decided it would be quicker to just answer it

A thin young dark-haired woman in a black T-shirt and jeans, her arms full of boxes, stood there. Kate was just about to speak to her when Sylvie hurried down the hall. 'What is it?'

'Delivery, I think,' said Kate.

'But we weren't expecting . . .' Sylvie stopped and turned to the delivery woman. In French, she asked, 'Yes, what is this?'

'Your order,' said the woman, in a halting French, with an accent that sounded Eastern European. She nodded towards the pile of boxes she was holding. 'Ten frozen pizza bases.'

Sylvie stared at her, as did a startled Kate. Even with her own halting French, she could see what was written on the boxes. Frozen pizza bases! Why on earth was the Paris Cooking School ordering things like that?

'There is a mistake,' said Sylvie, tightly, to the delivery driver. 'We made no such order.'

'But, Madame . . .' With one hand, the young woman tried to reach into her pocket while, with the other, she tried to keep a hold on the boxes. Finally she pulled out a piece of paper and consulted it. 'Is this the Paris Cooking School? Are you Madame Sylvie Morel?'

'It is. And I am. But I made no such order and . . . Wait!' Her eyes narrowed. 'How did you get the entry code into this building?'

The young woman's eyes widened. 'Your assistant gave it to us, of course.'

'You mean Yasmine? Or Damien?' Sylvie's voice was sharp.

Kate knew she should leave. This wasn't her business. But she couldn't help hovering.

'I don't know, Madame. I wasn't the one who took the call.'

'Okay, enough,' said Sylvie, then, gesturing to Kate, she said, in English, 'I'm sorry to ask, but can you please go and get Damien? He's in the basement, dealing with the rubbish.'

Kate headed downstairs and found Damien sitting on a bin in the basement, smoking. He looked startled, then guilty, as she came in. Stubbing out the cigarette, he said, 'Oh, hi.'

'Sorry about intruding,' Kate said, in English, 'but Sylvie asked me to find you. There's a problem. An unexpected order of frozen pizza bases.'

Utter astonishment filled his face. 'Frozen pizza bases?' he echoed, blankly. 'We never order such things.'

'Yes, that's what Sylvie says. But the delivery driver says you ordered it.'

'*I* ordered it?' Now Damien was outraged.

'Well, she said an assistant, and . . .'

But Damien had already gone, rushing for the lift.

Kate made her way back up via the stairs. She needed to get her bag and head off to her hotel, but she wanted to leave time and space for Sylvie and Damien to work out the misunderstanding.

Back upstairs, Kate found Damien and Sylvie in earnest conversation in the hall. A little uncertainly, she asked, 'Is everything okay?'

Sylvie gave her a tired smile. 'Yes. We gave that poor girl money to cover the delivery—she isn't paid any commission unless she delivers—and told her to give the pizza bases to her friends. That seemed to be acceptable.'

'Of course,' grumbled Damien. 'Free money, and free pizzas! Okay, okay,' he added, when Sylvie glared at him, 'I know you had to do it, but it really is annoying!'

'It is more than annoying,' said Sylvie, quietly. 'But we will get to the bottom of it.' She looked at Kate. 'I am sorry that you had to witness all that.'

'Oh no, it's quite all right . . . I'm just sorry for you.' She hesitated, then went on, 'If I can be of any help . . .'

'Thank you. But it's fine. You don't need to worry. You are here to enjoy yourself, not be dragged into tiresome administrative details. At least,' Sylvie added, 'I hope you *are* enjoying yourself?'

'Oh yes! So much! This is truly . . .' Kate struggled to find the words. 'Truly one of the best things to happen to me in quite a while. I love what we're doing. I love what you do. And I'm so happy we're only at the beginning and still have so much to learn and experience.'

Both Sylvie and Damien were beaming now. 'Well,' Sylvie said, 'that is wonderful to hear. It is exactly what we hope for.' She looked at Kate. 'Damien, Yasmine and I usually have a drink about now, to unwind. Yasmine's gone home early, but would you like to join us?'

Kate smiled. 'I'd like that very much. Thank you.'

Eight

During Gabi's visit to Guernsey, in the week before she'd come to Paris, her mother's sister, Melanie, had shown her a battered, stained book that was a guide from the 1900 Paris Exposition. It had been brought back as a souvenir by their ancestors Thomas and Beatrice Ogier, who had been enterprising enough to run a cheese stand somewhere within the massive exposition grounds in central Paris. The exposition had gone on for months but the Ogiers could only afford to stay for three weeks and had returned to Guernsey with a bit of money to show for their time, but many more memories—not all of them good, apparently. Their trip had passed into family legend, embellished and embroidered by their descendants as time went on. As far as actual documents went, though, there was just one small photo, which showed them posing in front of the Petit Palais, one of the few buildings constructed for the exposition which still stood today; and the guidebook, which had been passed down through the family like a holy relic. After Gabi had told her aunt that she intended to do some research about the Ogiers in Paris, Melanie agreed to lend the book to her for the duration of her stay, on condition that she bring it back in person afterwards. 'I don't trust the post, and besides, this is a way to lure you back to see us again.' She'd smiled. 'It's been too long between visits.' But she hadn't lent the photo; too easily lost, she'd said. Instead, Gabi had taken a photo of it with her phone.

Now, on this sunny Wednesday afternoon, she stood, open book in hand, in the middle of the grand Alexandre III bridge whose elegant steel arch, bookended by carved stone pillars topped with golden statues, spans the Seine, linking two of the city's most famous quarters: the Champs-Élysées on the right bank and the Esplanade des Invalides on the left bank. On both sides of the river it was a magnificent view, but back in Thomas and Beatrice's time, it would have had the added excitement of being at the centre of the globe's biggest and most ambitious show, with a huge stage of superb but ephemeral pavilions and palaces, painstaking reconstructions of the distant past and exciting portents of the electric future.

Gabi took several pictures, from all angles. Despite the brisk wind coming off the river, the sunny afternoon had brought out lots of people, a tide of humanity flowing across the bridge. The pictures from 1900 that Gabi had seen online also showed crowds of people milling about on the bridge. She could almost see Thomas and Beatrice standing there, taking in the panorama before them, lost in awe and trepidation. Guernsey was a quiet little place even now, but she imagined coming from there back then and finding yourself here, in the middle of the huge crowds come to gawk at the world's wonders—talk about culture shock! And moving among the crowds, with his tray of cakes slung from a leather strap around his neck, would have been a young man from another part of Gabi's family tree: Ander Picabea from the equally quiet Basque hills in the hinterland of Biarritz. The family story went that he'd rented time in someone's oven and got up in the middle of the night to make the little cakes that he hawked around the exposition. He'd managed to earn enough to return home with money to help set up his own small bakery, and for a dowry for his sweetheart Maïté, daughter of a local farmer. For him, Paris was just somewhere to make money fast, and the only souvenirs he'd brought back were a pretty lace collar for Maïté—and an enduring dislike of the city, which, Gabi thought, smiling to herself, he'd passed on down the generations to her own father. But not to her. Being here, on such a beautiful day, looking, imagining—it was wonderful. It took her outside of herself . . .

'Hello.' The voice behind her made her jump. She turned to see a man in a hooded jacket and sunglasses. He saw her wary expression, took off his glasses, and smiled. 'Sorry. I didn't mean to startle you.'

She knew him now, those very dark eyes, the light brown hair under the hood. It was the cheese guy—Yasmine had said his name was Max. 'It's okay,' she said, in French. 'I was a long way away. In 1900 actually. Imagining being at the exposition.'

His smile was broader now. 'Really? That's cool.' His glance fell on the book she was holding. 'Did you find that at one of the *bouquinistes*?' The bookstalls lining the Seine were one of the great attractions of the riverside.

'No. It's a family treasure.' And Gabi found herself telling him the story of how both sides of her family tree had found themselves in Paris in 1900.

He listened intently, showing no trace of boredom, and when she'd finished he said, 'That is quite something.'

'Isn't it?' replied Gabi, pleased by his genuine interest. She had told everyone back home that she was looking into her ancestors' time in Paris as research for her new show. It was a fib, of course, designed to deflect nosy family questions, but that didn't matter.

'I wonder if they ever met, even without knowing it,' Max said, and she smiled.

'Yes, I wondered that too.'

Their eyes met and Gabi had the strangest feeling, a feeling she hardly recognised, it had been so long. *Joy*, she thought wonderingly. *I do believe it's joy*.

'It's a bit chilly standing here, don't you think?' he said, his eyes still on her face. 'And there's a great café in the Petit Palais that serves pretty good hot chocolate. What do you say?'

'I say that I am suddenly in dire need of a hot chocolate at the Petit Palais,' said Gabi, looking boldly back at him. 'But only with someone I have been formally introduced to, of course.'

'Of course, Mademoiselle from 1900,' he said, giving her a mock bow. 'My name is Max Rousseau, citizen of this fair town and cheesemonger by trade.'

'Pleased to meet you, Monsieur Max,' said Gabi, pertly. 'My name is Gabrielle Picabea, only my friends call me Gabi, citizen of the world, and apprentice cook.' The half-truth about her work tripped off her tongue, and she didn't feel bad about it at all. It was just part of the joyful moment and the sunny afternoon.

'Pleased to meet you too, Mademoiselle Gabi,' he said, 'and now that we are formally introduced, let us proceed to the halls of refreshment.'

'Very well, Monsieur,' she said, with a mischievous sideways glance.

They walked across the bridge back towards the Petit Palais, just a short distance away. Along the way, Max asked how Gabi was finding the course, and she told him how much she loved it. 'There's always something surprising—today, for instance, a woman called Annick came to speak to us. She works in the local library, but she's an excellent fish cook, too.'

'I think I know who you mean,' Max interrupted, 'she's from St Malo originally, right?'

'Yes, that's right. Anyway, she put on an amazing show, all around this one fish.' And she told him how Annick had chosen the fish known in France as the Saint-Pierre, the Saint-Peter, but also occasionally as 'Jean Doré' or, literally, 'Golden John'. 'We call it John Dory in Australia and, though I'm bilingual, I'd never realised that's where the name came from.'

'She must have told you the legend, then?' Max said. 'About Saint Peter forcing the fish to give up the golden coin it was hiding in its mouth?'

Gabi nodded. 'And that ever since the imprint of the saint's index finger and thumb has stayed on every one of those fish.'

'He is a fish of France and a fish of the world, a fish called John and a fish called Peter, a fish with a gold coin in the legend and a fish worth his weight in gold in the kitchen,' Max said, in English, making Gabi draw an appreciative breath.

'That's wonderful,' she said. 'Almost a poem.'

'*Almost*?' he exclaimed, pretending to be insulted.

'I'd need to hear it again to be sure,' she said, teasingly.

'Very well. For your ears only,' he added, as she took out her phone, 'not for TikTok.'

'Just for me,' she said, 'I swear. And I hate TikTok anyway.' She snapped a video of him saying the words again.

They were in the Petit Palais now, and Max led her through its spacious museum rooms to a peaceful colonnaded interior courtyard paved with mosaics, where café tables clustered between the pillars, looking out onto a beautiful garden. 'We could have it inside if you're feeling cold,' he said, but Gabi shook her head. 'It's perfect here.'

'One of my favourite places,' Max agreed, gesturing to a table. 'Will this one do?'

Once they were seated, Max picked up the guidebook and started leafing through it. 'Seems like your ancestors had the right idea,' he said, 'all those hungry exposition tourists needing quick snacks! When you look at the list of restaurants, you can imagine how packed they must have been. And it seems like they had *le pop-up* down pat, too,' he added, 'most of the *restos* sound like they were just temporary installations.'

'Just like all the other stuff they built for the exposition,' Gabi said. 'Dozens, even hundreds, of buildings, all over central Paris, and in the Bois de Vincennes. Can you imagine? It must have cost an absolute fortune.'

'Most of it would have been paid for by foreign governments eager to show off their country's splendour,' said Max. 'Paris was the centre of the world at the time, remember. Everyone wanted to be seen here.'

'Everyone still does,' said Gabi. 'Except for my dad.'

Max laughed. 'Of course! What southerner worth his salt would waste one word of praise on this city?'

'And what Parisian would care?' Gabi countered.

Max shrugged. 'So they say. But I'm not really from Paris, so I can't be sure.'

The cups of chocolate arrived then, richly dark and fragrant, with a cloud of whipped cream on the top. 'Oh,' Gabi breathed, reverently, as she took the first sip and rolled the smooth beverage around her mouth, 'I haven't had hot chocolate this good in a long time.'

'Told you,' said a smiling Max, sipping at his own cup.

'So, then, Max,' she went on, 'where are you really from, if not from Paris?'

'I grew up in the Loire,' he said, 'but when I was thirteen, I moved to Paris to live with my grandmother. So I suppose I am from both, or neither.' He saw her expression, and added, 'My parents wanted me to go to a particular high school in Paris.'

'Oh.' Gabi took another sip of the divine chocolate. 'Do you have any siblings? Did they go to that school too?'

'I've got two brothers, both quite a bit older than me. My parents had other plans for them.'

'That must have been hard, to be separated from them like that.'

'Not at all,' he said. 'My grandmother was very kind. And I wasn't close to my brothers, maybe it was the age gap.'

'I'm the youngest too,' Gabi said, 'but my sister, Joana, and brother, Ben, we're close, even though we've gone on different paths. They're both in professional jobs, and they're both married, with kids, whereas I . . .' She paused, flushing a little.

'Do go on,' he said, smiling.

'Whereas I'm not married and I don't have kids,' she said, with a little smile.

Their eyes met. 'I'm glad to hear that,' he said, quietly. 'Same with me. No kids, anyway. But I was married, once. A folly of youth, or rather an attempt to please my parents. It didn't work: the attempt, or the marriage.'

'I am sorry to hear that,' she said.

He smiled, knowing full well she wasn't sorry at all. 'So you're not married.' He looked her in the eyes. 'But is there someone, back home?'

Her pulse raced, but she held his gaze. 'No. There isn't.'

'Me neither,' he said, and he touched her hand, fleetingly, sending a rush of warmth through her.

'We'd better finish our chocolates,' she said, quickly, 'or they'll get cold.'

'You think so?' he drawled, his eyes still on her.

'I do.' She managed to keep her voice steady. 'And if we drink them quickly, then we can go quickly too. And then—'

'Yes?'

'And then we can have a leisurely promenade along the river,' she said, teasingly. '*Sympa, non*?'

'*Sympa, oui*,' he replied with a grin. Swallowing the last of his chocolate, he stood up and held out a hand. 'Shall we go for our promenade, then, Mademoiselle Gabi?'

Nine

That afternoon, on her way back from class, Kate noticed a place calling itself the Museum of Magic and Automata, and on impulse went down the stairs and into the dimly lit interior. Her niece, Mia, had recently acquired a magic set for her ninth birthday and become obsessed, so Kate thought she'd take some pictures to send her. But with its creepy transforming automata, 'open mouth of hell' mirror and sinister stories, the dimly lit museum was clearly appealing to an adult and adolescent audience. It wasn't so much a jolly Halloween vibe as a horror movie. But Kate managed to secretly video a few seconds of a live magic show that her niece would love.

Emerging into the bright air with some relief, she took a deep breath. After being down in the sorcerer's dark den she needed a walk. Yesterday she'd taken a stroll to the fabulous BHV department store on the Rue de Rivoli and spent a happy hour or two browsing; today she decided she'd walk a different way, to the Place de la Bastille, where the famous old prison had once stood.

It was a fairly short walk in theory but in practice it took her quite a while because she kept stopping to look in shop windows and take photos of their displays. It didn't matter what the shop was, all their displays were so beautiful. Some were quirky and intriguing, others elegant and glamorous; some full of colour and pattern, others restrained and cool. But all showing an imaginative attention to detail that was quite enthralling, and so individualistic: no same-old-same-old brand marketing here. It was all part of the charm of this city, that individuality, that diversity, and it was exactly what she'd yearned for that first time she'd been here, but had not achieved. She still could not quite get over actually being in this gorgeous place, able to explore it at leisure. Not even the thought of the stiff email she'd got earlier that day about the Resmond shares could spoil that. It was signed by the board chair but everyone knew he was just a rubber stamp for Josh. *You are being quite unfair, Kate. Three hundred per cent over our offer is not on. We might go to 100 per cent over, but that's being very generous.*

She hadn't bothered responding. The words had sent a prickle of fury through her, but it would annoy Josh more if she didn't react to his patronising bullshit.

And she didn't care. That's what they didn't seem to realise. They desperately wanted her to sell her shares, but she didn't care one way or the other. Even if Resmond tanked and she lost her shares, she didn't care. It was a liberating thought.

Presently, the street she was on opened out into the big Bastille square. Several streets converged here, and buses, cars and motorbikes whizzed past noisily on all sides. To reach the island in the middle, with its towering 'July' column commemorating the fall of the Bastille, you had to cross two times. It wasn't at all what she'd expected and she didn't linger. She'd spotted a way down to what she thought was the river, so she headed there and eventually found a set of steps leading down into a covered walkway to the water.

It wasn't the river. It was a canal. The beginning of the Canal Saint-Martin, she realised, after checking her phone. Walking further, she came to an area where the water was closed off by a lock, forming a peaceful little port, where dozens, no, perhaps hundreds, of boats were moored in single file. This was the Port de l'Arsenal, and these were houseboats, of varied size, type and colour. Most were inhabited, judging by the cheerfully curtained windows and pot plants on the decks. Some had fairy lights hung around them, others were painted in bright colours, still others were sober but very neat. Enclosed on all sides by high walls that had no discernible exits, lined by quays that were cobbled in some places, it felt almost like another world. A tranquil waterside village, perhaps, with the noise of the city far away, though its skyline towered above both sides of the port walls.

As Kate paused to take photos, a pair of swans appeared, gliding across the water between the boats, and she was so entranced by the sight that she almost forgot to capture it on her phone. She was about to walk on when she was startled by the feel of somebody nudging the back of her legs.

No, not somebody, at least not human; it was a small, solid dog, looking just like an illustration in a kids' story with its fluffy white coat and beady black eyes set in a cheerful face. It looked a bit like a poodle but not quite. Those black eyes regarded Kate with such innocent curiosity that her heart melted at once. Crouching down to its level, she put out a hand, which the dog promptly sniffed at, then it looked at her, enquiringly.

'Hello, what are you doing here?' she asked it in English. The dog gave a short bark as if to say, *What sort of question is that?* Or maybe, *Speak French, lady!*

She couldn't help smiling at the notion. 'Okay,' she said in French, fondling the dog's ears, 'where do you come from?'

'I'm sorry. Is she bothering you?' The man had seemingly come out of nowhere, but she soon realised he'd appeared from the waterside path behind her.

'No, not at all,' she said, getting to her feet. 'She is—she is so—' what was the word for cute? *Jolie*? *Belle*? No, that wasn't quite it. Then she remembered that French people used 'cool' a lot these days, so she finished by saying, 'she is very cool!'

He laughed. 'I think so too.'

She took him in properly: a broad-shouldered, stocky man in his forties, with short, thick dark hair sprinkled with a few threads of grey, and blue-green eyes in a strongly featured tanned face. He was dressed casually in a round-necked blue jumper and jeans.

'What is her name?' she asked, bending down to pat the dog.

'Nina.'

'That's a good name,' said Kate, as the dog nuzzled at her again. 'What—' she wanted the word for *breed*, but drew a complete blank—'what type of dog is she?'

'She's a *bichon frisé*,' he said, 'just five years old. A good companion.'

'She looks it,' said Kate, wistfully. Her family had once had a Jack Russell terrier. Jack, they'd called him, very unoriginally. Kate and her siblings had pretty much grown up with him. But one day, when they were teenagers, Jack had been bitten by a brown snake and he'd died. No one had the heart to replace him. He'd been loved too dearly. And by the time Kate was an adult and had thought about getting a dog herself, she'd been married to Josh, who had a phobia about dogs. So that was that. Except now, she realised, it *wasn't*. 'Are they difficult to look after?' she asked.

'No. At least not Nina,' he added, smiling. 'She is very adaptable. She needs to be, living on a boat.'

'Oh!' Kate looked up at him, eyes widening. 'You live here?'

He nodded, gesturing to a trim green and white boat a short distance away. 'That's home, yes.'

Chez moi, he'd said. At mine. 'You're lucky,' Kate said. 'It's my father's dream to live on a boat. He has only a . . .' *How do you say 'tinny' in French?* 'He has a small boat, for fishing. Metal.'

'A tinny,' he said, in English. He laughed at her astounded expression. 'Is that not what you say in Australia?'

'Er, yes—yes we do,' said a flustered Kate, switching to English. 'But how do you . . .'

'I recognise your accent,' he said. 'I once spent six months in Australia. Many years ago. One of my friends, he had a tinny.' His English was good, although accented.

'Where in Australia were you?'

'Lake Macquarie,' he said. 'Near Newcastle. You know it?'

'No. I come from Victoria. Melbourne, actually.'

'I visited it once. It is a nice city,' he said. 'Are you here on holiday?'

'Yes. No. Well, sort of. I'm doing a course at the Paris Cooking School.'

He nodded. 'Ah yes! Sylvie Morel's business. It is good, I think.'

'It is very good,' she said, smiling. 'You know Sylvie?'

'A little. I have covered a book for her.'

'Covered a book?' she repeated, puzzled, then understood. 'Oh, I see, you are a bookbinder! That's such a cool thing to do.'

He smiled. 'Not always. But I like it.' At that moment, Nina, who had been standing there looking at them, her tail wagging, gave another of those short, sharp barks.

'I'm sorry,' the man said, 'it is time for her supper. She is not always patient.'

'Of course. I'm sorry for holding you up. It was nice talking to you. And to you too, Nina.' She bent down once more to fondle the dog's ears.

'It was a pleasure,' said the man, and looked for a moment as though he were about to say something else, but Kate didn't wait. With a friendly wave, she headed down the quays. It had been a nice moment, but they'd pretty much exhausted the small talk. Besides, she was getting a bit chilly as the shadows lengthened over the port. Time to get back to the comfort of the hotel.

She'd seen on the map that there was an exit a fair way ahead, onto a bridge that should bring her almost back to the Quartier Saint-Paul. It was when she was almost there that she saw them, leaning against a wall, arms around each other, totally oblivious to anyone else: Gabi and a young man. She couldn't double back, it was too far to retrace her steps. She had to pass them. As she drew near, they broke away from their embrace, and Gabi saw her. She gave her a smile. 'Hey, Kate, you out for a walk too?'

'Yep,' said Kate, trying for the same light tone, 'nice time for it, isn't it?'

'Sure is,' Gabi said. 'This is Max, by the way. Max, Kate is in my cooking class. Kate, Max is responsible for those goat's cheeses we had yesterday.'

'Oh, they were amazing,' Kate said, sincerely, forgetting to be embarrassed.

'I am not *responsible* for that,' Max said, laughing, 'the cheesemaker and the goats are. But I do choose well, it's true.'

'Max!' said Gabi, laughing too.

'I'm not boasting, I'm just telling the truth,' he said, looking at Gabi with a teasing expression in his very dark, almost black, eyes.

'Well it's nice to meet you, Max,' Kate said, 'but I'd better be off. Have a nice evening, both of you.'

Just before she reached the steps up to the bridge, she looked back. They were walking on, his arm around Gabi. The sight sent a twinge through her. It wasn't as if she wanted a Paris romance—she was done with romance, and honestly, Gabi was a bit of a fast worker, wasn't she? But her attempt at prudish tut-tutting didn't work. She knew the truth: she was a little envious of someone who was so light-hearted, so untroubled by problems, that she could simply do whatever she felt like, like having a spring fling with a hot French stranger. *Lucky Gabi*, she thought. *And stupid me, still allowing Josh's long shadow to loom over my life . . .*

Taking out her phone, she tapped out a rapid email to the Resmond board chair. *Okay, 100 per cent more than your original offer. Not a cent less. Kate Evans.* And that was it. She'd be done with it. Done with them. It was none too soon.

Ten

If there was something Sylvie never tired of, it was the markets, despite the fact she'd been to more than she could count! From sitting as a child at her grandmother's egg and poultry stand in the local market town, to being sent as a teenager to do the week's shopping in the Victor Hugo Market in Toulouse; from her first independent foray as an adult gathering ingredients for a special meal designed to impress friends, to now, guiding her wide-eyed students around the big Bastille markets, she'd always felt at home in the noise and bustle and colour of it all. And she loved helping others kickstart a lifelong pleasure.

The class had met early that Thursday morning, all set for the task of gathering ingredients for the week's final group lunch. Sylvie had split them into four pairs of two: two pairs to create entrees, and two pairs to create mains. The theme was spring, so everything had to be based around what was in season *and* based on things they'd learned during the week. There would also be a dessert, created by Damien. And there would be a couple of guests joining them: just Yasmine and Serge, this time. Claude had come along a few times before, but Sylvie had not invited him today. They hadn't spoken since the other night when they'd parted on the doorstep. Sylvie suspected Claude was expecting her to go back on her ultimatum, but she'd done that once before, to her regret. This time, she was not going to be swayed. Besides, she had more concerning things to worry about than a recalcitrant lover. For a start, she'd not been able to find out who had placed that fake pizza-base order. It had been paid for, that was all the shop it had come from knew and cared. But it worried her, and coupled with the Tripadvisor review, it felt like someone was trying to destabilise her business.

But she was determined not to allow a shadowy pest to spoil this session of the school. Especially as this was one of the best groups she'd hosted in recent times—all keen and quick to learn. She'd thought at first that Gabi and Ethan might be a bit more challenging than the others, but they'd both settled down. Shy Misaki had come out of her shell a little, while Pete had stopped being quite so loud. As for the rest, the Germans were always bright and pleasant, and Mike good-natured and jokey, even if a little tiring at times. But Kate was Sylvie's favourite student, and not only because of her undoubted talent. She was the kind of person Sylvie instinctively felt comfortable with: smart yet modest, hardworking yet able to relax, and neither too familiar nor too formal. And the other day, after the pizza fiasco, she'd been calming and helpful.

'A nice person' as the Anglo-Saxon term would have it, but Sylvie thought the French word *sympa* was much better than that limp English word 'nice'. It conveyed more human warmth, and much more individual quality. She could see Kate now over at a fish stall with her cooking partner Ethan and she smiled, thinking that, despite the Englishman's haughty manner, the Australian could more than hold her own. Being *sympa* didn't mean you were a pushover.

She looked around for the others. Misaki and Mike—a surprisingly successful pairing of opposites—were hesitating over the vegetables on an artistically arranged stand, while Stefan and Pete walked from stand to stand, clearly having trouble deciding what to buy. And the final two, Gabi and Anja, were over at Max's cheese stall, talking animatedly with him. That is, Anja was talking and Max was answering. But he kept glancing sideways at a silent Gabi, whose attention was apparently focused on his cheeses but who occasionally shot him a look back. *Well, well,* Sylvie thought, *good for them!* It was Paris, it was spring, they were young and free, and if you weren't allowed to fall in love or lust, unwisely or not, then truly life was a dreary thing. She only hoped Gabi wouldn't play fast and loose with Max, for underneath his light manner, he had a serious heart. *Bof, what am I doing, meddling with my students' lives, even in thought?* Sylvie asked herself. *They can take care of themselves, it's no business of mine.* Besides it would soon be time to round them all up and get them back to the kitchen to prepare what they'd chosen.

At the cheese stand, Gabi was having trouble stopping herself from telling Anja to take a hike. She desperately wanted to speak with Max but there was no way she could, with the woman babbling on in a mix of reasonable French and excellent English about caves and fermentation and rinds and what have you. Maybe Germany had a big dairy industry and everyone was familiar with cheesemaking. Gabi didn't know and frankly didn't care.

'Mademoiselle, what do you think?' Max had managed somehow to find a space in Anja's incessant chat to address Gabi.

Gabi felt a tingle sneak up her spine. 'Mademoiselle', he'd called her, all polite and formal, when yesterday . . . well! 'I think you are very good at what you do,' she said, demurely, and had the satisfaction of seeing a faint blush creep up his neck.

'I am glad you think so,' he said, looking back at her quite steadily, 'but it is up to you to choose the way you want to go.'

'Oh, but we would value your honest opinion,' Anja broke in, clearly unaware of any double entendres in the conversation. 'As an honourable member of the great cheesemaking fraternity,' she added, and seemed nonplussed when both Gabi and Max laughed, releasing the tension between them.

After that, as they finally decided on the cheeses, and Max packaged them up carefully in waxed paper, Gabi was filled with a great lightness of spirit. She'd thought that maybe facing him today, in an ordinary situation, in the midst of all these people, she'd feel differently. Or that he would. But no. It was extraordinary, this instinctive connection. It was so unexpected. Things like that didn't happen to her. Oh sure, she'd had her share of affairs in the past, and a long-term relationship with a writer called Sam, which had lasted for five not altogether happy years before fizzling out just over a year ago when he'd moved to Perth. Since then, she'd shied away from hooking up, even casually. She knew how some people would interpret that: that she'd lost her libido along with her muse. But she didn't think it was as simple as that. There had been something else inhibiting her. Boredom, perhaps, with the guys she met in her normal circles. Or boredom with the whole dating scene. Or boredom just generally . . .

But Max didn't bore her. Max was *very* far from boring her. And if he kept looking at her like that, Anja or no Anja, she didn't know what would happen. It didn't feel like just a case of simple sexual attraction, strong as that was. She *liked* him, in the real sense of the term. And she felt he liked her too. The lovely ease she felt with him, free of the baggage of the past—that was new, and wonderful, and intoxicating.

'Well, then,' he said, in English, when they had all the packages stowed away in their basket and Anja was looking around to see where the others were, 'are you all set now?'

'Yes,' said Gabi, adding, 'and you?'

He looked quickly at her then at the oblivious Anja, who was waving at the rest of the group, fast approaching with Sylvie. 'Yes,' he said, quietly, in French, looking back at Gabi. 'Yes, I am.' A beat, then just before the others arrived, he added, rapidly, 'Unfortunately I have to be away overnight in the Loire, but tomorrow—may I cook for you tomorrow? My place. I'll send you the address. Yes?'

She could only nod, her throat tight with excitement and nervousness. However was she going to wait till tomorrow?

Eleven

Kate stretched luxuriously, waking up slowly to the morning light slanting through the shutters. It was Friday, the first day of a three-day break from the course. No need to get up at the crack of dawn or oversleep and rush through the streets to class. She could take it easy, explore, poke around, go on a shopping spree, do whatever took her fancy.

The class had dispersed after yesterday's lunch, which had been a big success. Everyone had made different dishes, all quite simple, but all delicious. She'd been paired with Ethan that day, and they'd created a medley of two different types of fish, one grilled, the other roasted, served with a lemon and white wine sauce, based on the one Annick had taught them the other day, but tweaked to include chopped shallots. It had been pronounced pretty much perfect not only by their fellow students but by Yasmine and Serge. And they weren't hollow compliments for both Yasmine and Serge were fine gourmets, apparently. Sylvie and Damien had not been quite as effusive but they had smiled warmly and said it was good. Kate was content, because as far as she was concerned, if they said it was good, that was high praise indeed. Ethan had been a bit snarky about it afterwards, but that wasn't Kate's problem.

Nothing was Kate's problem, right now. She'd loved the markets so much yesterday she decided to visit a couple of them today, in two different parts of the city. One was close by: the old covered market known as the *Marché des Enfants Rouges*, the Market of the Red Children. The rather Gothic sound of its name had intrigued Kate, but when she looked it up, she discovered it was a reference to the red coats worn by children in a nearby orphanage in the nineteenth century. The first market she was going to visit was further afield, in the 6th arrondissement on the left bank. It was at least forty minutes' walk, but it was a nice day and most of the route was close to the river. If she was tired, maybe she'd catch the Metro on the way back, or a bus.

Yawning, she got up. A quick shower, a quick cup of coffee and a croissant downstairs, and then she was off.

It was indeed just as nice a walk as she'd hoped. She kept to the right bank of the Seine for most of the way, then crossed the river at the Carrousel bridge, near the glass pyramid entrance to the Louvre. The Louvre had been one of the places she'd gone to during that first whirlwind visit to Paris, and she didn't intend going there this time, but it was still an imposing sight. She was walking down a long street, pausing now and then to look at shop windows, including Deyrolle, the famous Paris institution specialising in taxidermy that had been going for nearly two hundred years, and which housed a museum as well.

'Careful!' she shouted, forgetting, in her agitation, to speak French. A speeding scooter had come barrelling down the road, narrowly missing a little white dog that had chosen that moment to run across. Yelping, the dog somersaulted, landing in the gutter close to Kate, who hurriedly pulled it out of harm's way. It was only then that she saw who it was.

'Nina,' she said, stroking the trembling animal. 'Nina, what are you doing here on your own? Where's your papa, eh?'

Nina licked her hand and feebly wagged her tail. Kate looked up the street. The man from the canal was nowhere to be seen. Then Nina gave a short bark and Kate looked behind her in time to see him hurrying across the street, a short distance from where his dog had crossed. And he did not look happy.

'What the hell!' he said, furiously, in English, before Kate could utter a word. Bending down, he clipped a lead on Nina's collar and pulled her to him. 'Why did you do that?'

'Why did I do what?' replied an astounded Kate.

'Call her!'

Kate stared at him. 'I did *not* call her.'

'She would never have crossed the street otherwise,' he retorted, eyes narrowed.

Kate could feel her anger rising. 'I did *not* call her,' she said, biting off the words, 'and you are totally irresponsible, not keeping an eye on your dog! What was she doing loose in the street without a lead, anyway?'

'We were in the shop across the road,' he said, gesturing in that direction, his voice tight. Kate saw it was a bookshop. 'It's never been a problem before.'

'Well, it is now, clearly,' said Kate sharply.

He frowned. 'Are you sure you didn't call her?'

'Of course I'm bloody sure!' she snapped. Turning away from him, she gave Nina one last pat. 'Sorry, Nina, I'm sure you don't like loud voices.'

'No, she doesn't,' he said, his voice noticeably calmer. 'And I'm sorry, I didn't mean to . . .' He would have said more, only Kate didn't wait to hear it. Honestly! Who did he think he was, blaming her for his own incompetence? But as she walked on, she thought of how Nina had dashed across the road, straight towards her. Why had she done that? She'd only met Kate once. And Kate sure as hell hadn't called her. She'd make damn sure not to go near the Port de l'Arsenal again.

When she reached the market soon after, it took her a while to cool down. Then the buzz of the market warmed her up and the chill of the strange incident washed off her. She ended up staying longer than she'd intended, lunching on grilled pork ribs with a side of ratatouille. The salt-crusted pork was unbelievably succulent, the ratatouille bursting with fresh flavours and colours, and she ate it all slowly, lingering pleasurably over each mouthful. She followed that up with a couple of juicy little clementines for dessert and after that decided she'd forget about the other market for today. Instead she strolled in the Luxembourg Gardens, which weren't far away. She sat by the big pond there in the sun, watching kids—and some adults—manoeuvre wooden toy yachts across the water with long sticks. She spied Stefan and Anja, laughing as they tried to race each other's yachts. Anja saw her and called her over. 'Want to join the race?' she asked.

'Really? Can I? You don't mind?'

'Of course not,' Stefan said, sounding puzzled, 'or why would we ask?'

Why indeed? Kate thought, smiling to herself. Choosing a boat with blue and white sails from the rental stand, she happily joined in. Afterwards, they had a drink together in a nearby bistro and talked about the course and the food they'd cooked and what next week was going to be like. At least, Stefan and Anja talked, finishing each other's sentences and laughing at each other's jokes. After a while Kate started to feel like the captive audience of some wacky rom-com. Managing finally to get a word in edgeways, she took her leave, but not before they'd invited her to come to dinner with them, Ethan, Mike and Misaki that night at *Le Train Bleu*, a legendary restaurant in the Gare de Lyon.

Back at the hotel, the receptionist called her over. 'This was left for you.' She pulled out a small square parcel, wrapped in brown paper and string.

'For me?' Kate asked. 'Are you sure?'

The young woman raised an eyebrow but didn't bother replying, just handed over the parcel. Sure enough, it had Kate's name on it. And a sender's name. It was Kate's turn to raise an eyebrow. For the sender was 'Nina'.

'This isn't for me,' she said, firmly. 'There has been a mistake.'

'Your name is Kate Evans, yes?' replied the receptionist, in a tone that suggested Kate was, in her dad's immortal words, 'a sandwich short of a picnic'.

'Yes, but . . .'

'Then it is for you. We have no other Kate Evans here,' said the woman, impatiently.

'But how did he know who . . .' Kate began, but the receptionist was not interested.

Nina, indeed! she thought when she reached her room. She should just chuck it in the bin. But curiosity got the better of her, and she could not help exclaiming as she saw what was inside the brown paper wrapping.

It was a small thick square book, beautifully bound in deep green leather, stamped on the front with an embossed design of a stylised flower. Inside, the pages were creamy and blank. But there was a short note, tucked inside. *Nina says this book is good for writing down recipes. It comes with humble apologies from her servant Arnaud.*

Kate looked at the book, and the note, for quite a while. Then she took out her phone and called Sylvie.

'Sorry to disturb you on your day off,' she said, when Sylvie picked up, 'but I need to know if you gave my name to someone called Arnaud? He is a bookbinder and has a dog called Nina,' she added, just in case.

'Yes, I did,' Sylvie said. 'Arnaud Rocca. He called me a couple of hours ago. Said you'd bought a book in the shop that sells his stuff but had left it behind, and he wasn't sure of your name.

He said he knew you were in the class, and described you, so I knew it was you. I told him that he should deliver the book to your hotel. Did he?'

'He did indeed,' said Kate, a little grimly.

Sylvie must have caught the tone of her voice because she said, 'I'm sorry, did I do the wrong thing? I know Arnaud, he's a good man. And a brilliant craftsman.'

'That he is,' Kate said, with a glance at the book. 'No, you didn't do the wrong thing at all. Thanks. I just wondered how he'd known where to send it.' She paused. 'Do you have his number? I would like to thank him for taking the trouble.'

'Certainly. I will text it to you.'

Sylvie was as good as her word. Kate took a deep breath and looked at the number. She was going to press *call*, then changed her mind and hit *message* instead. *Thank you for the book, Nina, it's beautiful. Please tell your servant Arnaud that I accept his apology but not the book, it's too much. Kate.* She pressed send before she could reconsider then waited for an answering message. None came, and she felt absurdly disappointed.

She picked up the book, ran her fingers over its silky surface, opened it, touched the paper, then closed the book again and carefully rewrapped it. She couldn't keep it. It would give the wrong impression. But oh, it was so beautiful, and she could just see the pages covered in notes about food, recipes, impressions. It needed a fountain pen, a proper one from the stationery and art shop she'd seen nearby. And even if she didn't keep Arnaud's book, she could still get the pen and a lovely notebook to write recipes and food notes in, rather than using the cheap spiralbound one she had with her. Being at the school, here in this glorious city, was an experience that warranted the best of everything. Time to ditch the penny-pinching and treat herself to beautiful things!

Twelve

Max lived in the 11th arrondissement, a supposedly easy walk of about fifteen minutes from Gabi's hotel. But the backstreet where he lived was small and not easy to find, even with Google Maps. Or perhaps *especially* with Google Maps. Gabi took a wrong turn a couple of times and by the time she finally found his place, she was in a sweat. She punched in the code he'd given her for the street entry door, and then pressed the button for his apartment. His voice crackled over the speaker. 'Gabi?'

'Yes, it's me,' she said, horrified to find herself squeaking. 'Sorry if I'm late.'

'You aren't,' he said, and his voice had a smile in it. 'I've unlocked the door. Come on up.'

His building was shabbier than Sylvie's: the paint on the walls was peeling, the treads of the stairs a little worn. But when she reached Max's landing and saw him standing in the open doorway of his apartment, all other thoughts fled.

'Well,' he said. 'You're here.' His face was full of light.

'I am here,' she agreed, without sarcasm, her pulse racing.

'Come in.' He stepped aside so she could enter, then he closed the door. Their eyes met. And then they were in each other's arms, kissing fiercely, and everything in her was melting. He said, 'Shall we . . .' And she couldn't speak, only nod, as he took her by the hand and led her to the bedroom. They undressed each other, quickly, kissing voraciously, panting, feeling each other's skin, the touch like fire rushing up their limbs. Then they were on the bed, bodies interlaced, nothing mattering but the glorious hot sweetness filling them as they came together in a rush of passion.

Afterwards, they lay together on the bed, her head on his chest, his heart close to hers, and he whispered, 'You are lovely, so lovely, I can't believe it, I can't . . .'

'Neither can I,' she whispered back, 'but we don't have to *believe*, because here we are.'

He laughed and drew her to him, kissing her softly on the lips, then gasping as she kissed him back, hard, and then it was happening again, and it was a little while before they spoke another coherent word.

Later, as they lay quiet again, holding each other, Max said, 'Well, maybe I had better go and see that the chicken's not burning,' and Gabi kissed his naked shoulder, saying, 'Absolutely, burnt chicken should not be on the menu,' and he smiled and stroked her hair. But this time, they got up and he dressed quickly and went off to the kitchen to attend to the meal while she followed more slowly, pulling on her clothes, running her fingers through her hair, touching her lips which felt a little swollen but deliciously so.

Before going into the kitchen, she wandered around. His apartment was light and spacious, though it wasn't exactly large. Maybe, she guessed, around forty or fifty square metres, broken into three small rooms: bedroom, bathroom, study; and a main room that functioned as a living room with a kitchen/dining alcove. But it was a good size for Paris, especially for a single person. The floor was made of creaking polished wooden boards, with a couple of good rugs scattered over them: a deep grey and white modern one in the bedroom, a lovely blue Persian one in the main room. The furniture was simple but comfortable, the walls painted a soft creamy colour. Pictures hung on the walls: in the tiny study, some rather good black and white photographs, arranged in a circle, of different views of Paris; and two paintings, one in the bedroom, one in the main room. In the bedroom was a striking small abstract in blues and greens, making her think of deep water; in the main room a large, beautiful figurative painting, showing a group of people sitting around a table playing cards. From their dress, she judged it to be probably very early twentieth century, post-Impressionist, maybe. Under this was a bookcase, stuffed with books: mainly novels, with a sprinkling of non-fiction, nearly all of them in French, except for a couple of English-language paperback thrillers. On the bottom shelf, three or four large photograph albums were shelved next to some travel books. She took out one of the albums and leafed through it briefly. It contained more beautiful black and white views of Paris, and some colour ones too. She put the album back and glanced at the couple of framed photographs on top of the bookcase. One showed a family group—parents and three boys—standing under a tree; the other was of a rather beautiful woman with a 1940s hairstyle. Peering at the family photograph, she could recognise Max in the smallest boy. The woman, she thought, was probably his grandmother when she was young.

She entered the compact kitchen, where she found him mixing mustard, white wine and tomato puree in a bowl, with the savoury smell of chicken cooking in a pot on the stove. 'What are you making?' she asked, sitting on a stool at the bench. 'It smells great.'

'It's something my grandmother used to make for me when I was a kid,' he said. '*Poulet au vinaigre*, vinegar chicken. The vinegar is added later,' he added, forestalling her question. 'And then you add the wine mix to make the sauce. A bit of a classic.'

'Yet I've never had it before,' she said, as he took a couple of glasses from a cupboard.

'Good. Then you won't know what it's *supposed* to taste like,' he said, smiling. 'So, what do you think of my apartment?'

'It's lovely,' she said. 'Very peaceful. Serene, even.'

He smiled. 'It doesn't reflect its inhabitant then. But I'm glad you like it.'

'The photographs of Paris in the study,' she said, 'are they yours?'

He nodded. 'I went through a photography phase some time ago.'

'They're very good.'

He shrugged. 'I lost the urge. Would you like an aperitif? Or just a glass of wine?'

'Wine, please,' she said. 'That white you have there—Sancerre. I've heard of it but it's something else I've never tasted. It's not just for cooking, right?'

He laughed. 'Oh, if my family could hear you! They'd be scandalised. No. Sancerre isn't just for cooking, but as I'm sure Sylvie would tell you, a good dish deserves the best wine. Making this one with inferior white is just not right.'

He poured them each a glass of the beautiful light gold wine and handed one to her. She sniffed. 'They will tell you citrus, elderflower, flint,' he said, with a grin, 'but to me it just smells . . . familiar.' He raised his glass. '*Santé*!'

'*Santé*!' she echoed, as they clinked. Then she said, 'You said your family would be scandalised if they heard me. Are they wine buffs?'

'They grow the stuff, actually,' he said, and turned the bottle around to show her the label. 'This comes from the family vineyards.'

Domaine Taverny, Sancerre, Loire, she read.

'I thought your surname was Rousseau.'

'It is. And Taverny too. I just don't use that bit.'

'Oh.' She looked at the label again. It showed a small castle rising up from lush vineyards. 'Your family has a *castle*?'

'A fortified manor house, actually. With one tower on one side. It's old, sure, but you can hardly describe it as a castle. Not like the real castles in the Loire: Chambord, Chenonceau, Azay-le-Rideau.' His tone was light.

Yesterday, he'd said he had to go to the Loire overnight. To visit his family, no doubt. Who he'd hinted he didn't get on with, aside from his grandmother. 'What does your family think of you being a cheese merchant instead of a wine grower?' she asked, taking another sip. It really was a very nice wine. She knew Sancerre was made with Sauvignon Blanc grapes, but it tasted different from the New Zealand ones she was used to. Those were nice, but this one was more delicate; drier, too. And more aromatic.

He shrugged. 'They don't think about it. At least, not anymore.' His tone was still light but there was something in his eyes that told a different story.

'Cheese and wine—they go well together, though,' she persisted.

'So they do. But it's not what the family does, you see.'

She nodded. 'I do. Families, eh!'

'Families,' he agreed, smiling, and the sadness that had been in his eyes vanished like a shadow in the sun.

Lunch was as delicious as it had smelled: tangy, garlicky vinegar chicken over plain boiled rice, the herby mixed salad Max had served as a first course, and the melt-in-the-mouth crème caramel he'd made for dessert, with fresh whipped cream on the side. And of course the cheese, which he'd served in the French way, between the main course and the dessert, had been superlative. There had been four of them, each of them from a different region of France: slices of a creamy blue from Auvergne, a pungent washed-rind Munster from Alsace, a herb-rolled fresh goat's milk Chavignol from the Loire, and a delectably buttery Ossau-Iraty sheep's milk cheese from the Basque country and Bearn. Beautifully chosen and diversely delicious. A mini Tour de France, he'd called it. He had served the cheese with a lovely Burgundy pinot noir. And then, after the dessert, they retired to the sofa with a Cointreau, which Max said was to round off the meal. Gabi teasingly said that if he was trying to make her drunk, he should know that she held her liquor very well, better than many men, and he laughed and kissed her, saying, 'Then perhaps it's true what they say, that the way to a woman's heart is through her stomach, after all you seemed to quite like the lunch I made!'

'I thought it was the way to a man's heart,' she retorted, snuggling into the crook of his arm, 'but your food is pretty good, I'll give you that!' And she pulled cheerfully at the waist of her velvet skirt, saying, 'My peasant ancestors on both sides didn't bestow on me the gift of excessive slimness, but they did pass on a good skill in fork-wielding.' The French saying, *avoir un bon coup de fourchette*, literally meant wielding a fork well, and metaphorically meant you enjoyed eating: having a good appetite and an appreciation of good food.

'I think your peasant ancestors passed on exactly the right things,' said Max, with frank appraisal.

'And what about you? What did your aristocratic ancestors in their castle pass on?' she asked. 'Clearly not a dislike for the descendants of peasants.'

He laughed. 'My ancestors weren't aristocratic, just wine growers with long memories and even longer grudges. Just like peasants, in fact.'

She laughed. 'So did they pass on those memories and grudges to you?'

'No.' He gave a darting smile. 'Well, I try not to give in to them, anyway.'

'Where did your love of cheese come from, if not your family?' she asked.

'I didn't say it didn't come from my family. We always had good cheese at home. What French family doesn't? But wanting to be a cheesemonger came from one time when I went with my grandmother to the Salon de l'Agriculture.' Gabi knew the salon was an annual event in Paris that had been going for more than one hundred and fifty years; one of the biggest agricultural shows in the world. 'We went into one section that was full of cheeses from all over the country,' Max said, 'and they had sample plates you could try. One of the guys took time to talk to me about the cheese they produced in his area, in Brittany. It was magical, listening to him, but exciting too, because he wove in stories about the villages and farms. It made me feel like I was actually there. He was so knowledgeable and so imaginative. I was fourteen then but I knew that was what I wanted to do with my life.'

'That sounds amazing,' she said, softly. 'But your family didn't agree?'

'I didn't tell them. Not for ages. It had been expected I'd go to the Sorbonne and do law. My parents felt it would be useful to have a son who had legal training, even if he was no use in the vineyards.' There was that sadness again. 'But when I finally plucked up the courage to tell them I wasn't going to go to university but instead travel around France and learn as much about cheese as I could—well, you can imagine. All the family joined forces to try to stop me ruining my life, as they saw it. Even my grandmother—she was kinder about it than my parents, but she still felt it wasn't the right thing for me.'

'Oh, Max,' she said, squeezing his hand. 'It must have been so hard for you.'

'It was,' he said, quietly. 'I tried to go to uni, to knuckle down to legal studies. It was there that I met Floriane—my ex-wife—she came from the kind of family my parents approved of, and we got married. We were just over nineteen, the pair of us.'

Her eyes widened. 'So young!'

'It didn't last. Eighteen months later, we had broken up and gone our separate ways. I dropped out of university, bought a motorbike and set off around France, to do what I'd dreamed of when I was a kid. And you know what?' he added, his eyes on her, 'I didn't ruin my life. I enriched it. I met the most amazing people all over France, people who lived cheese, breathed cheese, but who were also the most extraordinary human beings I'd ever met. And I got to taste the most wonderful variety of cheeses in farms and villages and small-town markets all over the country. I felt like the luckiest man in all of France, maybe even the world.'

'That is so marvellous, Max.' The passion in his voice moved her almost to tears. 'And has it always stayed the same for you, that feeling?'

'Yes,' he said. 'Always.'

'Then you are very lucky,' she said, and sighed, without meaning to.

He glanced sharply at her. 'But what about you?'

'Me?' she shrugged. 'I'm still—well, I'm still looking.' She had been about to tell him, it had been on the tip of her tongue, but something had stopped her, a fear of putting into words the thing that haunted her, that she couldn't break free of. Yet how ironic was it that she, who'd never had to withstand parental pressure to be someone she wasn't, who'd always been encouraged by her family, her teachers, her mentors, should be the one struggling now, while he, who'd had to fight so hard for his dream, had ended up feeling like the luckiest man in the world? Or maybe it wasn't ironic at all. Maybe it was logical. *Perhaps we don't value the thing we don't have to fight for?* she thought. No, that was too easy. She *did* value her art, she valued it very much. She just couldn't do it, not anymore. And that scared the hell out of her. Because if she wasn't an artist, then who was she? An apprentice cook, she'd told him. Or someone still looking for her path. Both were untrue, or at the very best, half-truths.

'You'll find it, whatever you are looking for,' he said, gently. 'You will. I am sure.'

She swallowed. He had cut closer to the bone than he realised. 'I hope so. In the meantime, I intend to have a very good time while I wait.'

He laughed. 'Excellent plan! And do you have any ideas for that good time?'

'Oh yes,' she said, climbing into his lap and putting her arms around him. 'Quite a few, as it happens.'

Thirteen

Le Train Bleu was even more stunning in real life than Kate had imagined from seeing it in photographs. Stepping into its extraordinary interior, with its richly, even extravagantly, carved and gilded woodwork on the walls and on the ceiling, inset with beautiful landscape paintings, simply took your breath away. Set within the barrel-vaulted precincts of the Gare de Lyon in the 12th arrondissement, the restaurant had originally been built for the 1900 Paris World Exposition, serving as a luxurious station buffet for well-heeled crowds. You could certainly imagine elegant ladies in big hats, long dresses and lacy parasols and gentlemen in top hats here, Kate thought, happily, as she followed an immaculately turned-out waiter down the royal-blue carpet to the two tables Ethan had reserved. She might not be as elegant as those long-ago ladies, but she had tried to dress for the occasion. Late that afternoon, she'd gone back to the BHV department store on the Rue de Rivoli, a short walk from her hotel, and bought a beautiful navy-blue wraparound dress with cream-coloured daisies fade-printed on it, matched with a slim cream cardigan in very fine cotton, as well as silver drop earrings. If she'd had more time, she'd have gone on a proper shopping expedition, but that would have to wait. The outfit, teamed with her own low-heeled slingback sandals, a simple clip loosely tying back her fair hair, looked okay, she thought—maybe even just a little bit Parisian.

She was a bit late and everyone else was already there, though Mike and Stefan were up and about, taking pictures. They weren't the only ones, and the staff seemed well-used to paparazzi tourists going crazy with their phones. As Kate sat down on the supremely comfortable plush seat next to Misaki, Anja said, eyes shining, 'Isn't it just so wonderful here!'

Kate nodded. 'Like being transported into a glamorous old film,' she said, 'or a *Poirot* episode.'

'Ethan's sister was in a *Poirot* movie,' Anja said, turning to Ethan. 'Wasn't she? Tell Kate.'

He smiled. 'Yep, back in 2005 my sister Chloe was in an episode called *The Mystery of the Blue Train*.' He gestured around him. 'Not that this place appears in the episode, but I know she'd love it here. She's not very well—' he paused—'so we're seeing it for her, and sending pictures.'

'I'm sure she'll love that,' said Anja, warmly.

'And I must tell my mum to watch out for your sister in the show,' Kate said. 'She loves that series!'

'Blink and you'll miss her,' said Ethan, lightly, 'she's in a crowd scene at a hotel, you can just about catch a glimpse of her in a satin dress twirling on the dance floor.'

Mike plonked down beside Ethan. 'Okay, let's order. But not the seafood platter, folks!' When everyone except Ethan looked puzzled, he added, grinning, 'It's a scene in *Mr Bean's Holiday*. Check it out online, you'll see what I mean.'

Kate could just imagine what disaster-prone Mr Bean would do to a plate of crustaceans. No seafood platter appeared on the real menu, however, and the food, when it came, was very good: traditional French in inspiration, but with some contemporary touches, such as spelt risotto and pear and chervil biscuit. And the wine was excellent. Kate had just finished her starter, a lovely confection of scallops with black truffles, when her phone pinged with a message. Thinking it might be her family back in Australia—they often texted at this time—she excused herself and went to the bathroom to read it. But it was an MMS, showing a cute picture of Nina, her black eyes gazing right at the camera, and a speech bubble coming out of her mouth, reading, *The book's surely not too much for saving my life. Please do us the honour of keeping it.*

There was a catch in her throat, and a smile in her eyes, as she texted back. *Then I will keep it. Thank you, Nina. And . . .* she hesitated, then went on, *please thank your servant Arnaud too.*

A text came almost instantly back. *He says it is a pleasure, Kate.* She waited a moment, but nothing else came. Feeling just a little deflated, she pocketed the phone and went back to the table where the main courses had just appeared, including her own order, *blanquette de veau*, a classic, richly tender veal stew, enrobed in a savoury velvety sauce, with pilaf rice accompanying it.

'Everything okay?' Stefan asked, as she sat down, hungrily inhaling the savoury smells from everyone's food, especially Anja and Stefan's choice, a spectacular share dish of slow-cooked lamb in its rich, deep, slightly spiced juices, served with a tangy cream sauce and a deliciously nutty spelt risotto. It could almost have given her food envy: if her own dish hadn't been as good!

'Sure, all good,' Kate said, starting in with relish on the *blanquette*, 'just a text from a friend back home.' Why had she told the fib? It wasn't as if anyone was going to interrogate her. Though it had to be said, Stefan was a bit of a stickybeak, but the kind you didn't mind, as he was so genuinely interested in others. As conversation swirled enjoyably among them, to the tune of busy knives and forks, Stefan skilfully drew out from her the fact she'd once been involved in Resmond, and from Misaki that she had two grown children back home and that one of them had gone into the restaurant business, like his mother, but the other, a girl, made set models for anime movies. And from Ethan and Mike he winkled out that they'd met at a fancy-dress Halloween charity ball where Mike had been a waiter, obliged to wear a zombie outfit, and Ethan had been a guest, a very glamorous Dracula. Mike recounted their unlikely meeting in such a hilarious way that you couldn't help laughing your head off, while Ethan just sipped his wine, looking indulgently affectionate yet ironic, his default mode when it came to Mike.

Kate had been quite glad that Stefan's probing hadn't ventured into more private areas. He hadn't heard of the Resmond app, and neither had Anja or Misaki, but Mike and Ethan had, and Ethan said they'd even used it on holiday. Then everyone wanted to know how it worked, and that was a safe enough topic, so Kate brought up the app on her phone and showed them how you could both search for and reserve tables at a long list of restaurants around the world, although not yet at *Le Train Bleu*. She found herself giving the kind of spiel that was familiar to her from a million marketing meetings, talking about how it was different from similar apps because of its personalised approach, how when you downloaded the app, you built a profile of yourself and your likes and dislikes, not only about food but atmosphere and location, and that then paired you up with restaurants, 'like matchmaking'. Then Misaki asked where the name had come from, and she said quite truthfully that it had been her idea, built around 'reservation' and '*monde*', meaning 'world' in French. The original name Josh had given his brainchild was Foodworld, but marketing said it sounded like a discount supermarket and so they'd brainstormed other ideas. Resmond had come up tops. She had been quite proud of it. Maybe she could have demanded extra for her shares, but she hadn't. And wouldn't. She was free and clear of it all, now that the board had agreed to paying her out at 100 per cent over market value.

The email from the chair had been brief: *Okay. Please find attached our agreement for the sale of the shares, which we request you complete and sign at your earliest convenience. Payment will happen on signature.* Her earliest convenience had been straight away, as soon as she'd read over the short document and confirmed it was all fine. And now all she had to do was wait for the money to come into her account. Quite a lot of money, actually. She didn't know what she was going to do with it . . . Go on a shopping spree, certainly—after all, she was in the perfect place for that! But long-term . . . The practical part of her said to invest it in something secure. But what did security mean, exactly? She'd thought she was secure in her marriage, her work, her role. And they'd turned out to be illusions.

~

'*Merde*, all you care about is that damn school of yours!' Unusually, Claude didn't seem to mind who heard him. 'It matters more to you than people, than *me*!'

Sylvie looked at him. 'You're creating a scandal.' Her voice was cool, but she didn't feel cool at all. He'd invited her to dinner and, against her better judgement, she'd agreed. But after the first moments, when he'd said how much he'd missed her, he had gone on and on about how difficult things were as he tried to cut connections with Marie-Laure. And rather than fruitlessly argue with him about it, she'd tried to deflect him by telling him about her own issues at the school. But all it had done was make him explode.

'So what?' he retorted, now. 'I bet they're used to scandals in this ridiculous place you've dragged me to.' He gestured around him at the noisy restaurant with its crowded tables and pop-art décor. It was a new place in the 3rd arrondissement, and she'd suggested it.

'Claude, calm down.' She put a hand out to him. 'Of course I care about you. But right now, I don't have time for more stress in my life. I told you what's been happening with the school, and—'

'Just because some idiot is playing games with your precious school, does it mean you can't focus on me, on us?' Fortunately, he'd lowered his voice now, but his words stung Sylvie.

'Does everything always have to be about you?' she hissed.

'No, clearly it has to be all about *you*,' he flashed back.

'Oh, for God's sake.' She gestured to a passing waiter for the bill.

'That's right, run away.' Claude got up, pushing his chair back dramatically. 'You might as well.'

'Actually it's you who is running away,' she said, tightly. 'Like you always do when things get tough.'

He glared at her, then threw his napkin on the floor and stalked out. Sylvie stayed impassive as she waited for the waiter to come back. But inwardly, she fumed. This was it! She'd had enough. It's true she'd felt like this more than once. And still they'd limped on. But this time it felt different.

She'd given him the ultimatum, and clearly, though he'd claimed he couldn't wait to be out of his ex's reach, he'd not done anything about it. And his response to the incidents at the school—the Tripadvisor review, the fake order, and now another bad review, this time on Google—showed that he didn't have any notion of what things were like for her. Worse, he didn't care. Claude had accused her of only caring about the school. That was not only untrue and unfair, but it was also a clear sign that he saw her business, her livelihood, as not mattering at all. He clearly felt she should keep things as they had been between them—convenient and comfortable for him, despite his ex's unreasonableness. Maybe he liked the feeling of being fought over by two women. *Well, I'm not in the fight anymore,* she thought, as she paid the bill and stepped back out into the street. *I just don't have time for petulant tantrums and self-centred grandstanding. I'm tired. So tired.* And what an irony, that he thought she only cared about the school when she was starting to think that maybe she could take a step back, slow down a bit. She hadn't told Claude, she didn't want to, not after the way he was behaving. He'd only think it was because she wanted to concentrate on him, and that definitely *wasn't* the case.

She thought about the photos Julien had posted on his Instagram feed the other day, of a snorkelling trip he'd done on the Great Barrier Reef, and it had reminded her of being there herself, twenty-five years ago. She was delighted her son was having such a good time on his backpacking holiday, but she also felt slightly envious. Imagine having the time and headspace to just step away, enjoy yourself, plan some travel, or just sit and relax . . . But she couldn't. She had responsibilities. Not her son now that he was grown up and managing well. But there were her staff and her students to consider, and of course, Claude. But it shouldn't be *of course, Claude*, she raged inwardly, it should be Claude giving occasionally. Not just taking, taking all the time. Not just presents. Not just sex. But *support*. Understanding. Knowing when to take a step back. Knowing when to offer help, when needed. For God's sake, her neighbour Serge was better at that than her lover!

It was Serge who had told her about the Google review. He'd been checking the internet, in case there was a repetition of the Tripadvisor review. 'Google are harder to get onto than Tripadvisor,' he said after he found the latest review. 'But we can send them a message. I have heard that occasionally people have been able to get reviews taken down.' He said it wasn't unknown for businesses to be targeted by scammers who posted bad reviews then emailed the business offering to delete the review for an extortionate sum, of course. Sylvie had checked, but she hadn't received that kind of email, not even in her spam folder. In a way that made her more anxious, because what did it mean if the scammer wasn't after money? Serge was reassuring, but he didn't have definite answers, and why should he? But he tried to help. And he didn't dismiss her anxieties. He didn't make it all about him. He understood. He was a good friend, a real one. Whereas Claude . . .

No more thinking about him, she told herself severely, as she stepped off the train and headed through the streets for home. *Put him out of your mind, at least for tonight. Go home, make yourself a* tisane *with maybe a drop of brandy to spice up the herbs, relax in front of a movie, and plan a weekend away. By yourself.* Yes. That's what she needed. She wouldn't go far, just to Giverny, to Monet's garden. She had been there a couple of times before and loved it. And it was spring so many of the flowers would be out, it should look glorious, and the forecast was for the sunny weather to continue over Saturday and Sunday. She'd never stayed in Giverny overnight but she knew there was a nice little hotel close by the garden. The more she thought about it, the more she felt excited. It was exactly what she needed.

Fourteen

On a sunny Saturday afternoon, the small park in the centre of the Place des Vosges is always full of people, sprawled on the grass, or strolling down the gravelled paths, or cycling around the lovely enclosure bordered by the ancient buildings and graceful arcade that make the place such a beautiful, peaceful small world, away from the hustle and bustle beyond it. People seem to walk slower here; birds hop about on the grass and splash in the fountains, unafraid; small children and dogs frolic about, attracting the occasional frown from more serious folk.

Kate sat on the grass, the leather-bound notebook open in her lap, writing the last bit of the first pages she'd filled in. Last night at *Le Train Bleu* had been lovely but finished quite late and then they'd gone for a drink in a bar so it was well past midnight when she'd got back to her hotel. She'd had a bit of a sleep-in and a coffee, then decided to take it easy, just mooching around the local area, poking into various little shops. After an enjoyable couple of hours, she'd ended up with a small haul: a smart dark red fountain pen, a pretty blue bangle, a bunch of quirky postcards, and a vintage poster of a Citroën DS for her father, who loved those classic French cars. In a bakery, she bought an excellent *jambon beurre*—a half-baguette simply filled with fresh unsalted butter and delicious locally made cooked ham—and set off for the Place des Vosges with it, a bottle of water, her notebook and fountain pen.

After finishing her lunch, she'd experimented first with the pen on a scrap piece of paper to make sure she'd know how to use it and not shake random blobs of ink around. Then she'd carefully drawn up a title page, creating a simple decorative ink frame, and inside the frame, a title, in her fanciest handwriting: *Paris Cooking School Impressions and Recipes, by Kate Evans*. The pen was lovely to use, the black ink flowing so satisfyingly onto the creamy paper! She'd waited a moment for it to dry—in the sun it didn't take long—then turned the page and wrote, in a careful print this time, *This book is not a diary or a complete report, it will just be bits and pieces, written whenever I feel the urge. Thanks to Nina and Arnaud for the inspiration.* Underneath she drew a quick cartoon of a boat with a little dog perched on the deck. It wasn't great art, but it was recognisable as a boat and a dog and would therefore pass the muster of her sternest critic, her nephew, Billy, who had very decided ideas about what a drawing should be like. He'd been quite scathing once of a horse she'd drawn for him, opining firmly that it looked much more like a camel. Smiling to herself, she turned to the next page and began writing down the recipe for the fish course that she and Ethan had made the other day, complete with sauce. One page wasn't big enough to fit it all in, so she had to go over to the next one too. The paper was thick but smooth, so the ink didn't go through on the other side, and she had to admit that, when it was all finished, it didn't look bad at all.

She took photos of all the pages but sent only the ones with the recipe to the family WhatsApp group, with the caption, *In case anyone wants to try this, this is something we made the other day.* She didn't want to send the whole thing because it might look childish and she didn't want questions about who Nina and Arnaud were. Then, on impulse, she sent the recipe pages to Arnaud's number, with a caption, *As you can see, Nina, I have taken your advice.*

A text came back quickly. *Good! And the fish sounds delicious.*

It was, she answered. *Simple too.*

If we buy the ingredients, said the text flying back, *will you teach my servant to make it?*

Kate stared at the text, her heart beating a little faster. Then she wrote, *Maybe one day.*

Tomorrow lunchtime? said the next message.

I'm busy, she wrote, untruthfully, then scrubbed it out, and wrote, *A bit soon maybe.*

Okay. We understand.

Kate thought a moment, then sent the photo of the page where she'd thanked Nina and Arnaud. There was a pause, then another text came through.

Thank you.

Nothing else. *You're welcome,* wrote Kate. She was going to write more, then decided against it. They'd clearly said all they needed to say. But now she wished she hadn't been so quick off the mark, declining the invitation for tomorrow. She could have said, *Can I get back to you*, or *Let me check my diary*, or other stalling tactics that help you make up your mind. But now she couldn't very well go back to him and say, *I've changed my mind, yes, it would be a lovely thing to do.* Which it would have been. But also dangerous. Because the last thing she wanted was for Arnaud to get the wrong idea about her, to misunderstand her intentions. It was fun, this game of pretending to speak through Nina. But it was just that, a game. Not real life.

Oh, I was so right to come here, Sylvie thought as she walked slowly along the meandering paths at Giverny. Monet's garden was always beautiful, even in the bareness of winter, but right now, in the explosion of April flowers, it was a place of sheer enchantment. Everywhere you looked there were sights to make you catch your breath: splashes of purple pansies and blue forget-me-nots; the smooth brilliance of multicoloured tulips; daffodils and narcissi nodding their yellow heads while white meadow daisies starred the grass. Cherry and crab-apple trees threw up armfuls of pink and white blossoms, and the fragrant flowers of jasmine and laurustinus shrubs attracted clouds of butterflies. The ponds sparkled and trees in new green leaf offered smudges of soft colour against the brighter green of benches and the lovely little bridge that featured in so many photographs of this place. And, of course, there was Monet's beautiful old house in its pinks and greens, floating serenely in the tide of spring colour.

The beautiful weather had enticed quite a few other people out, but Sylvie hardly noticed as she breathed in the soft perfumed air, allowing the calm beauty to fill her every pore. She'd arrived at Giverny late the previous afternoon and had a quick walk in the garden before having a delicious meal in the hotel restaurant and a restorative sleep. This morning, she'd decided to do the garden properly, soak it all in. She had always loved it here. But it was more than just love. It was here one day with Julien, sixteen years ago, when he was just six years old, that had first crystallised in her the idea that until then had been a vague dream. They'd wandered through the garden, or rather she'd chased after her son through the gardens as he clapped his hands at birds and tried to pick flowers and rolled laughing in the grass, and then they'd gone into the house, and she'd felt there a spirit that rejoiced in the extraordinary, joyful splendour of nature and life itself. And, by chance, she'd learned that Monet, as well as adoring the garden he'd designed, had loved good food. It had been central to his family life: you saw that so clearly in his paintings where people gathered around a table, or picnicked al fresco. She had a reproduction of one of those paintings in the dining room at the school now.

Back then, Sylvie had read about how, after awakening at dawn to paint, Monet tucked into a substantial breakfast; about the delicious dishes his devoted cook Marguerite had created for him and his family; about the hallmarks of food in the Monet household: beauty, abundance, flavour and splendid simplicity. And as Sylvie took it all in, her spine tingled as her own memories of her grandparents and their kitchen mingled with what she was reading about Monet. In a rush of excitement she had thought, *Yes, I am going to do it, it is not going to be dream anymore but reality.* It had taken nearly a year after that to get everything ready, to persuade the bank to lend her the money, to get all the permissions from the city and adapt the apartment before the Paris Cooking School could be launched. But it had been in the dining room of Monet's house that the idea had stopped being labelled with 'One day maybe, perhaps' to 'This is happening, no matter what'.

She was standing there now, remembering, when her phone pulsed with a message. She gave a surprised exclamation when she saw who it was: Julien, wanting to video call from Queensland. Hurrying out of the house into the garden, she swiped into the call.

'Hello, darling,' she said, as his face filled the screen. 'It's so good to see you.'

'And you too, Maman,' he said, a smile filling the bright dark eyes he'd inherited from his Mauritian father.

'End of the day, then?' she said, noting how the sky behind him looked streaked with pink.

'Yes, I've gone for a sunset walk. Look.' The view swivelled wildly as he moved his phone around. She could see a shoreline, waves breaking, a dog running on the sand, some people vaguely in the distance. The view swivelled again and his face reappeared. 'Isn't it lovely?'

'It is,' she said, softly. 'And look where I am.' Now it was her turn to make him feel dizzy as she moved the phone around.

'Let me guess,' her son said, smiling broadly as she moved the phone back again. 'Could it be your favourite garden, by any chance?'

'Good guess.' She smiled back. 'So, how's it going over there?'

'Good. Excellent, in fact. Maman . . .' he hesitated, an uncharacteristic uncertainty in his voice, then plunged on, 'actually that's what I want to talk to you about.'

Puzzled, she asked, 'What do you mean?'

'I've been offered a job, Maman. It would mean staying here longer than I thought.'

Her throat was suddenly dry. 'How much longer?' This trip was the first time she and Julien had been separated since he was born. Her fling with Julien's charming father, a young airline pilot, had been just that, a fling, before he went back to Mauritius and married his childhood sweetheart. He knew about Julien and had met him once, when they'd gone to Mauritius to see him. But that was it. Her parents had heartily disapproved of her pregnancy, and hadn't shown much interest in their grandson except on occasional visits, so Sylvie and Julien had been a tight little unit. And yet, he had gone off quite happily on his own to explore the world . . .

'I'd be away another few months,' he said. 'Maybe a year.'

Dismayed, she said, 'But, Julien . . . your studies . . . you were going to start your master's in September.'

'That might still happen,' he said, calmly. 'And if not—well, I can always start it the year after.'

Her voice rising, she said, 'Julien, you know that's not possible.'

'Why not?' His voice was getting an edge to it, and his eyes flashed. 'Surely you of all people, Maman, understand that isn't a philosophy to live by. If someone had told you that it wasn't possible for a single mother with not much money to start a successful business, you'd have sent them off for a walk!' *Envoyer promener*, he'd said, literally to send them for a walk, metaphorically to tell them to get lost.

'Yes, but—'

'Well, it is the same for me. I have been offered something that excites me.' He paused. 'And I've said yes.'

For a moment, she was tempted to say, *Why bother discussing it with me then, if you've already decided?* But thankfully, she stopped herself. Instead, she tried to keep her voice neutral as she asked, 'So what is this amazing job? Is it in an art gallery?' His bachelor's degree had been in art history, which he'd done very well in. And he'd also completed a successful holiday internship at the Paris office of Sotheby's. It was why he had been encouraged to consider undertaking a master's in the same field.

'No,' he said, and then, rather guardedly, 'it might surprise you. Or not.'

'Don't keep me in suspense,' she said, lightly. 'Are you planning to be a bush stockman? A hunter of crocodiles? A deep-sea diver?'

He laughed, the tension leaving his face. 'Ha ha, very funny, Maman! Hold tight—I've been offered a cooking job.'

For a moment, she didn't think she'd heard right. As a child Julien had loved hanging around the kitchen when she was cooking, and later he turned his hand to simple dishes. He'd enjoyed it. But he'd certainly never expressed an interest in working in the field. 'A *cooking job*?' she repeated.

'Yes. I thought it would surprise you.' Behind him, the night was growing, the light fading from the sky. 'There's this little restaurant I've been going to—they are really nice people and we got talking, I told them about you and how I loved watching you work when

I was a child and I described the kinds of things you cooked. One day out of the blue they asked if I'd make eggs *mimosa* for them, and without thinking I said okay. I was terrified, but you know what, I did it and it worked really well. It was like—I knew what to do. I must have just absorbed it watching you, without even realising it. I did look up a recipe too, just in case,' he confessed, with a laugh.

'Oh,' she said, slowly, 'so that picture on your Instagram feed the other day of eggs *mimosa* on the sunset plate . . . they were yours?'

'You saw it?' he asked, sounding delighted. 'Yes, they were. Anyway, well, after that, they asked me to make a couple of simple classic things based on my memories, and I did, and they worked . . . and customers apparently liked them so yesterday they asked if I'd like to cook for them two days a week to start with, just lunches for the moment.'

Sylvie had a lump in her throat. *Two days a week, and lunchtime only, that's not exactly enough to live on* . . . But she said nothing. He'd saved a lot for this trip, and he was careful with money, despite his easygoing nature. 'Oh, Julien,' she said, softly, 'that's . . . that's wonderful.' And suddenly, she knew it actually was. 'It is really wonderful.'

His face lit up. 'You really think so?'

'I do. I am astonished, yes. But also proud. Very proud of you.'

'That means a lot to me, Maman,' he said, softly. 'It really does.'

'My darling son.' She felt a little choked. 'I—I only wish I could taste your food myself.'

'Then do,' he said, with a twinkle in his eyes. 'Come here for a holiday. Let me look after you for a change.'

A pang went through her. 'Oh, Julien, I can't! I have students till October, you know that.'

'Delegate,' he said. 'Let Damien take over for a while. He's perfectly capable and he's been working for you long enough to know what's what. Come when this month's session is over, for a few weeks. This is a great time of year to be here. You can even swim without worrying about the jellyfish, which you couldn't after October.'

'But it's too much work for one person,' she protested. 'I can't leave Damien to do it all.'

'Of course not. But you can get someone else to help him. You know enough people. Come on, Maman, no more excuses.' A pause. 'You can even bring Claude, if you like.'

That was a big concession. Julien didn't think much of Claude. 'We'll see,' Sylvie said, carefully.

'Then you will think about it?'

'Yes. I promise I will. It's not a guarantee, mind,' she added.

'Of course,' he said, with a grin. 'Oh, hello.' This was said to someone behind him, who Sylvie could only see a bit of: a brief glimpse of a vivid face, black hair, a flash of bare brown shoulder. 'I'll be there in a second,' he said, in English, then turning back to French and his mother, 'I have to go, Maman. But we'll speak again soon. Yes?'

'Yes, of course,' she said, wondering if the girl she'd glimpsed was part of why he wanted to stay, but knowing better than to ask. 'Big hug to you, my darling, and good luck with the job!'

'Thank you, my dear maman,' he said, giving her a flashing smile. 'Big hug to you too.' And he ended the call, leaving Sylvie looking down at the blank screen, a smile on her own face. Julien had a sunny nature that made him friends wherever he went. Yet he was also surprising, coming out with perceptive observations and unexpected insights even as a young child. And this time, he'd *really* astonished her. *I'm so tempted to go there*, she thought. *I need a holiday. And it would be fun.* Then her shoulders drooped. *But I can't go. Not when all this stuff is going on, with Claude, with the harassment against the school. It has to be sorted out, all of it. I can't just run away.*

'To us.' Max raised his glass and leaned across the table to Gabi.

'To us,' she echoed, clinking glasses. It was Sunday evening and they were having dinner in a cosy restaurant near the Seine, not far from Gabi's hotel. It was a classic Parisian place, of the kind that you don't find a lot of anymore, with a zinc bar and a twisty metal staircase leading to a top-floor dining area that overlooked the boulevard and the river beyond. The waiters were also classic Paris, sharp-featured and sharp-tongued, with a nice line in repartee.

It had been an extraordinary weekend. She'd spent all of it with Max, aside from a couple of hours on Saturday morning when she'd returned to the hotel to pick up some clean clothes and tell the indifferent receptionist she wouldn't be back till Sunday night. On Saturday afternoon, Max had taken her to the place where he stored his cheeses: it was a small cellar deep in the basement of an old building, not far from his flat. Dim and quiet and cool, kept at a constant temperature, the cellar had slatted wooden shelves where the cheeses rested. On some shelves were the wheels of hard cheese: cow's, goat's, sheep's, mixes; on others soft cheese and rinded cheese. There was a lovely smell in there, and a timeless feel. Max said that the cellar was much better for storage than fridges, though he did use a portable one to transport cheese to markets. As well as his market stands—one at Bastille, one at another market, in the 20th—he also supplied the Paris Cooking School, and several local restaurants, including the one they were at right now.

'I'm sorry I have to be away in Normandy tomorrow,' Max said. 'If they weren't potentially interesting new suppliers, I would reschedule.'

She waved that away with an airy gesture and a teasing smile. 'You do have a business to run and we do need some sleep. There's not been much of that this weekend, has there?'

'No there hasn't,' he agreed, squeezing her hand, his eyes alight. 'No regrets, then?'

She gazed boldly back. 'What a question! None at all.'

'I'm glad,' he said, simply.

She had not had this feeling for a long time. Maybe not ever. Even at the beginning of the relationship with Sam, there had been awkwardness alongside the desire. Not with Max. She felt completely at ease, as if she'd known him for ages, and yet hot with the discovery of him. And even when they weren't in each other's arms, making love, when they were just sitting here eating, or strolling in the park and wandering the streets, every moment felt touched with a golden glow of passion *and* contentment. She felt a twinge of fear; something as beautiful as this couldn't last.

But she dismissed the thought as quickly as it had come. What was the point of second-guessing the future? She'd done that for much too long. Now she was going to live in the present and enjoy every minute of it.

Fifteen

'Pigs and poultry,' Sylvie said. The class was gathered again on a chilly grey Monday morning, glad to be in the warm school kitchen. 'Along with a dairy cow or two,' she went on. 'They were the mainstay of the small farms that for centuries covered the French countryside like a living patchwork quilt. Yes, there were big landowners with large properties too—but it was the myriad of small farms that really made the life of the countryside.' She clicked the remote, bringing up a picture on the large screen that Damien had wheeled in. 'My maternal grandparents had a small farm in rural Haute-Garonne, some distance from Toulouse. When I was a child I spent a lot of time there.' The photo showed a pigtailed child, laughing as she scattered grain for chickens pecking around her feet, while just behind her was a smiling short-haired woman in a sleeveless flowery pinafore over a dark jumper and skirt. It was a frozen moment of homely joy, and Kate really wanted to take a photo of it but thought maybe that was intrusive. She had her ordinary notebook with her, and jotted down a few things as Sylvie was talking, so she wouldn't forget when it came time to write it down properly in Nina's green notebook.

'My grandparents kept chickens and ducks, and a few pigs,' Sylvie was saying, 'and they had a couple of cows, for milk for themselves and the pigs. One of the things I learned from my visits there was that good food doesn't happen by chance. It comes about as a slow growing of local knowledge, experience and understanding. Even now, despite the disappearance of too many small farms, it still persists in our country, in a rich pattern that goes back hundreds, even maybe thousands of years. And so, these next couple of days,' Sylvie went on, 'that is what we are concentrating on. Pigs and poultry. Or, to be more precise, chicken and *charcuterie*.'

She clicked the remote again, bringing up a map of France dotted with pictures of different kinds of chickens. 'These are all French breeds.' She pointed at a corner of central eastern France which featured a white-plumaged chicken with blue feet and a bright red comb. 'And this is the bird known as the *Bresse Gauloise*, a meat breed celebrated in France since the seventeenth century. It's made the region of Bresse famous across not only the country, but the world as well.' She looked at them. 'The *poulet de Bresse* is rightly called the queen of chickens, but we're not going to begin with royalty, especially not at royal prices!' There was a ripple of laughter at this, and she continued, 'We're going to start with a humbler but still good kind of chicken, which you can easily find in markets and supermarkets at not too high a price.' She nodded to Damien, who went to the fridge and brought out two chickens. One had yellow flesh and the other white.

'Both of these are *poulets fermiers*, farm chickens, certified free-range and grain-fed,' Damien said, pointing at each in turn, 'but the colour and taste of the meat depends on what type of grain the chicken's been fed—sorghum for the white, corn for the yellow.' He began carving each chicken, commenting on what he was doing as he went, with the class crowding around.

'Now, we are going to cook each chicken, in one of two basic ways,' Sylvie announced, once he'd finished. 'Roast; and stewed. But that's just the base. From there, we are going to end up with four different dishes.' She picked up a folder lying behind her on a bench, and withdrew four handwritten, laminated recipe cards. 'You'll be working in pairs again, and Damien and I will be here to help and advise. And here are the dishes you'll be working on.'

This was one of Sylvie's favourite sessions when it came to meat cooking. The students weren't to know—because she wouldn't tell them till after the dishes had been made—that all the recipes, bar one, had been her grandmother's. The originals, written in sepia ink in her grandmother's fine hand, were in the battered old notebook that had been kept in the drawer of the kitchen table in her grandparents' house. Her grandparents and the farm had long gone—her mother had sold it as soon as her parents had died, when Sylvie was in her teens. It had caused a chill between Sylvie and her mother that had never quite gone away. But the recipes in that old notebook still lived—not only in her memory and the pages of the book, but in lived, passed-on reality, as each succeeding class worked on those dishes, recreating the aromas and flavours of Sylvie's childhood. The only recipe that wasn't from that time was one Sylvie had picked up early on in her time in Paris: an unusual and delectable method of preparing roast chicken.

She had nearly finished going round all the pairs to see if they had any questions before starting on preparations for their allocated dish, when Yasmine came in from the office. She knew not to interrupt when the class was in full swing, so Sylvie knew it was something that couldn't wait. Leaving Damien in charge, Sylvie went with Yasmine to the office and closed the door.

'What is it?'

'We just got a call. A Monsieur Pham, from the local office of the DDPP.' This was the government health department overseeing hygiene in restaurants and other food businesses. 'They've received complaints about the school, via Signal Conso.'

Sylvie knew that Signal Conso was an official website enabling consumers to make online complaints against businesses. The complaints could be anonymous.

'What?' she exclaimed. 'That's nonsense! Anyone can say any old thing on that site!'

'Yes, but they have to follow it up if they have more than one complaint about an individual business. And they've had two.'

'We've never had any issues with the DDPP before,' Sylvie said. Indeed, they'd had a surprise inspection just a year ago, and had passed it with flying colours. 'What do these so-called complaints accuse us of?'

'Monsieur Pham wouldn't say. He gave me a number, asked if you could call him back.' She looked at Sylvie, her expression distressed. 'What's going on?'

'I have no idea. But one thing I do know is that these guys rarely give you a warning if they're going to inspect you. I wonder if this so-called Monsieur Pham is from the DDPP at all.' She clenched her fists. 'Give me the number, please, Yasmine. And if you don't mind, can you step outside for a moment?'

'Of course,' said Yasmine. 'I had some errands to run, anyway.'

Left alone, Sylvie sat at the desk and rang the number Yasmine had given her. As soon as it connected, a recorded voice said, *You are calling the office of the DDPP, Paris region. Please press one if you want to be connected to our automatic information line. Please press two if you want to make a recorded complaint. Please press three to speak to an officer.*

She could have sworn it had been a fake call. Now she wasn't so sure. It did sound horribly like the rigmarole you had to go through to reach any government department. She pressed three and the recorded voice said, 'Please be patient. An officer will be with you soon.' She sat at the desk, tapping her fingers, as tinned music went on in her ear for at least five minutes. But she couldn't stay here forever. She had to get back to the class. She waited another couple of minutes, then put the phone down. She'd call back later. Or better still, go to the local DDPP office in person. That way, she'd be sure it was real. And oddly enough, despite the hassles it would undoubtedly cause if it was real, just now she hoped that was the case. Because the alternative was more worrying.

'I hope you don't mind, but Mike mentioned you were a bit of an IT wizard,' Sylvie said, as she handed Kate a freshly made cup of Lady Grey tea and a plate of thin almond-crusted biscuits. It was three thirty that afternoon, and the rest of the class had left, after enjoying a delicious late lunch of savoury chicken dishes, fresh bread and tangy green salad. Kate had been about to go too when Sylvie had called her over and asked if she'd mind staying a little while. Puzzled and intrigued in equal measure, she'd agreed.

'I wouldn't say I was a wizard,' she said now, 'hardly even an apprentice one. But I do know my way around some tech stuff. Mike probably overestimated it because I was involved in a tech start-up in Australia. It's called Resmond.'

Sylvie nodded. 'Yes. I've heard of it. One of my friends has a chic restaurant in the eighth which is listed on there. Anyway—I thought, as you created the app, that you might . . .'

'I didn't create it,' Kate said. 'My ex-husband, Josh, did. But I did have a hand in its development, so I know how they work.' She looked at Sylvie. 'Do you want to have an app built for the Paris Cooking School?'

'Oh no. No. Sorry. I didn't mean to give the wrong impression. I'm just wondering—you must have good security on Resmond, but I wondered if you'd ever had security issues, like people hacking into your systems?'

Kate nodded. 'We did have a scare one time,' she said. 'It happened years ago, when Resmond was still fairly new. People had turned up at the office demanding to be paid for restaurant meals they'd said had been ordered by Resmond staff. At first, we thought the app had been hacked.' She shook her head. 'But actually it turned out to be an elaborate hoax by a disgruntled ex-employee. He'd hired actors to play the parts of people turning up at the door.'

Sylvie's eyes widened. 'Wow, that *is* quite elaborate! What did you do?'

'Josh—who was the director—wanted to sue,' Kate said, 'but I advised against it. The man was broke, he'd spent the last of his savings hiring the actors. He couldn't have paid anything and pursuing him would have been bad publicity. So instead I went to talk to him. And we sorted it out.' She sighed. 'Turned out he just wanted someone to listen to him and take action on his claim of being underpaid. He'd tried before and nobody had listened. Anyway I did, promised to check. And he was right. He had been underpaid. Not deliberately, but through an overlooked glitch in his records. It wasn't as much as he claimed, but still, it was true. So Resmond paid up and apologised, the glitch was fixed, and that was that.'

'I see,' said Sylvie, nodding.

Kate looked at her. 'Is this about that fake pizza-base order the other day?'

Sylvie sighed. 'Yes. But there's more.' She told Kate all that had happened in the last few weeks. 'I am planning to go to the local DDPP office and speak to this Monsieur Pham. If he exists, that is,' she finished. 'But I'm beginning to wonder if whoever is behind this has somehow hacked into our emails or other technology. Or if that's the next thing we should expect, a cyber attack I mean.'

'It's possible, though it doesn't sound like that to me,' Kate said, reassuringly. 'But here's a few simple questions to answer. Have your suppliers or clients been getting weird messages from you? Has your website frozen or been taken down by your host? Has Google blacklisted your site as unsafe?'

Sylvie looked horrified. 'Oh my God, to think those things could happen!' She looked at Kate. 'My friend Serge said that sometimes a bad review can be a preliminary to an extortion attempt. I thought maybe all of it was building up to something worse, and I wanted to be prepared. Just in case.'

'That's wise,' Kate said. 'If I was you, I'd change passwords, as a precaution, on email, social media, your website, even on your bank accounts. But,' she went on, frowning a little, 'this doesn't sound like a developing cyber crime to me, it sounds like good old-fashioned harassment. Nuisance stuff, designed to stress you out, rather than actual extortion. Someone with a grudge against the school, for some reason. Because it's the school that is being targeted, not you personally, isn't it?'

'Well, yes, but the school *is* me, I suppose,' Sylvie said. 'At least, I'm the one associated with it. I did think it could be someone who tried to set up a similar business and failed . . .' She'd only thought of that this afternoon, when something had vaguely stirred in her memory. A man named Blanchard, Richard or Robert Blanchard, who'd contacted her a couple of years ago, telling her he wanted to set up a cooking school and wanting to meet her so he could ask her all sorts of questions. She'd put him off politely but he had then asked if he could send her his proposed plan, and then she could comment on it if she wanted to. She'd told him she couldn't really do that but suggested he get in touch with a business advisory service, and that seemed to do the trick, because he had stopped writing. Now, as she told Kate about it, she felt almost convinced that it was him.

'But why wait two years to target you like that?' Kate replied, not unreasonably. 'The guy who targeted Resmond did so not long after he left the company.'

Sylvie shrugged. 'Maybe he's finally given up on his dream and been brooding about it. I checked on the internet, and there is no cooking school or anything food-related run by a Blanchard, so he must not have gone ahead. Maybe he saw something about us online recently—there was a great article in *Le Parisien* in February—and it made him feel angry. And maybe he decided to pay us back, as he saw it.'

Kate nodded. 'It certainly could happen like that,' she said. 'In that case, maybe you should go to the police about it. Because he could escalate his campaign.'

'The police won't take any notice. Like you say, these are nuisance things, designed to stress me out. They're not crimes.'

'But someone impersonating a government official—that could be a potential crime,' Kate said.

'You mean our mysterious Monsieur Pham? Well, yes, if he doesn't exist, I suppose I could report it to the police.' But she didn't sound convinced.

'I think you should go to the DDPP office and take it from there.' Kate looked at Sylvie. 'I'm sorry. I suppose that isn't very helpful.'

Sylvie smiled. 'On the contrary. You've been really helpful. It's been so useful to talk about it with someone objective. But please excuse me for putting my troubles on you.'

'No worries at all,' said Kate, warmly. 'I'm not an IT wizard as Mike claims, but please let me know if there is anything else I can do to help.'

'I appreciate that,' said Sylvie, but before she could say anything more, the door buzzer sounded. 'Excuse me, I'd better answer that.'

'Of course. And I'd better go.' Kate jumped up from her chair. 'But thank you for the tea, and the chat. See you tomorrow.'

'Yes.' Sylvie smiled, following her to the door. 'May I say, Kate, what an asset you are to the class, in every way? And I mean that absolutely sincerely,' she added, seeing the red mount in Kate's cheeks.

'Oh. Thank you. I—I am glad you think so, but I don't know that I deserve it . . .' Kate was stammering, but Sylvie laughed.

'Of course you deserve it,' she said, 'And don't let anyone, not even yourself, tell you otherwise.'

As she went down the stairs, leaving Sylvie to usher in the red-haired man she had introduced the other day as 'Serge, my friend from next door', Kate thought of the other woman's words. *Do I tell myself I don't deserve praise?* she thought. *That I'm not good enough to warrant it?* The thought led her on to others. Had she also told herself she didn't deserve other things? Like the green notebook. Like Arnaud's hand of friendship. *Like too many other things I deny myself*, she thought, *because deep down I feel I don't deserve it*. Had that led her to believe that Josh was right to belittle her role in the company, belittle her role in his life, and, finally, replace her altogether, in both things?

Stop it, she thought, emerging angrily into the street, *no more pity party! I won't think like that. I won't. Not anymore. Not ever again*. And taking out her phone, she sent a text.

Hello, Nina. Ask your servant, how does tonight sound for that cooking lesson?

An answer came back almost immediately. *He says it is perfect. I will take him shopping now. Come 18h.*

She looked at '18h' for an instant, frowning in puzzlement, but then realised it was the French way of writing 6 pm. *Okay. See you both then.*

In answer, she got an emoji of a bunch of flowers, which made her smile and gave her an idea. On the way back to the hotel, she stopped at the local flower shop and bought a bunch of daffodils.

Sixteen

Gabi was sitting in the last of the afternoon sun in a little park not far from the hotel, missing Max. He'd just called her from Normandy and told her all about the dairy farm he'd been to, and the cream cheeses they made which were, he said, absolutely superlative. He didn't stock much cream cheese because he said it was so variable in quality, but these were wonderful, 'so delicate yet so distinctive you can taste the meadow flowers the cows ate', as he put it. To seal the deal, he would be having dinner with the young couple who ran the dairy farm, and the woman's parents, who had financed it. 'It's very much a family business,' he said, 'but the interesting thing is, though the girl is local, the guy isn't. He's from a rather tough suburb of Lille in the north, and his childhood, he says, was light years away from the green calm of Norman fields. His dad had been in prison a lot of the time and his mum struggled to put food on the table for him and his siblings. Meeting Clara, his wife, changed his life completely.'

'That's really sweet,' Gabi said, looking at Max's face on the screen, thinking how much she'd like to be listening to this while cradled in his arms.

'It was. People can be so cynical. To hear someone speak like that, openly, without making light of his emotions . . . well, it's quite touching.' He smiled. 'I think you would have liked them both. And loved their cheese!'

'I hope you're bringing me back some and not eating it all, then,' she said, mock-sternly.

He laughed. 'Not much chance of getting away with that, is there? So how did it go today, at the school?'

She told him then about the dish she'd made, or tried to make, with Pete. 'We had a recipe for stewed chicken with a wine, thyme, and walnut sauce, which was absolutely simple and should have been divine, but Pete put in too much wine, and then he insisted I hadn't salted the chicken, and then I got—well, I got a bit short with him so he got sulky and said it was best if we each dealt with our portions separately. Damien saw what was happening and he came over to have a word.'

'*Oh la la*,' Max said, trying to look solemn and failing. 'It sounds like you have had a hard day. How was the chicken, in the end?'

'It was fine,' she admitted, 'we rescued the sauce, with Damien's help, and Pete even apologised for getting cranky. And everyone said the chicken was good. Though they were rather more complimentary about some of the others.' That was especially so for a delectable roast chicken made by Kate and Misaki, whose unusual mustard, lemon, garlic and stock cooking mix produced a rich savoury skin and tenderly moist flesh reminiscent of *rotisserie* fare. 'Sylvie told us afterwards that most of the recipes came from her grandmother's old kitchen notebook. I wish we'd known that before. Maybe Pete would have been more careful.'

'Or maybe he wouldn't,' said Max. 'Was vinegar chicken among the recipes?'

She grinned. 'No. Lucky, eh? Or I'd have had a comparison.'

'How dare you,' he said in mock outrage, and then added, quietly, 'I wish you could be here.'

'So do I,' she said. 'Oh, so do I.'

Oh God, she thought, now, getting up from the bench. She had a long evening ahead of her and nothing much to do, except watch something on TV, and maybe go out for a bite somewhere. Or just buy some bread and cheese and have it in the room. But, just as she thought that, her phone rang again. No, not Max saying he missed her so much that he'd decided to forget about dinner with his cream cheese people and drive back to Paris. It was her agent, Nick. How had he got this number? She'd told her family not to give it out to anyone. She stared at the pulsating red and green buttons but didn't press either of them. She just waited until he gave up, until the phone stopped ringing. An instant later came the ping of a received message. But she just put the phone away. She would not look at the message. She might even delete it without looking at it at all. Stomach clenching, she walked away from the park, cursing Nick, and knowing at the same time that it wasn't the poor guy's fault that she was so bloody hopeless.

Monsieur Pham was a small fiftyish man with shrewd black eyes behind his glasses and neat greying hair. At first the receptionist had not wanted to let Sylvie and Serge through, saying that they needed to book an appointment. But then Monsieur Pham himself appeared and ushered them into his cramped office, where files were piled high on his desk. He saw them looking at the piles and sighed.

'Spring seems to bring out not only blossoms, but also problems,' he said. 'So, what can I do for you?'

'Thank you for seeing us, Monsieur Pham,' Sylvie said. 'We've come following your call to us earlier today. I'm Sylvie Morel, the director of the Paris Cooking School,' she added, seeing his uncertain expression, 'and this is my friend and associate Serge Jankowski.'

'Ah,' said Monsieur Pham, nodding. 'I am pleased to meet you. Though,' he added, with an unexpected smile, 'you may not be so pleased to meet *me*.'

Sylvie gave him a quick glance. 'I suppose not many people are overjoyed to get a call from a DDPP officer.'

'No,' agreed Monsieur Pham. 'Except when we call to give the all-clear.' He tapped something into his computer and looked intently at the screen. 'Here we are.' He looked back at Sylvie and Serge. 'Two complaints logged by Signal Conso, against the Paris Cooking School, complaining of poor hygiene, and both received within the last week.'

'The last week!' said Sylvie. 'That's impossible.'

'I assure you it isn't,' Monsieur Pham said, glancing at the screen. 'And they both say pretty much the same thing. That you don't maintain basic hygiene rules in your kitchen, such as sterilising knives between uses, that your bins aren't properly covered—and the list goes on.'

'It's all lies!' exclaimed Sylvie, angrily.

'Total lies,' chimed in Serge. 'I've known Sylvie and her school for years. You couldn't get a more scrupulously clean kitchen and better-run business!'

'You understand,' Monsieur Pham said, with a slightly raised eyebrow, 'that everyone protests their innocence.'

'Yes, of course,' Sylvie said, 'but—'

'But in this case,' interrupted Monsieur Pham, 'I'm inclined to listen. To you,' he clarified.

Sylvie's heart lurched. 'I'm glad, then,' she said. 'But . . .'

'But why?' he finished, accurately finishing her question. 'Because it struck me as odd that a business that has never had a single recorded complaint, and that easily passed its most recent surprise inspection, should suddenly receive not one, but two complaints, and in the same week.' He tapped the screen. 'It did not feel right, so I got our IT people to investigate. Their findings confirmed my suspicions. That is why I called.'

'What *were* their findings?' Sylvie asked.

'People send a complaint to Signal Conso via an online form,' he explained, 'but they are also supposed to put in their name and email address or phone number. But the email addresses of the complainants in your case do not appear to exist, so it seems reasonable to assume that the names are also fake. It appears that the complaints were sent over a period of two days from a large and very busy internet café in the eighth. But who sent them is unknown—there are no identity checks or bookings, people just walk in from the street. Unfortunately that's as much as we know, or indeed *can* know.'

Sylvie's shoulders sagged. 'But surely . . .'

'Look, Madame Morel,' he said, 'we don't have the resources to follow up things like this. Even doing this is beyond my normal remit. But I thought you should know.'

'Thank you,' she said. 'I am very grateful. But whoever this is has tried to damage my business. And this isn't the first thing they've tried. Isn't there anything you can do?'

He shook his head. 'I know it is frustrating, but it's not our job to look into malicious complaints. I would tell you to go to the police, but . . .'

'But they won't take any notice, if there hasn't been an actual threat made,' Sylvie finished for him. 'I know.'

'You could try a private investigator,' Monsieur Pham said. 'Wait a moment.' He tapped at his keyboard and then swivelled his screen around so they could see the page he had brought up. 'I've heard that these people are very good.' He smiled. 'Despite the name, or perhaps because of it.'

Sylvie and Serge smiled in their turn as they looked at the screen. *Renard et Cie*, the company was called. Fox and Co. There was an address in the 19th, which they noted down.

'Paul Renard and his staff get results, I've heard,' Monsieur Pham said, swivelling the screen back, 'he's ex-police, and he knows all the tricks.'

'That's good,' Sylvie said. 'I know you aren't allowed to give out names—but would it be possible for me to at least get the fake email addresses? It could maybe help Monsieur Renard.'

'I'm sorry,' said Monsieur Pham, shaking his head and tapping on the keyboard, 'but we aren't allowed to do that.' He stood up. 'But I will go and fetch some of our pamphlets which will inform you on steps you can take.' He left the room, closing the door behind him.

Sylvie and Serge looked at each other. 'Do you think . . .' Sylvie began, eyes alight.

'I do,' said Serge, smiling, and they went across to the other side of the desk. There on the screen was part of an online form, showing an email address. Quickly, Sylvie snapped a photo, then, as Serge scrolled down, snapped a photo of the next one. They were sitting down again when Monsieur Pham came back, holding some pamphlets. 'Here they are, Madame Morel,' he said, handing them to her. 'I hope they might be useful. And now, I'm sorry, but I really do have a lot to do. I wish you the very best of luck in tracking down this pest.'

They shook hands, and Sylvie said, 'Thank you. You've been very kind.'

He gestured vaguely, as if embarrassed. 'Not at all. Our job to protect the public from being poisoned or ripped off is important. And it's hard enough without malicious idiots throwing the system into chaos.'

'Wow,' said Serge, as they emerged onto the street, 'that rather changes my view of bureaucrats.'

She nodded. 'It was certainly unexpected.' She felt elated. At last she had something to go on. 'Do you want to come with me to see this Paul Renard?'

He shot a glance at her. 'Now?'

'Why not?'

'Okay. Let me just make a call.' And he turned away for a moment, while she looked at her own phone and the photos she'd taken. The names in the email addresses were nonsensical at first glance: quenunormande@hotmail.com and sagetragot@gmail.com but somehow they evoked faint echoes in Sylvie's mind. She couldn't for the moment think what though.

'All right, then,' Serge said, turning back to her. 'Let's go.'

Seventeen

Clutching the daffodils, Kate walked nervously down the quay. Buying the flowers had seemed like a fun idea at the time but now it felt like what her mother quaintly called being an 'eager beaver'. Maybe she should chuck them in a bin. But she couldn't see any around and there were people strolling up and down. She couldn't see Arnaud's boat yet but she'd be there in a couple of minutes. And it was almost six. Being there on the dot would look—well, somewhat like the daffodils, even though she was by nature a punctual person. To kill a bit of time, she stopped for a moment, refastened the clip that was holding back her shoulder-length fair hair, adjusted the turquoise-blue pashmina scarf around her neck, and pulled the soft grey jumper a little further down over her dark jeans. She'd dressed for warmth—the evenings were still pretty cool, and she'd assumed being on the water would be even cooler. But she hadn't brought her coat, thinking the scarf and warm Merino jumper would surely be enough. Perhaps it wouldn't be, she thought, as a little shiver coursed up her spine. Or was the shiver due to something else? *Don't be an idiot, Evans*, she lectured herself, as she walked on. It was now nearly four past six. Ha! Almost late!

And there it was, the trim green and white boat, whose name, she now saw, was *Eos*. The cabin was lit with a warm glow, the deck strung with fairy lights. Also on the deck was a table laid for two. And, as a centrepiece, there stood a pot of—daffodils. Argh!

She had just decided to stuff the flowers in her bag and close it tightly, when Nina came barrelling out of the boat, barking excitedly and jumping up at Kate. She had no time to hide the flowers, instead they fell from her hands, just as Arnaud came out, calling to Nina to calm down.

'Sorry,' he said, as Nina subsided. 'She could see you coming.'

'That's all right,' babbled Kate, trying both to pat Nina and to hide the flowers from view. But he'd seen them. So she did the only thing she could—scooped up the daffodils and thrust them at him. 'Nina asked for flowers, in her text.'

He looked at her, startled. Then he laughed. 'Oh, the emoji! Yes, of course. And what a good choice. Nina loves daffodils.' He gestured towards the table. 'She thinks everyone must love them as much as she does. And I have to do what she says.'

'Of course you do,' she said, quietly, as the dog nuzzled at her.

'Come in,' he said, smiling. He ushered her over the walkway and into the boat, which rocked slightly under their feet. Nina trotted after them, proudly wagging her tail. From the deck they walked down a couple of steps into the wood-lined cabin.

'I thought you might like a tour before we start,' said Arnaud, and she nodded, impressed at once by what she saw. With its accents of polished wood, deep blue upholstery, and cream-coloured blinds, the boat felt welcoming and cosy. Fittings, such as a fridge and stove and heater, were tucked neatly into spaces built for them, so that the cabin felt spacious and comfortable. The main room functioned as a combination of dining room, living room and kitchen—or galley, as Kate supposed you had to call a kitchen on a boat. Beyond were doors that led to a cosy bedroom—which also featured a basket for Nina; a small bathroom, which included a washing machine, and a tall open cupboard lined with shelves on which reposed neat wooden storage boxes.

'It's lovely,' said Kate, sincerely, looking around the main room. 'It really feels like a home.'

He nodded, clearly pleased. 'Thank you. It *has* been my home for—well, a little over seven years now. Seven years this February, actually.'

'Wow. That's great. The boat's name—*Eos*—what does it mean?'

'Eos is the Greek goddess of dawn,' he said. 'She was called that before I bought her . . . I liked it. Didn't want to change it.'

'Of course. It's an excellent name.' She went over to a bookshelf set against one wall, which was filled with a mix of old and new books. 'Are any of these your work?'

'These,' he said, taking two books out. 'This one's cloth—' it was bound in red, with a beautiful inset plate of a dragonfly on a leaf—'and I made it for a man who'd written poetry and painted watercolours all his life, but never published or exhibited. In old age he decided to collect all his work and have it printed for his children. And then he asked me to bind it. I made just five copies, and he insisted this one stay with me.' He handed her the book, and she touched the textured cover and leafed through the pages.

'It's lovely,' she said, because it really was. She couldn't understand much of the poetry, but the pictures were charming. And the whole thing, with its thick cream paper, soft red endpapers and cloth binding—was superb.

'Yes, it is lovely,' Arnaud agreed, without false modesty, 'and so was its author. He was one of my first customers, and making this book was a real joy, he was so happy with it.' He showed her the second book. This one was leather-bound, in a gorgeous golden tan, with the spine a deeper brown, and marbled endpapers. 'This one is an example of the opposite.'

'Oh, but it's lovely too!' Kate exclaimed.

'Well—the materials are good. But it caused me much trouble.' He opened it and leafed to a page showing a tipped-in old photo of a bearded man in nineteenth-century costume, standing beside a wagon reading '*Chocolats Marmand*'. 'It was to celebrate one hundred and fifty years of a small family company. But no one could agree on anything and then they made me do an expensive sample book before they could agree on the text—' he leafed through more pages and she saw they were blank—'and in the end they abandoned it and would not pay.'

'Oh dear,' Kate said. 'So these are the best to worst experiences.'

'Yes—at least from my early days. There are others since then, but I only keep these.'

'As reminders of what to expect?'

'Or not. Yes,' he replied.

'So—do you work here?' she asked, as he replaced the books on the shelf.

'Yes. At least, some of the time. I keep my materials and tools in the cupboard you saw.' He patted the built-in table and bench, and smiled. 'This has heard many swear words as I tried to learn my trade.'

'You haven't always been a bookbinder then?' she asked.

'No. I got hooked on bookbinding a few months after I bought the boat, when I came back from Australia. Before then—' he paused—'before that I was in the army. For ten years.'

'Oh,' Kate said. 'That's—that's a long time.'

'Yes.' He pulled out a vase from the cupboard under the sink and arranged the rather bruised daffodils in it. Kate saw from his expression that the topic of the army was probably closed. So she asked, 'What brought you to bookbinding? I mean, I can *see* the attraction, but how did you get into it?'

'It's simple. I was in an antique bookshop—that one you saw me in the other day—' he gave a rueful smile—'and I saw a notice for bookbinding lessons. And well, I thought, why not?'

'And the rest, as they say, is history.' Kate smiled.

He smiled back. 'I suppose so.'

Kate opened her bag, took out the notebook—which now had a couple more filled-in pages—and opening it at the fish recipe page, said, 'Now, then, I suppose we should think about starting *this* lesson.'

'Of course! *No*, Nina!'

Kate laughed. The dog had jumped up on the bench and put her front paws on the table, for all the world as though she were a café customer waiting to be served.

'Nina,' said Arnaud, trying to sound stern, 'you know this is not allowed—at least not when other people are around.'

Nina gave him a beady look and a short bark, as if to say, *Nonsense!* She didn't budge.

'She will supervise what we do, sorry,' said Arnaud, shaking his head mock-sadly. Kate smiled. 'Well, that puts the pressure on us, doesn't it! Okay, then—where's all the things we need?'

Nina was a treasure, she thought, as he pulled out implements and ingredients from the fridge and cupboard under the sink. Her presence somehow made any awkwardness go away. Without her, there was no way Kate could be standing here, preparing to give a lesson in cooking to a man she strongly suspected was more than capable of making the dish himself. As they started preparing the food, with Kate reading out bits from the recipe and giving her own comments, and Arnaud chopping and seasoning and frying as per instructions, the little dog watched them with her head to one side, occasionally giving another of her short barks, which might have indicated impatience, approval, or a simple, *Well, isn't this nice!* And so it was, Kate thought, as they successfully finished the delicious-smelling fish, plated it up and carried it, a tossed salad, a basket full of bread and a bottle of wine up to the deck, Nina following happily at their heels.

Over dinner, because she asked, Arnaud told her about life on the boat. He stayed there most of the year, except for one month.

'It's part of the rules of living here,' he said, 'you have to leave the port at least one month of every year, as the port authorities have to have occasional spaces available for visiting boats. But that's okay, I head off to a different place each time.' He told her there were about two hundred boats moored here, so 'it's like a village. People know each other, help each other.' He smiled.

'A village on the water, in Paris—it sounds ideal,' she said, wistfully.

'Well, there can be problems, like in any village,' he said, 'not everyone fits in. People fight sometimes.'

'And tourists stickybeak at you,' Kate said, mischievously.

'Stickybeaking,' he repeated, laughing. 'I have not heard that word for years! I don't mind the interest. And it all depends on the tourist,' he added, with a sideways glance, making her colour a little, pleasurably. 'But enough about me. Tell me about your life, in Melbourne.'

'It's nowhere near as interesting as yours,' she said, lightly. 'I live in a flat. I work in—in a tech business or at least, until . . .' She broke off, then added, quickly, 'It's weird, but I was born and grew up only a suburb away from where I lived before I came here. It's that kind of place, Melbourne. At least, for me and my family. We've been based there since, well, my great-grandparents emigrated from Wales. I guess I'm a real Melbourne girl! I did live in Sydney for a year after university, but I never settled—it's not my kind of city, really.'

'What about Paris?' he asked, looking at her.

'I love it here,' she said simply. 'I don't feel at home, exactly, but things just feel right, somehow. Like the city is so content being itself that it rubs off on you, and you feel good. Oh, sorry, I'm not explaining properly,' she added, seeing his expression.

'I know what you mean,' he said, and she saw that he wasn't being polite, he really *did* know. 'Paris has that effect. It is why I live here.' He smiled. 'Now, do you have room for dessert?'

'Always!' said Kate, fervently, and they both laughed.

Eighteen

Gabi looked across at Max, peacefully asleep beside her. Last night, he'd stayed over with her at the hotel. This evening, they were going to his grandmother's for dinner—Max always had dinner with her on Wednesdays, apparently. 'I hope you don't mind,' he'd said to Gabi yesterday, 'but she would really like to meet you.' Gabi had teasingly said, 'So she can see if I'm suitable for her favourite grandson, you mean?' and he'd laughed and said, 'Don't worry, she's not like that.' He'd told Gabi quite a bit about her, she sounded like an amazing woman—widowed fairly young, she'd kept the family business going, not easy at a time and in an industry where women rarely headed companies. Max said it was her smarts and determination that had ensured that Domaine Taverny had thrived. 'She had to put up with all sorts of nonsense at the start, but she ignored it and just kept on her path. Now she's one of the most respected growers in our region.'

'She still takes part in the business, then?' Gabi had asked.

He smiled. 'Absolutely! She's taken a step back now, and nominally my father's in charge, but anything bigger than the day-to-day running has to be referred to her.'

'She sounds formidable,' Gabi said. 'I think I'm a bit scared of her.'

'Don't be silly,' he said, and kissed her. 'She'll love you, I'm sure.'

They'd met after the class was over the previous afternoon, and headed straight back to the hotel and into bed. When they'd finally emerged they'd bought a selection of delicious ready-made dishes from the local *traiteur*—trout tartare and rabbit terrine, mini quiches and tangy celeriac salad, plus some of that beautiful Norman cream cheese Max had brought back, all of it washed down with cold rosé. They'd picnicked by the side of the Seine, among other couples and families also dining al fresco on this beautiful evening. As the lights of the city came on, tourist boats passed them with phone cameras flashing. People were taking pictures not only of the buildings and landscape but of the picnickers themselves. 'It's like we are part of the scenery,' Gabi had said, 'like seals on the rocks.'

Max had laughed. 'Let's give them a show, then.' And he'd got up and hauled her to her feet. 'Shall we dance?'

She looked at him for a moment then said, 'Why not?'

He found some schmaltzy tune on his phone and they danced as if they were in an old movie, cheek to cheek. People near them stared a bit but they smiled and cameras flashed on a passing boat. When they'd finished, everyone around them clapped, and they took a bow, laughing, and sat down again to finish the last of the wine. Yes, it had been a magical afternoon and evening, and it had almost made Gabi forget about the message from Nick, or at least put it out of her mind.

Gabi, I know you don't want to be disturbed. But please call me asap. Something urgent's come up. Cheers, Nick.

She should have deleted it without reading it, she thought now, as she went to the shower. But though her finger had hovered over the bin icon several times, she had never clicked it. She had no idea what the 'urgent' thing was, and she didn't want to know. But it nagged at her, anyway, an annoying little splinter of anxiety. She hadn't said anything to Max about it, of course. She still hadn't said anything to him about her dilemma or even about being an artist. She hadn't wanted anything to cloud this perfect time. But now, as she dried herself off and stepped into her clothes, she wondered if she was doing the right thing. Maybe he'd like to know. Maybe talking to him might even help. She went back into the bedroom and he was sitting up, smiling at her sleepily, holding out his arms, and the last thing, the very last thing she wanted, was to introduce the crap from her life back in Australia into this beautiful time with him.

At last, she was able to drag herself away and, skipping breakfast, took off through the streets to the school. It was a cloudy day and there was a chilly wind that got under her jacket, making her hurry even more. She reached the school just as the session was about to start, and with muttered apologies, took off her jacket, put on her apron and tried to focus her mind on what they were doing. Yesterday, the session had been built around sausages and ham, including fantastic Toulouse and Alsace sausages and fine Bayonne ham—today they were moving from pigs and poultry to soups. Gabi had grown up in a family where soup was popular, but only in winter. Yet Sylvie was telling them about how it could be a feature of spring too, with both hot and cold versions.

'In my grandparents' garden,' she said, 'sorrel was the first green thing to pop up after winter, and so it was also the first soup that appeared on their table in spring. Then would come asparagus, and spinach, and peas, and new garlic . . . There would be a base of chicken stock, made from the bones of a weekend roast chicken, or from stock cubes bought at the mobile shop that used to come round every Thursday. And by the way, don't feel ashamed to use stock cubes: good *bouillon* cubes, as we call them, are a staple of French pantries.'

Gabi tried to concentrate but found her attention wandering as she thought again of Nick's message. Finally, she cracked, and making an excuse about going to the toilet, she left the room. In the hall, bringing up Nick's message, she looked at it for a moment before hitting reply. *Make it casual*, she told herself. *Keep it light. Cool.*

Hey, Nick, time differences make it tricky to call, but what's up? Cheers, Gabi.

There, it was sent. She could stop thinking about it and go back to soups. She was about to do just that when her phone pinged with a message. Not from Nick, but from Max. Just one line, but it filled her with warmth.

The day is long without you.

And without you. Too long, she wrote. *Maybe I'll leave early.*

Don't. You might learn to make something I'll enjoy eating. ☺

Grinning, she typed rapidly, *You have a hide, Max Rousseau, Taverny, or whatever your name is!*

Always, he replied. *And especially with you.*

Stop it, she wrote. *Or how can I concentrate?*

At that moment, Damien came out of the kitchen and saw her. 'Are you all right?' he asked. 'You were gone a little while and Sylvie was concerned you might be feeling sick, she said you looked a bit pale this morning.'

'Oh. No, I'm fine.' She pocketed her phone without sending the message. 'Sorry. Didn't mean to be so long.'

'No problem,' he said, with a smile. 'Sylvie just worries, since we had a student three years ago who collapsed in the bathroom.'

'Oh no! That sounds awful.'

'It was a little frightening, yes. But they were okay. Just fainted—low blood pressure. But the ambulance came and there was all kinds of *tintouin*'—kerfuffle—'and it was a bit stressful.'

'I can imagine.' As they went back into the kitchen, Gabi caught Sylvie's eye. There was impatience in that glance, rather than concern. But she didn't say anything, and Gabi just gave an apologetic smile and returned to her place.

Sylvie had already been feeling jumpy, waiting for a promised update from the investigator Paul Renard that hadn't come. She knew her presentation this morning hadn't been as tight as it should have been. Gabi's lengthening absence had felt like just another thing going wrong and she'd genuinely thought that the young woman might be ill. But clearly that was not the case. Sylvie had a fair idea why Gabi was so distracted and that was of course fine, and absolutely their business, but she couldn't help feeling a little irritated too, at the disruption to the class. Or was that, she thought suddenly, because she was a little jealous? Of that first wild flush of love, that wonderful sexual exhilaration? It had been like that with her and Claude at the beginning. Not anymore . . . Even before their last row, things hadn't been the same between them, the shadow of Marie-Laure falling over them more and more. Had she been wrong to push him on that? Had she been prepared to trash what they did have for something that maybe they *couldn't* have, something that was purely on her terms and took no account of an imperfect reality?

No. That was rubbish. She was just feeling vulnerable at the moment, that was all. Once Renard got back to her with some proper information on who was targeting the school, then things would feel better. She'd see more clearly. And so, casting the uncomfortable thoughts away, she returned to showing the students how you might vary the taste and look of a spring soup to turn it into a memorable centrepiece of a meal and not just a humble palate-preparer for what might come next.

With some regret, Kate finished her bowl of sorrel and garlic soup, sweeping up the last delicious drops with a thick slice of buttered bread. 'Wow,' she said to Stefan and Anja, sitting beside her, 'that was amazing!'

They beamed. It was they who had made the soup. 'Thank you, Kate! My grandmother, she made sorrel soup too,' Anja said, proudly. 'This one is a bit different though.'

'Same, same but different,' quipped Kate, and they looked a bit confused but smiled. 'And how was yours?' They'd chosen to eat the asparagus and potato soup that had been made by Ethan and Pete.

'Excellent,' said Stefan, giving a thumbs-up so the soup's creators could see.

Pete laughed. 'Ha! Knew that bit of nutmeg would enhance the flavour,' he said.

Ethan raised an impatient eyebrow. 'I don't know why you always have to tweak things,' he said.

'Because that's what life's about,' Pete said, utterly unfazed. 'Tweaking things to suit yourself.'

Ethan shrugged but didn't reply.

Kate found Pete amusing, at least in small doses, but clearly Ethan didn't. It had to be said that pairing up with Pete did things to people: Gabi had made it quite clear, for example, that she wasn't keen to be partnered with him again. *Maybe it'll be my turn next*, thought Kate. *And that'll be a test of whether I really am as easy-going as I think I am.*

She looked down the other end of the table, where Misaki and Mike were chatting to Damien. During the class, Mike had been paired up with Kate to make a velvety lettuce and pea soup, and Gabi and Misaki had made a fabulous green bean and fennel gazpacho, sprinkled with dots of tomato and Espelette pepper.

All of it had gone down very well and looked brilliant too, like a lavish still life in various shades of green, contrasted with sprinkles of other colours: red, white, gold, against the blue and white soup bowls. There had been slices of leftover cold sausage and ham too, as sides, and bread and salad—those two went without saying at school lunches!—and there would be cheese and fruit to finish. Kate was looking forward to writing a few words about it in the green notebook. *There was a deeply comforting pleasure about making and eating soup*, she'd write, *the kind of thing you remember from childhood. I remember the chicken and noodle soup Mum made us when we were sick. A couple of times I even pretended to be sick just so Mum could make it for me. Leah thought it was silly, who cared about chicken and noodle soup? But now she can't get enough of it. It's weird how we can switch from not caring about a thing to being absolutely obsessed.*

But was it, really? For years Kate believed that she didn't care about not having kids, only to be crushed by the discovery that Josh not only had had an affair with the glamorous Resmond marketing manager Indira, but had made her pregnant—and was thrilled about it! He had told Kate from the beginning of their relationship that kids weren't on the agenda; they were a tie, an inconvenience, a distraction, and probably bad for the planet (not that he really cared about that). And because she loved him, she had pretended to agree, and to be fine with him having a vasectomy—at least he hadn't tried to make her get her tubes tied. She'd quashed the longing and, as time went on, she had made her peace with not having kids herself but instead enjoyed being an involved and loving aunty to Billy and Mia. They had loved her right back, and it had seemed enough—until Josh had dropped his bombshell. And then a wild mix of fury and grief had boiled up in her so strongly that she thought for a moment she was going to physically attack him. The scale of her reaction had shocked her, and momentarily frightened Josh, then she had turned away from him and left the house, their house. And she hadn't returned to it since. She'd sent someone to pack up her things and take them to the serviced apartment she'd rented after going to ground for a while back home with her parents. It had been the worst of betrayals; not the fact that he had slept with Indira, who she couldn't even despise as a bimbo, because the other woman was very far from being that; not the fact that he had tried to justify himself by claiming that Kate had lost interest in him and Resmond; not even the fact that he had made Indira pregnant—but that he had *wanted* to have a child with her. So much so that the bastard had had his vasectomy reversed, in secret of course. Any longing she might have had for their old life together had been completely burned away. That life had been a lie, a fraud, a grotesque parody, a waste of too many years of her life, and she only wished she could scrub it entirely out of her memory.

Her fury and grief had subsided over the months since, transmuting into something that she feared would probably be with her the rest of her life, a mix of mistrustfulness and melancholy. And she had also become attuned to it in others. It was something she'd sensed in Arnaud the other night, despite his friendliness and the great evening they'd shared. She had felt it when she'd asked him what he'd done before bookbinding, and on a couple of other occasions in their conversation, when she thought he'd only been half-listening to what she was saying, his hand brushing Nina's coat beside him, his gaze turned inwards, bleakness filling his face. Later, as he'd walked her back to her hotel, Nina trotting beside them, she'd wondered if he would expect her to invite him up and had prepared an excuse, but he'd left her at the street door with just a faint smile, and a '*Bonne nuit*,' which she echoed. Nina had made more of a thing of goodbyes than the humans, jumping up to be patted, but as they left, Kate had felt a lump in her throat. Unlike his dog, Arnaud cut a rather lonely figure. Despite what he'd said about the Port de l'Arsenal houseboat community's warm villagey feel, maybe he was more removed from it than he let on.

She had sent him a text the next morning, to thank him for the evening, and he had replied that it was a pleasure. But he hadn't suggested they meet up again, and neither had she. It was better that way. She could still go walking down at the Port, and if Nina and Arnaud happened to be around, she knew they'd be pleased to see her. But she didn't need to seek out a meeting. If it happened by chance, well and good. If it didn't happen—well, that was absolutely fine too. She had no expectations. And that felt like a good place to be.

Nineteen

Gabi and Max had decided to get the Metro to the Louvre and then walk to his grandmother's apartment from there, on a route that would take them about forty minutes on foot, via the Champs-Élysées to the street in the eighth where the apartment was situated.

It was a beautiful evening; the clouds had lifted in the late afternoon and everything seemed to glow in the soft light. They talked of Gabi's class and Max's morning sorting cheeses for the next day's market; of possible plans for a weekend away together; of books and films and music. And then Max asked Gabi about the Marguerite Yonan drawing she'd acquired, which he'd seen in her room. Not surprisingly, he hadn't heard of her, as her reputation, such as it was, had been made in Australia, not France. Gabi said lightly that she'd seen a work of Yonan's in an art gallery in Sydney a while back, so she'd recognised the style, and she'd thought that it might be a good souvenir. Max smiled then and said, 'Come on, Gabi, you don't have to pretend with me,' and then he'd casually told her that he had googled her and had discovered she was actually 'a famous young artist', whose sold-out last show had earned wide acclaim. He'd seen her stricken expression and added, 'Don't worry, I won't reveal your secret. I understand if you want to go incognito.'

She understood from the twinkle in his eye that he didn't know, *couldn't* know the *real* secret. There was nothing online to indicate the shameful, horrible truth that the so-called brilliant, original young artist Gabrielle Picabea was an impostor; a one-hit wonder who had lost her muse completely and would never create anything worthwhile ever again.

'Well, you know,' she said, with a sideways look, 'it gets a bit tiring being a famous artist; not that I am, I'm just lucky.'

It was the first time that she'd felt like she was acting a role with him.

'Lucky, my eye,' he said, and she laughed.

Then, linking her arm with his, she said, 'How very restrained of you, Max my darling, to say *my eye*, not the other thing,' meaning *mon cu, my arse*.

He looked at her with a slightly surprised look that changed to one of those sexy darting smiles as he said, 'Restrained? That describes me perfectly, yes?' and the dangerous moment passed in more laughter and a kiss. It was only afterwards, when they were almost at his grandmother's, that she realised he hadn't actually said anything about her work, whether he'd liked what he'd seen of it. But she could hardly ask him now without looking needy and blowing the image of the artist taking it all in her stride, could she?

Gabi had expected something grand: the apartment was, after all, in one of the most expensive areas of Paris. The street was lined with those classically Parisian, desirable nineteenth-century blocks of apartments designed by the famous Baron Haussmann, with their decorated cream-coloured limestone façades, carved balconies and steeply sloping silvery slate roofs. It was in one of these that Max's grandmother's apartment was situated, on the second floor. And when they stepped into the apartment itself, Gabi could not help a small gasp. It was grand, yes, with high ceilings and gorgeous Persian rugs on polished parquet floors, a lovely crystal chandelier and a glorious Art Nouveau mantelpiece mirror in the living room, classically elegant furniture upholstered in white satiny fabric with pale brown stripes, and several superb traditional paintings, including one that looked to be the original of the picture on the label of the Domaine Taverny bottles. But it wasn't the sort of grand that felt intimidating, or forbidding: this was simply beautiful, a place you just loved stepping into. That was partly because of the warm golden light that flooded in through the windows, and partly because the apartment had just the right amount of furniture, none of it heavy or too ornate, but instead looking both comfortable and elegant, quite a feat.

Max's grandmother had buzzed them in, but told them they should make themselves at home, as she was just finishing off in the kitchen. 'She doesn't like anyone to interrupt her when she's in the final stages of creating a meal,' Max said as they took off their shoes in the hall and slipped on the red leather slippers that were kept there for visitors, to protect the parquet floors. 'So we'll just have to wait. I'm sure she'll have some drinks out for us.'

She had indeed. On the low glass table in the living room lay a lovely carved wooden tray with two bottles of aperitif, crystal glasses, and two small crystal bowls containing chips and nuts. Max poured them each a drink, but Gabi couldn't just sit there sipping her drink, for she had caught a glimpse of the view from one of the windows and walked over to see it better.

'Will you look at that!' she said. 'You can even see the Eiffel Tower from here!'

Max smiled. 'You can indeed.'

'And this is where you lived, when you were going to high school?'

He nodded.

'That must have been quite a hardship,' she said, raising an eyebrow.

'Yes,' he said, deadpan. 'To see that tower all the time, it becomes boring after a while.'

'I'll bet it does.' Gabi was about to say more when a door at the end of the room opened and a woman came in.

She was small and slim, and though Gabi knew from Max that his grandmother had just turned eighty, she looked at least ten years younger. She had caramel-coloured hair artfully cut in an elegant style, fine-grained creamy skin with hardly any wrinkles, a straight nose, a small mouth enhanced by dark pink lipstick, and the same bright dark eyes as her grandson, only in her case they held a hint of steeliness. Dressed in a navy-blue silk shirt over cream-coloured pants, the only jewellery she wore were two rings, one a wedding band and the other a signet ring. She extended a hand to Gabi, after having first greeted her grandson with a kiss on both cheeks. 'Good evening, Mademoiselle Picabea, and welcome,' she said, in a pleasant, even voice, with the crystal-clear enunciation that was said to be typical of people who came from the Loire, at least in her generation.

In her op-shop red velvet skirt, black jumper, rope of Murano glass beads and dangly earrings, Gabi was feeling decidedly out of place beside the chic confidence of this woman. She stammered, 'Oh—thank you so much, Madame Rousseau—er—Taverny, er . . .' She shot a desperate glance at Max, but before he could answer, his grandmother said, 'It's Rousseau de Taverny, actually, but just Madame will do.'

Gabi wasn't sure what to make of this—she had not expected the old lady to invite her to call her by her first name, and nor would she have felt comfortable doing so, this was France, after all. And of course she couldn't call her by the name Max did, Mamieli, which was an unusual combination of 'Mamie', the equivalent of Nanna or Nanny, and 'Liliane', his grandmother's first name. But 'just Madame'—well, that felt a bit odd. And Rousseau *de* Taverny! Max hadn't said the names were joined by the *particule*, the 'de' that showed you came from a noble family. Well, clearly he didn't use it, even if his grandmother did. 'Of course, Madame,' she said, 'but please call me Gabi. Or Gabrielle, if you prefer.'

'I *do* prefer,' said Max's grandmother, calmly, 'if you don't mind.'

'Of course,' Gabi said, 'that is absolutely fine, Madame.' *God, girl, don't gush*, she told herself, the formidable lady doesn't look like the sort to appreciate it. And Max wasn't being much help.

He seemed quite at ease, wandering over to the low table to pick up a handful of nuts, while his grandmother and his girlfriend stood there, sizing each other up.

'So, Gabrielle,' Madame said, 'you are from Australia.'

'Yes. But my parents—'

'Come, let us sit,' the woman interrupted her, gesturing a little impatiently to the sofa, as if Gabi had been keeping her standing around. 'We can talk a bit more comfortably here,' she added, her tone softening. 'And Max,' she said, turning to her grandson, 'please stop eating those nuts, you will spoil your appetite. Go and set the table and put the entrées out.'

He grinned and popped another nut into his mouth. 'Sure, Mamieli.' In his face, Gabi could see the boy he'd been, who'd lived happily here with this woman, away from his difficult parents. And that made her feel less intimidated when he left the room and Madame faced her across the low table, giving her a coolly assessing look.

'This is a lovely apartment, Madame,' she jumped in, before the other woman could start interrogating her. 'Such an amazing view!'

Madame's lips twitched. 'Thank you. Yes, it's not bad.'

Gabi gestured at the painting behind her. 'The estate in the Loire looks beautiful too, with that lovely castle surrounded by vineyards.'

Too late she remembered that Max had called it a 'fortified manor house' though to anyone else's eyes it would have definitely deserved the name of castle. Madame raised a beautifully groomed eyebrow and said, 'Yes, the estate is beautiful, and so is the *house*.

It's been in the family for quite a long time.' The emphasis on house was clear, and Gabi winced.

'It must be very interesting, to produce wine,' she said, nervously taking another sip of her aperitif, which bore a name she didn't recognise but tasted pretty good.

'*Interesting*?' The eyebrow went up again. 'Well. I suppose so. Mostly, though, it's hard work.'

'Of course. It must be. I wondered if—'

'Your parents,' Madame cut in, 'you were going to tell me about them.'

No way of escaping the interrogation, then. 'Oh. Right. Yes. Well, my brother and sister and I, we were born in Australia, but my parents, they are from here.'

Madame looked at her. 'From Paris? But I understood that—'

It was Gabi's turn to interrupt. 'Sorry. No. I mean, Europe.'

'Europe is a big place,' Madame said, a question mark in her voice.

Gabi coloured. 'The Basque country, near Cambo, for my father. And Guernsey, for my mother.'

'How interesting. Quite a contrast,' Madame began, but just then Max came back into the room. 'Everything's ready, Mamieli,' he said, giving Gabi an enquiring look, to which she gave a tiny shrug.

'Good.' Max's grandmother got up. 'Then we'll eat.'

The dining room was just off the kitchen, and like the main room was both elegant and comfortable, with a small round table surrounded by four Art Deco chairs with padded dark green seats, and a beautiful Art Deco ceiling lamp for lighting. The table was laid with an embroidered pale green linen cloth and set for three with white plates edged with silver, steel cutlery with dark green handles, and crystal glasses for wine and water. A basket of bread, a carafe of water and an open bottle of Taverny Sancerre were in the centre, and on each dinner plate was a smaller plate that bore the entrée: a slice of smoked salmon on a fresh green salad. 'I thought you would appreciate something simple and fresh,' Madame said, smiling, looking much less formidable than she had a few moments before.

The salmon salad was as good as it looked, and the Sancerre was perfect with it. As they ate, Max and his grandmother talked about the dairy that he'd been to, and Gabi listened, thinking that the two of them seemed to have a good relationship. Clearly, even if Madame had been against his unconventional cheese career at the start, she didn't seem to be anymore. It made her think of her own two grandmothers. She didn't much remember her mother's mother, as she'd died of cancer when Gabi was only four or five, but she did remember her father's mother, who'd only died two years ago, a mere year after her husband of more than fifty years had passed on. *Amatxi*, Basque for grandmother, had been a bit of a hard case, flinty-eyed and tough, but occasionally showing an unexpected tenderness that was as touching as it was rare. And it was even rarer after Gabi's grandfather, her *aitatxi*, had died. He was such a lovely man, kind, affectionate, and when he died, it was like the sunlight had gone out of the red and white house in the hills. *Amatxi* hadn't lasted long, after that.

'Sorry, what?' They were both looking at her expectantly, obviously she'd been asked something, but hadn't taken it in.

'Mamieli asks if you like Sylvie's course,' Max said, earning himself a cross I-can-speak-for-myself look from his grandmother, which he cheerfully ignored.

'Oh. Yes, I do. She's—it's very creative.'

'But why do it?' asked Madame. 'Didn't your mother teach you how to cook, or is she maybe from the English part of Guernsey?'

'Really, Mamieli!' Max said, with a laugh, but it was her turn to ignore him now.

'I ask because you are French, at least partly, and yet you go to a cooking school, in Paris. You understand?'

'I think so,' said Gabi, carefully. 'Well—' She looked at the two of them, so alike yet not alike, and went on, 'I did learn to cook at home, from both my parents, who are good cooks, but I think you can always learn something new.'

'True enough. But are you planning to make a living from it? Or is it just for entertainment?'

Gabi glanced at Max, who shook his head, slightly. He hadn't told his grandmother about her being an artist. She thought about making something up that would impress the old lady but decided not to. 'Neither. I just want to learn.'

'Hmm.' Madame didn't seem satisfied, but she didn't press any further. Instead, she said to Max, 'Take the plates away and get the main course, will you?'

'I can help,' said Gabi, making as if to get up, but Madame frowned, saying, 'No. You're a guest.'

So she had to stay there, wishing she could follow him, wishing they could just slip out by a back door. She'd been nervous about meeting this woman, but Max's assurances and the look of the apartment had lulled her into a sense of false security. Now she felt nervous again.

'So,' Madame said, and this time her expression was definitely steely, 'do you know what you are letting yourself in for?'

'I beg your pardon,' Gabi said, staring.

'Ours is an old family, Gabrielle. And old families have different ways of operating.'

Gabi felt a rush of heat in her chest. 'All families are old, even if they might not all have the records and documents that some have.'

'Records and documents, is that what you think it is about?' She leaned across the table. 'It's about land. Roots.'

'My family has that in abundance,' Gabi said, feeling her anger rising. 'On both sides. Probably more than—'

'Yes?' Madame's look was challenging.

'It doesn't matter,' muttered Gabi, just as Max came back in, carrying a tray with three covered dishes.

He saw the looks on their faces and frowned. 'What's up?'

'Nothing,' said his grandmother, in her even tones. 'Gabrielle and I were just chatting.' She shot a glance at Gabi, who said nothing. She couldn't, or she'd have exploded.

'Okay.' Max remained determinedly cheerful, placing the dishes on the table and whipping off their covers to reveal an aromatic beef stew, another dish full of tiny new potatoes, and a third, smaller one, of fresh green peas. 'Gabi,' he said, 'you are in for a treat.'

'I'm sure I am,' said Gabi, trying to match his cheerful tone.

It was indeed delicious. The Sancerre again showed its versatility with this dish, and the conversation while they ate had gone back to safer subjects, so that when Max again rose at his grandmother's request, to take away the dirty plates and fetch dessert, Gabi had almost relaxed. Which was a mistake, because Madame had not finished with her. 'Have you ever been married, Gabrielle?' she asked, fixing Gabi sharply with her black eyes as if pinning a butterfly.

'No. Never.' *Not that it's any of your business*, she wanted to add, but didn't, because she still hoped to stay on reasonable enough terms not to have a massive blue.

'Then you don't understand the compromises one has to make,' Madame said.

'Compromises? What *are* you talking about?' Gabi was genuinely astonished.

Max's grandmother shook her head. 'It's hard enough when a man and woman come from the same background, but—'

Gabi interrupted her. 'This is absolutely ridiculous.' She got up. 'I do not understand what I have done to offend you, Madame, and I do not wish to fight with you. But it is clear that you would prefer me not to be here and so I think it is better if I leave.' And she marched out of the room and into the hall, where she flung off the slippers, put on her coat and boots and left the apartment, closing the door carefully behind her.

She had only gone a little way down the street when Max came running after her. 'Gabi, Gabi, please! Stop. What's happened?'

He looked utterly distressed, and she almost softened, but the anger still boiled in her, so she said, biting off the words, 'Your grandmother is a pretentious snob who doesn't want me anywhere near you, her precious grandson!'

'What? No. What do you mean?'

'Apparently I'm not good enough for you, because I don't come from the right sort of family,' she spat out, 'apparently we don't have the roots you lot have, though that's a pile of *merde*.'

'Of course it is,' he said, 'of course. But you have to understand. She's old, and sometimes, well . . .'

'Old enough to know better,' Gabi said, sharply. 'Or has she learned nothing from what happened to you?'

'I don't understand,' he said, running his hands nervously through his hair. 'This isn't like her. Are you sure you didn't—er—didn't misunderstand?'

Gabi looked at him. 'There was nothing to misunderstand,' she said, trying to keep her voice steady. 'She made it perfectly clear.'

'But . . .' He frowned. 'She said nothing like that to me. She seemed surprised that you'd left.'

'Of course she'd pretend to be. She made damn sure you were out of the room when she was hectoring me.'

'Gabi,' he said, 'for God's sake, you're talking as though she planned it like that.'

'I think she did. She wanted to warn me off, only not in front of you. That's why she sent you off with the plates.'

'That's absurd,' he said, his expression sharpening.

She looked at him. 'You think I'm exaggerating.'

'I don't know what happened in there, Gabi, to be honest. Look, I know some of the things I heard her say when I was in the room were a bit—direct, but she's like that. And yes, she does have some silly ideas about the family. But warning you off! She's never done that before.'

Gabi snorted, a stab of jealousy going through her, despite everything. 'You mean she hasn't done this to any of your long line of girlfriends?'

He coloured. 'Don't be silly. There is no long line, just a couple, after Floriane. But it is out of character for her to be so—to say the things you tell me she did. Did you maybe say something, do something—' He stopped abruptly as he saw the expression on her face. 'Gabi, I didn't mean . . .'

'Yes, you did,' she said, in a hollow voice. 'Your grandmother knew what she was doing. She knew you wouldn't believe me when I told you. She knew you'd take her side, because you can't help it, can you, Monsieur Max Rousseau *de* Taverny, coming from that *old* family, with that castle that you all pretend is a *house* like any other, and—'

'Gabi, stop. Please. You don't know what you're saying.' His face was twisted with emotion.

'Ha, I don't, do I?' She clenched her fists. 'You didn't warn me what she was like. You even encouraged me to think she'd be happy to meet me. That was a lie.'

His eyes flashed. 'A *lie*? It was what she told me. I thought it was the truth. Like I thought your story about being an apprentice cook was the truth. But it wasn't, was it?'

Stunned, she opened her mouth to speak, but he hadn't finished. 'Why make up that stuff? Is it because the real truth is that I'm just part of the exotic scenery, just a part of the whole glamorous, sexy incognito artist in Paris story?'

Her stomach churned. 'You . . . how can you even . . .' But the words stuck in her throat, and she turned sharply and walked away, tears she furiously refused to shed clouding her vision and making her stumble as though she was tipsy.

He didn't follow her. And she didn't look behind her. Not once.

Twenty

It was a blustery, chilly morning, and padded jackets had come out of premature hibernation, but the crowd at the market was just as cheerfully busy as usual and Sylvie's class moved among it with notebooks and baskets at the ready. Today their task was to find products that came from no more than fifty kilometres from the centre of Paris, in any direction, and to build a group meal from that back at the school.

The previous afternoon, Sylvie and Damien had drawn up the list, and told the students who had what this morning, as they all gathered at the edge of the market. Everyone had seemed satisfied. Well, everyone except for Gabi. Sylvie had thought she'd be pleased to be allocated cheese—but she'd shaken her head and said, bluntly, 'I'd prefer something else.' Kate had seemed happy to swap with her—she, like Pete, had been allocated vegetables—but it troubled Sylvie. Yesterday, Gabi had seemed distracted but happy, but today she seemed distracted and sad. Or maybe not sad but angry.

You could see it in the shadows under her eyes and the tightness of her jaw. Sylvie sighed. Max was due to give a presentation to the class next Wednesday. It was always a popular session and there was no way she wanted some lovers' tiff, if that was what it was, to throw a stick into the school's well-oiled wheels.

She made her way to his stand. Kate had not yet got there—she was checking out other cheese stands first—but Max was busy with other customers. He didn't seem different from usual, but she would still discreetly raise the subject of next week's presentation. But as she stood there waiting, a memory popped into her head. It was an episode from a book she'd been fascinated by in her teens, *Le Ventre de Paris*, *The Belly of Paris*, by the classic nineteenth-century author Émile Zola. The novel was all about the vivid, chaotic community of producers, buyers and sellers at the legendary fresh food markets of Les Halles, which, until the early 1970s, had been in central Paris but were now out at Rungis. There was a famous passage in that book which was known as the 'Cheese Symphony'. She had loved that passage, with its exultant, extravagant descriptions, such as 'three bries, on their wooden boards, looking like extinct moons', and 'roqueforts under their crystal bells, putting on princely airs yet pockmarked with blue and black, like the shameful maladies of rich people who have eaten too many truffles'. Then there was an extraordinary bit about the stinky cheeses, such as red-tinted *livarots* whose smell caught at the throat like a puff of sulphur, and another cheese whose stink was so high it had actually killed flies. But what struck Sylvie right now was not so much an equivalence with Max's stand—there were no dead flies around his cheeses, anyway!—but that it awakened an echo of something she'd half-thought the other day at Monsieur Pham's office.

She took out her phone now and scrolled to the photos of the fake email addresses of the so-called complainants to Signal Conso: quenunormande@hotmail.com and sagetragot@gmail.com. Yes, she was almost sure of it! Moving away from the stand, she rapidly typed in *quenu Zola*, then *saget Zola*, and came up with references at once. Yes! The Quenus were important characters in that book and 'Normande' was the nickname of another character, while Mademoiselle Saget was a notorious gossipmonger in the novel, and 'ragot' means 'gossip' in French . . .

Sylvie called Paul Renard's office and was put through to him almost at once.

'Ah, Madame Morel,' he said. 'I was about to call you myself.'

'Are there developments then?' she replied, sharply.

'In a way. We found the man you thought might be behind this. Robert Blanchard.'

She tightened her hold on the phone. 'And what does he say?'

'Nothing.' A pause. 'He died a year ago, of cancer.'

Her throat tightened. 'Are you sure it was the Blanchard I knew?'

'One hundred per cent. I went to see his sister. She told us that her brother had indeed been bitter about you not helping him, as she put it.'

'It was not like that at all . . . oh, never mind. What about her? Do you think she'd be capable of doing this to avenge her brother?'

'No. She was quite dismissive of his claims. She said her brother always exaggerated things.'

'And there's no one else in his life who might have—'

'No,' he broke in. 'None that we have found, anyway. We'll keep looking, but I'm afraid that trail is most likely a dead end.'

She sighed. 'You're probably right.' Then she brightened. 'But I may have another lead for you. It's to do with Zola.'

'*Zola*?' Now it was his turn to sound startled.

'Let me explain.' And she did, quickly.

'Interesting,' he said, when she'd finished. 'But it could just be that it's a favourite book of whoever is behind this.'

'Yes, but that in itself might mean something, no?'

'It might—but it is rather like looking for a needle in a haystack. Or a single word in a Zola novel,' he added, and she could hear the smile in his voice.

'Of course. But you never know,' she said, a little deflated.

'You don't,' he agreed. 'Don't worry, we will look into it.'

'Thank you, Monsieur Renard.' As she ended the call, Sylvie caught sight of Kate heading for Max's stand. Not the best moment to have a discreet word with him about Wednesday. Never mind, she'd call him some time before then.

Kate had seen Sylvie hovering by the stand, phone clamped to her ear. But before she reached her, the other woman had taken off. She wondered if the preoccupied look on Sylvie's face meant something else had happened in that campaign against the school. *Poor Sylvie*, she thought. It couldn't be an easy time for her, trying to work out the identity and motive of someone who meant her ill.

'Good morning,' she said, cheerfully, to Max. 'I'm here to choose a local cheese. Or two. For our class today,' she added.

He gave a fleeting smile. 'Of course,' he said, in English. 'It's the day you have to choose local produce. No more than fifty kilometres from here, yes?'

She nodded, rather relieved that he knew exactly what she wanted. 'That's right.'

'Well, as you know, in French we use the word *terroir* to mean the particular place where a crop, like wine grapes, or a food product, like cheese, originates. Soil type, climate, farming practices, centuries of experience, all these are part of *terroir*. And the great classic cheese from the local Ile de France *terroir* is of course the Brie de Meaux, which is made in Meaux, a town fifty kilometres to the east of Paris.' He pointed to a beautiful big round of the cheese, with its thick, pure white crust. 'It's said to be one of the oldest cheeses in France, mentioned in a document of the eighth century. And supposedly Louis XVI asked for it for his last meal, before they guillotined him.'

'That's quite some pedigree!' Kate said, peering at the cheese. 'I love Brie and I'm sure yours will be excellent.'

His smile was a bit less fleeting. 'It certainly is,' he said. No false modesty there, how typically French, Kate thought, amused. 'There are lots of producers of Brie, as you might imagine,' he went on, 'but I get this one from a superb small producer. It's fully organic, and made of raw milk. So—you'll have some of this?'

'I think I have to,' Kate said, returning his smile. 'What else do you suggest?'

'This one,' he said, pointing to a cheese with a pale brown crust, labelled *Cabrichou*. 'It's a delicious raw-milk goat's cheese from another excellent local producer, this time from the beautiful

Chevreuse Valley, just forty kilometres to the south-west of Paris. I'll give you a bit to try.' And he cut a sliver, put it on a half-slice of bread, and handed it over to her.

It had an aroma of goat, but not overwhelmingly so. Its washed rind crust was soft, and the texture of the interior, the paste, was unctuously melt-in-the-mouth, with a rich taste. 'Oh. It's absolutely gorgeous!' she exclaimed. 'I'll certainly take some of that too.' She looked longingly at the other cheeses. 'Sylvie said no more than two, for the class . . . but I might get a couple of others, anyway. Something suitable for an evening picnic by the river, maybe.'

Something like sadness flickered over his face. But then his expression righted itself back to its professional calm. 'Then best not to have too soft a cheese, if you need to carry it any distance. Are you still needing it to be local?'

'No, I think we can branch out a bit,' she said, nodding when he recommended a blue from Normandy and a semi-hard cheese from Brittany. She tried each, and they were delicious. Watching as he cut and wrapped each cheese, she thought how wonderful it must be to live your life knowing and loving something so much, like he clearly did with his cheeses. And even better when it was something that gave pleasure to other people, and enabled all those rich food traditions to continue to thrive all over the country, in hundreds, thousands, of farms and small businesses.

'Thank you,' she said, when he handed the parcels over and she paid. 'Do you mind if I take some photos and put them on Instagram?'

He shook his head. 'No problem.'

'And I really appreciate you taking the time to advise me,' she added.

'It is a pleasure,' he said, with another of those fleeting smiles. He seemed about to say something else, but then his smile vanished and his face went blank. He barely acknowledged her *au revoir*, turning instead to fiddle with something behind the counter. Had she somehow said the wrong thing? But now she saw what he'd seen: Gabi's vanishing back. Kate thought of how she'd seen them that first night when she'd met Arnaud, down by the port. They'd been all over each other, their mutual attraction incandescent. Now—well, there was clearly trouble in paradise.

Gabi hurried back to the hotel, throat tight, gut roiling. She didn't feel well; she'd hardly slept at all last night. She'd not meant to go anywhere near Max's stand, but Pete had caught up with her and wanted to know what she'd bought, 'So we don't buy the same thing,' he'd said, and he'd insisted on taking her to some special stand or other, and that's when she had realised that she was much too close to Max's stand, where she could see Kate talking to him. She'd thrust her basket at Pete, saying, 'I'm so sorry, but I don't feel well, can you tell Sylvie I'm going back to my hotel to rest.'

'Oh no,' Pete had said, 'are you okay?'

It was a silly question, but kindly meant, as was the expression on his face, so she said, gently, 'Not really, but I will be okay if I can rest. Don't worry.'

He nodded. 'That's the best thing to do, sure, and I'll tell Sylvie.' Then he frowned and asked, 'But will you be okay to get back?

I mean, it's quite a way.' She assured him she'd get the Metro, and that she'd be fine, and he nodded again. He let her go because by then he'd seen Kate, with whom he was much more pally, but then Kate was pally with just about everyone, wasn't she, little Miss Sunshine, that was her . . . *God, I'm a bitch*, Gabi thought helplessly, as she walked rapidly away. But it wasn't Kate she was really thinking of, it was Max, and how easy he'd looked, chatting to Kate, as if nothing had happened, and then he'd looked up and seen her and the frozen expression on his face had sent such a sharp pain through her that she had immediately fled.

Reaching her street, she got a takeaway coffee and went into the hotel, where the receptionist looked up and said, 'There was a call for you, Mademoiselle, I took a message,' and handed her a folded piece of paper. *Max*, she thought at once, *Max, trying to excuse himself, and thinking that if he called my mobile, I wouldn't answer, which damn right I wouldn't*. And, anyway, she'd left her mobile here this morning so he couldn't call her. But the receptionist's eyes were on her so she restrained herself from screwing up the piece of paper and chucking it in the bin, and instead smiled and thanked her, then went up to her room where she put the coffee on the table, threw her bag and the paper on the floor and herself on the bed and just lay there for a moment, eyes tight shut, willing herself to stop being so pathetic. He was just a man she'd fancied for a while, that was all, good at sex and cooking but that's it. She was well shot of him, like she'd been of other guys who'd turned out to be douche bags. But all her defiance couldn't stop the little voice deep inside that told her that Max was *not* a douche bag, and that no man had *ever* made her feel like he had, not in the good times or the bad. The pain she felt now was not just righteous anger about his behaviour or hurt pride, it was loss, pure and simple, and it hurt, it bloody well hurt.

She fell asleep, without even knowing she had. She woke with a jump a couple of hours later, disorientated and gritty-eyed. Getting up to splash water on her face, she caught sight of the piece of paper she'd flung on the floor and picked it up. Unfolding it with shaky fingers, she saw it wasn't a message from Max at all, but from Nick. *In Delhi for arts festival, time difference easier, we must Zoom today. DON'T ignore this. Nick.* She sighed, took out her phone from the drawer of the bedside table and wrote, *Hi Nick, don't have Zoom on this phone.* An answer came back almost at once. *No worries. Download the app. Will email meeting link.* An instant after, when she was looking crossly at the message pondering how she could refuse, the phone pinged again. *No excuses, Gabi. It's urgent. But good.* She was still about to make some excuse, but paused. Nick wouldn't be put off, so she might as well get it over and done with, whatever it was. *Okay,* she wrote, *give me five minutes.* She could almost hear his sigh of relief as the reply popped up. *Great. Speak soon.*

Damn it. What time was it in Delhi? She looked it up. They were three and a half hours ahead of Paris. So it was midafternoon there. She downloaded the Zoom app, sent him one word: *Done,* then went to the bathroom to wash her face and brush her hair. Returning, she found Nick had emailed her the link, so she turned the table around so that she could sit with her back to the window, where you could see the street outside, and set the phone up on the table. Sitting down, she took a deep breath and pressed the link.

Almost at once, he let her in. His broad dark face with its thatch of greying hair appeared on the screen a moment before his voice boomed, 'Hello, stranger!'

'Hello yourself,' said Gabi, trying to look and sound bright and cheery. She liked Nick, he was a decent bloke, and he'd taken her on well before *Shadow Life*, so it wasn't like he was some shonk trying to cash in on her newfound success. 'So, where's the fire?'

'The gallery wants—' he began, but she cut in.

'Look, Nick, I'm working on something.' *Liar, liar.* 'But I'm not ready yet to even talk about it.' *Pants on fire*! 'I'm here for another two weeks, and even after that—'

It was Nick's turn to interrupt. 'You can be ready when you're ready,' he said. That easygoing attitude was not at all what she'd expected, given the last conversation she'd had with him a few weeks ago. She was about to say something about it when he went on, 'This is something else. The gallery has been invited to nominate a promising young Australian artist for a prestigious art residency in Provence. And they want to nominate you.'

Gabi stared. 'What?'

'Three months, starting in late May, all expenses paid, and a weekly living allowance. There's no compulsion to produce something finished, just feed your creativity and hang out with other artists, apparently. It's bloody brilliant, Gabi—and you'd be perfect for it, especially as you're in France already, you're a dual national and you speak the language. But nominations close the day after tomorrow. They need your agreement to nominate you. So what do you say?'

'I . . . I don't know,' Gabi stuttered, her mind whirling. 'I . . . I need to think about it.'

Nick frowned. 'Don't think too long. An opportunity like this doesn't come along every day. Or year, actually. I need to give them an answer by tomorrow afternoon at the latest. Today would be better.'

'But I can't . . .' she began, then changed tack. 'Why is this happening so late? I mean, surely applications must have been open earlier than this?'

'They're not applications, they're nominations,' he said.

'Whatever they're called, it sounds weird to me. I bet I wasn't their first choice. Some other more famous artist must have fallen through.' She knew she sounded ungracious, but she was too discombobulated to care.

'Look, Gabi, I know you've been struggling—'

'I haven't,' she lied, not sure why she did.

'But I can't keep making excuses for you,' he went on. 'You've been out of touch for ages. You don't answer emails or phone calls. You've turned off your social media. The gallery can't get hold of you. *I* couldn't get hold of you, until I put the hard word on your mum and she gave me this number. You're in Paris, taking a month off to *cook*, she told me. For God's sake! And now you're looking a bloody big gift horse in the mouth. Are you trying your hardest to blow your career up? Please tell me if so because I for one am not going to go down with you.'

'Nobody's asking you to,' said Gabi, her anger rising, 'certainly not me!'

'Yes, well, you haven't exactly . . .' But whatever Nick was about to say, he thought better of it, and simply added, 'Just think about the nomination, and let me know asap, okay?'

She nodded, reluctantly. 'Okay,' she said, but by then he had already ended the call.

Swearing under her breath, she jumped up and walked up and down the room, her thoughts tumbling over each other, her stomach in knots. She'd have jumped at this residency in the past. Now, she couldn't sort out her thoughts and her feelings, not with this, not with Max . . .

But at that moment, quite unexpectedly, an image came into her mind. Kind blue eyes, bushy black eyebrows sprinkled with grey, thick grey hair, a smile that rose slowly, beautifully, like the sun . . . More images came—a long easy stride that waited for little legs to catch up, callused hands that were surprisingly gentle as they lifted a little one onto slightly stooped shoulders, and a voice, deep and rich, telling stories, singing songs, as he walked with his grandchildren among his beloved ancient hills. Her Basque grandfather, her lovely *aitatxi*, who had died three years ago but was still sorely missed by the family, and who her *amatxi*, her tough grandmother, had loved so much that she had only lingered in this world for less than a year after his death. Her *aitatxi*, to whom she could have confessed her troubles, because he would have understood; he who was so wise and saw so much about people and the world, despite never having been further than Bayonne.

And suddenly she knew what she needed, more than anything. Picking up her phone, she booked a return train ticket on a TGV that left in just a couple of hours, bound for Biarritz. From there she'd rent a car and head out into the hills.

Twenty-one

It was a bright breezy Friday morning at the Bassin de la Villette, and Kate, Pete, Stefan and Anja were waiting in a queue at a boat hire place. Stefan and Anja had rented a boat for the day to cruise up and down the canals, and they'd invited everyone in the class to come too. But Gabi had gone away, Mike and Ethan had already made plans, and Misaki said she wanted to spend the day at the Musée d'Orsay, soaking up the Impressionists, so it was going to be just Kate and Pete with the German couple.

When they'd first told her of their plans, yesterday, Kate had immediately thought of the Port de l'Arsenal, but apparently Stefan had already checked that out and it wasn't a place where you could rent a boat for a day trip; you had to go to the Bassin de la Villette for that. 'And we could have booked a private cruise,' he said, 'but then we found a company that rents out electric motorboats, which you can easily pilot yourself, so we decided that would be much more fun.' But clearly when it came to fun, he and his wife believed in making sure everything was well prepared. They'd hired a guide because otherwise, Stefan said, they wouldn't know what they were looking at, and they'd also organised for a substantial picnic lunch with all the paraphernalia. And they'd rented an eleven-person boat, which seemed a little excessive if there were only going to be four of them, or rather five if you counted the guide—who hadn't yet turned up. But, as Anja said, better to have too much space than not enough. And given that, apart from Kate, everyone was fairly big and tall, that was definitely true.

It must have cost Stefan and Anja a fortune, but they'd refused to take any contribution towards it. 'We are celebrating forty years of marriage on this day,' Anja had said, smiling, 'and as Katrin and her family are far away—' she'd mentioned before that their daughter had married an American and lived in the US—'we decided we'd like to celebrate with friends. And we do not ask friends to pay for this.'

Now, Kate looked around her, at the red and white open boats already out on the sparkling water, a pair of swans nonchalantly gliding among them, tourists and family groups milling about, the world's languages babbling all around, the whole cheerful bustle of it, and she was glad she'd come rather than spending the day mooching around the shops, which had been her original plan. Yes, it meant she had to put up with Pete for the day, but he was fine, and she really liked Stefan and Anja, they were so genuine and so full of joy about everything. She glanced at them in their matching navy and white stripy tops, cream canvas pants and jaunty caps—they had really got into the whole marine thing—and couldn't help smiling. Anja caught her glance and gave her a thumbs-up. 'Isn't it lovely!' she exclaimed.

'You wouldn't be dead for quids,' Kate agreed, channelling her dad.

Anja looked a little puzzled, then laughed. 'Oh yes!' Then a slightly anxious look came over her face. 'Our guide should be here. I hope he won't be late.'

They reached the top of the queue and picked up the keys, life jackets and handbook and were directed towards the briefing area where a young woman in a stripy top rather like that worn by Stefan and Anja gave them instructions and advice on how to navigate, what to avoid, what the restrictions were, and so on. Still the guide had not turned up. It was just as the groups were being directed towards their individual boats that he finally arrived, apologising for his lateness. 'I am very sorry, I was delayed at home—small problem with . . .' Then he saw Kate, and his eyes widened. 'Oh. Hello.'

'Hello, Arnaud.' Kate tried to mask her pleased surprise. 'Nina not with you then?'

He shook his head, smiling. 'She'd take over the whole trip. I left her with a neighbour. They have a dog too.'

The other three had been listening to this with some surprise, and now Stefan said, 'You are friends?'

Kate looked at Arnaud, and he looked back at her. 'Yes,' he said and Kate found that she didn't want to demur. Did it really matter whether they were friends or acquaintances, or just ships passing in the night, as it were? She was glad to see him just as he seemed to be glad to see her. There was nothing more to it than that, but nothing less either.

'One more friend to add to our day then!' Anja said, delighted. She smiled broadly at them all. 'Okay. Time to go, friends!'

Arnaud proved to be the best kind of guide—informative, entertaining, but not intrusive. Clearly he had done this before. Pete was on his best behaviour—it turned out he was a bit nervous on water so he dialled down the Tigger boisterousness. Stefan and Anja exclaimed over everything and held hands and looked so ridiculously happy it brought a lump to Kate's throat. And as they glided across the water, taking it in turns—except for Pete—to steer, Kate herself felt the beauty of the city, the undemanding warmth of the company, the quiet motion of the boat, steal deep into her bones, making her feel utterly relaxed. It was perfect.

They had a glass of Champagne on board the boat but pulled into a mooring to have a sumptuous lunch on the grass: cold roast duck and fresh bread, pork *terrine* in a glass dish, smoked salmon and *jambon de Paris* in succulent slices, tiny tangy gherkins, artichoke hearts and steamed white asparagus, a selection of cheeses—including the ones Kate had bought from Max—and finally, jewel-like tarts: lemon, strawberry, chocolate, caramel, almond. All washed down not with wine but instead very good fruit juice, and coffee hot from a thermos—Stefan had said there were strict limits on alcohol for the boat hire, and the Champagne they'd had already was all they could have for the day. But it didn't seem to matter, the talk bubbled along just as cheerfully as they sat on the sunlit patch of grass and watched people nearby play a game of *boules*. Pete went over and chatted to the players, who smiled and invited him to join them. Then Stefan went over too, and Anja, and finally it was just Kate and Arnaud sitting among the wreckage of lunch. Kate felt far too full and lazy to do anything more than sit, and Arnaud looked perfectly content too. They talked quietly and she learned he'd done the guiding regularly over the last couple of years, in the spring and summer, to supplement the bookbinding, which was pretty irregular. He enjoyed it too, he said, and Kate thought then about how the other day she'd thought he cut a lonely figure. But now she thought she'd been wrong—he was just a self-sufficient person.

She told him about the previous day's session at the school and the local-themed lunch they'd had to create and how much fun it had been, and interesting too, because it included the stories they'd all picked up along with their ingredients, like the one Max had told her about the Brie de Meaux, and poor Louis XVI requesting it for his last supper. Arnaud told her then that the famous classic gourmet Brillat-Savarin—after whom another cheese was named, and whose celebrated book on food was still in print nearly two hundred years after his death—had a story about how, as an aristocrat, he'd been on the run from soldiers during the French Revolution but stopped for lunch anyway at an inn. And the soldiers themselves had stopped for lunch at another inn, before the pursuit continued in earnest. A good meal was serious business in France, no matter what the circumstances!

Twenty-two

Gabi sat on the rocky hilltop, breathing in the scented spring air. It was the most extraordinarily beautiful sight she looked down on. Below in the valley, and on the next few hills, red and white houses dotted the vivid green of pasture, while in the distance the sharp line of the Pyrenees, still capped with snow, scribbled a stern reminder against the bright blue sky that winter had not yet quite left the high places. She could hear the tinkling sound of a cowbell, the questioning bleat of lambs calling their mothers and the distant hum of a tractor. It was cold but bright, and she could feel her grandfather's spirit on this hill they'd climbed together so many times. And that was a bittersweet comfort. 'Oh, *Aitatxi*,' she said aloud, 'I am happy to feel you here, but I would give so much to see you, to speak to you. I am lost, *Aitatxi*, and I can't seem to find my way back.'

This morning, after visiting her grandparents' joint grave, she had gone back to the house where they had once lived, but it was closed up, the people who owned it now were away. Her grandparents had also once had a small grocery shop in Cambo, but that had been sold a long time ago. When her widowed grandmother had died, Gabi's uncle Mikel, as the elder son, had inherited the house with its two acres of land, while her father Ander, the younger, had inherited the money they had saved up over the years. It sounded like something her practical, hard-headed grandmother had thought fitting, that the son who'd stayed in the Basque country should get the land while the one who'd moved so far away needed money more than anything else. It was a decision that had caused some friction between the brothers after their mother's death though eventually they'd sorted it out, agreeing informally to split both. But Mikel had insisted on selling the house and land, and Gabi's father had had to reluctantly agree. *Oh, Aitatxi*, Gabi thought now, *I know you and Amatxi thought you were doing the right thing by us all, but I wish . . .*

But what did she wish, in truth? There was no way she, or indeed any of her family, were going to come back to live here permanently, as her uncle had sharply pointed out to her father. Nostalgia wasn't a golden ticket to paradise, after all. Mikel had left the hinterland as quickly as he could, to a job in a cousin's garage in nearby Bayonne, and over the years he'd built up a flourishing freight business, with a sideline in van and truck hire. You sometimes saw his vehicles in the region, with their distinctive red logo and *Picabea et Fille*, Picabea and Daughter, written on the side. Because it was his daughter, Amaya, rather than his son, Marc, who had followed him into the business. Gabi was fond of both her cousins but it was Marc whom she got on with the best.

Ama was a tough nut, like their grandmother, but even more brisk and hard-headed, and though she was always friendly, Gabi knew that her cousin thought she was rather self-indulgent trying to make a living as an artist when everyone knew that wasn't possible. Not that Ama actually knew the realities of the artistic life, but she always had a firm opinion about everything. Like her father. Marc was more like their mother, Gabi's aunt Aline, quiet, smiling, easy in manner.

They'd all welcomed Gabi though, when she had turned up unexpectedly on Thursday night. Marc would have come with her today, only he had shiftwork at the hospital where he was a senior nurse. So he'd lent her the binoculars and Aline had packed her a fresh baguette filled with thick slices of *jambon de Bayonne* accompanied by pickled local peppers, and a slice of her wonderful *Gateau Basque*, the rich custard-filled pie emblematic of the region.

Gabi had eaten her lunch al fresco, washed down with a bottle of Orangina, the fizzy orange drink that reminded her of her childhood. It was always handed out as a treat by her grandfather after a hillside climb. 'My little *pottok* loves her Orangina,' her grandfather said, likening her to one of the sturdy Basque mountain ponies known as *pottok*, because he reckoned she climbed better than any of them, including him. Which wasn't true, not really, but as a kid she liked being called *pottok* because those little ponies were absolutely awesome and brave as anything. As a teenager she realised it could also imply you were kind of stocky and sturdy, the very opposite of the slim willowy type that you were supposed to look like. Not that it bothered her much even then, because being slim and willowy meant you had to be on a diet all the time and that was too damn boring when food was such a pleasure. And besides, she knew that her grandfather definitely meant *pottok* as a compliment.

Suddenly, high in the clear sky, she saw a dark speck. Its movement made her pulse race. Picking up the binoculars her cousin had lent her, she looked up, focusing on the speck and its nonchalant, almost lazy glide through the eddies of air. The breath caught in her throat as the speck resolved itself in the binocular sights. 'Oh, *Aitatxi*, look,' she whispered, 'I can still tell what it is.' Her grandfather had taught her and her siblings to recognise the difference between two of the great birds of prey of the region: the griffon vulture, known as *vautour fauve* in French and *sai arrea* in Basque; and the *arrano beltza*, the black eagle in Basque but golden eagle in English and *aigle royal* in French. The eagle was rarer than the vulture, but they were often confused at a distance. *But you don't need to see them up close to know*, her grandfather had said. *You can tell, if you are patient, and wait, and watch.* And now, absurdly pleased that she still remembered, she sat watching, waiting as the eagle drew large circles in the air high above her, its keen eyes no doubt nailing every detail below it.

What would it be like to soar so high, to see so sharp, to be so completely, utterly focused? The binoculars she held to her own eyes gave her a tiny taste of that, but nothing of the power of that wild bird way above her as it unhurriedly pinpointed its next meal. Or was it just enjoying the clarity of the sky, the purity of the air and the sheer exhilaration of being an eagle?

Her grandfather had told them how when he was young and out in the mountains with his own grandfather, they'd found an injured young eagle and looked after it till it was well again. The bird had not been an easy patient, and more than once it had lashed out in fear and anger. When they had let it loose, it had circled them three times, before flying off forever. *But didn't he ever come back?* the children had wanted to know, and when he told them no, they had said that must have been so sad, but he'd shaken his head. *No, you see, even if I did not see him with my eyes, I saw him with my heart, and I knew that would never leave me, not even when I grew very old, like now.*

There was a lump in her throat. She could hear his voice in her ears, his gentle touch on her hand, as she kept watching the bird circling again and then hanging in the air like a benediction, or a warning. And then suddenly it plunged, so fast it was just a dark blur in the binocular lens, and she lost it completely from sight. But she knew that down below somewhere, some little creature's life had ended as abruptly as though it had been shot. She shivered slightly, put the binoculars down, picked up her phone, went to Nick's original message and typed rapidly, *Okay to the nomination. Thanks*, and sent it before she could think too much about it. Somehow, in that moment, it had felt right. It had felt like that was what her grandfather was trying to tell her, though she'd never have confessed that to anyone else.

Then she sent a message, with photos, to her family's WhatsApp group. *Weekend break with the fam here, everyone says hi. And just saw an eagle on Aitatxi's hill!* Replies came almost immediately from her parents, but then they always were up early, earlier certainly than her siblings. *An eagle, lucky! Glad you're having a break, say hi back to them*, from her mother. And from her dad,

Good to know you're having time out from the Parigots, but then you have to put up with pompous old Mik, eh? :) The brothers still didn't have an easy relationship—according to her dad they'd never had one because they had diametrically different views on pretty much everything. Some of that came from their very different lifestyles: Mikel was a successful, even at times ruthless, businessman while Ander was a high school teacher who had never been interested in making money, just having enough for his family. He didn't think that being rich made you special, while Mikel thought his prosperity meant he was entitled to throw his weight around. But it was more than simple arguments about things like that which made the brothers rub each other up the wrong way. They were both so sure of themselves, and stubborn as well, that they clashed head on, like combative rams.

He's been busy, she answered, *haven't seen much of him, but he seems pleased to see me*. A short pause, then her dad's reply, *And why shouldn't he, eh?* Smiling, she wrote, *How's everything at home?* That started her mother on the family news, such as Ben's twins winning a prize at school, and Joana's little boy saying his first words—she was a very proud grandmother—with her father interjecting from time to time with remarks designed to annoy her mum, which always worked. It was all very familiar and funny and frustrating, the way it always was, and when at last Gabi wrote that her phone battery was about to give up and she'd better go, she felt as though she'd been back at home, sitting around gossiping after Sunday lunch, which was comforting. They hadn't asked her about her art or even about how she was liking the cooking course, and that was good too.

But she was really getting a bit cold now, so she got up, a little stiffly, and headed down the hill towards her car parked on the road quite some distance away. She was halfway there when she stopped suddenly. The eagle was just there, only about fifty metres away, but it hadn't seen her, so intent was it on the rabbit it was tearing to bits. Not moving a muscle, hardly daring to breathe, spine tingling, she watched it until quite suddenly it seemed to become aware of her presence. It lifted its head up and stared at her. It was electrifying, that hot golden stare, and seemed to go on forever. But in reality it was only a fraction of a second before the eagle jumped up, spread its great wings, and flew unhurriedly away.

Twenty-three

Claude had come hangdog to Sylvie's apartment that afternoon, apologising for his behaviour the other day. He had sworn he'd spoken to Marie-Laure, 'very firmly', and that though she was still being difficult, he thought that he had made progress in making her understand that things were definitely over between them. He had told Marie-Laure that he had met someone else, but he hadn't given her Sylvie's name. *I thought it was best*, he said. And he'd looked at Sylvie then, smiling tentatively, as if seeking her approval of his bravery, and she didn't have the heart to tell him that he should have done all this long, long ago. Just as she didn't have the heart to resist him when he put his arms around her and started to kiss her and then the familiar pleasurable rhythm of their bodies together took over. Now, as she sat up and looked at him, asleep beside her—he'd always had an enviable talent for falling asleep almost straight away after sex—she thought that, once again, he'd succeeded admirably in changing the subject and putting off the moment of truth. But the issue with Claude felt minor compared to her worry about the business, which was escalating again.

She'd received an email from a supplier—one of the small *charcuteries* she dealt with—asking for immediate payment of their invoice, which wasn't due for payment till next week, and which Yasmine would deal with as she usually did. Sylvie had called to object to the sudden change of policy, only to be reluctantly told that they'd heard there were financial difficulties at the school. Stung, she told them it was completely untrue, and asked where they'd heard the rumour. After some more prevarication, they revealed it was on some local Facebook group page. Which made her even angrier, because why on earth would they believe some troll and not check with her? 'You'll get your money in full today,' she said, sharply, through the woman's embarrassed twitterings, 'but I do not think our commercial relationship can continue, under the circumstances.' Then to her horror the woman burst into tears, saying that they had been having hard times themselves, that it had caused a lot of stress and they hadn't been thinking straight as a result. Sylvie heard the note of real desperation in the woman's voice and softened her own tone. It had all ended with an agreement that the invoice would be paid as normal, but that Sylvie would also put in a new order. She'd also got the URL of the page and texted it to Paul Renard, with an explanatory note. She didn't want to look at it herself, it would just make her too angry. But she'd told Serge about it, and knew he'd be diligently looking at it for her, making his own investigation. She wasn't on Facebook herself and never would be. She disliked all social media.

Yasmine kept up the school's page on Instagram and Sylvie followed it and Julien's, too, but that was as far as it went.

Ping! A message. She snatched up her phone and took it out of the room with her. Claude had looked as though he might be stirring and she didn't want him to put his grain of unhelpful salt into the matter.

It was from Serge. *Sylvie, I found that chat. Took a screenshot, here it is.*

And there it was, the sly poison of the troll. *Trouble at PCS, not paying their bills, I've heard.* Then someone else saying, *Who's PCS?* And someone else, not the original poster, said, *Paris Cooking School.* Another one chimed in, *Not surprising, they must spend so much money*, and then someone said, *And make it too, taking it off stupid rich foreigners!!* And yet another added piously, *But it's poor locals who don't get paid*, and someone else agreed, *If I was a supplier of theirs, I'd be worried.* And then the chat had moved on to something quite different as another topic of innuendo, gossip and rumour was introduced by somebody else keen to tear another reputation to shreds.

Sylvie called Serge, thanked him, then asked, 'The person who posted that first message—they didn't write anything more, did they?'

'No,' he said. 'I checked on that page and several before and after. They haven't contributed to any other discussions at all. At least,' he added, 'not under that handle.' Which of course was some made-up thing, but not something that awakened any memory in Sylvie this time.

'That means they went on the page specifically to do this,' she said.

'Yes,' he agreed. 'I suppose it does.'

So, whoever it was had just deliberately thrown in a stone and watched the ripples grow. Easy enough to do in the murky pond that was internet chat. And there was nothing she could do about it, other than hope that no other supplier read the posts and was gullible or paranoid enough to believe them.

'There *is* something we can do,' said Serge, as if he'd read her mind. 'That troll might have a made-up name but other posters on this page are using their real names. I can contact a couple of them and see if they have any idea who the troll is.'

It seemed like hanging on to a very slim thread but Sylvie said, 'I suppose you might as well.' And she sighed.

'Do you want to come over for a drink?' he asked, gently.

'No. That is, not today.' She had become aware of Claude moving about in the next room. 'Tomorrow, though. But let's go out.'

'Okay,' he said, and she heard the smile in his voice.

'Who were you talking to?' Claude asked, as he came into the room just as she'd ended the call.

'A friend,' she said.

He pulled a face. 'Should I be jealous?'

'Don't be silly,' she snapped. 'It was Serge from next door.'

His lips lifted in a sneer. 'Ah. Serge the loyal *toutou*.' He and Serge had met a couple of times and hadn't exactly clicked. But, even allowing for that, the rudeness of calling her friend a 'doggy' made Sylvie see red.

'Don't you dare speak about my friends like that,' she spat. 'They're worth more than . . .' She stopped, but too late.

'Worth more than me, eh?' Claude stared at her. 'Worth more than your lover? Ha, your little *toutou* trots along beside you wagging his tail and does your bidding, but I bet he hasn't even tried to seduce you in all those years he's been your neighbour! He's half a man, a damn eunuch!'

Cold fury flooded over her. 'Get out,' she said, fists clenched, pulse racing. 'Get out, right now!'

He looked at her, eyes blazing. He seemed about to say something, then marched out of the room without a word. Moments later, she heard the front door slam.

She leaned against the wall for a moment, bile rising in her throat. What a fool she was! What an unutterable fool. Claude was bad for her, he did not love her, she was just a convenience for him. Serge was worth a hundred of a man like Claude!

Impulsively, she picked up her phone and called Serge. 'That drink today—are you still free?' she asked.

'Of course,' he said, sounding surprised but pleased too. 'Shall we go out?'

'Yes,' she said, 'let's go now.'

'Okay. Where?'

'That little place near the Pont Marie,' she said, 'where we've been to before. Where your parents met for the first time.'

'Oh. You remembered,' he said, and again there was that smile in his voice. He'd told her how his dad, Filip, newly arrived in Paris from Poland, had asked about a job at the café near Pont Marie, but instead had ended up chatting to a young waitress called Delphine, whose family had always lived in that area . . .

'Of course,' she said, lightly, 'it was a great story, a real Paris story, how could I forget?'

'I'm glad,' he said, matching her tone. 'But let's not waste a moment more, or they might run out of your favourite wine.'

It turned out to be a lovely evening. Sylvie didn't mention anything to do with Claude—she could hardly bear to even see his name in her mind, let alone talk about him—and they talked a bit about what was going on with the school. Sylvie had just remembered someone in a previous class two or three years ago who had kicked up a fuss about being refused a refund for a day they hadn't attended, despite it being clear in the school's cancellation policy that was not a reason for a refund. The person hadn't been happy about it, and even threatened to go to court over it. But they hadn't, in the end. It didn't seem like much, but Serge said she should look up her records and give the person's name to Paul Renard.

But soon the conversation turned to other things, as one drink turned into two, then to dinner. From Julien's news and whether Sylvie should take him up on his offer to Serge's correspondence with a newly discovered cousin in Poland who might come and visit him, to a light-hearted discussion of how spring in Paris signalled not only the return of flowers but also of noisy demonstrations, to a friendly argument about the relative merits of Tintin and Asterix (he was an Asterix fan since childhood, she a Tintin one): the talk flowed easily, cheerfully between them. And as they walked the short distance back to their apartment building, Sylvie could not help reflecting, with a pang, that she had rather neglected Serge. Before she'd met Claude, she and Serge would sometimes meet up for a drink or a meal, and it had always been fun. *I missed that*, she thought, now. *I missed it more than I realised—being with a real friend, with a person who takes pleasure in my company, as I do with his. I took him for granted.* And he must have known that. It must have stung. But he'd never shown any sign of annoyance, never been anything other than his usual *sympa* self. But tonight, as their conversation roamed enjoyably around, as in old times, and he gestured, making a point, his wiry hair standing up on end, his grey eyes lit up with laughter, he seemed positively light-hearted. And that made her feel both glad, and guilty.

Twenty-four

One of Kate's favourite places in Melbourne was the Block Arcade. Her fascination had started in childhood, and summer holiday treats of visits to the arcade's amazing Hopetoun Tea Rooms, with her mother and Leah. With its vaulted ceilings, mosaic floor and glass canopy, the Block, and the nearby Royal Arcade, had been her first taste of a glamorous world far from her ordinary suburban street. Gaping at the window displays of those arcade shops, she had felt so grown-up and sophisticated, and of course the glorious cakes in the tea room had made her feel like she was being presented with food from fairyland. All of it continued to have a special place in her heart, and now, gazing around at the peaceful beauty of the Galerie Vivienne, she thought that this is where the Melburnian builders must have got their inspiration to recreate a bit of Paris at the other end of the world . . .

The Galerie Vivienne, built in 1823, nearly fifty years before the Royal Arcade and seventy years before the Block Arcade, is a jewel of pre-Haussmann Paris, and one of the city's few remaining classic *passages couverts*, covered passages or arcades. Famous as an elegant, well-lit shopping haven away from the dirt and noise of the early nineteenth-century streets, it had gone through a period of steep decline later on, before being restored to its former glory. And now, elegant as ever, it housed contemporary fashion designers, antique and art galleries, a bookstore, and upmarket home decor stores, alongside a long-established fine wine shop, and a couple of small restaurants. On her previous visit to Paris, Kate had, of course, not managed to get there, but on this rather drizzly Saturday morning, here she was, about to do more than just window-shop and gape at the architectural beauty of wood and glass, wrought iron and mosaic. She would splurge, on whatever she felt like. It would be the sort of day she'd not been able to treat herself to for years, not since . . . but all thoughts of the past would be banished today, she told herself firmly. This would be a day of pure indulgence, on her own, and she intended to make the most of it.

For a couple of hours, she wandered happily from shop to shop, gathering wonderful things as she went. In one boutique, she fell in love with a pair of soft flared pale-green trousers, assorted with a short-sleeved buttoned knit top in a deeper shade of green, with pink detail on the edge of the sleeves and buttonholes, and tiny embroidered leaves on the collar. In another boutique, she selected a cute cloche hat made of paper straw and silk, and next door to that, she found a glorious scarf for her mother. She lingered in the bookshop and bought a couple of pop-up dioramas of famous

Paris arcades: this one, and the next one she was going to, for Billy and Mia.

Then, after a restorative cup of coffee, she went on a short walk to the next covered passage she'd earmarked, the Galerie Véro-Dodat. She was under strict instructions from Leah. 'You've just got to go to shoe heaven,' her sister had said, 'or you'll have me to reckon with!' So Kate had laughingly promised she'd go, though Leah's idea of 'shoe heaven' wasn't exactly hers. Flashy, eye-wateringly expensive and just not her style, was what she'd thought of the famed Christian Louboutin brand, and imagined sniffy assistants looking down their noses at her humble self. But she'd promised Leah, so she'd go, take a few photos, and leave.

Yet it did not turn out like that at all. The store might look at first sight like a fashionista art gallery of over-the-top shoes, but the assistants were friendly and helpful, the glimpse into the workshop was fascinating, and browsing through the range of shoes amazing. The stilettos and boots were still not her style, but she could certainly admire the craft of them now. And then she saw her own perfect pair: fabulous silver mesh rhinestone-studded ballet flats. How could she possibly resist? *And another thing*, she WhatsApped rapidly to Leah as she sat waiting a little later for a simple but delicious lunch of salmon and spinach quiche, followed by a vanilla and honey madeleine, *though I couldn't afford a pair of shoes for you too :), I did find a pretty cool souvenir for you, same colour as those stilettos you love.* And she sent through a picture of the bright red lipstick in its beautiful container, signed Christian Louboutin.

It was still cloudy but the drizzly rain had stopped when she emerged from the bistro, nicely reinforced for the walk to her next destination. Soon, she found herself in front of the smart green frontage of yet another Paris legend, E.Dehillerin, the most famous cookware shop in Paris. Founded in 1820 by the family who still owned it, E.Dehillerin had been in its current premises since 1890, and had acquired a stellar list of clients over the centuries, from famous chefs to presidents, movie stars, five star hotels and ocean liners. Kate had read that a bain-marie dish signed E.Dehillerin had even been recovered from the wreck of the doomed *Titanic* . . . It had also been one of the favourite haunts of the famous American food writer Julia Child, and to this day often featured in scenes in films and on TV. Sylvie had confirmed that it was absolutely a must-see for cooks, whether professional or amateur. She herself had bought many things there over the years. Indeed, Sylvie said the very first good piece of cookware she'd bought, a lovely small copper sauté pan, which she still used, came from there.

And now, here Kate was, entering through the narrow doors into the cheerfully crowded kingdom of the kitchen, with its creaking ancient floors, dazzling array of copper pots and pans in various sizes hanging up, floor to ceiling shelves holding gleaming steel pans and bowls, decorative moulds, cake tins, whisks, rolling pins, salt and pepper shakers, baking dishes, aprons, racks of knives and utensils of all kinds, absolutely everything you could possibly imagine for the kitchen plus other things you had probably never thought of. But everything was useful for something, and much of it had a practical, timeless beauty that made her wish she could draw. Instead she took photos, as she wandered down narrow aisles, from shelf to shelf, row to row, exchanging smiles with fellow customers, or with the friendly black-aproned staff who asked if she needed any help. Finally, emerging back into the main part of the shop from the huge basement where more amazing things were displayed, including the biggest paella pans she had ever seen, Kate selected an olive-wood spoon and a lovely wood-handled cheese knife, both stamped E.Dehillerin, as well as a madeleine baking tin—that madeleine at lunch had whetted her appetite!—and a couple of small copper moulds. She would have picked much more but she couldn't carry anything else right now. She was just about to follow the assistant to the counter when a soft familiar voice said behind her, 'So you found it, too, Kate!'

It was Misaki, looking a little flushed, her eyes bright, her hands full.

'Yes, and isn't it wonderful!' Kate exclaimed.

'It is heaven,' agreed Misaki, seriously. 'I have dreamed of this for many years.'

Misaki had been a professional chef, Kate remembered. 'You've never come here before?'

'Never. Not here. Not Paris. It is a dream, while I run the restaurant and raise children. My husband,' she said in a burst of unusual confidence, 'he left while the children were still young. He never came back. I had to work. All the time.'

'Not easy,' said Kate, nodding.

'No. But worth it. For the children,' said Misaki, seriously.

Kate swallowed down a sudden lump in her throat as the sharp pain of Josh's betrayal knifed through her again. Something must have shown in her face, because Misaki asked, a little anxiously, 'Are you okay, Kate?'

'Fine. Fine, thank you,' Kate said, trying to sound it. 'I am just a bit tired.' She indicated her bags. 'Much shopping today, not just here.'

'Yes, I see that.' Misaki's face lit up with a smile. 'Maybe,' she said, 'after we finish here, we have a cup of tea? It is very refreshing, I think.'

'That's an excellent idea,' said Kate, smiling back. They left the store with their purchases and found a quiet café nearby where they sat down to chat over a pot of what Misaki declared to be surprisingly good green tea. Kate felt the hazy pleasure of her indulgent day slowly returning, cauterising the edge of remembered pain.

Gabi sat back in her seat, watching the landscape flashing past the window as the train gobbled up the kilometres between Biarritz and Paris on the fast-diminishing Sunday afternoon. It had been a good weekend, but she didn't regret having to go back. It could be restful with family because they took you for granted and you didn't have to explain too much, especially when it was extended family—you just took up where you'd left off last time. But it was also clear that there were large differences between the lives of her uncle's family and her own. Not that it mattered, really; it was just something you had to accept. You enjoyed the moments sitting around a table laden with good food and good wine, when shared memories and instinctive blood knowledge created an atmosphere of familiarity. And you didn't judge the differences. They were part of the mix. But you didn't have to accept everything. You could call out bad behaviour or offensive words. Of course, you might well face consequences but that was also part of the deal of family.

The thoughts conjured up a memory of a story her mother, Genevieve, had told, about the first time she'd met her husband's family, when the young couple had come to Europe on their honey-moon. It had started rather rockily, because her mother-in-law had not been at all happy that they'd married in Australia. 'She thought it was all my doing, when in fact it was a mutual decision,' Gabi's mother said. 'Apparently I'd made sure that her beloved younger son would never return home, not even so his parents could help celebrate his wedding. It drove me mad—it was so unfair.' Ander had been confused by his mother's anger and it had been his father who had gently made Genevieve understand what lay behind his wife's unwelcoming behaviour. Not to excuse it, just to understand. 'It wasn't about me,' Gabi's mother had explained. 'She didn't dislike me on sight, though it felt like it. But she'd thought her restless boy would be only away for a short time, but instead he'd made his home on the other side of the world and would raise a family far away. She felt she had lost him, and any potential grandchildren, forever.'

That had been why saving to go to Europe for family visits had been such a priority for Gabi's parents. It wasn't just about the Basque side, either, for even if the Guernsey family was more diplo-matic about their feelings, and more realistic about the unlikely prospect of their daughter staying put on the island, it had still pained them. Anyway, it had all worked out and certainly led to fabulous holidays for Gabi and her siblings, who loved going back to see family in both places. And, over the years, the relations between Genevieve and her mother-in-law had markedly improved from that shaky start. And it wasn't just because Genevieve was the mother of the beloved grandchildren. Gabi remembered with a smile how her *amatxi* had even helped to plan a surprise party for her mother's fortieth birthday, at which she'd raised a sincere toast to her daughter-in-law.

Loss. That was what her grandfather had made her mother understand. He must have felt it too, but he was such a kind man that he would never have blamed his feelings on anyone else. *Loss* . . . Gabi felt a prickle in her scalp as an unwelcome thought came into her mind. Was that what Max's grandmother felt? Was that behind her unpleasant behaviour? Surely not—after all, Gabi and Max were not in the same position as her parents had been. They were just at the start of their relationship. And there was no question of Max moving to the other side of the world. It was much too soon to even consider anything like that. Besides, he must have had other girlfriends, even serious ones. And apparently the old woman had never acted like that with them. *Because,* a little voice whispered, *because you are different, and she knows it. And she thinks you* could *take her grandson away.*

No. Gabi sat bolt upright, glaring out of the window in such a fierce way that the person next to her shifted slightly closer to the aisle in alarm. It was ridiculous. The woman might be old but she was a confident, successful businesswoman, for God's sake. She wouldn't be afraid of losing her grandson. She had him well wrapped around her little finger. Besides, she had all the rest of her family around her.

Or did she? Gabi thought of her in her beautiful city apartment, far away from the family home—castle or house, whatever!—back in the Loire. Maybe when Max was growing up and going to school in Paris, she needed to live there all the time. But later—she could have gone back, just kept the apartment for breaks in the city. Why hadn't she?

Who cares what the answer to that is, Gabi thought, defiantly. Even if the old woman was lonely or scared of losing Max, or not warmly connected to her family, it didn't excuse her arrogant behaviour. *But it didn't excuse your amatxi's behaviour either*, the little voice told her. *And yet your mother chose to understand. And you yourself loved your amatxi, and would have defended her against all comers, despite knowing what a difficult woman she could be. Just as Max loves his grandmother, despite knowing that too.*

It's not the same, she protested, to herself. *And he should have warned me.* But the thoughts kept whirling, making her stomach churn. Had her reaction been so strong because she was too much like the old woman, only seeing her own point of view? Had she been trying to test Max? And when he was found wanting because he declined to condemn his grandmother, even while he was bewildered by her behaviour, did Gabi even *try* to understand? What did that say about her?

But it shouldn't just be up to me, she hit back. *It should be up to that old battleaxe too.* And Max should understand that. But he didn't. Or wouldn't. Just like he didn't get why she hadn't told him about being an artist. *Yet why should he get that,* the little voice persisted, *when you don't even get it yourself?*

By the time she got to Paris, the cacophony inside her head had quietened. And she'd made her decision.

Twenty-five

Monday morning, and Kate had woken much too early. She lay there, thinking about the day before. Arnaud had invited her to a talk and demonstration on bookbinding he and a friend were giving that afternoon and it had been a fascinating experience. It wasn't just the skill and the materials of this ancient art that were so interesting. It was also the stories. Arnaud and his friend had showed four books, from the eighteenth century to the 1930s, whose production history they had researched. They talked about what they'd discovered, and how it had influenced some of their own work. And they told stories about people involved in the books. One story especially touched Kate: about a talented young bookbinder in the nineteenth century who had created a beautiful marbled pattern for the endpapers of the book he was working on. He'd called the pattern 'Mathilde' after his sweetheart and intended to give her the original template book he'd created as a sample for the publishers. But he'd been killed by a runaway horse, just a week before the book was published.

What had happened then, people wanted to know. Had his girlfriend still received his gift, and did the publisher honour his memory? 'We don't know,' Arnaud had said, gravely, 'but we can hope it was so. And even if it wasn't, we still have the pattern he created out of love, and it influenced us to recreate something like it.' Everybody crowded around to look at the original Mathilde endpapers in the old book and then at the recreation Arnaud and his friend had made, oohing and aahing over the peacock colours and swirling design.

Later, when Kate was accompanying Arnaud back to his boat, she asked him more about the creator of the Mathilde pattern. He smiled. 'We knew that was the name of the pattern. We learned too that a young employee at the publisher had made it. But the rest—well, it felt right.'

For a moment Kate felt disappointed. She was used, of course, to the notion of 'the right story' created for the purposes of marketing, but it didn't *seem* right, in this context. Then she thought of Sylvie's stories around food items, and the little narratives she wove around recipes and instructions. 'People remember stories,' she said, thoughtfully. 'More than just straight facts and information.'

'*Exactement*,' he said. 'We humans have always learned through stories. And not only words. Many years ago,' he went on, 'I went to the painted caves at Niaux, in the Pyrenees. Not as famous as Lascaux, but superb too. And oh! The goats, bison and horses on the walls—they were so beautiful, so alive! They sprang out at you with such vigour! And I thought, those people who made these beauties thousands of years ago . . . maybe they saw them as stories. To teach. To warn. To amuse. To delight. To comfort . . .'

His face was alight with undimmed wonder, and it made her spine tingle. 'It sounds wonderful,' she said, softly.

'It is still bright in my mind.' He hesitated, then added, 'I went at a time in my life when there was much darkness. But in that cave I found . . .' He broke off, and shook his head. 'It is ironic, is it not, that in a dark place underground there should sometimes be more light than under the sun?'

She glanced quickly at him. 'I know what you mean,' she said. 'It is strange, but it can happen like that. Like sometimes—peace can be found not in a quiet forest but in a city full of noise.'

'Like here, you mean,' he said, smiling, as a scooter whizzed loudly past.

She smiled back. 'Perhaps.' They looked at each other and, in that moment, Kate felt something had changed between them. Two days ago, when Stefan and Anja had asked if she and Arnaud were friends, she hadn't been sure. And she'd thought it didn't matter. Now she knew. It *did* matter, and they *were*. This was a real friendship. And it balmed her bruised heart.

Nothing was said. Nothing needed to be said. There wasn't a question of whether it could lead to anything else. Neither of them might be ready for 'anything else'. She didn't feel like she was, anyway. It was enough just as it was, for the moment.

Now, she stretched luxuriously. It might be rather too early—5.30 am—but she had gone to bed early and slept really well.

She felt great. But that feeling was not to last, for just then her phone pinged with a private Facebook message from Leah. *Did you see this?* It was followed by a screenshot of a small article whose headline read: *Resmond boss to face civil suit*. It went on to say:

> *Founder and CEO of high-rated tech company Resmond, Josh Hannon-Bell, is facing a possible lawsuit over alleged intellectual property infringement. Freelance designer Jaime Noura claims Hannon-Bell knowingly infringed her IP in the creation of a new look for the Resmond app, which was due to be unveiled this week. News of the lawsuit has already caused a drop in Resmond share prices. Hannon-Bell denies the charge but refused to comment.*

She'd just finished reading it when Leah messaged again. *You up already? Free to chat?*

Yep, Kate wrote, and hit the video call button. Her sister's face appeared, wearing a characteristic crooked grin. 'Hey, how's it going in Paris?'

'Great. I'm loving it. All of it.'

'I can tell that from your Insta pics. Place looks ridiculously gorgeous. And that shopping spree you went on—I'm jealous! Sure you're not just making it all up?'

Kate laughed. 'Promise, there's no tricks, sis. All real life. All of it.'

'Lucky you. Wish I could jet over straight away. Billy and Mia are absolutely hectic at the moment and their father is being his usual nonchalant self, driving me crazy.' Kate knew not to take Leah's complaints too seriously. She adored her family.

'That's life, eh?' she said. 'How are Mum and Dad?'

'Same, same. Mum's blood pressure seems to have settled down, pills are kicking in like they should, so all good. But this thing with Josh, eh!'

'Yeah,' Kate said. 'Not good.'

'So, is it true? Did he do it?' Leah asked, all agog.

'Leah! How would I know!'

'Do you know the woman making the complaint?'

'No, not really. But the name rings a bell. I think she might have come for an interview once.' In fact, she remembered the name *and* a vague impression of the person who went with it: young, pink-haired, nervous. And instead of the usual portfolio on an iPad, she'd been carting a huge, old-fashioned black leather folder, crammed with pieces of paper. The incongruity was why Kate had remembered her. She'd come to the office well over eighteen months ago, before everything blew up between Kate and Josh.

'Did you interview her?'

Kate shook her head. 'I never interviewed designers. I sometimes sat in on marketing interviews. Josh did the design and development ones, usually with another staff member. But not always. I can't remember, in this case.'

'So he could have interviewed her on her own, seen her designs, and asked her to leave some to think about?' Leah suggested.

'He might have. But I don't remember anything like that. He rarely asked people to leave stuff. Didn't like to be bothered with their pesky emails afterwards asking if he'd had a chance to look at them.'

Leah laughed. 'That sounds like Josh! But, you know, if she did leave a design or two and he decided to pinch it, he could be in big trouble.'

'It'll be her word against his.'

'You're not defending that scumbag, are you?' Leah asked.

'No, I bloody well am not!' Kate flashed back. 'I'm just pointing out the obvious. I have no idea if this Noura woman is telling the truth or not.'

'It's a shitshow for Resmond, either way. At least you cashed in your shares in time, eh?'

'Yeah.' The money was in her account now, too. 'But can we talk about some news other than bloody Resmond and Josh now?'

Leah looked a little surprised. 'Sure, sis. Want to hear about my very exciting hassles with the council over water rates? Or Billy's missing school report?'

'Okay, okay,' Kate said, laughing, 'I'll tell you about what I've been doing instead.' And she did, telling Leah more about the Saturday shopping spree until her sister sighed and made her promise to send even more photos. Kate wove in a carefully edited version of everything else noteworthy, mentioning Arnaud only in passing and not even by name because her sister would have been on to that at once, extracting all kinds of information that she'd then build up into a great big exaggerated story. Fortunately, Leah didn't appear to really clock the Arnaud bit, and soon the sisters ended the call with cheery goodbyes.

Kate lay there for a moment longer, thinking. Could Josh really be guilty of something like that? Eighteen months ago, she would have said no way. He might be ruthless and ambitious, but a pathetic bit of thieving like this wasn't his style. Now, she wasn't sure. She wasn't sure about anything to do with him. But another thought worried her more. If what he was accused of was true, then would she also be subject to suspicion? It could easily be claimed by a lawyer, couldn't it, that she and Josh must have had no secrets from each other—ha bloody ha to that!—and therefore, as his wife at the time *and* an executive in his company, that she could have colluded in the alleged infringement. Yes, she had stepped away from the company well before the 'new look' had been in more than its initial phases, but that might not be a valid defence . . .

Just then, her phone buzzed again. She froze. The number was Josh's extension at Resmond. Her finger hovered over 'Decline', then over 'Answer'. In the end, she just let it ring and it cut out by itself. An instant later, she got a ping announcing a voice message. She looked at it for a while, then decided she might as well hear what he had to say. She didn't have to respond, just listen.

I'm assuming you've heard, the familiar voice said in her ear. *We gotta talk, Kate. Please.*

Her pulse raced. *No*, she told herself. *Think of the lovely time you've been having in this wonderful place where you have found peace. Real peace. And you aren't going to give it up. Not for anything. And certainly not for that bastard. Let him stew in his own juices. Let karma get him. Don't answer. Don't answer.*

But she knew she wouldn't be able to stop thinking about it. And she wanted to immerse herself in the smells of the school this morning, the tastes, the preparation, the feeling of good busyness, the camaraderie in the class. She had to put this behind her, not have it sitting at the back of her mind all day. So, sitting up, the pillow behind her back, she called him.

'Kate,' he said, before she could speak. Obviously he'd been waiting anxiously. 'Thanks for calling back. It must be rather early there.' His voice was unexpectedly gentle, and she bit her lip. She was glad this was just an audio call. 'It's early,' she agreed, keeping her voice steady.

'Look, I know this is probably the last thing you want, but if you can put together a statement for us, about how you met that woman and definitely saw that her design wasn't—'

'Hang on,' Kate cut in. 'I didn't actually meet her, I just glimpsed her, and I never saw her designs. You know that.'

'Yeah, yeah, but you did see her, right? So—'

'So nothing! I have no idea what she had in that portfolio of hers.'

'Really?' His voice was hardening.

Kate fought to keep her self-control. 'You know perfectly well I didn't. And I'm not going to tell a lie. So look, Josh, if you did the dirty on Jaime Noura and took her design—'

'As if I would!' he shouted. 'What do you take me for? Don't you know me at all?'

She said, very calmly, 'No, I don't, Josh. I thought I did. But now I have no idea what you are capable of.'

'You stupid cow,' he growled, 'don't you see this could damage your reputation too? Just write the bloody statement.'

'Get fucked, Josh,' she said. She was famous for never swearing, and before he could recover from the shock, she cut the connection, and turned off the phone completely, flinging it on the bed.

She was so angry she could hardly breathe. It ran in her like lava, spreading through her body with poisonous speed. Jumping up, she went to the bathroom and stepped into the shower, making it as cold as she could bear. If hot tears ran down her face, they mingled with the chilly needles of water running down her body, washing away anger, disgust and pain, so that by the time she stepped out again, she felt much calmer. After dressing, she left the room and went down and out into the street. It was still a little chilly, but it was going to be a nice day.

She almost turned to go in the direction of the Port de l'Arsenal, then thought better of it. It was far too early to go knocking at Arnaud's door. And it would send the wrong message. So she went in the opposite direction and had gone a little way before someone unexpectedly hailed her. It was Sylvie. Flushed, wearing a T-shirt and soft trousers and joggers, her hair bunched up in a clip, she looked different from the groomed, casually chic woman Kate saw in class. Maybe she'd been running. Or power walking. 'Good morning,' Sylvie said, 'up early like me then?'

Kate nodded. 'Needed to walk off some things,' she said. 'Not food,' she added.

Sylvie sighed. 'I know what you mean.' She looked at Kate. 'Are you ready for a coffee yet?'

'Always,' Kate said, lightly. 'But nothing's open yet, is it?'

'I know a place.' Sylvie smiled, and led them through the streets to where a rather battered van was parked. A tall red-haired man in a beanie was standing by the open back of the van, arranging boxes, but as they approached, he turned, saw them and smiled. Kate recognised him as Serge, Sylvie's friend and neighbour.

'Are there maybe another couple of cups left in your thermos, Serge?' Sylvie asked, in French.

'You know me,' Serge said, eyes sparkling behind his glasses, 'I always make too much.' He smiled at Kate, who he'd now met a couple of times at the school. 'Bonjour, Kate.'

'Bonjour, Serge,' she said, with an answering smile.

Serge pulled out a thermos and two cups from the back of the van. Smiling, he handed her a cup. It was hot and fragrant, not like most thermos coffee she'd ever drunk. She said, in careful French, 'It is good coffee. Thank you.'

'Thank you,' he echoed, then added, in equally careful English, 'Sylvie says Australians love coffee. And you do not think much of our coffee here. So it is a nice compliment you give.'

Kate took another sip. 'But it is true. The coffee *is* good.'

'Compliments are not true words in Australia?' Serge replied, a little mischievously.

She blushed. 'I don't know.'

Sylvie felt a pang. Was Serge flirting with Kate? Well, if he was, surely that was a good thing. He was a good man. And he'd been alone too long, since his ex had walked out on him nearly five years ago. So why did she feel a little—bereft? Thrusting the thought aside as unworthy, and even worse, silly, she drained her coffee and said to Kate, in English, 'Well, I had better get going. Preparations for the day and all that.' By now, it was nearly 7 am.

'Oh. Of course.' Kate hesitated, then said, in a rush, 'Could I maybe—maybe help you with that?'

Sylvie looked at her, surprised. Then she nodded, smiling. 'Okay. If you're sure that you don't prefer a nice rest at your hotel instead.'

'No,' Kate said, at once. She'd left her phone on the bed in her room, and there it could stay. She wanted to be well away from any more attempts Josh might make to contact her. She wanted not to think about any of it. 'I would love to help. If you don't mind.'

'Another pair of hands is always good,' Sylvie said.

'Take care Sylvie doesn't make you work too hard,' Serge said, with a teasing sidelong glance at Sylvie. Serge *was* different this morning, she thought. Maybe it was the spring air. Maybe it was Kate. Maybe it was because he'd done good deals at the market. Whatever it was, it suited him. He looked younger, brighter.

'It was nice to see you, Serge,' said Kate, smiling. 'And thank you again for the coffee.' She added, cheerfully, 'I can work hard now.'

As the two women walked away together, Sylvie turned once to see Serge still looking after them. He gave her a wave, and a smile. And she felt a great lift of the heart, as if his own mood had filled her, and the shadows of anxiety that had lain on her all night, keeping her from a good sleep, had melted away.

Twenty-six

Gabi had stayed up till 3.30 am and had consequently only slept four hours but as she showered and got ready to go down to breakfast she felt surprisingly good. She smiled as she looked at the scattering of pages on the little table where she'd been working all night. She hadn't finished, not yet, but it could wait till she got back from class this afternoon.

Yesterday evening, after getting back into Paris, she'd bought some bits and pieces at the station: scissors, a couple of magazines, a glue stick, some coloured pencils. She'd found a late-closing shop nearby that had printing and photocopying facilities and printed out some photos from her phone—her own photos and website photos she'd downloaded on the train. She had a quick bite to eat in a nearby café then took a taxi straight back to the hotel. Back in her room, she went straight to work, her mind buzzing with anticipation.

As she worked, it felt as though she couldn't keep up with what was bursting out. Her pencil flew over the paper, sketching outlines and patterns; she cut bits out of magazines and stuck in photos. Each page followed from the one before, it was like a story, or a reel of film, unspooling. *What I couldn't tell you*, she'd called it, and it started with a photo of herself at the launch of *Shadow Life*, taken from the gallery's website. Only she'd changed the photo, cutting out half of her body and replacing it with smudged black shadow, while leaving the rest—the people around her, the gallery director, her agent, her family, some bigwig, some randoms she couldn't remember—untouched, as they raised their glasses, while behind them Gabi's artworks loomed large. Artworks in mixed media, collage, paint, ink, bits of found objects, creating a strange dreamlike world where buildings and interiors and objects seemed to have more substance than the people who were mere shadows against them. Not silhouettes, nothing as sharp and definite and human as that—and not even the kind of shadow you might see at midday on a sunny day, clear and black. No, these were wavering dusty grey shadows, the kind you see when the light's not good, or it's early, or late, or in moonlight. The shadows were engaged in all kinds of everyday tasks, but there were also some that were distinctly odd, like a shadow with a bed on its head, or another shadow trying to hold up a skyscraper.

The *Shadow Life* artworks were either very large or very small and together they had formed a stunning effect that had had both audiences and critics raving. All kinds of meanings had been ascribed to them by all kinds of people, when the truth was that it had started as a playful project. It had come out of her childhood memory of reading a story in which someone's shadow had detached itself from its person and run away. It had been a vaguely threatening idea to Gabi back then but also fascinating and funny. What if those shadows finally managed to ditch their people altogether, what would they do in their shadow lives? Those feelings had been very much in her mind as she'd developed the art of *Shadow Life*. But few people seemed to see the playfulness. And critics took it all so very seriously, seeing it as a portrayal of emotional disconnection, or cultural decline, or an anti-capitalist manifesto, or an erasing of human diversity . . . It wasn't just the critics though, *Shadow Life* went viral on social media, and people endlessly discussed their theories on it. So it wasn't really an option for Gabi to protest that she'd just been having fun pursuing that *what if* from her childhood. Nobody would have believed her. Or they might have done and then painted her as some kind of freak who didn't even know what she was doing. Nick advised her not to respond to any of it. 'Being mysterious is more interesting,' he'd said. And the gallery director had agreed. Even her family had agreed. Leave it all to the professional explainers, was the general gist. You can just be the artist, above it all, letting your art speak for itself.

Letting my art speak for itself was what I thought I was doing, Gabi had written, last night, on the second page. *But people were putting words into my art's mouth.* She'd illustrated that with cutouts of celebrities from magazines with speech bubbles saying the kind of stuff that had been said about her work. Then, on the third page, she'd drawn a cartoon in black texta of a shadow puppet play, and herself as one of the shadow puppets, with a caption simply reading, *Turning into shadow*. She'd followed that with a page featuring scraps of jumbled images from the artworks and bits of reviews, overlaid with a black scrawl reading, *Art under new management*, and then a page with a rapid sketch of herself standing in front of a blank canvas, only she was just a small wavering shadow against black bars while the canvas loomed large and threateningly white. She hadn't captioned that one. The next page had herself again as a shadow, only now she was a long thin one running after the blank canvas that had become much smaller and was disappearing into the distance. Everything was in black and white on those three pages and then on the following page that had faded to grey and she was just an outline in grey fog while all around her were speech bubbles coming from unseen people, in red pencil: *Eagerly awaited second show!* And *Give it to us now* and *Stay relevant* and *One-hit wonder.* The last phrase was repeated three times in speech bubbles, first in small writing, then in medium, then in large shouty letters that looked like they'd been dipped in blood. The next page was blank except for one word: *Escape*, in small letters down the bottom of the page, as though it was heading for a mouse hole to hide in or vanish altogether.

And that was as far as she'd got, last night. But this afternoon after class, she was going to keep going. She knew where she was headed with this. And that filled her with a deep pleasure of the kind she hadn't known in such a long time, not only before *Shadow Life*, but even stretching back from that. It was pure creative pleasure of the kind she'd felt as a child, when she would spend hours drawing, painting, cutting, gluing, making scrapbook journals and little books and cards for her family and friends. What she was doing now would never be shown, never be put out there in public; it was private, meant for Max only, as an explanation, an apology, a gift, without strings attached. But it was for herself too, she had come to understand as the hours went by long into the night. This was helping her to speak, to explain what had happened. She was letting the art speak for itself, yes, but for herself too. And that's what she needed. She had no idea if the pleasure, the ease, of doing this meant that the block she'd been suffering was going away. But it didn't matter. Not right now, anyway.

Everyone had gathered in the kitchen bang on time. They all seemed pretty cheerful, Kate thought, even Gabi. There was chit-chat about weekends—exclamations about Gabi going all the way down south, though Mike and Ethan had also gone on an overnight trip to Rouen. There was a bit of good-natured ribbing of Pete who had apparently met a Scotswoman at the Tuileries Garden, whom he'd really liked but had neglected to ask for her number or name. And Stefan and Anja spoke warmly about how Misaki had guided them around yet another amazing museum she'd discovered. Paris was full of amazing museums of course!

No one had commented on Kate being at the school before everyone else. They just assumed she was early. But Kate had loved being there before the class, seeing the kitchen in its early-morning hush, helping with preparations, however menial. Damien had arrived about twenty minutes after her and had looked a little surprised to see her there, but discreetly didn't ask any questions, just took it all in his stride. There was a nice rhythm to the prepping that Kate really enjoyed. It was calm yet busy and the very best way to forget about that conversation with Josh, so that by the time the others arrived, she was quite relaxed.

As part of prepping for the morning session, Kate had helped Damien gather together examples of the best fats from the school's stores: butters from Normandy, Brittany and the centre; olive oils from Provence, all of which had earned the coveted AOC label, or *appellation d'origine contrôlée*, which meant the product was guaranteed not only in terms of quality, but also in terms of local origin. There was also goose and duck fat from small organic farms in the south-west. Now she watched and took notes as Sylvie spoke about butter first and the six examples lined up on the bench: salted, unsalted, demi-sel. She got them each to try a tiny bit of each butter on a small piece of bread, and asked them to describe it in one word. That was quite a lot of fun as everyone cheerfully vied with each other to reach for more and more colourful descriptions. And then she got them to try a bit of what she'd called 'generic' butter, and even those who'd looked sceptical about whether you could tell the difference seemed quite convinced. Or maybe that was just the force of Sylvie's personality, Kate thought. The other woman was certainly one of the most grounded people she'd ever met, at ease in her skin, not trying to be someone she wasn't. And yet . . . As they'd worked that morning, prepping before the others came in, Kate had asked Sylvie if there'd been any more hassles for the school. And Sylvie had filled her in, briefly, almost casually. But it was nevertheless clear that she was rattled, and no wonder. Someone was hacking at the roots of her confidence, at the place she'd made for herself. Kate understood that feeling too well. Her own roots had been sliced clean from under her—no, not clean; it had been jagged and painful.

The call from Paul Renard came during a coffee break, between the butter and the oil, as it were. 'You remember mentioning that Zola novel to me the other day, Madame Morel,' he said, 'in regard to those email addresses used by the person who made those complaints to the DDPP?'

Sylvie didn't need to look them up to remember they were quenunormande@hotmail.com and sagetragot@gmail.com, allusions to Zola's *The Belly of Paris*. 'Yes, I do. What have you found?'

'It looks like the man from the DDPP was right. They are fake addresses. However,' he went on, 'in a wider search using those keywords from the email addresses, we turned up something else: the name of a little restaurant called Chez Quenu. It's in a backstreet in the fifth. Do you know it?'

The back of Sylvie's neck prickled. 'Never heard of it.'

'It's a small unpretentious neighbourhood place, just a few tables, and a rather limited menu. There's no website, just a minimal Facebook page, but it does say that the name of the restaurant was inspired by Zola's novel. And the owner/chef is a man named Martin Cahuzac. Does that name mean anything to you?'

'Nothing at all,' she said, bemused.

'You are sure? He didn't work for you, or attend a class, or supply you with any goods?' At Sylvie's request, Renard had checked up on the woman who had kicked up the fuss about the refund, but it had come to nothing. She didn't have a French name, anyway. It had been another dead end.

'I am pretty certain,' Sylvie said. 'But I will look in my records.'

'It may be nothing, of course, just a coincidence of names, but it's worth checking.'

I'll do more than just check in my records, I'll go to the restaurant today, Sylvie thought, but didn't say.

'I'm sorry we couldn't find anything more definite,' Renard said. 'But I thought it was worth mentioning to you anyway. And of course we'll keep looking.'

After the call had ended, Sylvie sat for a moment, her mind working furiously. She quickly texted Serge and let him know the news. He texted back almost immediately. *Interesting! But don't go to that place on your own. Let me come with you.*

She was going to text back telling him not to be silly, what danger could she possibly be in, when she thought again. Just turning up out of the blue to ask questions would be a bad idea. *Okay. Let's have dinner there.*

Good idea. I'll book under my name, then they won't realise it's you. Just in case.

If you like. But it's probably nothing.

Then we'll just have dinner. Let me check on their page if they're open tonight.

Many restaurants were closed on Mondays. In her haste, she hadn't even thought of that. A brief pause, then he was back. *Closed tonight. But open tomorrow, and you can book online. I've booked for 19h tomorrow. Let's meet at 18.15h. Okay?*

It would have to be. There was no point even going to check the place out today, everything would be shut up and she'd learn nothing. *Absolutely. Thanks, Serge.*

See you tomorrow.

As Sylvie put the phone away and returned to the class, she felt her spirits rising, buoyed by the thought that maybe, just maybe, she might have some answers tomorrow. If Chez Quenu had anything to do with it. In any case, it felt as though she were taking control of her life. And that was enough for the moment.

Twenty-seven

Gabi sat back in her chair and looked at the finished project. Those final pages, which featured her trip to Paris and meeting Max, had taken quite some doing. She'd stayed up late and then overslept, meaning she hadn't arrived at class till ten thirty and she'd missed the allocation of tasks. That wasn't so bad because it was really just a follow-up from the day before, but it threw her a bit, plus she had to work on her own as everyone else was already in cooking groups for the day. Even then it wouldn't have mattered if she hadn't been thinking mostly about her project, with only half her attention on the cooking, so that she ended up spoiling the butter, garlic and red wine sauce she'd intended as an accompaniment to the sauteed artichoke hearts and mushrooms that Stefan and Anja had made. They said it didn't matter, they could make a quick sauce for the dish themselves, but Gabi knew she'd let them down. Yet all she could think of was the project, and as soon as class was over she had raced back to the hotel to continue work on it, stopping only for a short walk and a quick snack. The work had gone on for hours and only now, late on Tuesday afternoon, did she feel she had truly finished.

Those last five pages had graduated from black and white and grey and red to more colours, so that the Paris experience glowed with brightness. But then, on the second-last page, she'd pasted a photo of the Marguerite Yonan drawing she'd bought, and sketched a woman in a red skirt and black jumper peering at it, her back to the viewer. Underneath was a caption: *Pretending can sometimes just be protection.* It was a reference to what Max had said to her, as they'd walked to his grandmother's place, before they'd had their big bust-up: *Come on, Gabi, you don't have to pretend with me.* On the last page, she'd drawn the same figure standing at a crossroads, beside a signpost with faded, smudged, illegible words on it. The figure wasn't looking at the signpost but at something perched on top of it: an eagle, sketched in bold black strokes from memory, from that amazing moment on her grandfather's favourite hill, and underneath two lines: *Where the road leads, we do not know. So we can only follow the heart.*

She hadn't been sure of that, she had written those lines many times on a piece of paper, each time in a different variation. Was it close to kitsch? Banal? One of those trite 'inspirational quotes' you saw on social media? She'd almost decided not to write anything, but then she thought, *The hell with it, it's what I feel and I don't care if it sounds like something people have said before.* Because they probably had but also they would have felt it too, that feeling of being lost, then coming to a crossroads, not knowing where to go, looking for a sign, then taking courage and plunging on. Wherever it might lead.

Now, she took a deep breath and photographed each page, carefully. Then she clipped all the physical pages together, put them in a large envelope, wrote his name and address on them, and set off through the early evening streets.

There's nothing like a dog to make you feel instantly more cheerful, Kate thought, as Nina greeted her with great excitement and a furiously wagging tail. Arnaud had messaged her earlier that day to ask if she'd like to come over for an impromptu dinner on the boat: a bookbinding friend from Normandy was visiting his architect brother in Paris, and Arnaud thought Kate might be interested to meet them. She'd readily agreed, and turned up a little earlier than he'd said. He was in the middle of cooking but didn't seem to mind her watching him work as she poured them both a glass of wine and made herself at home on the bench seat near the galley. It was so easy to feel at home in that small cosy space, smelling the good smells of the dish Arnaud was conjuring up, and stroking Nina's curls as the little dog sat with her head on Kate's lap. Arnaud himself seemed quietly happy that she was there, and the wine, a rich dark Bordeaux, was excellent too. So perhaps it was a combination of all those things that suddenly made her feel like it was okay to open up about what had happened with Josh.

She didn't speak of everything, and not in detail either, but it felt right to tell him, at that moment. He listened in attentive silence, still working at the stove, and stopping occasionally to take a sip of the wine, and that felt right too. She didn't need him to comment or commiserate or console, just listen. Everyone else she'd talked to had been too close to the centre of the explosion of her marriage: her family, her friends, her colleagues, the lawyers. Now, to this man, this almost stranger becoming a friend, she found she could speak clearly, without bitterness, but not without pain, either. He listened quietly as he continued his cooking, but when she'd finished, he closed the lid of the pan, picked up his glass, and came to sit by her and Nina. He put a hand briefly, gently, on one of hers, and said, 'The wounds of life strike deep, don't they?' And when she nodded, tears in her eyes, he began to speak of being married young but the marriage almost cracking under the strain and frequent absences of an army life. But when he finally left the army, determined to try to make a go of civilian life with his wife and their young son, he'd found it almost impossible to fit in. He'd become very difficult, he said, he was drinking too much, was full of anger, and finally his wife left, taking the boy with her. 'I thought they were better off without me,' he said, 'so I didn't try to hold them back. And I didn't try to contact them, not for months, not for nearly a year. And then, it was too late. They'd left France. I found out they'd gone to Canada. But that was all. I never saw or heard from them again.'

Kate saw the pain in his face, and any questions she might have wanted to ask, about why he hadn't tried to track them down, how he could bear to leave it like that, could not be voiced. He'd suffered PTSD, clearly, and she couldn't probe at that wound. Besides, he hadn't questioned her, either. He had just listened, which was exactly what she'd needed. So she did what he had, touched his hand briefly, gently. But she stayed quiet, and simply refilled his glass and hers, the silence lengthening between them but not uncomfortably, until shortly Nina sat bolt upright, there was the sound of footsteps above and a jolly voice called out, 'Arnaud! Where are you hiding?'

The atmosphere changed from one of melancholy reflection to a cheerful conviviality, a sudden shift that almost gave Kate emotional whiplash but she found, rather to her surprise, she could cope with it well. The bookbinding friend was a large, lion-maned man named Marcel and, in contrast, his brother Matthieu was a spry, short, almost bald guy. They didn't look much alike, aside from similar pairs of brown eyes, but it turned out later that was because they had different fathers, although they had grown up with the same stepfather, their mother's third husband. And they both proved to have pretty decent English, even cracking quite funny jokes, which Kate truly admired, as she certainly had not attained anything like that sort of proficiency in French. It was an entertaining dinner, up on the deck, around Arnaud's delicious Corsican lamb, red wine and tomato stew, mopped up with bread, and with a chocolate and mint mousse to follow that was quite the most delicious mousse Kate had ever eaten.

The 'two Ms' as Arnaud called them, left around 9.30 pm, but Kate stayed on a bit longer, for a quick nightcap and to help Arnaud with the washing up—though he tried to protest she didn't need to. After that he walked her back to the hotel, Nina scampering at their heels, and it was just as they arrived at the door that he said, quietly, 'Thank you for trusting me with your story.'

She looked at him, and said, 'And thank you for trusting me with yours.' Then she reached up and kissed him—on the cheek, not the lips, but that felt right too. He clasped her hand warmly in his and she saw the same expression in his eyes that she knew was in hers. Then he smiled and said, 'Goodnight, and see you soon.'

'Yes, very soon, I hope,' she replied, in French, smiling back at him. He called to Nina, who was nosing busily around on the footpath, and the pair of them left, while Kate stood watching them go. Before they reached the corner, Arnaud turned and gave her a wave, and she waved back until they were out of sight.

Chez Quenu was a rather cramped space into which fitted only a couple of long bench tables and three small round tables. A high wooden counter formed the serving area, with neat rows of glasses and plates on the shelves behind it, and the kitchen was through a door just beyond. Though small, it was a cheerful space, and despite its location tucked away in a quiet backstreet, it seemed to be popular—all the tables aside from the one Serge had reserved were occupied when they arrived. There was one young waitress who dashed around smilingly taking orders and bringing meals—she was clearly known to most of the customers there, so they must be regulars. She also seemed to be managing the bar. The owner, Martin Cahuzac, was nowhere to be seen, but then they'd already learned from Renard that he was also the chef so he must be hard at work in the kitchen.

The menu was simple and short, featuring just four entrees, main courses and desserts, plus two daily specials. The standards were all French bistro classics; the specials, at least that day, a little more unexpected, with a definite touch of the exotic: a Georgian pork shashlik, an Argentinian fish soup. Normally, Sylvie would have found that off-putting—she was of the opinion that mixing too many influences was rarely done well. But tonight she had other things to think about than a possibly over-ambitious cuisine. And the food, when it came, was good. For a main course, she'd ordered the safe but generally satisfying *steak frites*, and it was excellent, the steak tender and juicy, the chips both crisp and melt-in-the-mouth, and the bearnaise perfect. Serge opted for the Argentinian fish soup, which he pronounced truly delicious. 'I like this place very much,' he said, 'good ambience, good food, and I really hope it has nothing to do with what's been happening.'

'Me too.' Sylvie looked around her, at the cheerful tables of diners, at the nice young waitress bustling about, and felt a little foolish. 'I'm almost certain it's pure coincidence.'

As they waited for their dessert—both had opted for a slice of Pithiviers almond pie, a classic pastry Sylvie had loved since childhood—Serge poured them another glass of the pretty decent house rosé. 'We got a nice dinner. And we've discovered a new place.'

Sylvie smiled. 'Yes. And on a Tuesday night too!'

He laughed. 'Let's drink to that.' He raised his glass. 'To Tuesday nights! And may there be many more like it!'

'Absolutely,' she said, clinking. They looked at each other and Sylvie felt an unexpected frisson of excitement under her skin.

At that moment, a nuggety man in a cap and long apron came out of the kitchen. With his wavy dark hair, sharp nose and hazel eyes set in a smiley face, he was like an older, stockier, masculine version of the young waitress, clearly a relative, very possibly her father. This must be Martin Cahuzac. Sylvie was certain she had never set eyes on him before. Plus, Yasmine had checked, and no one of that name appeared in any of the school's records.

Cahuzac came out from behind the counter, heading first to the bigger of the long bench tables, where a party of people had been celebrating a birthday. Clearly he knew them, and stayed there for a moment, chatting; then visited the other long table, then the other two round tables, and finally came to Serge and Sylvie's table. Sylvie had been watching in fascination as he did his rounds; this was a really traditional restaurateur in action. She hadn't seen this sort of thing in quite a while. Now, as he stood there smiling and they'd exchanged a pleasantry or two, she said, 'We've only just discovered your restaurant. Have you been going long?'

'Just over a couple of years,' he said. 'I had another place before, in the south. But my daughter was accepted into the Sorbonne and I didn't want her to be on her own—it's always been just us since my wife died—so I relocated here too.'

'It looks like you have built up a loyal clientele in just two years,' Serge said.

Cahuzac's eyes lit up. 'Yes. We have been very fortunate. People in this neighbourhood seem to like us. Some people come almost every day. They feel at home here. We never need to advertise.'

'Then you have the perfect touch,' Sylvie said.

He shrugged. 'We're a modest local restaurant. We are lucky enough to have a good landlord who doesn't charge us a high rent, and we are a family business—a cousin of mine helps out during the day, when Amandine is at university. It's not hard to make a go of it that way.'

'On the contrary, Monsieur, I think you have done really well,' she said, warmly. 'Countless restaurants fail in Paris where we are so much spoiled for choice.' She paused. 'The name of your restaurant—I believe it relates to Émile Zola's novel, *Le Ventre de Paris*?'

He nodded. 'I read the novel at school and enjoyed it. It felt like an appropriate name for our new restaurant here.'

'So it wasn't the name of your restaurant in the south?'

'Oh no. That was called *Le Clin d'Oeil*.' He suited the name to the gesture and winked.

They laughed. 'That's a good name,' Serge said. 'Why not keep it?'

A shrug. 'A new start. A new name.'

'And you don't want to go bigger?' asked Sylvie.

He shook his head. 'Thank you, no. We are satisfied. Our customers are satisfied. Our suppliers are satisfied, and our landlord too. Why change?'

'Very wise,' said Serge, and shot a look at Sylvie before saying, 'I'm in the business myself.'

Cahuzac's eyes sharpened. 'You are also a restaurateur, Monsieur?'

'Oh no. I am not gifted like that. I supply organic vegetables and fruit to restaurants and other food businesses, though. Such as the Paris Cooking School.'

Cahuzac frowned. 'We are quite satisfied with our suppliers, Monsieur. As they are with us.'

'Oh, I didn't mean that,' Serge said hastily. 'Just that I do understand what a lot of work a food business is. It's not just a matter of being lucky.'

It was then that Sylvie had an idea. 'Monsieur Cahuzac, we were impressed by the standard of your food and the atmosphere here. I run the Paris Cooking School that Serge mentioned. Would you be open to giving a short presentation to my students if I bring them, after which we would lunch here?'

Cahuzac stared, bemused. 'Me, give a presentation?' he asked at last. 'But I don't cook *cordon bleu.*'

'And I don't teach it,' she replied, briskly. 'My school concentrates on teaching students—foreign students—a simple but satisfying French approach to food. Which is exactly what your restaurant demonstrates in ample measure.'

Cahuzac flushed with pleasure. By this time, his daughter had noticed how he'd lingered at their table and walked over to see what was going on. 'Is everything all right?' she asked.

'Absolutely,' said Sylvie. 'I was just asking your father if I could bring a party of foreign students to lunch on Thursday, and if he could talk about his cooking to them.'

'Oh.' Amandine Cahuzac looked at her father. Then she said, to Sylvie, 'You are a teacher of foreign students?'

'Yes. But I teach cooking to them at the Paris Cooking School.'

Amandine's eyes widened. 'Oh. *Wow.*' Clearly she had heard of it, even if her father had not. 'I've heard so many good things about your school! I can't believe you're here.' She glanced at her father again. 'Papa, of course you've said yes.'

'I can't give a talk, I'm not academic,' he protested, but Amandine brushed that aside. 'You're good at talking, you'll manage. Lunch on Thursday, then. How many people?'

'Ten, possibly twelve,' Sylvie said, promptly. 'Eight students, myself, and my friend Serge here. It's possible my assistants Damien and Yasmine might come too, I'll have to let you know.'

'We might be already full,' said Cahuzac, looking a bit panicky.

But Amandine shook her head. 'No, there's the usual regulars, but the big table isn't taken.' She looked at Sylvie. 'Right, Madame . . . er . . .'

'Morel,' Sylvie said. 'Sylvie Morel, director of the Paris Cooking School.'

Amandine's smile lit up her whole face. 'Thank you, Madame Morel. Your group is booked in for eleven thirty on Thursday, for the talk, followed by lunch at twelve thirty. Does that suit?'

'Perfect,' said Sylvie, smiling. There was no way these nice, genuine people were in any way involved with her mysterious persecutor. And right now, she didn't care that she was no closer than before to discovering who that was.

Twenty-eight

'Today, we have a special guest,' Sylvie said as the class gathered around her the next morning. 'His session is always popular with our classes: and no wonder, as you'll see!' She wouldn't say anymore, merely smiling at intrigued questions, and starting on the first task of the day, which was to get everyone talking about what they'd had for dinner last night, and specifically about a dish or an ingredient they'd noticed or enjoyed in particular. This caused a great deal of lively discussion, because everyone had apparently enjoyed amazing meals.

All except for me, thought Gabi, half-ashamed that her dinner had consisted of a very basic *croque-monsieur* grabbed from a little place on the way back from Max's building. She had heard nothing since then. Not a call. Not a text. Nothing. Maybe he hadn't found the package in his mailbox. Or maybe he had, but it had meant nothing.

It didn't matter, she told herself. She'd done it as much for herself as for him. If he didn't get it, well, she could cope. She could accept. This morning, before breakfast, she had sat down with pencil and paper and, with a few deft lines, sketched his face from memory. Her pulse had quickened, looking at it, and she wasn't sure if it was because of his face, or because the drawing growing under her fingers allowed her to hope that maybe, just maybe, the drought *was* beginning to break.

She was only half-listening to the others recounting their food stories, so when Sylvie called her name, and all the expectant faces turned her way, she was startled into blurting out the truth, or at least part of it: that she'd been so busy drawing she'd half-forgotten to eat and had to resort to a *croque-monsieur*. 'My siblings and I used to love them when we were kids, because of the name more than anything,' she said. 'We loved the gruesome sound of it, *crunch the gentleman*, but my mother said it was just a silly French name for a disgusting ham and cheese fried sandwich that had probably been invented by Americans. Sorry, Mike,' she added, to the burst of laughter that followed.

Mike shrugged and said cheerfully, 'The good old US of A is happy to claim the *croque-monsieur* and *croque-madame* too, no problems, folks!'

'A good *croque-monsieur* is a very fine thing indeed,' said Sylvie, smiling, 'and I loved them as a child too, for the same reason. *Poor Monsieur*, I would think, hypocritically, as I crunched ruthlessly into his cheesy heart!'

At that moment, the doorbell buzzed. 'Right on cue,' Sylvie said. 'I think our special guest has arrived. Damien, will you come with me?'

'You said you were drawing,' Misaki said, as Sylvie and Damien left. 'You are an artist?'

Gabi nodded. And a weight seemed to lift off her shoulders. 'I'm a conceptual artist, mostly,' she said. 'But I do love drawing.'

'Ah yes.' Anja nodded vigorously. 'It is so portable!'

'I don't mind a bit of drawing myself,' said Pete, happily, 'but not for anyone else to look at. You know what I mean?'

Gabi looked at him and smiled. 'Yes, I do.' She was about to say something else when the door to the kitchen opened and the words died on her lips.

'*Bonjour, tout le monde*,' said Max, carrying a slatted wooden box into the room. His greeting was for everyone but his gaze was for Gabi, who found herself tongue-tied, unable even to form a simple *Bonjour* back. But he didn't seem to mind. Laying the box on the bench, he turned to Damien, who was carrying in another box that looked just as heavy. 'Can you put that one over there?' Max asked, in French. 'Oh, and Sylvie, I am going to need your screen. Can you set it up?'

Sylvie seemed surprised by this but did as she was asked.

Gabi watched, mesmerised, as Max bustled about, getting things ready. He seemed perfectly at ease, unlike her. The boxes of course contained various cheeses, all of them under pottery cloches, so you couldn't see what they were. But you could smell them. At least some of them. Gabi's thoughts whirled. What was Max thinking? Had he got her package? Was he going to say anything? *Not in front of everyone*, she thought. No. Maybe not at all. Maybe . . .

~

Everyone else was crowding around, exclaiming, chatting, questioning. But Gabi was standing there as if she couldn't move. Sylvie sighed. Because it wasn't just Gabi; Max was behaving a little off-key too. Usually his preparations weren't so elaborate. Usually, he just talked and told stories about each cheese. Also, he never usually brought so many cheeses. There had to be at least fifteen here. How could he talk about so many, let alone leave time for tastings? She caught Damien's eye. He was looking puzzled too. She just hoped there wouldn't be trouble, a scene. She didn't need that, on top of everything else.

~

'We can talk about cheese in many ways,' Max began, in English. 'We can speak of provenance, of *terroir*, of process. We can tell you about the differences between cow's and goat's and sheep's milk. We can explain what cheese the Romans made, and the ancient Egyptians and Sumerians.

'Or I could simply tell you this.' He clicked the remote and an image came up on the screen. It showed a boy of around thirteen or fourteen, holding a big wheel of cheese in his arms, with an equally big grin. Clearly, it was a young Max, Kate thought. He hadn't changed a lot, except he was taller. 'I could tell you about my own story with cheese. That was my plan. But last night, I changed my mind.' He clicked the remote again and the image vanished.

With a faint smile on his face, he said, 'I decided to speak of two things that are at the heart of cheesemaking. As they are in life.' He paused, and in the expectant hush that followed Kate saw with some surprise that Sylvie and Damien looked as mystified as everyone else. She glanced across at Gabi, and saw how the other woman's hands were clenched together, her eyes deliberately not meeting Max's, though he seemed to be looking her way. *Oh dear,* she thought, *what is happening here? What is Max up to?*

'Are you going to tell us then or is this a guessing game?' It was Ethan who broke the spell, his drawl showing more than a trace of impatience.

Max smiled, more broadly this time, but didn't answer him directly. 'Love. Mistakes.' He paused again, and this time he looked around at them all, and not just at Gabi. 'That is what makes good cheese happen. Sometimes apart, sometimes together. Love. And mistakes.'

This time, Kate clearly heard Gabi's indrawn breath.

Love. And mistakes. The words hung in the air between them. *Last night, I changed my mind*, he'd said. *Last night*. She imagined him at the mailbox, finding the package, looking at it. Or had he? He certainly hadn't called. Or texted. He'd simply turned up here to his prearranged demonstration, without warning her, without telling her. Her mind whirled. Her blood rose. She felt angry. Sad. Foolish . . . But she couldn't stop listening.

'Without love, the only cheese we'd have would be the plastic factory kind,' Max went on. 'Without mistakes, many great cheeses would not exist. Love is what turns fermented milk into a beautiful, delicious cheese. Mistakes are what make us learn a perfect process isn't always a guarantee of good cheese.'

He moved to the table and lifted up the lids of the first two cloches, revealing their contents: a green-veined Roquefort and a soft cheese in the form of a heart, with a white crust like a Brie. Pointing at the soft cheese, he said, 'This is a *Coeur de Neufchâtel*, a Neufchâtel heart, the only cheese in that shape to be honoured with an AOC.' He clicked on the remote and a picture came up, a painting of a group of girls in medieval dress in a meadow while in the distance horsemen were approaching. 'The cheese was created during the Hundred Years War by the young women of the town of Neufchâtel, as secret tokens for their English lovers. And if they'd been discovered—' he smiled—'they could have eaten the evidence.'

Everyone laughed, even Gabi, startled out of her paralysis. 'Perhaps it *is* just a legend,' he continued, looking directly at her. 'But the love is real; the love that makes this cheese what it is. And now—' he turned to the Roquefort—'let us hear it for mistakes.' Another click, and this time the picture was of a charcoal drawing of men in sheepskin coats crouched around a fire in a cave, eating hunks of bread and cheese. 'More than a thousand years ago, the story goes, some shepherds made cheese from the milk of their flock and left it in a cave to mature. But they forgot about it, and also forgot bits of the dark bread they had been eating. When they returned, the bread was mouldy and so was the cheese. They threw away the bread and were going to throw away the cheese too. But then they tasted it . . .'

'And the rest, *as they say*, is history,' said Gabi, finding her tongue at last.

It was Max's turn to be startled into laughter. 'Exactly,' he said, and the expression in his eyes made her understand what he was doing. Just as she'd created those artworks for him, to try to explain, to try to make amends, to try simply to reach him, so he was doing this for *her*. Because he'd understood what her artworks meant. And now—now he was hoping she'd understand too.

'Which is the greatest of those two, the love or the mistake?' Sylvie asked Max, quietly, pointing at the cheese. It was going to be all right, she thought, feeling relieved. There wasn't going to be trouble. There was going to be—something else. And it wasn't her business, but it still made her smile to see the looks on the faces of the two young people. Love. And mistakes. Well, the latter, whatever it had been, was maybe transforming, and the former beginning again. It made her glad. Even, if for her, the mistake was more the theme of her life right now. Not a Roquefort mistake, either, but one of those awful processed cheeses where they'd added something inappropriate, like sweet biscuit crumbs, or flakes of chilli, to be 'different'. The thought made her smile. Claude would hate to be compared to one of those ghastly cheeses. Only the best for him!

'Perhaps we had better make the experiment,' Max answered, nodding to Damien who brought out a bread board and cut thin slices of baguette for everyone, 'and each of us decide.'

'Let our tastebuds decide, I like that,' said Pete, the first to help himself. 'Not that I love that kind of soft cheese, mind you. Baby stuff.'

'A mistake to ask you, then,' retorted Mike, cutting a slice of the Neufchâtel.

'I love all cheese,' confessed Stefan. 'Maybe I am too fond,' he added, as he cut a rather too-large piece of Roquefort while Anja shook her head, indulgently.

'In my country, many people think all cheese is a mistake,' said Misaki, trying little bits of each, 'but I think it is magic.'

'I once read a spell in this book,' said Pete, hoeing into a piece of the Neufchâtel, despite his earlier disdain, 'that said to enchant a woman all you needed was to give her a piece of cheese.'

'Well, you'd better fill your pockets with cheese then,' said Gabi, 'but beware of the mice.' Everyone laughed at her bad joke, even Pete.

'But what if the love is misguided, and the mistake just a mistake?' Kate asked, finishing off the last of her Roquefort.

'It happens,' said Max, equably, 'in cheesemaking, just as in life. But if we want guarantees before we start—then we never do anything. We never try. We allow mistakes to dominate us. And we are afraid to take a risk on love. And then . . .'

'And then, we don't live at all,' Gabi said, softly, adding, with a twinkle in her eye, 'plus we don't get to eat decent cheese because we are afraid of the smell!'

'Exactly.' Max's face was full of light. Any remaining tension left the room entirely as he carried on with his presentation, taking them through all the cheeses, filling them with stories and jokes and surprising insights. And, of course, the most delicious array of tastes. Though by the end, it had to be said (so Anja whispered to Kate) that the cheeses started to merge into one another.

Afterwards, Sylvie and Damien agreed it was the best presentation Max had ever given. Eccentric. Risky. But inspired.

Twenty-nine

Twilight on the river, and people were gathering to salute the balmy evening with picnics on the quays. Some carried the bare minimum of wine, baguette, cheese and ham; others went the full deal, baskets groaning with lovingly prepared dishes in individual containers, checked tablecloths and actual crockery and cutlery. Couples, families, groups of friends, students and tourists: the Seine drew them all into its orbit, the river serenely carrying its cargo of history and legend past the chatting groups of humans and attendant pigeons keeping a beady eye on carelessly dropped crumbs.

'I never get tired of this sight,' Max said to Gabi, as they walked arm in arm through the picnicking crowds. 'It is like an updated Bruegel painting—so much to see, and every time you see something else that you missed last time.'

Gabi knew exactly what he meant. She could also see the scene as a painting—and perhaps somewhere in a corner, as in Bruegel's

Landscape with the Fall of Icarus, there would be some great drama happening, almost out of sight, unnoticed by most of the people in the picture. 'Maybe it's been done already,' she said, with a smile, after she voiced the thought, and he smiled back, saying, 'Or maybe not, and it's just waiting for you.'

'Maybe it is,' she agreed, calmly. 'Hey, this is our spot, don't you think?'

They'd come to a miraculously unsquatted-on piece of quayside, just a few spare metres but near the water. They spread out the simple but sumptuous meal they had gathered: fresh bread, Bayonne ham and duck *rillettes* that Gabi had bought, with a salad of new potatoes, peas and mint that Max had made, a bottle of cold Beaujolais from a local wine shop, and a deliciously sweet and sticky *baba au rhum* to share. No cheese; they'd had enough of that for one day. It was perfect, sitting there on the cobblestones, feet dangling over the water, eating deliciously simple food, drinking the light, lovely wine that went straight to Gabi's head because of her tiredness and the emotions of the day, but it didn't matter, because here they were, together again, and there was no hurry for anything, not even to explain, there were just these moments, just as there would be more moments, stretching on . . .

Earlier that day, after the class had finished, she had found Max as he was packing up his boxes and said, very simply, in French, 'I missed you. So much.'

He had not said anything at first, just taken her in his arms, and for a moment they had stayed tightly entwined, breathing each other in, then he said, very softly, 'Forgive me.'

'It is me who should be saying that,' she murmured, and he'd protested that wasn't so, then she'd laughed and said he just wanted the last word, and he'd kissed the top of her hair and said, 'Something tells me that could be difficult.'

And just like that, it was all right again. No, not just like that, Gabi knew. In her artworks and his presentation they had said much that couldn't be expressed in any other way. And they had come to an understanding that would never have happened if they hadn't been apart at all.

She found she could ask after his grandmother then, without any bitterness; and she could tell he was glad, though he did not whitewash the old lady's rudeness, either. He said that he'd let his grandmother know that she'd crossed a line, and even though she hadn't exactly apologised (not in her nature!), she had expressed regret that the evening had ended in the way it did. Perhaps some day, he said, Gabi might feel inclined to accept an invitation from her again, but Gabi said no, it was *her* turn. When he looked at her, surprised, she added, 'A restaurant of my choosing. Lunchtime, Saturday. All right?'

He whistled. 'Really? Are you sure?'

'Wouldn't say it if I wasn't,' she'd retorted, smiling. 'But this time, she'd better be warned: I am not running away. Or letting her get away with patronising me.'

'And neither am I,' he'd said, quietly.

Now, as they sat drinking the last of the fragrant wine and watching a couple of pigeons trying to hoover up every last stray crumb of their feast—not that there was much there—Gabi felt a peace she hadn't known in a long time. In a little while, she and Max would be making their way back to the hotel, where he would stay the night with her, but for the moment it was enough to be sitting here together as the ancient river flowed past and the convivial groups of picnickers celebrated a perfect spring evening.

They were celebrating it too, some distance away on a boat moored at the Port de l'Arsenal, where Kate, Arnaud, and a couple of Arnaud's neighbours who he'd invited for dinner polished off the last of the confit pork, rotisserie potatoes and green salad he'd provided, and started on the exquisite little cakes Kate had found, courtesy of everyone's favourite patisserie in the Marais. For their part, the neighbours had brought along a rather amazing Armagnac as a digestif to follow a full-bodied red from Provence, and afterwards Arnaud turned the fairy lights on and put records on his old turntable (no way was he going to stream music, he said).

First it was classic French singer–songwriters, like Edith Piaf, Jacques Brel and Maxime Le Forestier. Their rich, powerful voices, full of emotion as they sang of life, love and loss, swelled over the canal, making Nina bark excitedly and attracting other boat people, who came up to chat and laugh and share in a glass of Armagnac, until Arnaud put on a record by a brilliant 1970s Senegalese band called Orchestra Baobab, which Kate had never heard of before but which everyone there seemed to know well. That got everyone dancing, and when the deck wasn't enough, it flowed on to the quay, while Nina, giving up on the barking, sat on the deck and watched them all with what looked like rueful indulgence. Kate couldn't help laughing at the dog's expression. It was all part of the evening—it didn't matter that she didn't know the music or most of the people, and that she felt ever so slightly tipsy, she just danced and danced, feeling the joy of it, the wildness, the power of letting go, letting it all out, just dancing, dancing, dancing. She'd loved it as a teenager, as a twenty-something, but Josh hated dancing, said it made people look silly. He never wanted to go anywhere where dancing might be in danger of breaking out. She'd accepted it like she'd accepted too many things. She'd repressed so much. Too much! But now she was sloughing it off—the acceptance, the restrictions, the limitations. *Enough! Enough!*

As she danced, her silver Loubi shoes flashing, her face red from exertion, her hair flying, people started clapping, cheering, and she was not embarrassed at all, but full of joy and power, feeling like she could do anything, go anywhere, be anyone. No, not anyone. Be *herself*. The person she was finding again after too long.

She could see the look on Arnaud's face, the warm smile that held a little sadness, and she held out a hand. 'Come on, don't be shy!' And there he was beside her, dancing too, circling close to her within the circle of dancing neighbours. There was nothing in the least self-conscious about it, he clearly was someone who loved to dance too. She hadn't known that about him, and why should she? But it seemed right. Her feet would ache later, her head throb, and she would fall into bed exhausted, but it didn't matter, not one bit of it, not now, not ever.

Thirty

Sylvie had made herself a simple but juicy herb omelette, mopped up with bread and washed down with a sparkling Perrier, for a change. She had washed up and was about to sit down and relax with the novel she'd been trying to find time to read for the last couple of weeks, when her phone rang. An unknown number. Well, she certainly wouldn't answer. An instant after the caller rang off, her phone pinged with a message. Voicemail received. She hesitated, then clicked through and listened. The message was in English.

Madame Morel, my name is Christine Clements. I'm not sure if you remember me, but I'm a freelance journalist, specialising in food and travel writing. I wrote a piece about the Paris Cooking School a couple of years ago.

Yes, Sylvie remembered. Christine Clements had been pleasant, if brisk; she'd not stayed long, but had certainly given the school a good write-up. The article had been published in a prestigious

British food magazine, and the school had received quite a few bookings from the UK that year.

The message went on: *I'm calling because I've received information that the school is experiencing some serious issues, and I just wanted to check in with you to verify the information.*

Sylvie didn't hesitate. Hitting 'return call' she waited as the phone rang and rang before at last ringing off. So she left a voicemail, also in English.

Hello, Ms Clements, this is Sylvie Morel. Sorry I missed your call. Please call me as soon as you can.

Now her evening was ruined. She couldn't concentrate on the novel. She turned on the TV and tried to watch a movie but her mind kept wandering. Finally she turned it off, put on a jacket and left the apartment, heading for the river and a walk along the quays just to clear her head. But even as she walked she was acutely aware of the phone in her pocket, willing it to ring. When it did, however, it wasn't the Clements woman returning her call—she had stored the contact—but her son.

'Hello, my darling,' she said, in French, as his face appeared on the screen.

'Hello to you too, my little maman,' he replied, smiling. 'Oh—you're out! Not disturbing you, am I?'

'Not at all. Just went for a walk. Alone. And you—where are you?'

'Take a look,' said Julien, moving the camera around so she could see two unmistakeable sights.

'Sydney! You're in Sydney,' she exclaimed. 'But I thought you were in Queensland.'

'We're on a few days' break,' he said, and before she could ask, *Who's we?* he had swung the camera around again so Sylvie could see a dark-haired woman near the water, looking out over the harbour as she spoke on the phone. Her back was to them but then Julien called out, 'Mila!' and she turned. Sylvie glimpsed a striking, smiling face, amber-coloured eyes startling under black eyebrows, before the young woman waved then turned back to her phone.

'Oh,' Sylvie said, remembering the girl she'd half-glimpsed last time she had spoken to Julien. 'I see.'

'Maman, I'm in love,' he said, simply. Her son had always been able to speak his feelings directly, honestly, sometimes shockingly so.

She smiled, tears pricking at her eyes. 'I'm so glad, my darling. You look very happy. And she looks lovely.'

'Inside and out,' he said, 'she is the most beautiful person I have ever met. I can't believe it. I mean, how lucky I am.' A pause, then he said, looking directly at her, his face full of light, 'Maman, I have just asked her to marry me.'

Sylvie almost dropped the phone. 'You . . . oh . . . my God, Julien . . . this is . . .' *A shock. Too soon. Crazy. You're too young. You hardly know her.* Those things raced through her mind before it cleared and she saw his expression, clouding now, and knew what she had to say, what she *wanted* to say. 'This is certainly a surprise, Julien Morel,' she went on, mock-sternly, 'but then, you have always been one for surprises, haven't you! And surprise is a joy of life. As it is now. Oh, Julien, what did she say?'

His face cleared as he heard the real pleasure in her voice. 'She said yes, Maman!'

'That's wonderful. That's so wonderful.' Now the tears that had just pricked at her eyes started to flow and she said, 'And look, you've made me cry. From happiness.'

'My darling little maman,' he said, tenderly, 'you don't know how happy you've made me. Not just now. All my life.'

'Oh, Julien.' Now she was almost bawling, and she had to turn away from a couple of people about to pass her on the quay, looking at her curiously. 'You—you have made me happy all of your life too. Always.'

'Even when I was an annoying adolescent?' he replied, laughing.

'Well . . .' she said, struggling to regain her composure, 'there *were* moments, I admit.'

He laughed, then grew serious again. 'Maman, we're going to get married here in Australia.' Before she could say anything, he hurried on, 'Mila is from Mexico. I'm from France. Trying to choose between them is too hard. But Australia is where we met. So it seems right. And we hope—we hope our families will understand.'

There was a lump in Sylvie's throat as she said, 'I do understand.' And she did, though it also hurt a bit. She would have so loved to see them married here, in Paris. She could have planned such a beautiful wedding for them by the river. 'And of course I will come,' she added, seeing the unspoken question in his eyes. 'Even if it's next week.'

'Wow,' he said, laughing. 'Maman, what's come over you? Don't worry, it won't be till September. By the sea, in the Australian spring.'

'It sounds perfect,' Sylvie said, as a wave of pure and unexpected happiness swept over her. 'And what of Mila's family?'

'She's telling them now,' he said, 'and it sounds like it's going well.'

'Of course it is,' said Sylvie. 'What parents would not want their daughter marrying Julien Morel?'

'You are just a little biased,' Julien said, smiling, 'but look, here she is, she can tell us herself.'

Now Mila came into the picture on the screen. '*Bonjour, Madame*,' she said, shyly.

'No Madames for me, please,' said Sylvie. 'I'm Sylvie. And I am very happy to meet you, Mila.'

'Oh, me too,' said Mila, then added, in an English only slightly accented, 'Forgive me, but my French is not good enough yet to say more. So much that is in my heart.'

'Then we speak English,' said Sylvie, touched. 'And in that language, as well as my own, I tell you that I am very happy for you and my son. And that I am delighted you will be part of our family.'

'Thank you so much, Sylvie,' said Mila, softly. 'I am so happy you think so. This means much to me. I know how close you and Julien are. So my heart is overflowing.'

'And mine is too,' said Sylvie, the tears threatening again. 'I am so happy for you, and I look forward so much to celebrating your special day with you soon.' She paused. 'I wondered if perhaps I could come before that?'

'Oh Maman, come any time! Come next week if you want,' Julien exclaimed, also in English.

She laughed. 'Well, maybe not next week, but in a couple of months' time. That will give me time to arrange things here, make sure Damien's happy to take over for a little while, find someone to assist him.'

'That sounds like a good plan,' said Julien. She could see the mischievous expression in his eyes and knew what he was thinking.

'Okay, so you had the idea first,' she said, smiling. 'And that way I'll have a chance to experience your cooking. I suppose that job you told me about last time is still happening?'

'It certainly is, but now Mila's agreed to marry me, maybe I will resign,' he said, eyes twinkling. 'She's just finished medical school, with distinction. She's going to be a brilliant doctor. Much better prospects than me. Maybe I can just stay home and make nice meals for her.'

'I hope you understand what a cheeky fellow you've chosen there, Mila!' Sylvie said, laughing.

'I think I've learned that already,' answered Mila, looking up at Julien. 'But I can give as good as I get, I assure you.'

'Glad to hear it.' Just then, a notice flashed up on Sylvie's screen. Christine Clements was trying to get through. 'I'm so sorry, my dear ones,' she said, 'but someone I've been expecting a call from is on the line. I'll have to go.'

'Okay, Maman, we have to go too. Speak soon,' said Julien, and he blew her a kiss, as did Mila, and then they were gone.

Filled with the elation of their conversation, Sylvie found herself clicking through to Christine Clements' call without the anxiety she had earlier. 'Hello, Ms Clements. Thank you for calling me back.'

'Thank you for answering, Madame Morel.'

'So, what is this about?'

'I received an email with certain information. May I be frank?'

Sylvie sighed to herself. 'Of course,' was all she said.

'It made some serious allegations. That you had been recently investigated for poor hygiene. That you had not been paying suppliers and were in financial difficulties. That complaints had been made against you. That you had bought factory-made products to substitute for—'

'Stop right there,' said Sylvie. 'Not one of those things is true. Except that complaints *have* been made. Malicious complaints. Fake ones. It's all part of a concerted attack.'

There was a small silence, then Christine Clements said, 'That sounds a little . . . dramatic.'

'Perhaps it does. Because it is.' Sylvie took a deep breath, then plunged on, 'Someone has been targeting the school, Ms Clements. I don't know who. I don't know why. But it's being investigated.'

'By the police?'

'No. A private investigator.'

'And?' The journalist's voice had sharpened. Perhaps, Sylvie thought, because she was sensing a story more interesting than the one she'd imagined.

'And he is still gathering final evidence. But it is already very clear that whoever it is has been deliberately targeting us.'

'That is extraordinary!' Christine Clements exclaimed. 'I know you say you don't know who or why—but surely you must suspect someone.'

'Suspicions don't help, Ms Clements. I need firm evidence and that is still being gathered. May I tell you what's been happening?'

'Of course,' said the journalist. 'Do you mind if I record it?'

'Not at all.' Sylvie quickly sketched in what had happened. After she'd finished, there was a brief silence, then Christine Clements said, 'That must be pretty stressful, Madame Morel.'

'Sylvie, please,' said Sylvie. 'And yes. Frankly, Ms Clements, it's been hell. Thank God I have good friends. And a good investigator.'

'Please, call me Chris,' said the journalist. 'And maybe I can help. It sounds like a great wrong is being done to you. I don't like to see that.'

'Well. Thank you.' Sylvie tried to hide the surprise she felt. Sure, Christine Clements had been pleasant enough and the piece she'd written had been complimentary though not gushing. But this was different. There was real feeling in the other woman's voice.

'I hate character assassinations,' the journalist said, as if sensing an unspoken question. 'Especially when conducted anonymously, online.' She hesitated, then added, 'It's happened to people I care about. And it's horrible. It's got to stop.'

'I am very grateful for your words, Chris,' said Sylvie, 'but I'm not sure what you can—'

'I can forward the email to your investigator,' said Chris, 'as a first step. And I can also ask contacts I have here to look into some of the incidents. Also, I can—'

'Wait a moment,' said Sylvie, whose mind had been busy with possibilities. 'Yes, please do forward the email. I will send you the details. But also, please reply to it yourself. Tell the person that you would be interested to talk to them. Tell them that you are in Paris on a job and that you could meet them in person. Then let me know what they say. You won't need to meet them. I will do that.'

'No problem for me to come to Paris, in any case,' said Chris. 'But what if they won't meet in person?'

'Tell them there is no deal if not, that you can only interest a major magazine if it's a verified conversation with a real whistleblower.'

Chris gave a small laugh. 'Goodness, Sylvie, you have the instincts of a journalist yourself!'

'Perhaps, but I'm not one. Whereas you are. They reached out to you because they know you had written about the school in the past. They are trying to destroy our reputation with everyone who is important to us: customers, suppliers, staff, government departments, reviewers . . .'

'And in reaching out to me they know they can go public,' said Chris. 'Yes. It makes sense. I will do it. And we'll see if we can catch this miscreant red-handed!' There was real enthusiasm in her voice, and Sylvie couldn't help smiling. Christine Clements might be known for food and travel writing, not investigative reporting, but Sylvie suspected every journalist worth the name had the hunting instinct or the curiosity gene.

'Thank you so much, Chris.'

'It's a pleasure. I'll be in touch. Have a good night, Sylvie.' And she ended the call.

Well, thought Sylvie, pocketing her phone and walking slowly back home, that was certainly another surprise. What an evening it had been! Not ruined at all, but full of possibility.

On an impulse, when her steps took her back to her building, she didn't turn towards her own door, but Serge's. It was a little late but she thought he might still be up.

When he answered the door, she said, in a rush of words, 'Serge, I have good news, Julien's getting married, and she's lovely, his girl, and I'm so happy,' and then for the third time that night she was utterly surprised, by herself this time, as she flung her arms around him and lifted her face to his. 'I wanted you to be the first to know,' she said, and reaching up, kissed him hard on the lips. His response was immediate, the kiss went on, and on, then he pulled her inside, shut the door behind them with one foot and together they stumbled into the bedroom. They fell onto the bed, and then it happened as it absolutely must. And it was as Serge had dreamed of for years, but as Sylvie had never imagined till now—or maybe she had. Because right now she was exactly where she wanted to be.

Thirty-one

Gabi had woken early in the hotel bed with Max beside her still asleep, arms and legs outflung—it was a double bed, only just enough space for two, especially if one person, like Max, was a rather exuberant sleeper, like a kid. She felt laughter bubbling inside her as she sat on the edge of the bed and looked at him. Then she bent down and kissed him gently on the top of his head. He didn't stir, so she got up, showered and dressed. Heading out into a grey early morning that threatened rain, she picked up a couple of still-warm croissants from the bakery and two takeaway cups of coffee and went back to the hotel.

When she got back, he was awake, looking a little bewildered, but he smiled as she came in. 'How's that for service,' he said, as she put a coffee and a croissant on the bedside table.

'I know, it looks like I spoil you, but really, it's so you don't tempt me to spend all morning in bed,' she responded, pertly, taking a bite of her own croissant.

'Because you can't resist me, right?' he said, giving her such an outrageously sexy look that she almost threw the croissant across the room and jumped on him.

'True enough,' she managed, 'but I have to. Because I have to get to the school and, rather more to the point, you have to get to the market pretty soon. It's Thursday.'

'*Oh merde*!' He scrambled out of bed now. Looking at the endearingly old-fashioned watch he'd left on the bedside table, he said, 'Oh shit,' again, and raced into the shower. Moments later, he was dressed and brushed. After gulping the last of his coffee, and inhaling the last crumb of croissant, he kissed her, hard, hot, then he was heading for the door, saying, 'I'll pick you up at the school this afternoon.'

'Actually we're going to hear some guy talk in a restaurant in the fifth and then we're having lunch there,' Gabi said, 'so I'll meet you at your place, around three, okay?'

'Absolutely okay,' he said, smiling, then he was gone. Left on her own—it was too early still to go to the school—she sat down at the table with pad and pencil and, in a few deft strokes, sketched a picture of the bedside table as he'd left it, an empty paper cup drunkenly askew, scattered flakes of pastry, and the watch he'd forgotten to take. It was an unusual still life, she thought, surveying the drawing, but one that worked. Humming to herself, she was about to put in the finishing touches when her phone buzzed with an audio call. It was her mother.

'Darling, I hope I haven't woken you.' Her mother's voice, with that intonation of the Guernsey accent she hadn't quite lost despite all her years in Australia, sounded a little anxious.

'You haven't, Mam. What's up?'

'It's your father,' her mother Genevieve began, but Gabi interrupted at once. 'What's wrong? What's wrong with him?' As a kid, she'd had a nightmare about her father dying in a car crash. She hadn't been able to shake off the horror of it for days and though it receded in time, she had never forgotten it. And now . . .

'It's all right,' her mother said, quietly. 'He's fine. And so am I. It's just that—'

'You're not getting divorced,' interrupted Gabi, sharply, 'are you?'

'For goodness' sake!' Her mother gave a surprised laugh. 'Why would you think that?'

'Because I've always thought it's too perfect between you two,' said Gabi, at once. 'It's like—something could happen, to smash that.'

'Well, it isn't,' said Genevieve, with the ghost of laughter in her voice still, as well as a kind of wonder. 'Not smashed, and not perfect either. We're just good. Anyway, sweetheart, what I wanted to tell you was that your father has bought tickets. For us to come to Paris and see you. I couldn't stop him. They're non-refundable. And,' she added, sounding a little nervous now because Gabi hadn't said anything, 'they're for next week. I mean, we'd arrive in Paris next Tuesday. I told him you'd still be doing your course, that you'd be busy, and you couldn't just drop everything, but he has gone ahead anyway, because it was a really special deal or whatever. I'm sorry, and—'

'Don't be,' Gabi said, the laughter bubbling up in her again. 'Don't be sorry. I'm really happy. I can't wait to see you both.'

'Really? You don't mind?' Her mother's astonishment couldn't have been plainer, and Gabi felt a twist of guilt. What had her family had to put up with these last few months? Had she really been such a self-centred cow that they felt they had to tiptoe around her? Maybe. Yes. She'd been a real bloody pain, actually. And she'd hardly been in touch this last month, apart from the occasional text or email. Well, that crap was ending now.

'I don't mind at all,' she said, firmly. 'I'm over the moon! It's time Dad got to see the real Paris, not the caricature of his Southern prejudice. *And* time he took you on a really romantic holiday. Plus,' she hesitated a moment and plunged on, 'there's someone I want you to meet, and a lot of things to show you and tell you, and that's so much better face to face than over the phone. Right?'

'Right,' said Genevieve, happily. 'I'm so glad. I've been—'

'I know, dearest Mam,' said Gabi, gently. 'You've been worried about me. And you were right to be. I was a bit . . . lost. But it's okay now. I'm okay. More than okay.'

'Oh Gabi. Darling.' And to Gabi's immense surprise, the 'switch to video' request suddenly came up, and accepting it, she saw her mother's face smiling at her, though her blue eyes were suspiciously shiny. 'Oh my goodness. I *do* know how this gizmo works,' Genevieve added, a hint of pride in her voice.

'Yes, you do, Mam,' said Gabi, 'and it's so nice to see your face.'

'And yours,' her mother said, a little distractedly, as the picture went out of shot a little, giving Gabi a glimpse of the top of her mother's head rather than her face. 'Prop it up a bit against something, Mam, yes, that's right,' she said, and now her mother was back in focus, and they talked for a bit more until Genevieve said she had to start thinking about dinner, but she'd send all the details of their flights by email. 'And don't let Dad book the hotel, he doesn't know Paris and he'll choose the wrong spot,' Gabi said. 'Tell him I'll do it.'

'I'll try,' said her mother, grinning, 'Well, darling girl, good night, or good morning, rather. And we'll see you soon. Can't believe it!'

'Neither can I,' said Gabi, grinning back. 'Good night, Mam. And much love to you and Dad. And the sibs, when you speak to them.'

'Same to you, darling, bye-bye,' said Genevieve, first blowing her a kiss then waving so hard the movement on the screen made Gabi feel dizzy. But she was still smiling as the screen went blank and the call ended.

Sylvie woke from a deep dreamless sleep in an unfamiliar bed as a familiar voice called her name and the smell of freshly brewed coffee filled her nostrils. She struggled up and found herself in a room she'd only glimpsed before. Serge's bedroom. And there was Serge, dressed, shaved, smiling, handing her a cup of coffee.

'Good morning,' he said. 'I didn't like to wake you but it's nearly eight o'clock.'

'Oh my God!' Sylvie swung her legs out of bed and reached for her clothes. 'I'm going to have to hurry.'

'Have your coffee first,' he said, gently. 'Then you can head across the landing. At least you don't have far to go! I have to leave, though. I have an appointment at Rungis in less than an hour.'

He was the same as ever, friendly, kind, practical. Sylvie gulped, and it wasn't just because of the hot coffee coursing down her throat. 'Thank you. I, last night . . .'

'Don't worry,' he said, in that same gentle tone. 'I understand. And I don't expect anything.'

'Oh no, I don't mean that.' Sylvie took another sip of the coffee. 'It was—oh, I don't regret it. Not at all. In fact I . . .' She broke off.

He looked at her, but when she didn't say any more, because she couldn't, he didn't try to press her. Instead, he said, 'Nothing will change, Sylvie, if you don't want it to. I am and always will be your friend, no matter what.' Before she could answer, he went on, 'Now I really must go. Will you be all right locking up? It's the same mechanism as your door.'

'Of course,' she said, wanting to say more than that, but now he was heading out of the door with a smile and a wave, so normal, as if nothing had happened.

But it had. It had. And Sylvie had no idea yet what it meant. But Serge did. Or at least, he knew what it meant for *him*. After that first time, they'd lain together on the bed, and she'd told him more about Julien and Mila. He had been as happy as she was, for he knew her son well, and had always got on very well with him. They'd made love once more then, and before she'd fallen into her dreamless sleep, she thought she'd heard him whisper, so softly she barely heard it, *I love you, Sylvie* . . . Now, finishing off her coffee in between getting dressed, she knew she hadn't imagined it. He *had* said it. Because for him it was clear. He loved her. And not just as a dear friend.

But he'd never told her. He'd never tried to get her into bed. He'd never shown that, for him, the friendship had turned into something more. Why? *Because I never gave any sign of wanting it,* she thought. *Because he is an honourable man, in the old sense. He is my friend. My true friend. And he wouldn't cross that boundary, if I didn't want to cross it too. And last night I did. Yet I had never imagined having sex with him. Or I hadn't until very recently; these last few days when I started to notice something more about my dependable, kind friend. I thought he looked different, brighter when he was talking to Kate, when probably it was just me not taking him for granted anymore, seeing him how other people might see him, the way other women might respond to him.*

Last night, the awful thing Claude had spat out about Serge being a eunuch, incapable in bed, had been proved to be so wrong it was laughable. Putting the cup down, she hugged herself for a moment, feeling a thrill run through her at the memories: the tender expression in his grey eyes, the sure feel of his hands on her body, the smell of his skin, his hair, the beautiful rush as they came together . . .

Oh God. She was still in a relationship with Claude, even if it was broken . . . Well, she *had* to end it, properly. Not because of Serge. That—well, she didn't know what would happen in the future, after last night, though she hoped that . . . She had to end it with Claude because she no longer loved him. She hadn't, not for quite a while, if she was being truly honest with herself. Giving him that ultimatum had been as much of a test for herself as for him—to test whether she still loved him, whether she still cared.

And she had her answer now. She didn't. It was over. And he had to know. Today.

Leaving Serge's flat, and letting the latch click locked behind her, as he'd said, she went into her own apartment. Nobody was there yet, though Damien would arrive soon enough and preparations would start for the morning's session. She had a quick shower, dressed in some fresh clothes, made herself another coffee, ate a couple of grilled pieces of yesterday's leftover bread with butter and jam, and sent a message to Claude: *We need to talk. Tonight. Meet me at our usual bar, 18h.*

He messaged back almost at once. *Tried to call you last night. Twice. I wanted to apologise. Why weren't you answering?*

I was out, she messaged back, annoyed, guilty. *Sorry.* She hadn't noticed the missed calls. But he hadn't left a voicemail, and he could have done if he really wanted to apologise. *But can you make it tonight?*

Yes. She could sense the grudgingness in his response but ignored that, texting back, *Okay. See you tonight then.*

He didn't answer. But he'd be there. Or he wouldn't be. She preferred telling him face to face, but if she had to, she'd do it another way.

Kate woke in a sweat, rather late. Stumbling out of bed, her head felt thick and she swallowed a couple of paracetamol to try to dislodge the ache. She'd drunk a bit too much last night. Not that she regretted it; it had been a wonderful night, and even now, she smiled at the thought of it. The party had ended well after midnight, then Arnaud and Nina had walked with her back to the hotel, and on the doorstep he'd said, 'I'm giving a workshop in Amiens this weekend. Leaving Friday morning, coming back Saturday afternoon. Would you like to come?'

'Going by boat?' she'd asked, and he'd grinned. 'No, hiring a car.' He looked at her with a twinkle in his eye. 'But Nina's coming.'

'Well, that settles it, then. I'm coming,' said Kate, also grinning, before saying, more seriously, 'Amiens is near all those World War One battlefields on the Somme, isn't it? My dad's grandfather fought there—Dad's always wanted to go, I could check it out for him maybe.'

'We could go there Friday morning,' he said. 'It is a place that holds much memory, both for you Australians and for we French. My father's family is from Corsica but my mother's family comes from the Somme. Her great-grandparents had a shop in Amiens. They liked the Australian soldiers they met . . .'

It was the first time he'd mentioned his birth family. She'd said, 'Maybe *my* great-grandfather met them.'

'Perhaps.' He smiled. 'So—shall I pick you up about eight thirty on Friday morning? I will book a separate room for you at the hotel in Amiens,' he added, 'of course.'

'Of course,' Kate repeated, smiling. Reaching up, she gave him a kiss on the cheek. 'Thank you, Arnaud. I look forward to it very much.'

'As do I,' he said, and taking her hand, he squeezed it gently. Then he whistled to Nina, who was busying herself with investigating some interesting smell nearby. Arnaud waved in farewell, and left.

Thinking of it now as she got ready to go out, she wondered if this weekend would change things between them. She couldn't decide whether she wanted that to happen—or not. Well, there were no plans, no blueprints, no templates. Just *que sera, sera*, as her dad would say.

Thirty-two

'Next week is our final week together,' said Sylvie, as the class gathered around her. 'And so next week, we'll be concentrating on the finale of a meal. The dessert. Cakes, pastries, mousses, ice creams, more. All the *douceurs*, as we call them in French. Sweetness, that means, but also softness, gentleness, kindness, pleasure. *Douceur* is a cardinal virtue, in France. We say *la douce France*, meaning that France is a lovely country to live in; *un temps doux*, meaning balmy weather; and *la douceur de la vie*, meaning the pleasure, the sweetness of life, the joy of being alive. In food, it's not always about sweet things: it can be about soft, creamy things, like that Neufchâtel heart that Max introduced you to. We'll be cooking cakes and making desserts that French home cooks put on the table for family and friends. But this weekend I want you to prepare by visiting shops that professionally celebrate *douceurs*: patisseries, bakeries, chocolate shops, sweet shops.

Now, we're not going to try to emulate the professional *pâtissiers* and sweet makers, you need a whole other course for that. But we are going to look at the place *douceurs* have in France. So take photos, make notes and taste where you want. Then tell us on Monday what the heart of *douceur* is, in France, for you.'

The class stared at her. 'Oh my God,' groaned Ethan, 'that's a dangerous mission you're sending us on!'

'Speak for yourself, dude,' said Mike, teasingly.

'It's easy-peasy,' chuckled Pete. 'Cakes, here I come!'

'We have already started this task from the first day,' said Anja, cheerfully, 'haven't we, Stefan?'

'I have even taken many pictures,' agreed Stefan, proudly.

'Me too,' said Kate. 'It will be no trouble at all.'

Misaki said, a little worriedly, 'But how many shops must we visit to get a good understanding?'

'As many or as few as you like, I'd say, Misaki,' said Gabi, and Sylvie nodded, smiling.

'There's no limit. No prescription. And now, let's move on to today's session, which Damien will lead.'

She'd planned for there to be only a short session for this morning, a discussion around the creation of everyday menus in the French household. They had to have time to get to Chez Quenu for Martin Cahuzac's talk at eleven thirty. She had no idea if the man would know how to talk to the students, but it didn't matter, it would be something different, and the lunch would be a good way to end the penultimate week of classes. It would only be her, Serge and the students going, as Damien and Yasmine both had other plans.

Just as Damien started to speak, Sylvie's phone buzzed. Giving Damien an apologetic nod, she hurried away. It was Chris Clements calling.

'Hello, Chris,' she said.

'Just wanted to tell you that the fish took the bait,' the journalist said. 'We have a rendezvous.'

Sylvie felt her pulse rate increase. 'Where? When? Who?'

'The cafeteria at Galeries Lafayette,' said Chris. 'Midday, Saturday. Do you know it?'

'I certainly do,' said Sylvie. The self-service cafeteria was big and crowded with tourists and Parisians alike. 'It's a good choice. Safety in crowds. Nobody would notice you.'

'Yes. As to who,' said Chris, 'the name given was Émilie Zola, which I presume is a pseudonym, because wasn't there a famous French writer by that name?'

'Yes,' said Sylvie, thoughtfully, 'but he was a man. Émile Zola. Émilie is a woman's name.'

'Doesn't mean it *is* a woman,' said Chris.

'I know. But it's interesting, still.'

'Well, whoever it is clearly stated they know what I look like and that I must come alone. I've booked a ticket on the Eurostar for tomorrow and will meet them as arranged on Saturday. Alone.'

'No. I want to be there too.'

'It could be dangerous,' Chris said. 'This person obviously has it in for you.'

'It could be dangerous for you too,' Sylvie said, 'if they are deranged.'

'I don't think they're deranged,' said Chris, 'just determined to destroy your business. But it seems personal, nevertheless. So I don't think you will gain anything by confronting them. Let me find out as much as I can about them and then we can make our move.'

'Okay,' said Sylvie. She had no intention of taking a back seat, but she didn't want to argue the case. 'And come to dinner tomorrow night at my place.'

'I'd like that. And we can talk strategy.'

After that call, Sylvie rang Paul Renard. Yes, he said, he'd received the email Chris Clements had forwarded, and was evaluating it. When she told him that Chris had arranged to meet the sender, he agreed that was a good idea but immediately added that Sylvie herself should not be involved at all. 'I strongly advise you to not go anywhere near this person,' he said. 'They clearly have a strong personal animus against you, and who's to know what might happen if you try to confront them? I can go instead, to back Madame Clements up if necessary. I'll stay in the background. But if there's any trouble, I can help.'

'Very well,' Sylvie agreed, after a moment's hesitation. Let them think what they wanted, she certainly wasn't going to pass up the opportunity to see her tormentor in the flesh.

They think they know what's best for me, she thought, as she wound up the call. *But they don't know what it's like. To them it's a job, or an intriguing story to be cracked.* Only one other person truly understood. And that was Serge. But she wouldn't call him. She was going to see him at lunchtime, as he was coming to Chez Quenu too. She could tell him then.

Douceur. The word ricocheted through Gabi's mind, lighting little sparks as it went. *Douceur.* She thought of gazing into patisserie windows, of biting into an éclair, or her mother's raspberry tart, her grandmother's Gateau Basque, the softness of the pastry, the luscious creaminess of its custard filling. There was the memory of the golden dense sweetness of greengages, picked straight off a tree in her grandfather's orchard, and the first time she'd tasted a proper hot chocolate in Bayonne. With a little twist of pleasure, she remembered Max, holding out a spoonful of crème caramel for her to try back at his flat, that first time, and how afterwards they could taste the dessert on each other's lips . . . She could see her ancestor Ander Picabea walking around the 1900 Exposition with his tray of cakes, imagining him walking by the cheese stall of her Guernsey ancestors, the Ogiers, and them buying a cake from him before he went on his way, without any of them aware what a momentous meeting it had been. And she thought, only half-listening to the discussion around her in the Metro carriage as the class headed to Chez Quenu, there was the *douceur* she'd encountered in this group of people. Not strangers anymore, not quite friends, not just acquaintances either, but maybe colleagues, or peers—all so different but united by a shared passion. Her spine tingled, her fingers itched for a pencil and paper, to get some of it down, the ideas, the images, the possibilities . . . *Shadow Life* had been all about darkness, fear, menace. About being erased. She'd created it playfully, without fear or darkness, and yet it had swallowed her. *Amertume*—bitterness—was the opposite of *douceur*, in French.

Shadow Life had been about *amertume*. Perhaps now it was time to look at the other side.

As they entered the restaurant, Kate was also thinking about what Sylvie had said that morning. But she was remembering that first afternoon in Paris, and the lovely little strawberry tart she'd bought on impulse and eaten in the street. It had been a symbol of her first taste of freedom, pleasure and possibility away from the bruising emotional battleground back in Australia. She'd been back to that patisserie several times since then, as well as exploring others in the neighbourhood. But before she and Arnaud headed to Amiens tomorrow, she would buy a couple of those little tarts in that same patisserie to share at lunchtime. She'd take a photo of them. And then, afterwards, perhaps even on Saturday, in the beautiful notebook he'd given her, which was already nearly three-quarters full of her observations and scraps of recipes, she'd write something about what that particular *douceur* meant to her, both at the beginning and now. Because she didn't know how it would go, the weekend. And she wasn't sure how she *wanted* it to go, even. That was both exciting and scary.

The restaurant was a small, cosy place, very simply decorated, and the young woman coming towards them was full of smiles. 'Welcome, welcome,' she said, ushering them to a prepared table. 'My father will be out shortly.' She spoke in a lightly accented English. 'He is feeling *le trac*, the stage nerves, I think.'

They were the only ones in the restaurant. The young woman, who introduced herself as Amandine, brought glasses and carafes of red and white wine, as well as water, and a couple of bowls of excellent olives, green and black. Sylvie left them to go to the kitchen, to see if she could calm the 'stage nerves' of Amandine's father, so the class was left to chat, eat the olives and sip the very drinkable wine.

'I don't mind if we don't get a talk but just lunch,' hissed Mike to Kate, his closest neighbour. 'I'm starving. Didn't have time to have breakfast. Ethan dragged me out for a walk. He reckons I don't do enough exercise.' He patted his incipient paunch. 'He's seven years older than me but seven years fitter too he reckons. But I reckon he can do the fitness thing for the both of us. What do you think?'

Kate smiled. 'Oh well, everyone has different feelings about exercise.'

'Yeah, but we're on a food course, for Pete's sake. I mean,' Mike added, quickly, as Pete, across the table, looked up from swirling the wine around in his glass, 'for heaven's sake.' Kate expected Pete to make some silly comment then, like *Pete and heaven are the same thing*, but he didn't. He just gave a vague smile and went on swirling his wine. He was uncharacteristically quiet this morning.

'It is a strange name this restaurant has, yes?' pondered Misaki, breaking into the conversation.

'It could be the name of the owner,' Kate suggested, but Mike was already googling it. 'It says here it's named after a character in an Émile Zola novel. Never read any of his stuff, I must admit.'

'One of my father's favourites,' said Gabi. 'Zola, I mean. A great writer of the nineteenth century, with a social conscience, kind of like Dickens only less all over the place.'

'All over the place?' Misaki repeated.

But before anyone could answer, Sylvie came back into the room with Amandine and a nuggety-looking man she introduced as her father, Martin Cahuzac, owner and chef at Chez Quenu. 'Martin will just give us a brief talk, then lunch will be served,' Sylvie announced, and sat down at the table.

Cahuzac cleared his throat, looked down at a piece of paper, shuffled it, looked up again and said, in very slow, very careful English, 'Thank you for coming. You are most welcome. My food is simple and I . . .' He broke off, reddening, and his daughter said, encouragingly, 'Don't worry, Papa. Speak in French and I'll translate.'

The restaurant's front door banged and Serge came in. 'Sorry,' he murmured to Sylvie, 'I had a last-minute order I had to fill.' She felt herself tense, but gave him a smile, whispering back, 'It's okay, it has hardly started.'

'Yes,' he said, his eyes meeting hers for a moment, and she thought she read a double meaning in his expression. But was she just imagining it? 'I have something to tell you later,' she murmured, and he nodded, but didn't answer, because just then Cahuzac finally started to speak.

And once he'd started, it seemed like he couldn't stop. He told them stories of growing up in Provence, how he'd wanted to cook from a tender age, about the many dishes he'd cooked, and how when it came to opening his first restaurant he returned to the food he'd known in childhood, and on and on it went. Some of it was interesting but other parts were too detailed and meandering. Poor Amandine was struggling to keep up with the translation, while the class began to look dazed by the torrent of words. And hungry too, a little tipsy with wine on almost-empty stomachs. Sylvie was just about to make a signal to Amandine to try to get her father to wind up when, glancing out of the window, she saw a couple walk past hand in hand. They had their backs to her, but she thought, no, she was *sure* that she recognised the man, and with a stifled cry she pushed back her chair and got up, making Cahuzac stop abruptly and the class look absolutely startled as their normally calm and collected teacher raced for the door.

But by the time she'd got out onto the street, the couple was gone. Into a building maybe, or round a corner, she didn't know. She thought for a moment of running after them, before dismissing the idea. It would be undignified. Ridiculous. Mad . . .

'Sylvie! What's happened?' Serge had come out after her. 'Are you all right?'

She swallowed. 'I'm fine. I just thought I saw . . .' He waited, but she shook her head. 'Nothing. It's nothing.'

He looked at her. 'Are you sure? You look pale.'

With an effort, she said, 'It's okay. Really. Please, let's go inside.'

She could see the disappointment in his eyes, but there was no help for it. This wasn't something she could share with him, not right now, not when everything was shifting between them. It would feel—wrong, somehow. To tell him that she thought she'd seen—no, she was certain she *had* seen—her lover Claude hand in hand with another woman, though all she'd seen of *her* from the back was a shining blonde head, pink top and slim short skirt.

And even less could she say that the sight had caused such a spurt of rage and anguish in her that she felt sick. Because that was shameful. She didn't love Claude anymore. She was going to tell him it was over. She'd even slept with another man. So why was she feeling like this, knowing he was cheating on her with someone else? It gave her an out, a way of ending things cleanly. She should be relieved. Instead, she felt gutted. And that was not something she cared to dwell on, far less talk about.

Thirty-three

'Well, did anyone else think that was a bit strange?' Pete asked. After lunch he, Anja, Stefan and Kate had adjourned to a nearby café for coffee while the others went their separate ways.

'It was enjoyable, actually,' Kate said. 'And the food was superb.'

'Sure,' Pete agreed. 'But I mean, the atmosphere . . . that chef going on and on until I thought I'd die of boredom or hunger, and Sylvie jumpy as a cat and then rushing out like that. What was it all about?'

'None of our business,' Kate said, tartly, though she had to admit it had been unusual.

'Yeah, but we can speculate, can't we?' Pete grinned. He seemed to have recovered from his previously quiet mood and was back to his irrepressible self. He turned to Anja and Stefan. 'What's your take on today?'

'We enjoyed it,' said Anja, glancing at Stefan, who nodded. 'Very nice food. Very nice owners.'

'But what about the rest?' Pete persisted. 'What did Sylvie see that made her bolt outside?'

'Maybe she felt unwell,' Anja suggested.

'Maybe she needed air,' added Stefan. 'It was quite hot in the restaurant.'

Pete shook his head. 'I despair of you lot,' he said, gesturing to the waiter for another cup of coffee. 'No imagination, that's your trouble.'

'It's not imagination, it's gossip,' Kate said, half-amused, half-annoyed.

He shrugged. 'A rose by any other name, is what I say, Ms Kate.'

'That is an interesting saying,' Stefan put in, earnestly. '*A rose by any other name*. I have heard it before but am not sure I understand the meaning.'

'It's from Shakespeare,' Kate said. 'And it means that a thing is a thing, even if it's called something different,' she added, deadpan.

They all stared at her for an instant, then Pete burst out laughing. 'Well, that sure makes it crystal clear!' Seeing Anja's and Stefan's politely bemused smiles, he went on, 'Like so many things in English, it's best to explain it with a story. So here's one from real life for you. On his fifteenth birthday a couple of months ago, the son of my next-door neighbour back in Toronto decided that he wanted to change his surname. His mother wasn't happy at first but eventually came round to it because, as she said to me, it didn't change the fact that he was still her son. What he is called doesn't matter as much as what he is. A rose by any other name.'

'I see,' said Stefan, slowly.

'It's a good explanation,' said Anja, smiling.

'Yes, but *why* did he want to change his surname?' asked Kate.

'Well, he had his mother's surname—she's a single parent—but he decided he wanted to add his father's name to his mother's, so he's now double-barrelled: Perret-Rocca. It doesn't quite roll off the tongue but there you go!'

Kate smiled. 'Yep, I reckon that . . .' Then something snagged at her memory, making her pause. 'What did you say his name was?'

'He was Lucas Perret, now he's Lucas Perret-Rocca.'

Rocca. *Rocca.* That was Arnaud's surname. He'd said his father was of Corsican origin. And his wife had taken their child to Canada. It was probably a coincidence. 'Are they Canadians, your next-door neighbours?' she asked. 'I mean, originally.'

Pete looked at her, a little surprised. 'Louise Perret is French, and her boy—I'm not sure. I mean, I don't know if he was born in France or in Canada. Why?'

Anja and Stefan were looking curiously at her now too. Kate coloured a little. 'I—it's just that Perret sounds like a French name.'

'Plenty of French people in Toronto,' Pete said. 'Don't know about the Rocca, though. Sounds Italian to me. Lots of people with Italian ancestry in Canada and the US. Maybe the dad lives there.'

Or maybe he doesn't, thought Kate, *maybe he is living on a boat on the Seine, and his ancestry's not Italian but Corsican.* 'They never said?'

'Nah. Louise is very private, she doesn't even use social media.' His tone sounded incredulous. 'And Lucas wasn't interested in his dad till recently. Something about turning fifteen triggered an interest. But he wouldn't talk about such things to the old man next door.' He laughed.

The rest of the time in the café passed by innocuously in friendly chatter before they all headed off in different ways.

Should I go straight to Arnaud? Kate thought, as she walked alone. *Should I tell him what Pete said?* But what if it was all a false alarm? Or rather, a false hope? It could just be a coincidence. She didn't even know what his ex-wife's name was. He'd just called her *my wife*, and he didn't even say the boy's name either, as if it would be too painful. He also hadn't said how old the boy was when his mother took him to Canada, just that he was young. Pete's teenage neighbour might be the right age, or he might not.

She had to say something to Arnaud. She had to mention it at least. But not today. Not till she and Arnaud were away, together. But—wait—he might already know about it. Maybe he'd looked his ex-wife up on Google, seen where she ended up, and still done nothing about it. After all, he said he hadn't tried to find them. He said he'd thought they were 'better off without him'. But did he still think that now? Or was he just too scared to find out? If he knew that his son had wanted to add his father's name to his mother's, might that change things?

I don't know, Kate thought. That was the trouble. She might do more harm than good if she interfered. *I should just leave it alone*, she told herself. She really wanted to enjoy their weekend together. But she also wanted to be honest with Arnaud. She didn't want to hide anything from him because she was scared.

She'd have to make up her mind what to do. Soon.

'I've got something to tell you,' Gabi said.

'That sounds ominous.' Max was smiling lazily at her. They hadn't even made it to the bed in his flat, just the sofa, and now lay in each other's arms, half-covered in the throw that had been on the back of the sofa, while most of their clothes lay in a disordered heap on the floor.

'It's not especially dramatic,' said Gabi, 'only it is, in a way. My parents are coming here next Tuesday.'

'Here?' echoed Max, gently disengaging himself and sitting up. 'To my apartment?'

'No. I mean, they are coming to Paris. It—I had no warning. My father—he just booked tickets. He's like that.'

'Oh,' said Max. 'Then I suppose next week—well, you are going to be very busy. With your parents. So . . .'

'So I need you to help me,' said Gabi, firmly. She knew exactly what he'd thought she meant, that she was telling him she couldn't see him next week because her parents were coming.

He stared at her. 'Help you?'

'They know France, of course, but just the South. They've never been to Paris. My father never wanted to and my mother never had the opportunity when she was growing up, even though she lived on Guernsey, which isn't exactly far from France. My ancestors who went to Paris, you know the ones I told you about back when we first met . . .'

'I remember, even though it is lost in the fog of time,' he said, grinning, and ducking her playful tap as she sat up.

'They didn't have the best time here and the story in the family was that you should steer clear of Paris.'

'Maybe that's why your parents clicked,' he said, still grinning, 'because of that shared dislike.'

'Ha, very funny,' she said, smiling back, 'but anyway, I want to show them around, show them the real Paris, not the usual tourist stuff. But I'm not a real Parisian, whereas you . . .'

'Whereas I am really a *plouc* from the provinces,' he put in, using a term that might translate as hick or bogan, 'but I do give a good imitation of a real Parisian, I suppose.'

Gabi raised an amused eyebrow. 'Then that will have to do. Will you?'

'Will I what?' he replied, teasingly. But when he saw her little frown, he gathered her up in his arms, and said into her hair, 'Will I devise a plan to make your parents fall in love with Paris, just to see you smile? Will I want to spend not only next week with you but all those that follow? Yes, then. And yes, again.'

'Oh, Max,' she whispered, the words clotting in her throat, joy rushing through her as she lifted her face to his and they kissed, tenderly, entwined in each other's arms.

Sylvie could see him sitting at a table near the window, a whisky in front of him. In France, whisky was the most popular form of spirits, but Claude wouldn't have dreamed of going near any of the popular brands. He would have picked the most obscure, the most niche, the most ultra-chic, from the smallest craft distillery available. He hadn't seen her yet; he was looking at his phone. Texting. Not to Sylvie, for her phone stayed silent. Was he messaging the blonde? A twist of nausea gripped her. She saw him as anyone else might have seen him: artfully groomed silver head bent over his phone, expensive linen jacket carelessly draped over the back of his chair, snob whisky in front of him, utterly confident in his own certain place in the world. It made her feel disorientated, as if she were looking at a stranger. What *was* she doing with this stranger?

She almost turned and walked away. But then he looked up, saw her and waved. There was the hint of a smile on his face, no doubt the lingering effect of texting whoever it was, Sylvie thought.

Pushing open the door of the bar, she headed straight to his table.

'Hello,' he said, the smile turned on for her now. 'What will you have?'

'Nothing, thank you.' She glanced at his phone, which he'd put facedown on the table. Of course. He wouldn't want her to see what he'd been doing.

He raised an ironic eyebrow. 'Nothing?' he repeated. 'Well, sit down, anyway.'

'No. This won't take long, Claude.'

He took a sip of his whisky, calmly, but there was the beginning of anger in his eyes. 'Don't be ridiculous, Sylvie. Whatever you have to tell me—and I can guess what it is—won't be told any better if you stay standing up. So sit down.'

There was a hard note in his voice that made her scalp crinkle. With fury, not fear. Without a word, she sat down. Not because of what he'd said, but because now there was going to be no quarter.

'See? Not so hard,' he said, taking another sip of whisky. 'So? Tell me you want to end it. That's what you've come for, isn't it?'

She still didn't answer, just looked directly at him.

'I see,' he said. 'You want to make me feel uncomfortable. So you don't feel so bad when you coldly break my heart.'

An ironic smile twisted at her own lips, but still she said nothing.

'Well, if you are refusing to speak, let me tell you this.' His hand tightened around the whisky glass. 'You might break my heart but you won't break my will, you won't emasculate me like you have tried to do from the beginning of our relationship.'

She shook her head, contempt flaring from her eyes, but still there were no words. And she could see her silence was beginning to disturb him. He was irritated, yes, but uneasy too.

'You wanted everything, didn't you?' he continued. 'Not content with having my heart, my body, you wanted my memory, my being. You wanted to own me. You did not want me to have had a life before you, you wanted to cut me off from everyone in my past life . . .'

'From Marie-Laure, you mean?' she asked, making him pause.

'Well, yes. And others.' He coloured, wrong-footed. But he wasn't finished. 'And yet you gave nothing of such value back. Because you never do, do you? All that matters to you is that shitty business of yours, and maybe your son, though I'm not convinced of that. You are cold as ice, Sylvie, I don't think you have a heart at all.'

'I saw you today,' she said, managing to keep her voice steady through the bitterness in her throat.

He stared at her, bemused. 'Are you feeling well? Of course you saw me. Here. Now.'

'At midday. In the fifth,' she said. 'You weren't alone.'

He went still. Now it was his turn to say nothing.

'That's what I came to tell you,' she said, getting up. 'You're free to screw anyone you like. To do whatever you like. Goodbye, Claude. I never want to see or hear from you again.'

'Now, wait here a moment,' he began, getting up. 'You can't do this to me, you can't just walk away . . .'

'Can't I?' she replied, mockingly, and walked briskly away, while he shouted after her, angrily, incoherently. As she strode past the window of the bar, she saw the barman come out from behind his counter to remonstrate with Claude. *I hope you try to punch him and he lays you out flat*, she thought, vengefully, *I hope you get blood all over your oh so lovely jacket and your oh so white shirt, I hope they call the cops on you . . .* The scalding white-hot fury in her was like an exultation, and it sustained her for several blocks before her legs started to give way and she had to sit down on a low wall. Her chest ached and her throat was so full of bile that she thought she might throw up.

How could she have stayed with him for so long? How could she not have seen him for what he was—a narcissist whose perverted sense of self could never allow him to really see anyone for themselves? Not her, not Marie-Laure, not the blonde woman, whoever she was—but not just women, everyone. The hateful way he'd spoken about Serge, the comments he'd made in the past about Julien, about her students, her friends, even random strangers in the street; comments he supposed were sharply witty but which were really just snide: everything was reflected through the mirror of his own diseased self-love. Why hadn't she seen it before? Well, maybe she *had* seen it, and been uneasy, but she had not really thought about what it meant. What it *really* meant. She'd closed her eyes to it in the beginning, because she had been dazzled by his good looks, his charm, his poise, and of course, the sex . . . But she had begun to fall out of love some time ago, she knew that. Yet to think she had given him the ultimatum about Marie-Laure because she'd wanted to put the relationship on a firmer footing! She had been deluded. Or maybe not, maybe subconsciously she knew that it would make him reveal himself fully: not as a committed lover, but as the narcissist he truly was. *I should be glad to know the truth*, she thought, but there was no gladness in her heart, and no more fury either, just a great weariness that made it seem like a long way back to her flat.

Arriving on her own floor, she saw a bar of light under Serge's door, but she didn't knock. This wasn't a time to be falling into his arms, just to blank out the anguish and pain. It wouldn't be fair to him. And it would destroy any chance they might have.

Later, crawling into bed after half-watching a couple of episodes of *Lupin* over a scratch meal of leftovers, she lay awake for quite a while before finally managing to fall asleep.

Thirty-four

TWINNED WITH ROBINVALE read the sign at the entrance to the village of Villers-Bretonneux. The mention of that small town in north-western Victoria was only one of the signs of the impact Australians had had here, in the Somme, during World War I. The museum in the old school, which had been rebuilt with Victorian donations after the war, was full of characterful faces, Australian and French, looking out from old black-and-white photographs. Photographs not just of war and death, but also of meals and meetings and of local kids gazing curiously at the tall, cheeky-looking young men who had come from the other side of the globe to fight. There were carvings of Australian animals around the walls and a sign reading proudly, in French and English, NEVER FORGET AUSTRALIA. Kate felt moved to tears. It felt so intimate—unlike the massive cemetery at the Australian National Memorial, just outside of Villers-Bretonneux, which they'd visited beforehand. With its endless rows of white headstones stretching out over the beautiful, undulating green countryside, it took your breath away—such a vast extent, such a mute yet graphic reminder of mass slaughter. But here, in the quiet little museum—she and Arnaud were the only people here at the moment—it was the individual human stories that caught at your heart.

'It's so hard to understand,' she said, shaking her head. 'Such a stupid, stupid war, and it solved nothing. Why didn't people rebel, refuse to fight, or run away?'

'Because they'd be killed,' he said. 'Shot for desertion or cowardice. In France, anyway.'

'So if you left, you were killed. And if you stayed, you were likely to be killed,' Kate said, sadly.

'Yes,' said Arnaud. 'There was no choice.'

'But Australians—it wasn't quite like that,' she said, gesturing to the photos around them, and thinking of her dad's grandfather, whom she'd never known. 'They weren't conscripted. They volunteered. And they weren't shot if they tried to escape. They went to prison. So . . .'

'So sometimes it's not as simple as it looks,' he said gently. 'Maybe they weren't conscripted. But there are other ways of forcing you to go. What your family expects. Your friends. Your society . . .'

Maybe it was the faraway expression in his eyes, but Kate found herself blurting out, 'Did anyone make *you* go into the army? I mean, why did you . . .' She broke off, horrified at herself. What right did she have to ask questions like that? 'I'm sorry,' she stammered. 'Forgive me.'

He held her gaze. 'There is nothing to forgive,' he said, quietly. 'You are right to ask. Nobody forced me. I joined the army to get away from my family. It was not a good reason. And I stayed because I had to. Not because anyone made me stay. But because—well, it was a matter of pride, to persist.' He smiled. 'Not very clever.'

She swallowed. 'Do you regret that you stayed? I mean . . .'

'No. If I did not stay, I would not have met my ex-wife. And so my son would not have been born. And I cannot regret that.'

She stared at him, her throat tightening. 'Even after they—they left?'

'Never,' he said, simply.

'But have you not tried to . . .' She was on difficult ground, she knew that, but she had to get a sense of what he really felt.

'To find them?' he offered, finishing her sentence, quietly. 'I think of him a lot. But—I do not think it is a good thing, a fair thing, to try to find him. Not good for him, I mean. After all this time.'

'Oh, Arnaud,' she said, a mix of hope and fear rushing through her, the fear of saying the wrong thing, the hope that somehow the right thing might come to her. 'What if—what if maybe he might be looking—wondering—what if for him it is a good thing if he could find you?'

He seemed nonplussed. Then he said, 'But he wouldn't. Try I mean.'

'Why not?' she asked, relieved by his response but also a little impatient. 'Do you know what he is like now?'

The sadness flickered into his eyes again. 'No. I don't.'

Kate felt uncomfortable about pushing him, but she knew she had to. 'Then how can you say for sure? If you don't try to find him, how can you ever know if he wants to see you or not?'

There was a silence. Then Arnaud smiled, a real smile that reached his eyes. 'You are a strong woman, Kate. You would not give up, I know.'

'I only give up on things that are not worth persisting with,' she said, fiercely. 'But I fight when I need to. And I think this is worth it. *You* are worth it.'

A small beat of time, which seemed endless to Kate, who was aghast and exhilarated at what she'd just revealed. Then, his face alight with feeling, he said, 'I hope you are right. Oh, I am so full of hope that you are right.' And then he took the three steps that separated him from her and she was in his arms, and they stayed like that for a long moment, heart against heart. Until Nina, who up till now had been more or less patiently sitting in a corner of the room, came to nudge between them. Laughing, they released each other.

'I think she's trying to tell us something,' Kate said.

'Yes, that it's time to head into Amiens for our lunch,' said Arnaud, cheerfully, as they followed the little dog trotting briskly out of the museum and down the steps, into the sunshine.

Amiens had nondescript outskirts but a pretty town centre with a beautiful Gothic cathedral and rows of picturesque houses set around the Somme canal, and their hotel was right in the middle of that. In the car, Arnaud had, unprompted, opened up a little more about his family—he knew Amiens well, he told her, because he'd lived there as a child until his mother died when he was eleven, and his father remarried just a year later. Things changed after that, he said, and it was clear he didn't just mean moving away from Amiens. Remembering what he'd said about joining the army to get away from his family, she didn't press him. He'd tell her if he wanted to. She hadn't told him what Pete had said about his neighbours, either. She had to find the right way, the right moment. It would come, she knew that, and now she was untroubled by it. She was happy, simple as that.

It was his company, it was the beautiful mild day, it was the feel of holiday, of freedom, and also, it had to be said, the new outfit she'd bought at Galerie Vivienne, which felt soft against her skin, so comfortable yet elegant. Everything felt right. They had lunch at a little place by the cathedral, and both had the same thing: the best mussels Kate had ever eaten. They both got a whole pot of them, deliciously fragrant in a light wine and cream sauce, which they sopped up with chunks of white sourdough bread, accompanied by a lovely salad of herbs and *mâche* with a tangy vinaigrette. Nina, in good French style, was also a welcome and well-behaved diner in the restaurant; her bowl neatly set near their chairs and smiles sent in her direction both by the waiters and other customers. Dessert, by the water later, featured the luscious little strawberry tarts Kate had brought from Paris. This was real *douceur*, Kate thought, happiness flooding over her. Not just the cakes, but all of it, the whole day.

Later, they went with three other tourists and a guide on a boat tour of a strange, lovely place called the *hortillonnages*—a tongue-twisty word Kate didn't even attempt pronouncing!—which was a series of community water gardens; little green islands where people grew flowers or vegetables or simply relaxed in the sunshine, all set within a network of water that stretched for kilometres. The boat was utterly silent, electric like the one they'd been on the week before in Paris. But here they had moved from the busy, noisy world of a modern town into a miniature archipelago, like a fantasy world come to life. The guide spoke about the history of the place and the people who had made it, but when she fell silent, no one spoke. It was so quiet that Nina fell asleep. And when Arnaud's arm came around Kate's shoulders, she nestled quite naturally into his chest, feeling the warmth of him so close. She felt completely relaxed with him, in this hidden green world.

That night, they had a simple soup in a little place by the side of the canal, and when it came time to go back to the hotel and their separate rooms, they said goodnight with a long hug, but neither he nor she suggested that they might come into the other's room. And that was as it should be. Both of them were still bruised, wary from past experience. For now, what they had between them was enough.

She didn't feel sleepy, though, so she wrote for quite a while in her notebook about the tarts, and *douceur*, and watched a film. It was well past eleven by the time she got ready for bed and then a message popped up on her phone. It was from Leah. *Did you see this?* It was accompanied by a screenshot of a short article with the headline, 'Resmond case to be settled out of court'. Kate scanned it, rapidly. Basically, it said that Resmond and Jaime Noura had issued a joint statement to the effect that they had come to an understanding and were settling out of court. There were no details as to what the settlement entailed. Kate messaged back, *That's the best outcome*, and Leah immediately answered, *Maybe, but sounds dodgy as, what's Josh been up to?* Thinking of her conversation with him the other day, Kate messaged back, *Dodgy is Josh's middle name, but I don't care. And no reason why the others at Resmond should suffer for his sake, so it's good they are settling out of court.*

As soon as she sent it, she thought, *Do I really think that, about not wanting people to suffer? Wouldn't I want Indira to suffer, at least? She broke up my marriage, after all, she and Josh.* And then she thought, *Nah, actually, I don't. I don't wish her ill. Because my marriage was broken before, only I didn't know it.* Indira was welcome to Josh. And good luck to her. She was going to need it.

You're very relaxed and philosophical, Leah's message pinged back, *Paris is obviously good for you, certainly looks good from your Insta pics.*

Kate considered before writing back, *I'm in Amiens actually for the weekend, north of Paris. With a friend.* She could almost see Leah's raised eyebrows before the next message pinged on the screen, *A friend! Ooh! Nothing on Insta about that! Do tell.*

Kate smiled to herself as she replied, *Some time. You'll have to wait. Tell Dad I went to the Somme battlefields this morning, where great-grandad fought. I'll send pics to the family WhatsApp.*

Leah wrote, *He'll be stoked. Shit—better go, Billy's up and making a mess. Love you, sis, and good luck with that friend xxx,* to which Kate sent a heart and a laughing emoji back.

Yes, she was happy, she thought as she lay back in bed and closed her eyes. So bloody happy, it was almost insane.

Thirty-five

Saturday morning had dawned brightly breezy in Paris. The day before, Gabi and Max had scarcely realised what the weather was like, for they had not left the flat except for a quick trip to the local bakery for some fresh bread. Although they hadn't spent quite the whole day in bed! Some of it had been spent talking about memories and plans and dreams, but also they'd spent time together in the kitchen, creating a series of little dishes for each other. That had been Gabi's idea, but Max had taken to it at once. Sweet and savoury, dishes from family memory and those learned recently: it had been a lovely impromptu degustation menu and Gabi had taken lots of pictures. She was thinking about the 'homework' Sylvie had given them, but also groping her way into her new artistic project. Max said he was delighted to be at the birth of it, but then Max was proclaiming everything delightful right now. Not that Gabi was far behind in that! It had all been so much fun. Too often, 'fun' was seen as something frivolous, inessential, but that was so wrong. For fun could be an absolute human essential, in the best, most beautiful way: playful, joyful, healing, and deeply satisfying to the senses, the heart, the mind.

Now, late on Saturday morning, they were walking through the busy, windy streets, heading to the lunch appointment with Max's grandmother. 'Ready?' Max asked when they arrived in front of the unpretentious little backstreet restaurant Gabi had chosen, with a lovely painted side panel on which the *menu du jour* was displayed on a blackboard.

'Absolutely,' said Gabi, trying to act nonchalant, but not fooling him in the least. She couldn't help being a little nervous. But only a little, because she truly felt she could stand up to the formidable old woman now. Still, she reminded herself, everything worth doing involves at least a bit of nerve-shaking. And besides, she could see Max was nervous too.

Liliane Rousseau de Taverny was already there, seated at a table in the centre of the room, an interesting choice, Gabi thought, as they followed the waiter. She looked immaculate as ever, caramel hair beautifully set, make-up perfect, clothes simple and elegant. But Gabi was intrigued to see as they approached that there was a sign of nerves there too, for the fingers of the old lady's beringed left hand were ever so slightly gripping the side of the table.

She saw them, and got up to greet them: Max warmly, Gabi politely. They sat down and the waiter handed them a menu, but both Gabi and Max had already decided that they wanted the day's special, the *menu du jour* they'd seen outside. 'It sounds like a good choice, I'll have the same,' Max's grandmother declared, more, Gabi suspected as she met Max's eyes, as a goodwill gesture than because that's what she might actually have chosen. And that thought put paid to the slight nerves she had been feeling, as well as the remains of any grudge she might have been carrying still.

'I think it is too, Madame,' she said, smiling. 'It's hard to go wrong with such classic dishes.'

'You'd be surprised,' said the old lady, a trifle tartly but also with a genuine smile, as if to show she meant no sting. 'Some people can get even a boiled egg wrong. But it isn't the case here. I have been glancing at other people's meals who also ordered the *menu du jour*, and they look most acceptable.'

'Lucky we have you as our spy, Mamieli,' said Max, smiling also, but with relief. Despite everything, Gabi thought in some amusement, it was clear he had been half-dreading a renewed sparring match between his lover and his grandmother. Now that it appeared both were going to be on their best behaviour, he could relax. But neither he nor Gabi could have predicted what his grandmother would say next.

'Max, I am going to ask you to be quiet while I say this. And Gabrielle, I am not going to waste your time and mine on offering or demanding explanations and apologies. I think us being here together is in itself both those things. Do you agree?'

The two women's eyes met, for a long moment. Then, slowly, Gabi nodded. 'I do.'

'Good. Thank you.' The old woman reached out her beringed hand towards her, and somewhat dazedly, Gabi shook it. 'There is something else I want to thank you for besides your graciousness, Gabrielle,' she went on. 'Something I only just discovered. Something I need to show you both.'

Both Gabi and Max stared at her as she bent down to her handbag, which was on the floor beside her: a beautiful Longchamp bag in soft tan leather with a gold clasp, as timelessly elegant as she was. They watched as she took out an envelope, carefully extracted what was in it and placed it on the table.

It was a small black-and-white photo with crinkled edges, showing two young women. They were standing a little awkwardly, staring into the camera, and behind them you could see the vague outline of a wall, with a couple of pictures hanging on it. Max picked it up and turned it over. On the back, in faded ink, was written: *Odette, 1938, et? (inconnue).* Odette, 1938, and? (an unknown person).

'I haven't seen this photo before,' he said, frowning, turning it over again. 'But it's of your aunt who was in the Resistance, isn't it?'

'Yes,' said his grandmother, 'and no, you won't have seen this photo because it's been in the trunk of loose photographs and trinkets that's been in the basement all these years. I only dug it out last night.' She turned to Gabi. 'This is a family photo,' she explained. 'Not a Taverny one. This is from my side.' She pointed to the young woman on the left. 'This is my aunt Odette Sabin, my father's younger sister. I never met her because she died in 1941 at the age of twenty-four, shot by the Gestapo after being captured.'

'My God, that's awful.' Gabi gazed at the young woman with her smart blonde hairdo and her soft, still face. She couldn't see her as a Resistance fighter. But appearances were deceptive.

'It is, but that is not why I am showing it to you. Look carefully.'

Gabi looked. At first she did not understand what the old lady was driving at. Then she looked again, and gasped.

'Yes,' said Madame Rousseau de Taverny. 'I felt like that too. Once I realised.'

'Once you realised what?' asked Max, bemusedly looking from his grandmother to Gabi.

'The unknown person,' Gabi said quietly. 'I know her. Or at least—I know her through her work. It's Marguerite Yonan.'

Max stared at her. 'The artist whose drawing you bought?'

Gabi nodded. 'She looks a lot younger than the only other two photos there are of her, when she was in Australia. But it's definitely her. And I'm almost sure . . .' She peered more closely at the photo, wishing she had a magnifying glass. With a catch in her throat, she added, 'I'm almost sure one of those pictures on the wall behind them *is* that drawing.' She pulled out her phone and, scrolling to a picture she had taken of the drawing, placed it beside the photo. 'Look.'

'It's hard to see well,' Max said, slowly, 'but it certainly could be.'

'The date's right,' said Gabi. 'It's the same year: 1938. And the inscription, *To OS, affectionately from MY*, that fits too. They were clearly friends.'

'More than that, I think,' said Max's grandmother, quietly. 'Affectionately might have just been a euphemism. Odette—well, she wasn't spoken about much, in the family, except as a Resistance heroine, which they were proud of, certainly, but there were intimations about her being estranged from the family because of something called *unnatural tendencies*.' She pronounced the last two words with great care, but the two young people knew immediately what she meant.

'She was a lesbian,' Max said, on an indrawn breath.

'And Marguerite was her lover.' Gabi thought of the second-last page of the artwork she'd created for Max, which she'd captioned, *Pretending can sometimes just be protection.* It had been a comment on her own dilemma, but now it felt prescient. She looked down at the photo, the awkward pose, the wary eyes of the two young women. Whoever had taken it either did not know, or didn't approve, of their true relationship. And Marguerite Yonan had left France in 1939, the year after this photo was taken. Something had happened to break them up. Family pressures, maybe. Or societal ones. Or simply something more personal. But the two women probably never had a chance to attempt a life together. Not then. 'Poor things,' she whispered.

'Yes. Indeed,' said Max's grandmother. She hesitated, then added, 'In 1938, Odette had moved to Paris, cast out by her parents. And that writing on the back—it's my father's. Maybe he didn't know who the woman was, with Odette. Or maybe he did, and couldn't bring himself to write her name, though he also could not bring himself to throw away one of the few photos he had of his sister. A photo that perhaps he himself had taken.'

There was a silence. Then Gabi said, quietly, looking at Max and his grandmother, 'The drawing. I do not know how it ended up in that shop—but I think it should come back to your family.'

'No,' said the old lady, decisively. 'I only knew—only realised—*because* you found that drawing. Because Max told me about it, and I looked up the artist's name and saw a photo of her online. And then I remembered this photo of my father's, and the unknown woman in it.' She hesitated. 'I always wish I'd been able to meet Odette. And I think my father regretted all his life that he had followed his parents in turning his back on her. That drawing doesn't belong to us. It belongs to you, Gabrielle. And maybe to those people in Australia who value Marguerite Yonan's work and might like to know more about her.' She picked up the photo of the two young women and held it out to Gabi. 'This is for you too.'

'I can't . . . it must be precious to you . . .' Gabi stammered, on the verge of tears.

'Please take it,' said the other woman, and Gabi felt the shock of it: that Max's formidable grandmother was actually pleading with her. 'Please take it. It has lain unregarded in the bottom of a suitcase for far too many years. But you will know where it should belong.'

Gabi met Max's eyes, and saw him nod, slightly, his eyes suspiciously shiny. She stretched out her hand and took the photo. 'Thank you, Madame,' she said, looking directly at Liliane Rousseau de Taverny. 'I will do my best to honour your trust.'

'I know you will,' said the old woman, with a lighter inflection in her voice. 'I know now what I should have seen from the start: you are a rare bird. And also that my grandson is fortunate to have met you.'

Impulsively, Gabi reached over and squeezed the old woman's hand. 'As I am fortunate to have met him,' she said, happily, as Max took her other hand, and the three of them stayed like that for a moment. Then—'No need to pray, Mesdames, Monsieur, the leek salads are honestly excellent today,' announced the waiter, with a cheeky Parisian smirk, appearing suddenly at their elbows with the entrées, startling them into laughter.

Life had a way of mixing the solemn with the comic, the profound with the everyday, Gabi thought, as the three of them began tucking in to what was indeed an excellent leek salad.

Thirty-six

Last night over dinner, Chris Clements had told Sylvie that, in her experience, the kind of person who conducts the kind of harassment Sylvie has been subjected to eventually wants publicity for whatever grudge it is they are holding. So she wasn't anticipating a no-show. But the journalist had been waiting for nearly half an hour now and from her carefully chosen vantage point Sylvie could see she was getting restless. Chris kept checking her watch, her phone, and looking around as if the very act could conjure up the person she was waiting for. Around her, the Galeries Lafayette cafeteria was packed, people chatting, eating lunch, squabbling with family, gossiping with friends, wandering around with trays trying to find an empty table . . . and casting an enquiring eye at the journalist sitting alone by the window, as if to say, *You've only got a cup of coffee in front of you, when are you going to leave?* But they didn't ask; Chris could look forbidding when she wanted to.

Sylvie couldn't see Paul Renard. But she knew he was there, somewhere. She herself hovered outside the cafeteria, pretending to look at the artfully arranged shelves of souvenirs nearby, and feeling a little silly in the beret and sunglasses she'd decided to put on at the last minute—just in case. The thirty minutes hadn't gone fast for her either, apart from the first five, when she had waited with growing impatience and dread for her persecutor to make an appearance. Now it felt like a foolish anticlimax.

Her phone vibrated in her pocket. She drew it out to find a message from Chris. *Just got an email. They're not coming today. I'm leaving.* Sylvie took a deep ragged breath and texted back, *Are you sure it's not just a trick?* The answer came immediately, *No. I think now they never intended to come.* Sylvie could see her getting up and gathering her things, and as soon as she'd vacated the table, a hovering, tray-laden couple had claimed it.

Sylvie took off the beret and sunglasses and was about to move when she spotted Paul Renard, appearing from nowhere, following Chris. Perhaps he thought she was going to meet whoever it was somewhere else. And in fact, Sylvie thought, *I've only got Chris's word—or rather, her text—that all she knew was that the person wasn't coming*. Perhaps they'd said to meet somewhere else. Chris was a journalist above all else, she wanted a story, and she'd tell half-truths or even outright fibs if she had to. She didn't know Sylvie was here but she did know Paul Renard was likely to be. *What should I do?* Sylvie thought. *Follow Chris and Paul, like I'm in some ridiculous spy movie? Or . . .*

'I knew you couldn't resist being here, even though you'd been told not to.' The voice close to her ear startled her.

She turned to see a youngish woman simply but stylishly dressed in straight-leg jeans, a blue floral shirt and slim navy cardigan. Her light brown hair was streaked with a darker colour and her round face would have been pleasant were it not for the way her jaw was set and the scorn—or something stronger—that flashed out from her pale blue eyes.

Sylvie stared at her. The woman was a complete stranger. Wildly, she searched her memory. In vain. She had no idea who on earth this woman was. Yet the woman's words indicated *she* knew who Sylvie was. 'Who are you?' she managed to ask. 'Why are you here?'

The woman gave an unamused smile. 'I think you know the answer to the second question,' she said, in a light, almost casual tone. 'As to the first, well, I'll tell you. But it might be more comfortable to be seated while we say what we have to say to each other.'

In a dream, Sylvie followed the woman to a table that had just been vacated. She motioned Sylvie to sit, and Sylvie, still in that hazy state, pulled out a chair and did so. The other woman sat down composedly, and looked enquiringly across the table at Sylvie, as if she were waiting to start a job interview. Trying to recover her scattered wits, Sylvie said, 'It was you. The bad reviews. The pizzas. The fake complaints. The trolling . . .'

'It was me,' agreed the woman, her pale eyes steady on Sylvie. 'All of it, including the meeting today. I knew that journalist would go running to you.' Her lips twitched. 'I've been several steps ahead of you all the time.'

Sylvie felt her rage mounting. 'Enough. Who are you?' she ground out.

'My name is Caroline Lamy,' the woman said, watching Sylvie closely.

Sylvie stared back. 'I still have no idea who you are. Or why you have chosen to target me. If it's money you want, you might as well know you've chosen the wrong target.'

Caroline shrugged. 'Of course you don't have any idea who I am. Nothing matters outside your selfish concerns and your right to do whatever you want, no matter how much it affects others.'

Sylvie's eyes narrowed. 'What are you talking about? If you are a disgruntled client or a business rival, I—'

The other woman cut her off. 'Is business really all that matters to you, Sylvie Morel? Then I was right to target your business. To make you feel what it's like to be threatened with the loss of what you care about most.'

Sylvie's gut churned. So, this wasn't about business. This was personal. Then she caught her breath as a fleeting glimpse of the truth came into her mind. She said, slowly, 'This is about Claude.'

Caroline mimed clapping her hands, silently. 'Bravo. You are finally there.'

Sylvie gave a short laugh. 'So it's that boring old tune, is it? You were dumped by Claude or you want to get together with him. And you seek to get rid of the competition by threatening my business. But here's the thing,' she added, leaning across the table, 'your efforts are pointless. You are welcome to Claude. It's over between us.'

For the first time, Caroline Lamy looked uncertain. But it was only briefly. Her lips curving into a sneer, she said, 'I have no interest in Claude. Except for one thing.' She paused, and now the tone of her voice changed. 'He is married to my sister.'

For a moment, Sylvie was completely lost for words. Then she said, blankly, 'I didn't know Marie-Laure had a sister.'

'Of course you didn't,' Caroline said, 'you never troubled to know anything about Marie-Laure, did you? Our mother died when I was very young and my sister always looked after me. And so now I look after *her*.'

An unexpected feeling rose in Sylvie then, a twinge of compassion. She said, quietly, 'But your sister is Claude's *ex*-wife. They've been separated over a year. She just took it badly. Claude told me all about it.'

Caroline's eyes narrowed. 'And you believed him. You are naïve enough. Or perhaps you didn't want the complications that come with an affair with a married man, unlike the other bitches who couldn't care less. He would have realised that pretty quickly. So he tried a different tactic with you. He pretended he was separated. He pretended she was making his life hard. I bet he never even took you to his place, but made some excuse why you had to go elsewhere. Am I right?'

Sylvie swallowed. She felt nauseous with the knowledge of her own blindness, her stupid trust in him. She looked at the woman sitting across from her and said, quietly, 'I don't understand. Why would you . . . why would you attack *me*, and not him? He's the one causing your sister suffering. Not me.'

'Just listen to yourself,' Caroline said, angrily. 'You're supposedly a good woman. I know he would have told you lies about

Marie-Laure. And yet you didn't trouble yourself to check, to find out if it was true. Because she didn't matter to you. You should be ashamed of yourself.'

But Sylvie had had quite enough now. 'Does your sister know what you've done?' she snapped. 'Has she asked you to fight her battles?'

'She doesn't have to,' said Caroline, tightly. 'She—'

'Stop,' said Sylvie, holding up a hand. 'You're facilitating him, don't you see that? You get rid of one lover and he just goes on to the next. I saw him, the other day in the street, with someone else. He's moved on from me already. So how have you changed anything for your sister?'

Caroline looked stricken, but then she rallied. Defiantly, she spat out, 'I've ended him and you. That's what counts.'

'*I* ended it, not you,' said Sylvie, but the other woman took no notice.

'You were different from the others. They were *bimbos*,' she pronounced the English word contemptuously, 'and he tires of them quickly. But he was fascinated by you, or rather, your success, even if soon enough he'd have grown tired of the fact you weren't fully focused on him—' Sylvie winced a little at that—'And I was sure you were the type to want respectability. Not marriage, necessarily, but a relationship in the open, not sneaking around. You'd put pressure on him. And he's weak. I thought there was a small chance he might really leave my sister. She's a gentle person, defenceless. She and Claude, they've been together so long. She loves him despite everything he's done. If he left her, it would break her heart. How could I let that happen?'

There was a small silence, then Sylvie sighed and said, wearily, 'For God's sake, Caroline, she'd be so much better off without him. Surely you must know that. If you really love her.'

'You don't understand. Because you can't. Because you don't know what love is, Sylvie Morel,' Caroline spat out. 'Your business means much more to you than Claude ever did. Than anyone has ever done, I suspect.'

Sylvie rose to her feet. 'You know what?' she retorted. 'You sound *exactly* like him. I pity your sister. I really do. Between Claude and you, my God, what chance does she have! And so for her sake, and her sake only, I won't take action against you, I won't go to the police or the media. I won't even tell my journalist friend, Chris Clements, what happened, or the private investigator I engaged who was getting very close to discovering who you were.' She saw Caroline's eyes widen and realised that the other woman had not known about Paul Renard. 'But this is what will happen. I will walk away from here. You will walk away from here. No repercussions. But if there is one more email, one more message, one more trolling, one more attempt, however tiny, to attack my company, ever again, I will know it is you. Then it will be no holds barred. And it won't just be you who is exposed to the consequences, or Claude. The pair of you, you deserve it.' She added, more gently, 'However, your sister *doesn't* deserve it. But she will still get caught up in the mess. Do you really want that to happen?'

Caroline visibly flinched and looked away. 'No,' she muttered.

'Then we understand each other?'

Caroline nodded.

'Then it's goodbye,' said Sylvie, getting up. 'And may we never cross paths again.'

Caroline said, hollowly, 'That is indeed devoutly to be hoped.'

'You know,' Sylvie said, 'you could help your sister, properly. If you had the courage.' And without another word, without a backward glance, she left.

She didn't get the Metro but walked all the way back to her apartment, a walk of nearly an hour, just to clear her head. Oh, she could waste time, wallowing in regret for her mistakes, anger at all that had happened, disgust at Claude, even pity for Caroline and Marie-Laure; but instead, she would spend that time walking and thinking about the future, and knowing that at the end of her walk, when she reached her apartment, she would knock at Serge's door. And she would tell him everything. Without evasion or reservation.

Thirty-seven

It was Thursday and the class was gathered for the last time in the school kitchen, getting ready to host the final lunch to which everyone, as was tradition, had invited a guest. At the Paris Cooking School, it had been a week of sweet delights like no other. On Monday morning, everyone had presented their ideas on *douceur*, and of all of them, Sylvie had especially liked Kate's inspired riff on a strawberry tart as a symbol of how Paris had transformed her understanding not only of food but of her approach to life. 'Taking superb but simple ingredients and turning them into something so exquisite it's like a little miracle, but it's also something everyday that's available to everyone. An enjoyment of the present moment, yet the joy of knowing there's always another one: that to me is the heart of *douceur*, and the heart of all I have learned here,' she had ended, to applause. The others' presentations had also been really good, from Stefan and Anja's funny video featuring a young apprentice baker with blue hair and a Belgian accent 'interviewing' various cakes in a local patisserie, to Gabi's lovely drawings of people queuing outside bakeries and patisseries, from Misaki's photos of Impressionist paintings showing people at a table, or having picnics, to Pete's shambolic quest for the perfect *macaron* in several different arrondissements, and Ethan and Mike's collection of photos of descriptions of cakes in the display cabinets of patisseries, allied to taste test notes. But Kate's offering had been truly special, as superb and simple as the strawberry tart she had focused on. As the other woman spoke, Sylvie thought about the idea she'd had, whose seed had been planted on that long walk back from the Galeries Lafayette, but which had now taken shape in her mind. An idea she hoped might flower . . .

All the *douceurs* the class had made this week had been inspired by recipes from Sylvie's and Damien's repertoires, each accompanied by its own story. There was a magnificent crème caramel, based on one Damien's aunt used to make, back in his home territory of New Caledonia; a simple, creamy yet light vanilla ice cream which never failed to work, based on a method Sylvie had gleaned years ago from a writer whose book launch she'd attended; a Pithivier pie, based on a childhood memory of Sylvie's, when as a puzzled five-year-old she'd misheard the name of the delicious pie her grandmother was making, thinking it was called *petit vieux*, little old man, and only years later realising it was named after a small town not far from Paris. There was a *quatre-quarts*, the homey golden-crumbed butter cake beloved of all French family tables, the very first cake Sylvie had attempted to make, as a seven-year-old; and, as a contrast, a flamboyant *moka*, with rich layers of coffee buttercream, which a sixteen-year-old Damien had first attempted to impress a girlfriend; a succulent chocolate mousse that came out of the battered cookbook he had brought with him when he'd stepped off the plane from Nouméa and into Paris for the first time; and a *tarte Tatin*, that famous upside-down apple tart with its caramelised, buttery crust, which years ago had featured as a symbol in a Parisian tabloid's weather forecast. Sylvie had kept a clipping of it: '*Le ciel en Tatin*', it had been headlined, or 'The sky as Tatin', meaning that the weather would be upside down in France that day, with the south being cold and wet and the north being warm and sunny. And the whole of the forecast had built on that image, like a playful prose poem that would have seemed quite incongruous in a popular tabloid newspaper anywhere but in France. To Sylvie, it was a perfect image of something timelessly French.

Now, as everyone buzzed around her, nervously getting ready to show off their skills to their guests, she thought of how she'd miss these people, a group of such different personalities yet who somehow had worked together so harmoniously. It was fair to say that she'd liked most of the people who'd passed through the school—certainly not all, mind!—but she felt this was a truly special group, one she would never forget. Perhaps that was because their time with her had coincided with such upheavals in her life—both bad, like the hate campaign against the school and the ugly secrets it had revealed, and good, like her recognition, finally, of the beautiful, loving man who had been under her nose the whole time. Thinking of that right now made a thrill of desire run up her spine as she remembered Serge's fingers slowly running down her back . . .

Yesterday, Julien had called her just as she was about to go to Serge's apartment, and it had seemed quite natural to tell him, then, that the two of them were 'seeing each other', as she rather coyly put it.

'At last!' Julien had exclaimed at once. 'I wondered when you would come to your senses, dear little maman, and see the real gold in front of you instead of chasing after tinsel and glitter!' She'd protested a little, for form's sake, telling him it sounded like their roles were reversed, and he was the sensible parent and she the reckless child, but he'd only laughed and said *somebody* needed to be sensible. Of course, he'd always got on with Serge, and very much disliked Claude—he even cheerfully admitted now his trip to Australia had been partly prompted by not wanting to be around the man—but she also knew that Julien had an instinctive perceptiveness about people, even as a young child. Serge might travel to Australia with her for the wedding, she said, if he could get away from his business, and Julien laughed and said he was sure there was absolutely no way Serge *wouldn't* be there. But what was going to happen with the school while his mother was away, he asked so she told him.

The long table in the dining room had been extended with two smaller ones and extra chairs brought from Serge's apartment, the guests and staff were standing around chatting and knocking back an aperitif, while the students made an anxious last check of the menus—entrée, main course, dessert—each pair had created. Out of the corner of her eye, Gabi could see her parents and Max having a good yack: there were no worries at all there, ever since her mum and dad had met Max on Tuesday, they'd clicked at once, much to Gabi's relief. They hadn't met his grandmother yet, so there could still be fireworks, but Gabi didn't feel too worried about that. She could cope, whatever happened.

Over in another corner, Kate's guest, a smiley man named Arnaud, had brought his lively little dog with him, and she was clearly making Damien's day, as well as that of Stella, the young apprentice with blue hair who'd featured in Anja and Stefan's video. Meanwhile Misaki's guest, Jerome, an art restorer she'd met at the Impressionist museum, was getting on famously with Sylvie, Serge and a horse trainer called Mathilde whom Ethan and Mike had met on a visit to Longchamp racecourse that weekend. And Pete's guest, Lily, the forthright Scotswoman he'd met in the Tuileries Garden and had serendipitously come across again, in a café just two days ago, was saying, loudly, that she was 'on a gap year—the gap between my son getting hitched and me being roped into grandma duties', while Pete beamed happily beside her.

The celebration was wonderful, Gabi thought, but it also felt a bit melancholy, to know that this was the last hurrah for the class. She thought back to the first time she'd come in here, how she'd been so caught up in her own stuff, so standoffish and unwilling to get into the spirit of it all, thinking of the course only as a way of blotting out her fear. How different it felt now! She was working at her art again, but also pacing herself, letting it come in a kind of slow joy that felt right. She'd sent a couple of samples to Nick, and he'd responded in a way that made her heart sing. She didn't know yet if she'd be awarded the Provence residency—though she hoped so—but if she didn't get it, she'd create her own, here in Paris, exploring it more, with Max and on her own. They had many other plans, to visit Guernsey, and the Basque country, and maybe Spain and Portugal, and certainly to head back to Australia maybe at Christmas or New Year. Max had already applied for a visa.

She'd sent an email to her old art school lecturer back in Sydney, the one who'd been instrumental in interesting her in Marguerite Yonan's work. She'd attached photos of the drawing and of the picture of Marguerite and Odette, and there had been an almost immediate response. He was as excited as she was by what she'd discovered. Apparently there had been talk of a retrospective. So, in a small way, she might be helping to bring the life and work of a gifted artist out of the shadows, and into the light . . .

Everything had been absolutely delicious. It had been so varied, all of it, and yet somehow it had worked brilliantly together, a symphony of colour and taste and texture laid out on the tables. Kate had tried to get at least a mouthful of everything, but to concentrate especially on those things she was most drawn to. She and Misaki had made a simple but spectacular menu: for an entrée, bright green asparagus with vinaigrette; a main of braised fresh broad beans with duck confit, cooked in its own juices, with thyme and garlic; and for dessert, a *quatre-quarts* with a glaze made of brown sugar, butter and lemon, then decorated with candied violets and rose nibs. It had looked and tasted wonderful but she'd left most of it for the others to try, while she indulged herself in other people's creations: a bit of trout with almonds here, a delectation of pea, mint and goat's cheese salad there; new potatoes with dill accompanied by a delicious veal sauté; a garlic soup of surprising delicacy, and a fish and vegetable stew full of colourful, homely cheer. And the desserts—oh, the desserts—and not just the magnificent *moka* that Ethan and Mike, also the creators of the veal sauté, had made, but also the sweet-smelling Pithivier created by Anja and Stefan and the luscious crème caramel Pete and Gabi had offered.

Before the desserts, there was a variety of cheese, selected by Max, each a reminder of some they'd got to know over these last four weeks. The wine had been supplied by Sylvie, carefully chosen to go with most things and not overwhelm. It had happily flowed as everyone ate and talked and laughed, and now only a few drops remained and the dishes were practically empty. The coffee was brought in and soon, Kate thought, everyone would be getting up and going on their way, and the busy small world that had been created for four weeks in this place, around this table, would only be a memory. The thought made her feel sad.

But no. There was no need to be sad. It would never be just a memory. Her life had changed here *because* she had been a part of that small world. Which wasn't so small after all. Because it had led not only to her becoming a much better cook—it had allowed her to turn away from the bitterness of the past. To stand up for herself. To regain her lost confidence. To make undemandingly warm friendships with lovely people like Anja and Stefan—who'd already invited her to their home in a small town near Hanover—and even to sleeping better. And of course, most wonderfully, it had led to her meeting Arnaud. And Nina, she smiled to herself. Yes, of course Nina, who in her innocently wise doggy way had enabled the joy of possibility to blossom between the two humans she'd brought together.

Kate gazed across the room to where Nina was at that moment busy creating a spark of friendship between two more humans, Damien and Stella. She looked across the table at Arnaud, who was busy trying to keep up with the animated flow of conversation from Serge, Pete and Stefan. He caught her eye and gave a rueful grin, his blue-green eyes full of warmth, making her catch her breath.

Yesterday, after dinner on his boat, she'd finally told him what Pete had said about his next-door neighbours. Arnaud had been silent for a moment, long enough for her to wish that she'd shut her mouth. Then he'd taken her hand, gently raised it to his lips, and kissed it. He said, simply, 'Thank you for telling me. Not easy, I know.' She'd looked at him with unexpected tears springing up in her eyes at the gentleness in his voice. 'I thought—it might not be—not be them—and I didn't want to give you false hope if . . .' she stammered.

But he replied, quietly, thrillingly, 'Oh it *is* them. I am sure of it.' And then, wonderingly, he added, 'And your friend—he is sure that Lucas—that he wanted to take my name?'

Kate had given him a mock-cross look then and said, 'Of course he is. It was the point of Pete's story. *A rose by any other name . . .*'

Arnaud had smiled, the Shakespearean reference lost to his French ears, but the reality of his son, far away, but possibly ready to know him, was clearly filling him with a happiness he was still nervous of wholly believing in. He said, 'Will you tell your friend that I would like to speak with him some time?'

'I'll do better than that. I'll call Pete right now and get him to meet us for a drink at that bar you like.'

Arnaud had looked panicked, but just for an instant, and then his face had cleared and he'd said, lightly, 'Why not?'

Pete was surprised but willing. When they reached the bar, she'd turned to Arnaud and said, 'I'll take Nina for a walk, you don't need me right now,' and he'd looked at her with that beautiful warmth in his eyes and said, simply, 'Thank you.'

When she came back, the two men were on their second cognac and it was clear all had gone well. Pete kept saying, 'Wow, that's so cool, so cool, man, just so cool,' while Arnaud patiently and amusedly agreed that yes it was indeed. He winked at Kate. He looked younger, or maybe it was just lighter, a weight lifted. They'd talked a bit afterwards, on the way back to her hotel, of possible plans, perhaps first an email to his son, or a call to his son's mother, because she had to be on side, of course. And then, maybe, later in the year, if things worked out, there might be a visit to Toronto, or maybe his son might come to Paris. It was all up in the air and there was still much to be done, and who knew if it would all work out? But as he was about to leave her on the threshold of the hotel, he had said, 'I will never forget what you have done, Kate. And I hope I can show that to you, in every way, for as long as you wish it.' She had not answered—she couldn't speak, her heart was too full—but reached up to him and kissed him full on the mouth, and he'd responded in kind, oh, in *such* kind! But she didn't invite him up and he didn't ask it, because both of them knew that they might have reached the end of the first chapter of their story and the second chapter was beginning, but also that it must not be written too quickly. She would be returning to Melbourne in under a week and neither of them wanted that final week to be, well, final, which it might be if they jumped into bed now. It was maybe old-school to wait, Kate had thought, as she went slowly up to her room, and it might not suit everyone. But for them, it was right.

Now, as she made her way to the kitchen with a pile of dishes and plates, she thought that, no matter what happened between her and Arnaud—though of course she hoped that their story would be a happy one—she would not have any regrets. And that was beautiful knowledge to hold within her.

In the kitchen, she found Sylvie alone, sorting out empty bottles and stacking the big dishwashers. She looked up as Kate entered. 'Oh, you didn't need to do that,' she said, as Kate put the plates down. 'Damien and Yasmine would have helped later.'

'It's no bother,' said Kate, 'and besides, they're having a great time out there.'

'And you weren't?'

'Oh yes, but it's pretty noisy,' Kate said with a smile, 'and getting a moment's peace and quiet in the kitchen didn't seem like a bad idea.'

'I feel exactly the same,' Sylvie said, smiling back. 'And I'm glad you came in. There's something I wanted to talk to you about.'

'Oh?' Wild notions of what it might be flitted through Kate's mind, but she was completely unprepared for what came next.

'Look, Kate, I am going to come straight out with it,' Sylvie said. 'And I understand if you think this is a crazy idea—but how would you feel about coming to work for me?'

Kate stared at her, lost for words. The other woman went on, hurriedly, looking anxious now. 'It would be just as an intern, at first, and just for a couple of months, later this year, but it could be extended. We couldn't pay much, but we would also cover accommodation and help with travel expenses. I've talked it over with Damien, and he absolutely agrees, like me, that you would be perfect to—'

'Wait a moment,' Kate interrupted her, and her voice was a little choked. 'I don't understand. Why are you—I mean—why would you—I'm just an amateur beside you and Damien, I'm just—'

'You are talented,' Sylvie said, interrupting. 'Naturally talented, instinctive about food but also not afraid to say you don't know, and willing always to learn. Plus you have something else—a gift for bringing out the best in people.'

'*Me*?' Kate replied, eyes wide, genuinely astonished. 'But I'm not really . . .'

'I've noticed it. Damien has noticed it. Serge too. Not to speak of Arnaud,' she added, smiling. 'And Anja and Stefan were telling me how genuinely kind you've always been to everyone, but not afraid to speak out when you need to.' She looked at Kate. 'You are exactly right for us. But of course the question is whether we are right for *you*.'

Kate swallowed. To have the chance to return, and not as a client, but as part of the school, working with people she admired and liked; a new start in a new profession, creating food she loved and learning more and more; being back once more in this beautiful city and building on the next chapter with Arnaud in such an unexpectedly wonderful way; oh, to be given a second chance at everything—it was as if a fairy had suddenly appeared and offered her wishes she had hardly even been aware of and yet now knew were all she wanted. She said, in a rush, 'I'd love it. I'd love it more than anything else—and I am also so deeply honoured, you can't imagine . . . But I don't know if I can live up to what you want.'

'The fact you even say that shows me absolutely that you will,' said Sylvie, and her face was filled with light. 'I am so glad you have not turned down our crazy idea, Kate. Of course, there will be things we need to discuss, arrangements we'll need to put in place. But for now . . .' From a cupboard, she took a tall thin bottle of Sauternes, filled a couple of small glasses with the deep golden wine, and handed one to Kate. Then she raised her own glass, saying, 'Until we have a proper celebration to welcome you, I would like to propose a toast: here's to the future!'

'To the future!' Kate echoed, and they clinked, just as a radiant-looking Gabi entered the room, hands full of empty coffee cups. 'Now there's a toast I could drink to as well, ladies,' she said, breaking into a big smile, 'if there's another glass of that gorgeous stuff going, of course!'

Epilogue

TWELVE MONTHS LATER

Standing in the sunny garden, looking down the long table, Kate felt a flutter of nerves from her throat to her toes. She'd worked so hard for this day, and now it was here. Shortly, the guests would arrive and everything would be put to the test. And not just for herself, either. This had been her idea, but Sylvie had encouraged her to run with it, had trusted her to not only develop it but bring it to life. *But what if it flopped*, Kate thought, nervously rubbing her hands on her apron. What if they hated it? Or thought it ridiculous, the daft idea of an antipodean interloper who had no real understanding of how things were done in France?

They wouldn't hate the setting, anyway, she thought, glancing around the peaceful green haven. With its banks of flowers, shady trees, grassy path and a fountain whispering to itself in a corner, the garden looked like it belonged in some rural retreat, not in the heart of Paris. Yet outside the Paris traffic growled as it rushed through the streets, while in the garden, protected from the street by tall stone walls almost covered in creepers, you only heard birdsong. A garden like this, in Paris, was certainly a rare and coveted thing. It and its attendant house—a beautiful, three-storey nineteenth-century stone building in the 16th—belonged to a woman called Juliette Marigny, and the garden had been designed by her niece, Charlotte, who was well known as a garden designer. Juliette herself had had a stellar globe-trotting career as a diplomat and later as a very successful travel and food writer, and even now, at over eighty years old, she was still a force to be reckoned with. She also happened to be a childhood friend of Max's formidable grandmother Liliane Rousseau de Taverny, which was how they'd managed to secure this unique venue. Since Kate's return to Paris to take up the job at the Paris Cooking School, she and Gabi had become, if not best friends, definitely friendly. And after Gabi and Max had come back from their travels following a successful artist residency in Provence, the two couples—Gabi and Max, Kate and Arnaud—had shared several meals together. It was during one of those, just two months ago, that Max had suggested approaching his grandmother's friend. 'She has an absolutely superb garden,' he'd said, 'and she knows so many people who could be helpful, it really would be the perfect place for the launch!'

Yes, it *was* perfect, Kate thought, now. But did what she'd planned match that perfection? The table under the blossoming tree looked beautiful, sure. It was covered in a superb antique embroidered cream linen tablecloth—a find of Kate's in the sprawling Parisian flea market that she'd haunted more than once now—and was decorated with strategically placed silk flowers that Leah had found for Kate in an artisan market in Melbourne. The flowers weren't European, but, rather, Australian natives—waratah, kangaroo paw, wattle, flannel flowers—exquisitely rendered in fine silk. Piles of cheerfully mismatched small plates—vintage black-and-white ones showing scenes from country life on the one hand, and contemporary plain yellow ones on the other—stood alongside a flotilla of chunky tumblers and elegant stemmed glasses, as well as black-handled cutlery. Striped yellow-and-cream napkins were to one side of these, and next to them a small pile of menus, decorated with the lovely sketch contributed by Gabi. Scattered around the garden were benches and seats, which Arnaud had commandeered from all sorts of quarters: as mismatched as the plates, they looked just as charming.

Kate breathed deeply. Sure, it looked great. And thank God, the weather was brilliant. It and the setting would put people in the right mood, even if nothing else did. Heading back through the garden, up the patio and into the house, she went straight to the kitchen. Damien was there, and Amandine from the Chez Quenu restaurant, busy with finishing touches, and Yasmine with her head bent over a clipboard. They all looked up and smiled as she came in. 'It's all still there then?' Damien asked, with a mischievous expression, and Kate smiled back. 'I think so.' She had, it's true to say, checked things in the garden more than once this morning. The four of them were alone in the house, Juliette having discreetly decided to take a walk until everything was ready, and Sylvie having made it clear from the start that she wasn't going to be hovering over preparations. She wanted Kate to feel she had full control. She and Serge would come along as guests, she said.

But the launch of the Paris Cooking School's boutique catering service was Kate's event, just as the idea of the new offshoot had been Kate's in the first place.

Kate glanced over the food waiting to go out. There were trays of small savoury tarts and pies, traditional and not: asparagus and tarragon, pork and prune, roast chicken and ginger, trout and leek, and a tart with a colourful piperade filling. There were tiny sandwiches whose fillings reflected an unusual mix: from goose *rillettes* with thin slices of preserved figs to prawn and avocado with a Marie Rose dressing. There was a plate of *charcuterie* from different regions of France and another featuring only local Île-de-France cheeses. There was a big bowl of seasonal salad vegetables—lettuces of different kinds, plus *mâche*, rocket, sorrel and herbs, with a traditional vinaigrette spiked with lemon myrtle, and a long plate with thinly sliced tomatoes, red and yellow, with a pomegranate molasses vinaigrette. French food, but with an intriguing, original Australian twist. The drinks—Champagne, and red and white wine, including a couple of Sancerres from the Taverny vineyard, and a couple of Australian reds, as well as water and orange juice—were all waiting. She had to admit it all looked pretty good. There was just one thing missing . . .

At that moment, the gate buzzer sounded, and Yasmine went to answer it. She returned with Gabi and Max, Sylvie and Serge, along with Juliette and Charlotte Marigny and Max's grandmother, Liliane. Dressed in colours that echoed the spring, they all looked great, thought Kate, with Gabi especially radiant, the baby bump just beginning to show now. There was a buzz of excited greetings and exclamations about the look of the food and the setting. But pleased though she was, Kate could hardly concentrate. Her nerves were fizzing again, and she couldn't help glancing at her watch. He should have been here a while ago.

Soon, everything was out on the table, and other guests started arriving, including a couple of the carefully chosen journalists Juliette had recommended. In a lull, Kate managed to brush her hair, put on some lipstick and take off her floury apron. She went around shaking hands and greeting people, including the journalists, who were hovering around the table, talking in low voices and reading the menus. It was hard to read their expressions but they certainly didn't look unhappy!

And then, finally, here he was: Arnaud, carrying a large cardboard box, with his son Lucas just behind him, Nina at *his* heels. 'Sorry we're late,' Arnaud said, giving her the smile that never failed to warm her all over, 'there were delays on the Metro.'

'It's all right,' she said, smiling back at him with a mix of love and relief, 'you're here, now. I've got a big plate all ready for it, just over here.'

'Wow,' Lucas said, as they approached the table, 'it looks amazing.' Adding in French, 'When can we eat?' Everyone laughed and Lucas looked pleased. He was quite a revelation, this boy, Kate thought. Arnaud *had* told her that Lucas was incredibly confident—his own first introduction to his son in Toronto last year, had, he said, made him feel like the roles were reversed and he was the tongue-tied adolescent, while his son was completely at ease. Kate had thought he was exaggerating, but in fact it had turned out to be pretty much on the money. The first time Lucas had met her, two weeks ago, she'd been a little nervous, but he not at all. He had chattered on to her quite happily about an eclectic variety of subjects, from whether Canada was like Australia to whether she preferred graphic novels or anime films, from naïve observations about Paris to poignantly candid ones about being thought 'weird' at school. He wasn't at all weird—unless weird meant being delightful—and Kate had liked him at once. And so, importantly, had Nina, who right now was sitting beside him looking very pleased with herself, her beady black glance only occasionally drifting to the source of the enticing smells.

'So then, let's have a look at it,' Kate said taking the box from Arnaud and opening it very carefully to reveal the cake she'd dreamed up and then asked her favourite patisserie to create. As she did so, there was a gasp of collective delight—including from the journalists. And no wonder! The 'Paris-Melbourne', as she had christened it in honour of her two favourite cities, was a delicate concoction of meringue layers sandwiched with cappuccino-flavoured cream, with the top featuring glazed strawberries and crystallised white rosebuds, studded like edible jewels in the pale brown cream. She sighed happily, all nerves gone. It looked exactly as she'd hoped it would. Perfectly, delectably beautiful.

Acknowledgements

I absolutely loved writing this novel, and that joy was greatly enhanced by the many people who have supported, advised, encouraged and inspired me on the journey towards making this book a reality, and I'd like to publicly acknowledge them here:

My wonderful agent, Margaret Connolly, who from the start has been as excited as me by this story and was always such a great sounding-board when I needed it.

My fantastic publisher Alex Craig, whose perceptive guidance, inspired suggestions and unwavering support have been second to none.

All the lovely Ultimo Press team, in editing, design, production, marketing and sales, who have made this book into such a beautiful object and worked so hard to bring it into the hands of readers.

Many grateful thanks to all of you!

Thanks and much love to my Paris-based family, for the many engrossing hours discovering unusual corners of the city in your knowledgeable company, and the same to all my family, whether based in the South of France, Australia or the UK, for your constant and loving support. And a special thank you to my sisters-in-law in England whose delightful pet helped to inspire the inimitable Nina!

Thank you to the Australia Council for the magical six-month Paris residency I was awarded several years ago which helped me to build on my knowledge of the City of Light.

And to my darling husband, children, and joyfully expanded family here in Australia, much love always, and thank you for always being there for me. You are all truly the light of my life.

Reading Group Questions

1. Sylvie says, 'The French way of home cooking is not *fancy*, or difficult, or even necessarily time consuming.' Thinking about Sylvie's approach to French cooking, does it differ from your own impressions of French food culture?

2. The food descriptions in this book are sumptuous—was there any particular recipe that you wanted to try?

3. Sylvie emphasises the importance of stories when cooking; do you have a family recipe with a story you'd like to share with others?

4. Cross-cultural connections—and occasional misunderstandings!—are important in the novel, and not only between French and English-language culture. What examples can you think of, and what do they show?

5. Do you think Gabi's creative block is due to fear of failure—or success? What else could she have done to overcome it?

6. Kate's strawberry tart is a recurring motif in the novel, and she reflects on its meaning to her at the end. But what does it represent for you, as a reader?

7. Gabi's and Kate's motivations for attending the Paris Cooking School are very different. Or are they?

8. Was Sylvie really guilty of deliberately closing her eyes to Claude's lies, as she's accused by Caroline, or was she simply too trusting?

9. Romantic love in its many forms is a central focus of the novel, but other kinds of close relationships—family, friends—also feature significantly. How do you think this affects the atmosphere of the story?

10. Paris can be seen as not only the setting of the novel, but also a very important character in its own right. How would you describe that character? Did you learn about any new places you would like to visit?

Sophie Beaumont is the pen name of Sophie Masson AM, who was born in Indonesia of French parents and was brought up in France and Australia. A bilingual French and English speaker, she has a master's degree in French and English literature and a PhD in creative practice. Sophie is the prolific and award-winning author of more than fifty novels for children, young adults and adults, many of which have been published internationally.